DON'T LOOK FOR ME

DON'T LOOK FOR ME

A novel based on the true story of
Hetty van Leeuwen and Jozef Jacobs

Ann Donovan

Matador
Unit E2 Airfield Business Park,
Harrison Road, Market Harborough,
Leicestershire. LE16 7UL
Tel: 0116 2792299
Email: books@troubador.co.uk
Web: www.troubador.co.uk/matador
Twitter: @matadorbooks

ISBN 978 1805142 690

British Library Cataloguing in Publication Data.
A catalogue record for this book is available from the British Library.

Typeset in 11pt Minion Pro by Troubador Publishing Ltd, Leicester, UK

Matador is an imprint of Troubador Publishing Ltd

This book is dedicated to Hetty and Jozef and to all people of all faiths and nationalities across our often broken world who have faced the trauma of unreasonable hate and persecution.

Author's Note

This book tells the story of two extraordinary people: Hetty Donovan (nee Van Leeuwen) and Joop (Jozef) Jacobs. I have used the names of the Van Leeuwen and Jacobs family in this book as well as those of the Lievegoed and Loggers families who were key in hiding Hetty and Jozef and that of Jan Schep the resistance leader in Zeist that Hetty would probably have worked for. Other names are fictitious.

I spent long hours talking to both Hetty and Jozef and writing down their recollections of this dark period in time. Their memories sometimes varied slightly but Jozef was always keen that I stick as closely to Hetty's version as possible as he had been a child at the time of his rescue. For both of them, as for millions of others, those terrible years scarred and haunted them throughout their lives. Theirs isn't the only story of that time: Loes and Hans, Hetty's brother and sister had other stories to tell as did Jozef's sister Trudi and many others who survived.

The story in this book of both bravery and tragedy, and extraordinary fortitude is the one I was closest to, as Hetty was my mother-in-law, although it was Jozef who first told me about the rescue. My aim has been to tell this story in a way that would enable their grandchildren and great grandchildren, to understand what they went through during the war. It is not a history or a biography, though it draws closely from both.

Hetty eventually talked to me about the war, the rescue, and how she survived, but it was Jozef who, as well as telling his side of the story, was able to add detail, and who understood and empathised with my aim in writing this book. He read and commented on it from start to finish as it was written and re-written and in one of his last emails to me, when he found it too difficult to read on the computer, told me that he trusted me, that he believed I had understood the heart of what had happened to him and to Hetty.

Acknowledgements

I am sincerely grateful to many people for their help but particularly to Hildebrand Lievegoed, youngest son of Bernard Lievegoed; Henk Schep, son of Jan Schep and particularly to my good friend and cousin-in-law Jacqueline, Loes' youngest daughter who has been on much of the journey of this book with me.

I am also grateful to my sister-in-law Karen, and her husband Bob and my sister Maggie for their encouragement. I am also grateful for the help of my writing friends Jenny Knight and other members of the not Morley group who have been positively constructive in picking up loose ends and to my friend Rhona Kyle who expertly edited my copy. Most of all I am grateful to my own family, my beautiful daughters, Isobel and Laura, their partners Chris and Will, and my husband Danny, all of whom have patiently listened to, read and commented on endless drafts of this book.

On 10ᵗʰ May 1940 Hitler's forces invaded the Netherlands. Ill prepared for war, it took the Nazis less than a week to cripple the country, reeking devastation on Rotterdam, and forcing the Dutch army to surrender. It would be five years before the entire country was liberated, during which time over 210,000 Dutch men, women and children died. Half of them were Jewish. This is the story of two of those that survived.

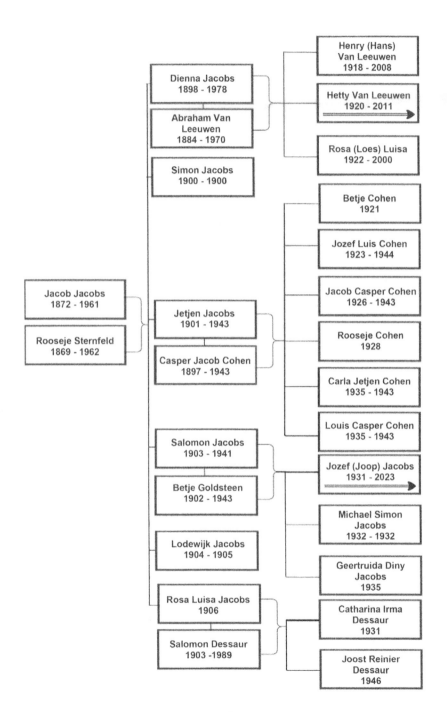

PART 1

1940
In the beginning

Hetty – May – Scheveningen

Could he be dead? The door shuts, the sharp final click of the latch, closing Hetty out into the street.

He can't be dead, not Hans, her tall dark, resourceful, too handsome 21-year-old older brother. Her thoughts swirl, tension and an uncomfortable settling of fear, making her head ache and her stomach churn. He's never going to get shot, killed, injured. Is he? She freezes in front of the polished glass front of her parents' perfumery, she has lived in the flat above it for every one of the 20 years of her life.

Her head spins with the last time she'd seen Hans, smiling as he put his cap on, shouting goodbye as he clattered noisily down the stairs two weeks ago, late back to his battalion, days before the invasion.

She looks across the street, heart racing as she watches three Nazi soldiers ambling along, talking and laughing. She better get used to them. She pushes dark curls behind her ears and looks down to do up the buttons on her blue wool jacket before striding determinedly down the street. It will take her 15 minutes to get to the clinic.

She starts to clock the changes around her home in the fashionable coastal town of Scheveningen near The Hague. Shops are open, well of course they are open. Her father had made them open up the perfumery this morning three days after the brutal invasion ended in surrender. It had seemed an extraordinary suggestion. But she and her sister Loes had done it. And yes, there had been a smattering of customers, asking after her mother and brother, toying with lipsticks on the counter, gossiping rather than buying. She had been amazed and shocked and relieved, and all the time feeling her insides knotting, holding her breath, waiting and hoping that Hans would walk through the door. As if!

At lunch the rising tension in the flat had escalated following news that their neighbour's only son had been killed. Her mother who had been fretting, waiting for every knock on the door, pacing the floor at night unable to sleep, worrying about Hans, was now in a spiral of despair, apoplectic with worry, and had despatched their father to check the main hospital in the Hague to see if Hans was amongst the injured and Hetty to the clinic.

Hetty's hope is that while she is out looking for him, he will walk into the flat and her trip to the clinic will become a joke, the sort of joke Hans liked, a story that would make them all fall about laughing.

There is a sudden rasp of an engine coming up behind her. A truck turns the corner, gears grating, black beetle-helmeted soldiers jostling shoulder to shoulder in the back. She looks up and sees two of the soldiers staring at her, elbowing their comrades. One smiles and winks as the truck rattles ahead. Nazis everywhere, peppering the streets like an infestation of ants.

She quickens her pace looking around for confirmation of normality, or what was normality. There is no visible physical damage to the street: the tall brick terrace of shops and flats with crenulated rooves and dormer windows is untouched. The florist is open, buckets lined up on the pavement spilling with red and yellow tulips, heady scented white freesia. As usual. A little girl, nose pressed to the window of a first floor flat, watches her and waves. There's a queue outside the bakery, the yeasty smell of fresh baked bread wafting into the street. The book shop looks closed, but the newsagent is open, a rack of newspapers reporting the arrival of the Nazi command, a grainy picture of Hitler on the cover. He looks so.... her mind flicks back to her father telling them of German cousins, one a professor, who had escaped the lockdown on the Jewish community in Berlin by fleeing to Rotterdam, their jobs gone, their world shattered. That can't happen here, can it? She passes her favourite dress shop and stops; the same blue wool dress hangs in the window that was there two weeks ago. "Same colour as your eyes," Loes had said, their arms linked as they strolled down to the beach. She blinks, two weeks ago none of this had happened.

She must get to the clinic which is up on the dunes, maybe a kilometre along the coast road. She can see the Steinberger Kurhaus, the hotel which dominates the seafront with its huge dome and turrets and almost bumps into a waiter in a starched white apron standing outside the café on the corner, serving someone in uniform; more nazis, officers, drinking coffee, easy as you please on the Gentsestraat.

She quickens her pace, passes the courtyard of the Kurhaus and head down turns onto the seafront breathing in the salty air, the vastness of the blue-black sea under a blanket of gathering grey clouds. There's an old man with a beard throwing a ball for his dog; two children running in and out of the lacy fringe of the sea racing across the hard packed sand. So....normal?

But it's not normal, behind her she hears a group of Nazi soldiers ordering drinks loudly in the bar across the road. Hard to believe that two weeks ago she was sitting on this stretch of beach with her friends: Wil marching up and down his shock of red hair flying in the breeze; Rosa laughing, blonde curls bouncing, dancing in the sand to music drifting down from the terrace of the hotel where silk dressed guests were eating dinner on the terrace in the early summer sun; Dirk pulling her close as they shared a bottle of beer, the scent of cigars, expensive perfume and rich seafood from the hotel mixing with the salt of the chips they'd bought from the beach café.

Wil and Dirk had been arguing, as always. "It will never happen," Wil had declared, taking a swig of beer, totally convinced, that an invasion by Nazi Germany of neutral Holland was impossible.

"You are so, so wrong." Dirk had tried and tried to change his mind.

And now? She thinks of Wil with his crazy laugh, fizzing with energy, Dirk biting the corner of his mouth as he thinks, refusing to give Wil an inch in the argument, black hair flopping across his eyes. Are they alright? Are her friends, her best, her oldest friends ok?

A sudden burst of laughter makes her look round and she inadvertently catches the eye of one of the soldiers, leaning against the polished brass bar, hat on the counter, downing large glasses of frothing beer. He wipes the froth from his mouth and seeing her shouts out. "Fraulein!"

She quickly starts to walk along the sea front, digging her hands in the pockets of her jacket, focussing on getting away, keeping her head down, praying that they won't come after her, dreading being stopped she bumps into someone.

"Sorry." She looks up, straight into the bullet-grey eyes of a man in uniform: Nazi uniform.

She swallows. "So, sorry." She tries to pass him, but he grabs her arm.

"I said… I am sorry…" She tries gently to pull away, but he doesn't let go. He's breathing heavily and she realizes he must have run down the street and crossed it to cut her off.

He smiles; "Can you help us?"

"Can I help you?…. What? How can I help you?". He's actually quite good looking and she suppresses a returning smile as he points back towards the Steinberger Kurhaus, towards the group of soldiers now gathered round the huge metal telescope bolted to the pavement of the promenade, swinging it back and forth, taking turns to scan the horizon.

One of them, plump, red faced, neck straining against the collar of his uniform, races towards them takes her arm. "Help! Help at last. Didn't you hear me call to you?"

He pulls her towards the telescope, pushing the others away, gabbling at her in a confusing mix of Dutch and German which she finds hard to understand. What is it? What does he want? He steps closer. Shouts. "England! Where is England?" His face is inches from hers.

"What?"

"Show us where England is," he shoves her towards the telescope. "With the telescope."

She swallows a giggle. "You can't see it from here." She shrugs. "Really you can't. It's too far, much too far away."

"I told you…" breaks in one of the other soldiers, tall, blonde, with an attractive smile. He winks at her.

"Sure?" The other soldier loosens his grip.

"Absolutely. Sure. It's over there…somewhere." She lifts an arm and points out at the empty black sea. "But it's much, much too far away to see from here."

The soldier suddenly lets her go, his taller companion clicking his heels and giving a slight bow. Her eye catches on the skull and crossbones on his cap as they turn, cross the road back towards the bar, laughing and clapping the fat soldier on the back.

She races down the promenade, a black Mercedes passing her with two men in uniform in the back, a red, black and white flag, fluttering from the front of the bonnet. Another truck rumbles past, exhaust fumes choking the air, more soldiers.

As she leaves the centre of the town she stops and leans out over the railings, fringing the promenade, remembering how her father would tell her off as she turned somersaults on the bars as a child, her cotton skirts flipping over her head, her brother laughing. She looks out across the wide beach, memories jostling for space: picnics, games of tag, building forts from sand, collecting shells, playing volleyball, screaming as they dived into the freezing water. She looks out to where sea tips into the sky and imagines all the places beyond the horizon, but she is trapped here now with Hitler's Nazis. Shivering she turns from the seafront, into the street leading to the clinic and gasps; a bomb has crashed its way through a terrace of houses, bricks spill across the pavement, broken furniture is upended amongst the rubble, a flowered curtain waving flaglike in the breeze; a woman in a torn grey dress picking her way among the debris, a toddler trying to grab on to her skirt.

Hetty holds her breath looks further up the street and sees by some miracle that the clinic is untouched. Wide white stone steps leading up to the entrance, a queue of people filing in and out.

She crosses the road and joins the queue going in.

Pushing through the swing doors she is slapped by the noise, the mayhem; people collapsed on the floor, a couple whispering and crying, an old man curled up, moaning, covered in mud and blood, a red-faced little girl struggling to get off her mother's lap. The mess collides with the acrid smells of blood, disinfectant and burned clothing. Weaving in and out of sprawled legs, jumping up and down, is a little boy oblivious, spinning and laughing, as a woman holding a wailing baby calls to him.

"Jaan, Jaan, stop that come here! Jaan!"

The little boy crashes into Hetty's legs. She bends down and holds him by his thin pale arms as his mother reaches her and grabs his hand.

"Bloody children," says an old woman pushing through the door behind her, limping, leaning heavily on a cane.

Hetty scans the room. At the reception desk a grey-haired woman with wire-rimmed glasses is both talking on the phone and with a bony finger impatiently directing people in a long queue in front of her. Queuing is not going to help. She starts her own search, turning down each passage, glancing into each examination cubicle, walking discreetly, confidently, defying anyone to ask what she is doing. Nobody stops her. There's a man on a gurney in military uniform, blood oozing from a gash across his face. It's not Hans. She walks on, pulls a thin blanket over a shivering boy curled up on another bed in torn grey shorts.

She's searching the last corridor when she hears her name being called.

"Hetty! Het! Is that you?" The cry is breathless, desperate.

She looks around at the human sea of misery and sees no-one she knows.

"Het?"

She looks again: a man, red hair matted with blood and grit, his arm and side a mess of charred flesh looks back at her.

"God Almighty! Wil?"

Jozef – the same day – Laag Keppel

Jozef sits on the red tiled kitchen floor, legs splayed out, trying to read his book, distracted by the constant chatter of his 4-year-old sister Trudi. He's been cooped inside reading and playing board games with her for the past ten days while his parents

9

listen to the news: towns taken, bridges defended, troops lost, catastrophic destruction, surrender. He can't believe it.

His father has just re-tuned the radio to broadcasts coming from the Reichstag in Germany, the honeyed voice of the newscaster is saying the Netherlands occupation will be peaceful, the Netherlands will be part of a greater Germany, part of something powerful, part of something strong.

He looks up as his mother stops chopping carrots for some sort of soup, wipes her hands on her apron, and strides across the kitchen, heels clicking noisily on the tiles, turning the radio off, glaring at his father: "They'll kill us."

Jozef looks intently back at his book. Not another quarrel.

"I was just getting a different viewpoint," says his father quietly.

"What the…?" His mother's voice begins to take off.

But before she gets any further there is a sharp knock on the back door and she marches across the room to open it. It's one of the teachers from the village school.

"Mrs Jacobs? The school is closed until Monday but a group of us are over there in the field at the back. We are telling families that the children are welcome to come over, get out, run about for a bit?" He smiles. "We'll watch them." He can see his mother struggling to compose herself, to smile graciously. The teacher continues talking: "There shouldn't be any danger, not here in the village. Would Jozef like to come over? Some of the boys want to get up a game of football." He spots Trudi hiding behind her mother's skirt and smiles at her. "And Trudi too of course."

"Jozef?"

He's up and ready to go, but his mother grabs his wrist and holds him back.

"Trudi? Do you want to go with Jozef?"

No, please no. He desperately doesn't want to be told to look after her. Trudi looks at him with round brown eyes but then buries her face in her mother's skirt.

"You go Jozef. Trudi can…." Before she has finished speaking, he is out of the door.

The gang are all in the field: Hendrik who's the unofficial leader and nearly 10, a year older than Jozef, is trying to organise a kickabout game of football. But it's Pim, Jozef's best friend who shouts out when he sees him. "Grab a ball from the games shed Jozef!" The game when it finally starts is a mismatch of ages and abilities and includes two 7-year-olds who drop out when Pim calls one of them an idiot for missing an obvious goal. They play on for a bit, but eventually when another player leaves they give up and collapse in exhaustion on the grass, swopping news about what they've been up to during the invasion; Pim getting the biggest laugh with a limping imitation of his grandmother, who lives with them, constantly turning the lights back on after his parents have turned them off in accordance with the instructions from the local police, and getting seriously cross when his father turned them off again.

"What's going to happen now?" says Jozef lying back on the grass.

"My dad says we'll probably be better off under the Nazis," says Pim.

Hendrik shoves him roughly. "Rubbish! He's joking."

Pim shrugs.

"You can't think that" says Jozef, leaning up on one elbow. "They invaded us. My cousin fought them."

"Did he kill any Nazis?" asks Hendrik.

"How do I know? I expect so." Jozef wonders where Hans is as he pulls at the grass, trying to find a long enough strand to whistle through. He starts blowing but after a not very successful minute gives up; he's bored. "What now?"

Hendrik stands up, brushing flakes of grass off his shorts. "Let's go and see what's going on."

"Like how?"

"My father says there are thousands of troops coming in on the main road from Germany. We can get to the canal path below the road and... maybe we can see what's happening....?"

"Isn't that dangerous?" Pim shakes he head. "We could get into real trouble...."

"How can it be dangerous? We're not going to do anything. Just," Hendrik shrugs. "Just look." He starts searching for a gap in the hedge. "Jozef you up for it?"

Jozef looks at Pim.

"Nobody is going to know, are they?" says Hendrik starting to push his way backwards through the gap he's just found. "They won't even notice we've gone and if they do they'll just think we've gone home."

Pim nods at Jozef who looks Hendrik in the eye. "OK."

"Me too," says Pim.

They slip through the gap and scramble down through the field behind the hedge to the main village road, running quickly the 100 yards to the bridge over the canal that borders the village. Once across and on to a footpath, Hendrik is garrulous with his plan. He's obviously been thinking about it all day realizes Jozef. Hendrik reckons it will take them 15 minutes to get to the path below the main road using the footpaths that network across the fields. They can then hide on the tow path and crawl up the bank where they should get a good view of what's going on without being seen.

"But stay low," Hendrik is emphatic. "We have to stay out of sight."

They climb over a wooden gate into another field and duck down running along the packed earth at the edge, past a group of black and white cows grazing methodically on the grass. Jozef stifles a laugh as Pim slaps his foot into a cow pat. Hendrik turns and beckons them on. They hurry giggling behind him, Pim dragging his foot in the long grass to clean off the mess. They climb a stone stile into another field, the ground dark and soft, newly turned, pale shoots of an, as yet unrecognisable, summer crop just appearing. There's a tractor in the distance, growling its way through the earth and they duck and run, not wanting to be stopped or asked what they are up to. They pretend they are Dutch troops, flattening themselves against the hedge of the next field, crushing banks of wildflowers, buttercups, pink and white campion, sprawling vetch. They start to crawl when they hear a car backfiring down a track leading to the farm bordering the field they are in. They run around the back of the farmyard, nearly tripping over an old tin tub filled with rainwater, skirting a pile of wooden crates. The farm collie, chained near the barn, hears them and starts to bark. Pim runs forward.

"Get back!" calls Hendrik

But Pim just turns puts a finger to his lips and continues to creep towards the dog, mumbling softly to it, holding out his hand for the collie to sniff. And suddenly the dog is on the ground, stops barking and is enjoying a scratch under its chin and between its ears, doleful eyes on Pim.

Hendrik sighs, steps out. "Come on!"

Pim grins, gets up and runs back to them.

Steadily they work their way across the flat landscape, a patchwork of fields, climbing wooden gates and stone stiles until they reach a small wood, not much more than a cluster of trees and stop to catch their breath.

"One more field after this and then down to the canal path near the main road. That's where they'll be." Hendrik is deadly serious.

Pim scuffs his shoes in the clean grass under the tree. Jozef wonders if they should be where they are.

"You ok?"

"Sure." Pim grins.

"Let's go," says Jozef

"Keep low and keep close."

Hendrik leads the way and they all duck as they come out of the wood and run for the shelter of the stone hedge edging the final field. They jog along, keeping down, only slowing as they reach the other side, climb over a gate, then scramble down a track which leads onto the canal path running parallel to the main road. They can hear the tanks now, grumbling, gears cranking, metal banging. The escalating roar makes them cringe back against the bank, excited and petrified. Jozef feels his heart pounding, he should not be there, he knows it now, his legs are turning to jelly and he should definitely not be there. Hendrik waves to them as the roar grows louder; slowly they move forward. They are less than 20 yards away and the noise is deafening. They push their way on their hands and knees through the undergrowth of leafy ferns and round clusters of hawthorn growing up the bank, pricking their skin as they push it back and peer over the top. Jozef thinks his heart will stop; the black armoured trucks and tanks snake along the road forever; soldiers bumping and jostling in the back, two at the front on look out, huge metal machine guns pointing in every direction.

A thundering overhead forces them to look up. Dozens of planes roar across the sky, blacking out the sun. Pim stands, head back, mouth open. Hendrik grabs his shorts and pulls him down. But it's too late. One of the trucks stops, pulls over, half a dozen troops jump out. The boys slide down the bank fast, a nest of nettles stinging their skin. Skin pierced and pricked they get up and start running. Hendrik first, head back legs pumping, then Pim. Jozef races down the path behind them feeling his heart thumping loudly in his ears, his head buzzing with fear. Hendrik is already on the stile that leads into the field before the wood.

"Come on!"

Blood pounding Jozef races on, past Pim, muscles pumping, sinews stretching, heart thumping. A shot cracks through the air. Someone shouts and he stops, turns. Pim yelps. He's on the ground, trying to pull himself up. Jozef takes three steps back grabs him by the collar, pulls him up.

"I've got him!"

"I wasn't hit," gasps Pim. "I slipped."

"Come on!"

They run. The soldiers are chasing them now, they can hear their heavy boots thudding along the path. Jozef gasps for air, slowing not stopping, not daring to look, ready to die first, but the soldiers stop.

"*Jungen. Nur einige Jungen.* Boys. It's only boys."

The air cracks open with another shot. Jozef freezes, turns, the Nazi soldier is so close he can see the stripes on his shoulders. He's laughing, shouting and shooting into the air. "*Laufen jungen. Laufen.* Run boys! Run!"

They run.

The soldiers don't follow.

None of them say a word as they make their way back through the woods, across the fields, behind the farm and on along the network of footpaths back to Laag Keppel.

Back in the school field they examine Pim's knee as he screws his face up with pain. It's twisted, but nothing serious, nothing that will surprise his mother.

Hendrik is soon garrulous with the events of the afternoon. They are all shaking but he reworks their recklessness into an expedition in which they are the heroes. Soon they are all laughing, teasing Pim who goes beetroot with embarrassment and then gets an attack of the giggles as he thinks about their escape.

Going home, Jozef is buzzing with the adventure, but when his mother asks about the afternoon, he tells her nothing. "Just playing football with Hendrik and the others". She mutters something about Hendrik being a reckless boy and asks him to read a story to Trudi.

He's grateful when it's time for bed. But memories of the day now won't let him sleep. He hears his parents coming upstairs arguing, going into their bedroom next to his. The floorboards creak familiarly under their weight, talking as they get ready for the night.

"So, what now Sam?"

"We wait. We go about our business and wait. Things won't change for us. Not here in the village, in Laag Keppel. I've lived here all my life. We are safe here, as safe as we can be."

"You are a fool if you don't think things will change." His mother's voice is bitter. Jozef doesn't want to hear the argument again. He wants it to end. He pulls his blankets up around his ears, but he can still hear them.

Then it's quiet. Jozef hears his father getting into bed, the springs complaining as he settles down. He pulls down the blanket. But he can hear his mother crying now, her voice choked with her tears. "We have to go Sam."

"Where to? Where do you think we can go? And what about my parents, my sisters, your sister?"

"You know Lea had to leave Germany."

"Lea lived in a city. It's different. They are not interested in us. We're not like her, we're not religious."

"We're still Jewish Sam."

Jozef pulls a pillow over his head finally blocking out the argument, his mother's sobs. He thinks of his Aunt Lea, how she'd looked when she and her husband had first moved to the Netherlands two years earlier. He'd been told to hug her, but she was so thin and pinched, not a person you wanted to hug. But his mother hugged her.

Hetty – The Hague – December

Hetty winds her way through the fug of the noisy bar, pushing past students from the Leiden University who seem to have taken the place over. The air is thick with argument and cigarette smoke. She squeezes past a large group who have clearly been drinking for some time, one winks at her and lurches forward as she passes, spilling beer on the polished mahogany bar. She pushes him away and continues towards a booth at the back where Dirk and Wil are sitting, navigating herself by the distinctive thick ginger brush of Wil's hair. Every time she sees him she feels a sense of relief that he is alive, that he survived, that he wasn't dying when she found him in the clinic in Scheveningen.

Dirk stands to greet her, envelopes her in a hug. She breathes him in – his defining scent of cigarettes, strong coffee and newspapers. He moves over and she slides into the booth next to him, taking off her woollen gloves, undoing her damp coat. It's freezing outside and she rubs her hands briskly together to get warm, then shimmies out of her coat and hangs it on a hook at the end of the booth.

The table is littered with books and newspapers, an overflowing ashtray, used coffee cups and glasses. An article on the front of a student flier complains about Nazi authority's ongoing intransigence in the face of student demands to re-open the university which has been closed for over a month. A notebook lies open in front of Dirk with the start of a scribbled letter to the University administration. He and Wil seem to have taken up temporary residence in the bar along with the other students.

Wil grins at her lopsidedly as Dirk lifts an arm and catches the eye of a frazzled looking waiter and orders three beers.

"How you doing nursey?" Wil winks at her.

She raises an eyebrow, splays her hands out on the table, the backs rough and red and leans into the back of the leather seat. After finding Wil in the clinic all those months ago she'd volunteered to help, working as an auxiliary and within a month had applied to train as a nurse at the major teaching hospital in the Hague. She'd been told on her first day that first year trainees got all the worst jobs and that's proved to be true, she has never seen so many urine-soaked sheets or stinking bedpans and sick buckets.

"It is what it is. It will get better."

"No regrets?"

She shakes her head and smiles as Wil leans across the table takes her hands and kisses her on both cheeks. She looks at the deep scar on his cheek, still livid at the edges after all these months. He drags a flop of his hair forward in an unsuccessful attempt to cover it.

Dirk pulls her close as the waiter puts three glasses of beer on the table and hands him the chit. Someone shouts at Wil and he gets up and pushes his way through the crowd to greet a girl coming into the bar in a red coat, waving and calling to him.

Hetty nods in his direction: "How's he doing?"

"Better, lots better, much more himself and less depressed. But still mad as hell that I was right about these Nazi bastards," he grins. "In some ways it has made him angrier, more committed to wanting to see them gone." He pulls her close. "But how are you really. You looked worried when you came in."

"I didn't think you saw me."

"Of course I saw you, I would have called out, but I could tell you'd spotted us and were making your way in the right direction."

She takes a long swallow of beer. "Nothing and everything is the matter," she puts her glass down. "My sister Loes and I went to register yesterday, and that was pretty weird."

"Register? As Jewish?"

"Yes. My father went on and on and on about it. They are talking about imprisoning Jews for five years who don't register and taking away their property. It's crazy."

"That serious?"

She shakes her head. "Look, I'm here. I'm working. Everything seems fine and it probably seems small with everything else that's going on but it feels… creepy. What's the reason for it? And I felt….marked I suppose. When we left the council office there were these Nazi soldiers standing at the bottom of the steps and they kind of eyed us up and down." We decided to take a walk along the promenade, breath in some sea air," she shakes her head. "And these Nazi soldiers just grab us round the waist."

"What?"

"Yes, odd eh? Kind of scary. They're everywhere in Scheveningen. It's going to be a major base, they walk around like they own the place," She takes a cigarette from a pack lying on the table, shaking her head. "Actually, they do own the place." Dirk lights the cigarette and she takes a drag, blows out a stream of smoke and sighs. "Anyway, they try to drag us into a bar for a drink, laughing and joking and asking us what we were doing in the Council offices, did we work there. They were not nasty, just jolly and friendly and slightly drunk. What are we supposed to do?" She takes another drag of the cigarette. "So we just go along with it." She looks at him, sees his frown, shakes her head. "You know the bar I mean, next to the council office? Huge place. And we go in and it's just packed…mostly off duty soldiers, a few locals, some being over friendly, others trying to ignore them, everyone looking at us. This fat guy, the one who had grabbed Loes drags us over to a table, makes us, well doesn't make us but insists we have a drink. And the other guy, his friend who had grabbed me asks me again whether I worked in the Council offices. His Dutch was good. He looked more sober than the others."

"What did you say?"

"I said, no, I was training to be a nurse….and actually…I couldn't really stay for a drink as he had just reminded me that I would be late for a shift."

"Did you have a shift?

"No, it was my day off…a really rare day off…but I needed to get out of there." She pauses, takes a gulp of her beer.

"And?"

"Well we left….but I felt….this is going to sound weird," she shakes her head. "I felt invaded."

He looks at her seriously. "We have been invaded Het…" He starts to laugh, a deep hopeless chuckle, but then stops when he sees how serious she is.

"They left you alone then."

"Yup." She takes a long sip of her drink. "In retrospect they were very polite really. One of them even clicked his heels and bowed as we left the table." She shakes her head at the memory. "So, we left. We grabbed each other by the arm and walked, actually half ran home." She turns her glass round in her hands. "You know the thing is, I actually thought because they'd seen us coming out of the council building…. I actually thought they were going to ask us for our papers which had just been stamped *Jood*." She stubs the cigarette out. "And I could feel the absolute terror of that inside me. Just…"

"But they wouldn't do anything. They couldn't do anything to you?"

She shrugs. "I don't know. I just know I was….scared. Really scared."

He turns her face to his with the palm of his hand. "I'm here for you Het."

She leans forward and kisses him gently. "I know."

"Sorry to break things up," They look up and see Wil has returned and is pulling out a handful of pamphlets from inside his coat. The girl in red is laughing, chatting to a group of students near the door of the bar.

Dirk looks at him and Wil passes across a pamphlet. Dirk scans it quickly. "So we go?" asks Wil. The pamphlet is written by students from Amsterdam who want to form an action group.

Dirk looks at Hetty. She shrugs. "I'm fine."

"I think we should," says Dirk. "We need to co-ordinate. And there's a lot more going on there. What does Anya say?" He indicates the girl in the red coat.

"She gave me the pamphlet. She hopes strength in numbers might force some changes. I'm not really that sure, but what else can we do? We've got to give it a go. If we support them in Amsterdam, they might support us here."

Hetty leans across and reads the pamphlet over Dirk's shoulder about a possible strike in Amsterdam being organised by the Communist party and a group of students.

Dirk takes a stray curl which has fallen across her face and tucks it back behind her ear. "You know they've closed the university? We thought it was just temporary...but."

"They're not going to re-open?"

"Seems unlikely. Anyway, we want to show them that they can close the university, but they can't stop us." He sits back and puts his hands behind his head. "The students are the university,"

He picks up the pack of cigarettes takes one and lights it, offering the pack across to her and Wil. "Everyone is so angry," Dirk shakes his head at the memory. "They've sacked professors, Jewish professors, arrested others... It is just wrong. Really wrong."

"They can occupy our country, but we won't let them occupy our minds," says Wil quoting from the pamphlet in front of him and drinking his beer. He leans forward. "There is much more going on in Amsterdam and we need to get together with the students there."

"You really think you can do something?"

"Who knows," Dirk looks across at Wil. "But we won't forgive ourselves if we don't try."

She nods. Someone turns on the radio, Glenn Miller's Moonlight Serenade starts up and a young woman in a yellow jersey standing near them starts humming to the tune. The student standing next to her grabs her round the waist and they try to dance, arms wrapped around each other, swaying to the gentle jazz sounds coming from a radio behind the bar, bumping into tables. The barman turns the music up.

Dirk leans into her puts an arm around her shoulders, rubs her arm. "You'll be ok Hetty? If we go?"

"Sure. The hospital keeps me busy 12 hours a day. I'm exhausted. No time for fun." she grins at them and drains her glass looking at her watch. "Actually, I've got to get back. Just wanted to see you both. Touch base."

"Ah the soft easy days of working for father are over!" laughs Wil.

Hetty leans across and punches him on the arm. "He was never, never soft. I pity Loes sometimes. She has to do lots more now I'm not there." She pauses shaking her head. "He wasn't that happy about my taking up nursing. And..." she shakes her head. "Hans is still missing. That's quietly breaking my mother's heart."

Wil turns his glass round and round on the table. "Have you heard from Rosa?"

Hetty reaches across and takes his hand, knowing he is still sore that Rosa broke it off with him. He'd got too clingy after the accident, and she'd decided to take a job in Zeist with the Zonnerhuis, the disabled children's home she'd been working for in Scheveningen who have moved there. Hetty can't tell him how they had sat in the park. tears rolling down Rosa's face as she'd explained that a clean break was the only option. Her parents' home in Scheveningen had been seconded by the Nazi army and they were going to live somewhere in the north with her grandparents. The offer of the job in Zeist had seemed like a godsend.

"Rosa's fine. You know...." Hetty starts to tell Wil.

"I don't want to talk about it."

Hetty shrugs. "I miss her."

"Me too."

There's a sudden commotion at the front of the bar as a group of Nazi soldiers walks in elbowing their way forward, a girl in a jaunty blue hat hanging on the arm of one of them, smiling and giggling. They all look as space opens up around the soldiers and the noisy chatter settles quickly into an almost unbearable hum. Only the radio keeps playing jazz.

Hetty looks at the group, mesmerised, and catches her breath as the girl in the blue hat turns her way. "I've got to go."

"What's up?" Dirk puts down his glass and stands up to help her.

"I'm going to be late back...and I know that girl," she nods in the direction of the Nazi group, the girl laughing and flirting with the tallest of the soldiers. "She was in the class above me at school. She knows....she knows I'm Jewish and she's a nasty piece of work."

Dirk looks at her. "I'm coming with you." He looks at Wil.

"Me too. Let's get out of here." They scoop up the pamphlets and notebooks on the table, stuffing them into a leather satchel. Wil slings it onto his back as they push their way out of the bar.

Wil turns to look at the girl as he passes, and she winks at him.

Dirk opens the door and as Hetty pushes through it, the girl recognises her. "Hetty!" There's surprise and mockery in the voice. "Hey, Hetty Van Leuven what are...." The rest of the sentence is lost as the door of the bar swings closed behind them.

PART 2

1941

Taken

Hetty – The Hague – March

Stepping out of the dark oak swing doors of the hospital Hetty shivers and pulls up the collar of her coat, pulling on woollen gloves. It's a miserable grey day, the sky flat and a fine drizzle combing the air.

She sees Wil before he sees her. It's been nearly a month since the strike, the march, since…since. She breathes, swallows, pushing down the emotions which still keep flooding over her, pulling down her black cloche hat. Part of her has been dreading this. Dreading knowing. Wil's standing across the road under the black skeleton branches of a plane tree, leaning against the trunk smoking, absorbed in his own thoughts. She smiles involuntarily. He turns and seeing her waves as she slips across the road, dodging an elderly woman on a bike. He tosses the cigarette stub on the ground, crushing it with his heel and opens his arms to greet her. It is a long hug and she sinks into the comfort of it.

"Shall we walk? Have you got time for a drink? A cup of coffee?"

She looks up, the rain is stopping. "Let's just walk. I haven't got a lot of time."

He puts his arm around her shoulders holding her close as they walk along in silence, matching each other's stride, deep in thought, oblivious of the few people on the street racing to get inside before the drizzle resumes its relentless onslaught. They turn down a side street leading away from the centre and then through black wrought iron gates into the park.

There are a handful of people in the park, two middle aged women sheltering in a wooden gazebo deep in conversation, Hetty recognises one of the porters from the hospital racing along in the opposite direction and smiles at him. They wind their way along a brick path dividing crescent shaped flower beds, clusters of red, yellow and purple crocuses poking out of the loamy brown earth. They pass a woman in a green coat pulling a little boy on a wooden tricycle as he makes train noises. In the middle of the maze of flower beds there is a circular shelter divided into sections and they find an empty corner, white paint flaking from its boards and sit down on the curved bench inside. Hetty takes her gloves off and reaches across to take hold of Wil's hand which is red with the cold.

"Tell me." She looks up into his dark eyes, haunted by shadows, knowing that he's seeing the shadows in her eyes, haunting her. "Tell me what happened."

He squeezes her hands before letting go and pulling a pack of cigarettes from his top pocket, offering one to her before sliding the pack back into his pocket and pulling out a pack of matches. "I'll tell you what I know." He takes a moment to light the cigarettes, and they both inhale deeply, but Wil says nothing.

After a minute Hetty breaks the silence. "Well, I know about the strike. Everyone knows about that."

The angry two-day strike, orchestrated by the Communist party in response to discrimination against Jews, and the lock down of everyone and everything that dared to question the absolute authority of the Nazis. It was finally prompted when 427 young Jewish men were arrested for a series of protests to the barbed wire fencing being put up around Amsterdam's Jewish Quarter. The outrage was widespread. Dirk and Wil had been part of the student action.

Wil looks up at her taking a second, long drag of his cigarette.

"At first, in some ways, it was amazing. Dirk was so full of energy, so full of anger. We all were. It was no longer just about the university; it was about everything. And it was great because for once in our stupid lives Dirk and I were fighting on the same side, in agreement with everything each of us said, and I suppose we felt closer than ever, like real brothers." He taps ash off his cigarette onto the ground. "I never really understood before how close we really were, that underneath all the arguing and shouting at one another, we actually cared about the same things, had the same set of principles."

He shakes his head, and blinks slowly remembering. "He felt it too. I know he did. Anyway, we were all up for carrying out some sort of protest march on the day of the strike. I mean it is kind of what you feel you can do, should do. We wanted to be heard. We needed to be heard; to be seen and heard. We felt so utterly abused and ignored – our university closed, professors dismissed, so many people arrested, the barbed wire around the Jewish Quarter...

"Those arrests in Amsterdam, so many of them! I knew a couple of the guys, not well, but I knew them from university. They were just ordinary guys protesting against crazy regulations." He takes another deep drag of his cigarette. "There were posters everywhere, flyers distributed by lots of people, including us, to everyone we could think of, stuck to lamp posts, walls, wherever."

"There were some here too," says Hetty.

"Really? Well, it seemed that as fast as we put them up, the Nazis pulled them down or painted over them. But there were too many. It was all organized by the Communist party, but we were with them, everyone was with them on this. What we didn't anticipate was the level of support the strike would have. It was huge. Extraordinary. We woke up on the day of the strike and there were no trams, no buses, nothing, shops were closed, cafes too." He shakes his head. "It was unbelievable. Awe inspiring. We'd agreed with some of the Amsterdam students that we would march. Anya – you remember her? I had a bit of a thing for her." He shakes his head momentarily absorbed in his own memories. "It's over now." He flicks some ash from his cigarette. "We had been painting, Anya and I had been painting, this banner in black and orange wanting to march with it on the day. Crazy eh?

"Anyway, we go out to join the march, carrying this banner…the paint still wet," he shakes his head. "And there are not just dozens of us, but hundreds, maybe thousands. All sorts of people decided to join in – women, men, old and young. There was a woman with a push chair and a man with his son on his shoulders. There was all this anger but mixed in there was a subtext of almost celebration, if that doesn't sound mad, like we, the people of the Netherlands were standing together against what'd happened, what was happening. Our country was occupied but we would not change our way of life… Or something like that. It was powerful, really powerful.

"We were with a group from Leiden and Dirk was saying we should be at the front of the march and Anya wanted to go with him, to take the banner, but my leg was killing me…you know…from before…it still plays up so I knew I was slowing them down, so I gave Dirk my end of the banner and said I would catch them up. And he looks at me, grabs my shoulder and says: "You alright mate?" And I give him a shove, tell him to go and they are gone, pushing through to the front. Dirk was jumping up and down, punching the air, waving this crazy banner we'd painted in the apartment where we'd been staying. He was so…. impassioned," he shakes his head, tosses the stub of his cigarette to the ground and grinds it out with his heel. "Not like him really, I've always been the crazy one in the past. But he was so full of energy, angry energy." He takes another cigarette from the packet and lights it. "I wish you'd been there, that you could have seen him." He flicks a look into her eyes.

"Anyway, they were gone, melded into the crowd, swallowed up and carried by this surge of people and all I could see was their banner waving crazily in the air as they made their way to the front.

"I stayed with some others. We'd already planned to meet back at the flat if we got separated. We started singing… everyone was walking and shouting and singing. Someone started singing the national anthem…little bit bold considering the occupation. But for those few hours we felt… unstoppable. Our heads told us we weren't, but our hearts…

"And in those mad moments we went with our hearts. We wanted to believe that something good, something positive, some change would come out of it all," he grabs her hand. "I wanted to believe, to hope against hope that things could get better? There were so many of us, linking arms, banners waving, people leaning out of windows, cheering us on. What could they do?" He shakes his head, exhales a long stream of smoke. "What could they not do."

She knows what happened next. The anger of the Nazi authorities had been incalculable. They'd sent in SS troops with machine guns to break up the march, ostensibly to frighten people, shooting in the air. But shots went into the crowd.

"It was horrific, deafening, the sound ricocheting around the streets, against the buildings, people screaming, running.

Terrifying. I was… terrified." Dirk rubs his eyes, pinching the top of his nose. "People were falling over each other to get away, get out of there, scattering in every direction. We were all petrified that they would never stop firing." He shakes his head.

"I got out, down a side street, ran, everyone ran, and I made my way back to the apartment and waited… and waited. And Dirk didn't come. Others appeared, but not Dirk or Anya. To tell you the truth I was more worried about Anya….

"Then eventually a knock on the door and it's Anya, looking terrible, blood streaked down her face and on her clothes, white as a sheet, limping, her coat covered in mud." Wil stops, breathes, puts his head in his hands but keeps talking.

"She told me they were running. He was pushing her ahead of him, away from the march, away from the shooting, still trailing that stupid banner. She ducked into an alleyway behind a restaurant and crouched behind bins. There was more shooting and she looked up and realised that Dirk hadn't followed her. He wasn't there. He wasn't behind her. But she couldn't move. Didn't dare move, not for ages. Not until it was all over, and she could hear the troops leaving, and even then she waited."

"And?"

"And then when it was quiet, she'd gone back. She saw him. She saw Dirk. She couldn't go to him because the Nazis were everywhere picking up people who were injured, arresting them carting them off in vans. He was just lying there, arms and legs splayed across the pavement, blood oozing from his head. She watched as they picked up his body and just threw it into the back of a truck like a sack of coal. I kept asking was she sure, was she sure it was Dirk and that he was dead not just injured. And she kept nodding, crying."

He looks up and sees the tears streaming down Hetty's face and realises he is crying too.

A list had been posted two days later of those killed and those arrested, a warning to anyone else who thought to do the same thing.

"I can't..."

"Don't. Enough." Hetty takes his hand as he wipes away the tears from his face with the back of his other hand.

"Het, I feel like I finally found the brother I'd always wanted, and always had but didn't know it. And then I lost him."

Neither of them says anything. And they sit like that thinking, remembering for ten minutes, until Hetty glances up at a woman shouting at two little boys chasing each other across the grass. She looks at her watch.

"I must go," she says gently. "I'm on duty in 10 minutes."

Wil takes a huge breath. "OK"

"But what about you? Are you going to be about for a bit now?" She gets up from the bench. "Are you staying here? Going back to Amsterdam?"

"I'm going back to Amsterdam for a bit, then maybe Utrecht. There's a group of us," he hesitates, looks at her. "We've got to stop this."

"Stop it? What are you going to do?" She shakes her head.

"Try to stop it Het, try to do something. I can't do nothing."

They walk silently, Hetty clenches her fists, pushes her hands into her pockets. The drizzle starts again, a dog is barking at a squirrel scampering up a tree.

"Yes, yes. I understand. You need to, for Dirk.for... everyone."

"I don't know where I'll be....Hetty..." He stumbles over his words. "Het it won't help you if you know where I am."

She nods feeling an emptiness opening up inside her, a loneliness. What can he do? What group will he join? She braves a smile as they reach the hospital. She pulls away from him. "Look, you know where I'll be."

33

She turns leaves, runs up the steps of the hospital, sadness seeping through her like ice. It's a final goodbye not just to Dirk and Wil but to everything that was. She pushes through the wooden door, holding it open for an old man in a Homburg hat wheezing his way in. She glances back as the door closes, but Wil has already gone.

Jozef – July – Laag Keppel

Jozef's late, they all are. But they are laughing, racing down the path by the canal, then up to the road, across the bridge. His shirt hangs out of his shorts, sticks to his back after the swim.

He waves to Hendrik and Pim as they turn left and he runs down the main street, past the family's butcher's shop, down the alley by the side and through the gate which leads to their dark green painted back door. He stops to catch his breath, runs his hands under the outside tap and combs wet fingers through his thick brown hair before quietly opening the door into the kitchen. He's surprised to see both his parents sitting at the kitchen table. He'd expected to find his mother making supper and his father to be still in the shop, scrubbing down and putting meat away. They look up.

"Jozef."

He stands still, smiling nervously waiting for the telling off, he knows he's late.

"Sit down," says his father indicating the chair opposite him.

He pulls the chair out, wondering why his parents are so serious, so quiet he can hear the ticking of the mantlepiece clock in the living room. "Where's Trudi?"

"She's at your Aunt Lea's, playing with Tina," says his mother softly, looking at him, her face blank, white. She's turning her wedding ring round and round, something she does when she's nervous. Something's wrong, very wrong. His mind sorts swiftly

34

through the worries of the summer, his grandmother's illness, his cousin's disappearance. But he was sure his mother told him Oma was better when she visited her two days ago. Hans, maybe it's something to do with Hans.

"Have they found Hans dad? Is he…."

"It's not about Hans." His father picks up a letter lying on the table in front of him and passes it across to Jozef.

"Read it."

It's from the head of the village school. He feels tense, he hasn't done anything wrong, he's a good pupil, that's what his form teacher told him at the end of term, roughing his head as he walked out the door and telling him to have a good summer. But his dad's face tells him it's not going to be anything good. He focuses on the letter.

"Dear Mr and Mrs Jacobs,

"I regret to inform you that Jozef and Trudi will no longer be able to attend this school…"

He feels dizzy and reads on where the letter explains that as a Jewish family they will now need to find an appropriate Jewish school for their children.

"What?….Why?" A mix of embarrassment and anger sifts through him.

"It's a new law Jozef. It affects all Jewish families," says his father quietly.

"But why?"

His father shrugs.

"It's not a surprise Jozef," says his mother bitterly as she gets up from the table. Her heels click as she walks across to the sink where she has been washing lettuce and tomatoes for a salad for supper.

His father reaches across the table and takes his hand. "I went to see the headmaster this morning, after the letter arrived and then the head of the local council. I appealed to their better judgement, their reason. But there is nothing they can do. If they don't obey this law they will get into serious trouble…and so will we.

"So, this afternoon I went to the synagogue, the one your aunt and uncle attend and asked what they were going to do. They are setting up a Jewish school in Doetinchem."

"Doetinchem! That's so far away! I won't know anyone." Jozef screws the letter up in his hands. "I don't know anyone who lives in Doetinchem." A lump forms in his throat, in his belly he feels sick. "I want to go to my school with my friends."

"You haven't got that option," says his mother turning around.

"I'm sorry Jozef, really sorry," says his father sadly. "I understand how you feel."

"How do you know what I feel? You don't know what I feel? No-one's telling you that you have to go somewhere else? This is….crazy." He kicks the chair leg. "Does everyone else know? Does everyone at the school know? My friends."

"They will."

Joseph yanks his hand from his father, scrapes his chair back and goes to the back door thinking about his friends, the swim that afternoon, the sun on his back, the chat about school, the teacher they'll get next year, who'll be in the football team and what position they each want to play, feel they should play. "Will I still be able to play in the football team?"

"It's a school team Jozef. There'll be another team at the new school…."

But he is already half out of the back door, banging it behind him, not caring what anyone says or thinks.

Hetty – September – The Hague

Hetty pulls open the door of the hospital, half smiling, reading the letter in her hand from Rosa that she's just picked up from the reception desk. She's waiting for a woman with two children struggling up the steps, opening the door for her to come in before she goes out. Rosa's clearly happy, settled at the children's home in Zeist.

"*...write and tell me more about the hospital. Loved the story about the old man who wore three pairs of pyjamas.... I told it to the children (adapted of course) and they thought it was hilarious... One of the little boys tried to put on two pairs...*"

There's a crash behind her.

"Damn it!".

She swings around, recognising Dr Meyer bending down to pick up a file of papers and books which have slewed across the polished black and white tiled floor. He always smiles at her on his ward rounds. She tucks the letter back into her pocket and goes back into the hospital to help him.

"Thanks," he says as she bends down to help pick up the papers. "It's Hetty isn't it? Thanks...just...can you put them over there on the bench...thanks."

He bends to pick up more papers, piling them on the long wooden bench that runs along the wall, the length of the reception area. He reminds her a bit of Dirk, the way his eyes crease when he smiles and she feels a sudden lump of sadness. But it feels as if an aeon of time has passed not just six months since he was killed. It feels that her friendship with him belonged to another lifetime, a time wrapped and folded away in her memory of 'before'. She straightens the pile of papers in her hands and passes them to the doctor.

"The box broke," he says indicating the collapsed cardboard next to him, fatally torn across two sides. "I probably shouldn't have stuffed it so full. Just.... Anyway, thanks." He smiles again and shakes his head.

"Where are you taking all this stuff?" She hesitates. "Can I help?"

He says nothing, he's absorbed in putting his papers into order.

"Dr Meyer?"

He looks up. "Would you?" He sighs. "Just out to the car. That would be great. A really great help. Thank you."

He scrunches the destroyed box into a nearby wastepaper bin and takes a pile of books and papers and puts it in her outstretched arms, picking up the rest of the pile and a small brown leather suitcase "Follow me."

He smiles gratefully as the receptionist slips out from behind her desk and opens the door for then. "Thanks Emily, thanks so much."

Following him Hetty remembers that's one of the things she particularly likes about him, that he remembers everyone's name, smiles at everyone, talks to the nurses and the patients in the same tone and with the same respect as he speaks to a fellow doctor.

She follows him out to a small old black Ford. He puts the pile of files he is carrying on the bonnet and then opens the boot which is already piled high with books and boxes. He takes the files one by one from Hetty and starts packing them in.

"You'll never get everything in there…" She catches a framed certificate as it slides from the top of the boxes of papers and looks at it. "Are you leaving?"

He stops for a moment and looks at her. "You don't know?"

"Know what?"

"I got the letter yesterday. I can no longer work here, according to the regulations of the Third Reich."

"What?"

"I'm Jewish Hetty."

"I'm Jewish."

"Well you should know then…" He looks at her sadly. "You'll get a letter," he stuffs more papers into the boot, tucking them round the side and then slams the boot lid down and opens the passenger door. The seats inside are crowded with more boxes. He scratches his head and starts pushing boxes about to make room for the small suitcase and the rest of his papers.

"But I'm in the middle of training." She wants to kick herself for the whine she can hear in her voice.

He half chuckles and picking up a bunch of files and tucking them in a small space on the floor behind the far seat he turns around, frowning and smiling at the same time. "What would that matter?" He stands up and looks at her. "You'll probably be transferred to the Jewish hospital in Amsterdam the Portuguese Israeli Hospital. Have you heard of it?"

"Yes..."

"Mmmm, it's not particularly good...that's not fair. It's not a teaching hospital like this one," he casts a look back at the huge mass of the Zeikenhuis Zuidwal. "But it's not bad. It's small, doesn't have the funding, the specialist equipment, the staff."

"Are you going there?"

He sighs. "Where else?" He stands and looks at her puzzlement. His eyes are very dark blue. "There is nowhere else to go."

"I just thought. God I'm stupid. I just thought they'd leave the hospitals alone."

"You're not stupid. I thought so too. But apparently not." He reaches out and takes her hand the way she has seen him take the hands of patients and relatives when he has news to give. "It's no one's fault, no one's fault here in any case. It's a law. They risk too much if they break it."

"But if you go... if all the Jewish staff go." She ticks them off in her head, those she knows are Jewish, the nurses, aids, doctors, surgeons, one of the receptionists.

"They'll cope.... I'm not happy, they're not happy, but we have to live with this." He spits out the last words as he walks around the car, checking he's closed all the doors properly. "You know I can't even technically own this anymore." He taps the roof of the car. "I've sold it – technically – to my neighbour on the basis that he loans it to me when I need it." He slams the passenger door shut. "Like now."

"What are your family going to do. Will they go to Amsterdam with you?"

"My wife? No, she and my daughter will move to friends in the country… sort of friends, she's going to work for them as a housekeeper, nanny, help…I don't know. It's safer though."

He turns and leans against the car and she realises that she doesn't really know how to say goodbye to him. He's looking across the road and she turns to see what he is seeing. A man in blue overalls is fixing a sign to the iron gate leading into a small public garden across the road. He stands back *"Joden Verboden"*.

"You see?" he shrugs, shakes his head and looks into her eyes. "This is probably not goodbye for us." He takes her hand again. "Sooner or later they'll get to the nurses and the trainees. Kick you out too. You don't want to contaminate anyone with your Jewishness."

"What!"

He squeezes her hand. "My little inappropriate joke. Don't think about it until it happens. Don't ask about it. Don't do anything. This is the best place to train, so stay here as long as… until the letter comes." He shrugs. "Then come and join me…. And the others…you know Dr Vanderham and Dr Levi have already left?"

"I. It won't be the same here."

"It's surprising how quickly the gap we might seem to be leaving will be filled." He shakes his head. "Somehow." He lifts her hand and in an unexpected gesture kisses her knuckles. He blushes as surprised as she is.

"You'll be fine. Thank you…for helping me," he turns to get

into the car and hesitates, looks back at the imposing shadow of the hospital and then at her. "It's been good to work with you."

"You're going now?" She wants to delay the moment.

"Yup. I've cleared my office."

"You're not going back in to say goodbye to everyone?"

He shakes his head. "I've said the goodbye's I need to…I can't do any more."

There's a sadness in his eyes as he gazes beyond her at the sign. Going on instinct she steps forward and hugs him, picking up the faint smell of carbolic soap and tweed jacket. "We'll miss you."

He pulls away from her and ducks into the car, a lock of black hair falling across his face as he slides into the driving seat, slams the door, turns on the ignition.

She stands back as he winds the window down. "I'll see you in Amsterdam."

Jozef – Laag Keppel – 8th October 1941

Coming downstairs, Jozef hears his mother talking softly to his sister in the kitchen, the click of her shoes, water running into a kettle. He looks at his watch, a present for his 10th birthday in May, unbuckling and buckling the leather strap, twisting it into place on his wrist. It's 7 o'clock.

In the kitchen Trudi kneels on the floor, chattering as she sorts and re-sorts the contents of her red schoolbag. She looks up, flipping long brown plaits across her shoulders and he grabs a book from the floor by her side.

"Jozef!"

"Don't Jozef," his mother warns without turning from the stove where she's making coffee. He drops the book into Trudi's hands.

Putting the coffee pot on the back of the stove his mother turns and looks him up and down, bends down to inspect his clothes, yanking the hem of his grey trousers and rearranging his shirt. She's so close he can smell the lemony shampoo she uses to wash her hair. She pulls at his braces; his trousers are too short but there's no mention of new ones.

She goes back to the stove and he goes to the huge oak sideboard to collect plates and knives for the table and then to the larder for bread, cheese, butter and apple jam. Finally, he slides into his chair, as the side door that links the house to the corridor between it and the family butcher's shop opens and his father walks in.

He watches smiling as his father creeps quietly over to Trudi, pulls her plaits and lifts her up from the floor as she squeals in delighted protest before depositing her in her chair and giving Jozef's shoulder a good morning squeeze before sitting down. Jozef eyes the creamy yellow wedge of cheese and the treacly black loaf of bread near his mother's place. He's hungry, he's always hungry. Furtively he picks at the bread crust, until his father pulls his hand away. His father rolls back the cuffs of his white shirt, stretches across the table and picks up the cheese. Balancing it in the palm of one hand, he trims the rind back with a sharp knife, and then with a bone handled slicer cuts crescent moon slivers from the edge letting the slices fan onto the blue patterned plate in front him.

Trudi leans forward, watching, yattering on about her school and a new friend she's made, drumming the heel of her shoe against one of the chair legs until their father tells her to stop.

His mother comes to the table with the coffee pot and smiles across at them all as she sits down. She's beautiful when she smiles thinks Jozef, wishing she smiled more often. She pours Trudi and him glasses of milk and slices the bread.

Trudi starts gently kicking the leg of her chair again. "We are going to be late Mama."

"No, you're not."

"I told Mrs de Wit I would be early."

"You will still be early."

His father sharing out slices of cheese looks at his daughter: "You like your new school Trudi?"

"I love it. I love Mrs de Wit. I love sitting next to Frankie. I don't want to be late Papa."

She goes on and on, Jozef says nothing, watching his mother spread the bread with butter before cutting one slice in two, passing half to him and half to Trudi and a whole piece to their father.

He tries to blank out Trudi's chatter: as much as she loves the new school, he hates it. He wants to be back at his old school in the village. He misses his friends, the kick-about before and after school with Pim and Hendrik and the others had been the best part of every day. He even misses some of the teachers.

Everything has gone wrong. Yesterday he'd bumped into Hendrik who'd told him about a football match they were playing on Saturday against the school in Doesburg. For a second he thought he was being invited to play, left wing his old position, but, Hendrik said he couldn't, someone else was now left wing.

"Jozef? His mother taps his arm bringing his attention back to the breakfast table. "What's the matter?"

"Sorry Mama, just thinking about school."

She knows he hates the new school, and he knows there is nothing she or his father can do about it.

His father reaches for the coffee pot. "It's a bit of a challenge eh?" Jozef doesn't look at him just stares at his plate and chews. What's he going to say? Then his father reaches across and pours a swirl of coffee into Jozef's cup.

"What?" He looks up and smiles at his father who shrugs.

"Me too?" asks Trudi.

"When you are the same age as Jozef."

Jozef sips. He's not sure he really likes the coffee, it adds a bitter edge to his milk, but he likes the partisan nature of the gift. And it's valuable. He saw his mother swop a generous piece of beef for their packet of coffee.

Things could be worse he thinks as he takes another sip and smiles at his father. He turns to tell his mother it's ok, he's made a friend, David one of the older boys from Laag Keppel has also had to go to the Jewish school. But as he starts to speak someone bangs on the front door, the sound reverberating around the kitchen.

"Sam Jacobs! Open up. Open up Sam Jacobs."

His father puts his cup down and gets up, rolling down his shirt sleeves striding towards the door. The shouts get louder and his father's jaw tightens as he goes into the hallway. Trudi slips off her chair to go with him, but his mother grabs her, pulls her onto her lap as his father turns around: "Stay. All of you stay here."

Jozef hears the rumble of a truck outside, the choking cough of its idling engine. Why hadn't he heard it before, why hadn't he heard it coming? He hears the click of the front door opening, pushing and shoving in the hallway, men speaking angrily in German and Dutch, their voices overlapping each other. His head buzzes. He wants to hear what they are saying but he can only hear the deafening thump of his heart. His father is saying something…his voice soft and firm. What's he saying? He wants to go out and see what's happening. He wants to move but his body is glued to the seat and he realises his mother has reached across the table and is gripping his hand, her knuckles white, his fingers cracking under the pressure.

Then she stands up, putting Trudi down, pushing her towards Jozef. His sister runs to sit on his lap and for once he lets her, holds her. "Don't move!" orders his mother, raising a warning finger as she goes into the hall.

Jozef hears the grinding noise of the lorry engine revving up then settling into a thrumming cough: waiting. It seems louder now he and Trudi are alone. He looks at her and sees tears bubbling in the corner of her eyes. He tries to smile to make it seem better but he can't and he holds her tighter. He isn't going to give in, he isn't. There are lots of people outside now, shouting over the noise of the engine. It sounds like the whole village is there. Trudi tries to wriggle off his lap but he won't let her. "Shshshsh… We must stay."

He hears his father's voice again, outside now.

"Papa!" Trudi calls out.

Their mother puts her head around the kitchen door, "Quiet." Then she's gone, talking so someone in the passageway, her voice icy.

Where's father?

She walks back into the kitchen. "Jozef. Trudi. Stay where you are. Don't move. Stay exactly where you are." She speaks through clenched teeth, eyes wide, face drained of colour.

She runs up the stairs and Jozef hears the firm slap of her shoes on the wooden floorboards as she crosses the hall and goes into her bedroom.

"Jozef," Trudi whimpers.

"Shshshshsh." She buries wet cheeks against his shirt.

"You're holding me too tight." He loosens his grip and smooths the knuckles of her small fingers in apology.

His mother comes downstairs, a small brown case in her hands which she hands to someone at the door.

"Good." A German voice. "We are leaving now Frau Jacobs."

Someone else shouts something and then a face peers into the room, ruddy, dark haired, square jawed. "Wife, two children!" he calls back to someone in the hallway. Then they go, their heels cracking across the stone floor and the door slams shut.

There is a commotion of some kind outside in the street. Jozef pushes Trudi off his lap, runs to the window and sees someone – his father – it can't be his father falling into the truck. There are maybe a dozen men in the truck. He spots his Uncle Mauritz in his navy cap with the yellow piping round the edge. Trudi is pulling at his shirt sleeve, jumping up and down. "Can you see anything? I want to see."

They both turn as their mother walks back into the room, her face white and hollow. They hear the truck jerk into life and accelerate away.

Trudi runs to her mother and throws her arms around her legs. His mother doesn't bend down to her or pick her up but just stands there, frozen. Trudi pulls on her skirt: "Where's papa gone?"

His mother doesn't answer, just grabs Trudi, draws in gasping breaths. The back door clicks open and his mother's head whips round. It's Lena the daughter of their Aunt Lea's neighbour panting as she steps into the kitchen.

"I am sorry…. I am so, so, sorry Bets…" She sucks in air, catching her breath, doubling up with the pain. "They came for Mauritz and Lea wanted to call, to warn you, but they cut the telephone line. She asked me to cycle up here instead. I came as fast as I could."

Bets looks at her blankly. "They are just taking them overnight Lena, just for one night." Her voice is dry and cold. "That is what they said. We must believe that. We must get on now as if… just like a normal day." She looks at Jozef. Her smile is icy her eyes watery. Please don't cry, please, please don't cry. "That's what Papa would want, for us to go on quite…. quite as usual." She untangles Trudi from her legs and bending down brushes away the tears pouring down the little girl's face. "Come on now. This is no good. Papa wouldn't like this. Jozef, Trudi, come on now, school. You'll be late. You don't want to be late Trudi?"

Sniffing and grabbing her mother's hankie to blow her nose, Trudi picks up her satchel, puts it on her chair and then picks up her glass to drain the last dregs of milk.

"Why have they taken Papa?" asks Trudi putting down the glass and easing the satchel onto her small shoulders.

"It's a mistake, just a mistake. He'll be back tomorrow. Now, school. Go."

On automatic, Jozef gets up from the table, puts on his coat, scarf and cap, picks up his school bag and calls to Trudi.

They stop outside the door. There are people everywhere. The whole village seems to have tipped out onto the street. Jozef hears old Pieter van Dam, their next-door neighbour talking, shouting, thumping his stick on the ground, on the paving stones, silver white hair slicked across his balding scalp. "They hit him! Did you see that! They hit him"

"Who?"

Jozef can't see who he's talking to, someone just inside the greengrocer's shop opposite.

"The soldiers. Those bloody Nazis."

"Who did they hit?"

"Jacobs. They pushed him in the truck – shouting at him."

"No! Who else was in the truck?"

"I couldn't see. About two dozen men maybe. Someone stood up to help Jacobs into the truck, but they hit him anyway – right across the back with the butt of a rifle."

"Why?"

"I don't know. I think he had turned to tell someone to look after the shop, to get his father to help Bets. Didn't you see it?"

Old Pieter looks up and sees Jozef on the other side of the street, listening, watching.

"On your way boy," the old man shouts waving his stick. "Go on. You'll be late for school. It's just us old folk chatting. Your father will be fine. He's strong Jozef."

Jozef grabs Trudi's hand hard and walks swiftly down the road.

"Where's Papa gone Jozef?"

Doetinchem – three weeks later

Bets Jacobs pulls her coat tightly around her as she waits in the queue outside the municipal offices in the center of Doetinchem.

She looks at the large notice pinned to the board. It's the same as the one put up all over the village shortly after Sam and the others had been arrested and explains that on the orders of the Third Reich, two tranches of men believed to be working for the underground had sabotaged vital army communications and had been arrested – one group from the district around Laag-Keppel and the other from Amsterdam.

She's read the story. Resistance workers had cut telephone links between guards monitoring the Dutch coastline for British allied aircraft and Nazi gunners manning a huge line of anti-aircraft positions built up along the German border. Alerted by the call, the gunners switched on huge bundles of searchlights which arced like ice tornadoes across the sky. British bombers flying under cover of darkness, suddenly became easy targets and were picked off and destroyed by a barrage of anti-aircraft fire. Since the telephone line between the coastguard and the gunners had been cut by the resistance the success of the anti-aircraft operations had plummeted to an embarrassing low.

Reading the poster on his way to school Jozef had been elated by the news. Some of his friends from the village who rarely talked to him anymore, had crossed the road and run up to him to ask if it was true. Was his father in the resistance?

Remembering his enthusiasm Bets bites her lip as the queue shuffles forward, the woman in front of her sneezing loudly into a blue handkerchief. Bets looks at her and wonders if her husband too has been arrested, if she too is waiting to ask Council officials if they can give her any information about her husband's whereabouts.

Part of her wishes she could have lied to Jozef, but she didn't, she knew without doubt that Sam had nothing to do with the resistance; whatever his feelings about the occupying force, he felt he had enough to cope with dealing with the onslaught of anti-Jewish regulations and protecting his family.

She remembers how Jozef's disappointment had been quickly replaced by hope, a hope that she keeps trying to feel too; that once they realise Sam is not a member of the resistance, they will let him go, let him come home. Her heart hopes but her head doubts it.

She's written to everyone she can think of to say that he had nothing to do with the attack on the telephone lines, but the disinterest she's felt in response is palpable. Being Jewish is considered reason enough for his arrest. But she's still going to ask where he is. She won't give up until she has an address for him so she can at least write to him, give him hope, tell him about the children.

The woman in the brown coat in the queue behind her taps her shoulder as the queue moves forward.

Hetty – The Hague – October

No-one is in the small bedroom in the nurses' quarters on the fifth floor of the old building when the brown envelope carrying the Ziekenhuis Zuidwal's smudged seal is pushed under the door. It is several hours later, close to midnight, when Hetty finds it. Climbing the stairs to her room after a 12-hour shift, pulling out the pins holding her cap in place, all she can think of is getting into bed, getting some sleep before the next shift begins. She pushes open the bedroom door, treading on the letter. She bends down to pick it up at the same time putting her cap on the chair and pushing the door closed with the heel of her shoe.

Her name is typed across the front of the envelope. It's formal. This is it.

She collapses on to the bed, putting the letter on her bedside table while she eases off her shoes. She doesn't bother to take off her dress, just lies down putting her feet up on the blankets, undoes her belt and crosses her ankles. She closes her eyes wondering if sleep will come or whether to open the envelope. She knows what's in the letter, she's been waiting for it ever since Dr Meyer left in the summer, swiftly followed by Dr Steinwald and her friend Anke as well as several other nursing staff. She is surprised it has taken so long.

She reaches across and picks the letter up, turns it over and slips the envelope open with her index finger. Inside is a neatly folded single sheet of paper. Opening it she sees the name of the Zeikenhuis hospital embossed in black across the top. She scans the single paragraph addressed to her above the hospital director's signature. No surprises in it, just a termination of her contract, telling her to report for duty at the Portuguese Israeli Hospital (PIZ) in Amsterdam, the Jewish Hospital, if she wishes to continue with her nursing career.

She has had a card from Anke telling her that the PIZ was cramped, poorly equipped, overcrowded, and understaffed, but the atmosphere was better than that at the Zeikenhuis, friendlier. Hetty wonders if people were whispering about her, wondering why she is still there, still at the Ziekenhuis, if she is Jewish. She hasn't hidden the fact, not deliberately. She just wanted to finish the year out, pass her first-year nursing exams and prove a point. She can't hide being Jewish: it is stamped in black indelible ink across the inside of her identity card and written on her contract of employment. So, it is inevitable that the administration has eventually realised their oversight, and having done so, acted accordingly. Anke hadn't waited for a letter; she had just gone quietly as soon as plans for segregating Jewish workers had been announced. But Hetty's not the sort to leave quietly, inconveniently, in the middle of her training. She had told Anke before she left that if the hospital wanted her to go, they would have to tell her face to face. She had imagined the scene a dozen times and it was always dramatic. But in the end, there was no drama just a letter.

She crushes the letter into a ball and surprises herself by finding tears running down her face: she feels humiliated, inadequate, hurt and angry but she knows the tears are as much from exhaustion as from disappointment. Well, what did she expect: thanks?

She sits up and undresses into the pale yellow pyjamas she keeps under her pillow. It's too late to do anything. She pads across the room to the small porcelain washbasin in the corner, brushes her teeth and washes her hands and face in the cold water with a sliver of hard anaesthetic green soap, feeling its rawness bite into her skin. Pushing her hair behind her ears, she climbs into bed, and feels an unexpected surge of sudden relief that she won't ever have to sleep another night in this room with its depressing brown anaglypta wallpaper and tiny window looking out over the courtyard where they keep the hospital bins. She sets her alarm for five: the first tram to Scheveningen is at six.

In the end she takes a later tram. Waking up she decides she won't sneak out down the back stairs before anyone is awake: she isn't a criminal, and she isn't going to behave like one.

She dresses in a favourite blue checked wool dress with a fitted bodice and full skirt fitting snugly into a wide black belt, showing off her slim figure, good legs and blue eyes to full advantage. She packs her suitcase and then strips her bed, folding the sheets and blankets for someone else to deal with.

She goes down to breakfast and determinedly sips a cup of coffee and eats a slice of bread and cheese, every mouthful an effort. There aren't many people in the canteen but one of the second-year nurses who she has worked with comes over to chat. Her eyebrows knit together uncertainly as Hetty tells her she's leaving, that she's received a letter terminating her contract.

"I didn't know. I'm sorry." She puts a gentle hand on Hetty's sleeve before checking her watch and leaving, other hospital gossip suddenly irrelevant.

After finishing breakfast Hetty goes to the director's office and tells a secretary she has never seen before that she has received a letter and is leaving. She asks for any necessary papers or correspondence to be forwarded to her parents' home. The girl peering at her from behind wire rimmed spectacles writes down her name and address and looks up Hetty's file to pin the note to it and put it in the director's tray. She has the decency to blush as she glances inadvertently at the carbon copy of the letter Hetty had received and Hetty wonders if she had typed it.

She takes the 10.40 tram to Scheveningen. Arriving, she walks swiftly past the coffee shop next to the tram, keeping her eyes forward, hearing the raucous laughter of a group of Nazi officers coming from inside. It's a five-minute walk to their home in the Gentsestraat, above the *Parfumhuis*. She walks slowly thinking of what to tell her family when they come up to the apartment when the Parfumhuis closes for lunch. The apartment feels exceptionally quiet. Riet the housekeeper who had worked for her parents for the past seven years had gone home to Amersfoort three weeks earlier and then sent a letter saying she wouldn't be back, her grandmother wasn't well and her mother needed help. Was that true, she wonders? Or an excuse? Whatever, she misses her gentle clattering around the house, humming a random tune.

Hetty climbs the carpeted second flight of stairs to her bedroom and unpacks her few belongings. She wants a shower to wash off the eau-de-anaesthetic of the hospital. She's looking forward to seeing Loes, finding out about this new man in her life, Jacques? Something like that. He too had lost his job because he was Jewish.

In the shower under the stream of steaming water she feels bitter about her dismissal. Her future is sliding off track....well not quite true there is always the Amsterdam hospital.

She worries her parents won't want her going to Amsterdam, not after all the trouble there earlier in the year, the rumours about the Jewish quarter, but they'll cover up any fears they have. That was the thing now, keeping up appearances, carrying on a performance of normality, even at home where a sort of tense bravado had replaced life before....God she could hardly remember what it was like before sometimes... the laughter and bustle that ran through the seams of the apartment; the smell of her father's nightly cigars and mother's lavender perfume and the talk, talk, talk about family, friends, work, the season in Scheveningen, returning customers, a new bar or café. It's a dream. The apartment is always quiet now, contained, without laughter: without Hans. His absence is etched on her mother's face and scrapes away at her father's natural good humour. They are living in an alternative universe, just using the same furniture. The streets are no longer their streets, they are owned by the Nazi occupation force, laughing loudly, talking and spitting with arrogant confident proprietorship. Some of the shop signs are now in German rather than Dutch, languages so close but not the same – open/offen, gesloten/geschlossen – a nod to who was in charge, who to curry favour with. The mind games involved in working out who was and wasn't sympathetic to the Nazis was exhausting.

She scrubs at her nails. She hates the Nazis 'we are all one nation' talk; she even hates the Nazi soldier with his polished black boots and immaculate uniform that offered to help her off the tram that morning with her case. She wanted, she needed to hate them all. No exceptions.

She gets out of the shower and pulls on clean clothes and looks at herself in the small mirror above the sink. Finding a stub of lipstick, she smears a little across her lips, checking the colour – rose blush – sounded very Loes, looked nice. Brushing her hair, she hears the click of the front door, the chatter of her sister and mother.

"Hello? Hetty?"

They must have spotted her coat in the hallway. She bumps into her sister as she comes out of the bathroom. "I didn't know you were coming back today." They link arms and go to the kitchen where their mother starts heating a pan of soup. Hetty walks around and kisses her softly on the cheek, feels the warmth of her mother's arm go around her waist.

"What brings you home so suddenly? I thought you didn't have a day off until next weekend?"

There is no point delaying things. She takes the slightly crumpled letter from her pocket and hands it to her mother.

"I got this last night. I left this morning. They wanted me to go immediately."

Loes takes the letter from her mother. "This is ridiculous Het." Loes' voice shakes with anger.

"Ridiculous?" She looks across at her sister and then goes and puts her arms around her, leaning her head on her shoulder, she can feel tears welling up inside of her, a coldness weeping through her. "Actually, I'm scared."

Jozef – Laag-Keppel – November

Jozef closes the back door leading into the kitchen behind him, stamping on the door mat to get rid of the damp autumn day clinging to the leather soles of his shoes. He unwinds his green scarf and listens to the silence, wondering where his mother is.

"Mamma I'm home. Mamma!" No reply.

He hears the click, click of the wall clock in the hallway and looks at his watch: 4.30. Where is she? They had a message about his father two days ago, an address where he was being held in Austria, near Linz. He'd asked at school where Linz was, how far away, and his teacher had pointed it out on the map.

'It's maybe 1,000 kilometres from here,' the teacher explained tracing the route with his stubby index finger.

"Why so far away?"

No-one knows the answer, not his teacher, not his mother. No-one. But they can write to him now, be in touch at last. All day he's been thinking of what to say, composing a letter in his head, trying to think of good things to tell his father.

The strain of not knowing his father's whereabouts had pulled at his mother, at them all. The house had been filled with short sentences, strained silences and tears and tantrums from Trudi who was totally confused by their father's unexplained absence. His mother hid her distress with a determination that everything should in all respects continue as normal, but this normality was eggshell fragile. Whatever he said or did, Jozef felt he was always doing the wrong thing. Whatever she wanted he did: at her request he had polished his father's good shoes again last night. Her anger had been almost apoplectic when she discovered last week that he had stopped cleaning them when doing his weekly chores.

He had been relieved when his Aunt Diny had appeared from Scheveningen to help for a few days, full of news about his cousins Hetty and Loes. He didn't want to ask her about Hans, even he knew she'd tell them if they'd heard anything. But with Aunt Diny around, the house seemed to return to a kind of normality: meals were made on time, nothing forgotten.

He had dreaded her leaving and it had been strange that on the last day of Aunt Diny's visit, she rather than his mother had gone to the Council Offices and returned with the address where his father was being held. His mother's relief had been palpable; she had smiled, really smiled at dinner that night after Aunt Diny had left for Scheveningen.

Jozef remembers that his mother had promised during breakfast to make chicken soup – his favourite. Coming home he had thought of the sweet curling aroma of the soup, just the thought making his mouth water. But there is no soup on the stove, nothing but a half-peeled onion and a couple of carrots on the side. Nothing cooking.

So, no soup. But where is she? Trudi's at a friend's house. Has she gone to collect her already? He pours himself a glass of water. Maybe she's gone to his grandmother's.

He slips his braces off his shoulders allowing his trousers to drop down on to his hips, rolling his shoulders until his clothes resettle before walking down the hallway to the corridor separating the house from the shop. He knocks with one hand and with the other twists the brass door handle, cautiously putting his head around the door leading into the shop.

His grandfather looks up from behind the meat counter, nodding for him to come in, while continuing to chat to a customer. He is serving the old lady who lives at the other end of the village in the house with the tall privet hedge. Jozef bids her good afternoon and watches his grandfather's square hands firmly holding a large hunk of veal, carving paper thin slivers, picking up each slice and placing it neatly on a crisp sheet of grease proof paper lying across the large brass scales. It is artful;

the slices spread out but overlapping one another, setting the illusion that life wasn't as bad as it is: customers could still have four slices of meat even if they were translucently thin.

Watching, Jozef remembers his father doing the same thing, his mother too sometimes when his father was out buying cattle.

He's jolted from his daydream by the shop doorbell ringing as the old woman leaves. His grandfather has put the meat away and is washing his hands in a bucket of cold water behind the counter, scrubbing his fingers.

"Jozef? What's up?"

"Where's Mamma? Is she round at Oma's?"

His grandfather's eyes flicker, thick grey brows pulling together. "I don't think so. She's not in the house?"

"No"

"Have you looked in the garden?" He squeezes out a damp cloth and starts to wipe down the counter. "Maybe she's having a lie down upstairs, have you looked?" His grandfather sighs. He's grown older, more bowed over these past weeks, thinks Jozef as he watches him turn to help a new customer coming into the shop.

"I'll go and look. Thanks Opa."

Jozef closes the door to the shop firmly and begins listening again for sounds in the house.

Maybe she's outside. He opens the back door and races down the slab-stone path alongside the house and into the garden. But she isn't there. Nothing, just an empty patch of sodden ground with a few overblown cabbages, recent rain drying on their worm-eaten outer leaves. He runs back, slamming the door behind him, hoping it will draw her attention if she is in the house.

He calls out again. "Mamma!" Nothing. He takes his shoes off and runs upstairs. It is quiet on the small upstairs landing, but he can hear his mother now, she's in her bedroom. Relief and worry run through him. Maybe she is unwell.

He knocks tentatively on her bedroom door. "Mamma…" he whispers. No answer, he knocks again louder, "Mamma!" and hears her blow her nose. No mistaking it. He turns the handle and pushes the door open.

"Mamma?"

She is crumpled on the bed. Her grey wool dress rucked up, twisted around her hips, black wool-stockinged legs curled up.

"Are you sick Mamma?"

She rolls woodenly onto her back and sniffs loudly as he steps towards her. Her face is red and blotchy.

"Is it Papa? Are you worried about him? We must be brave Mamma. That's what you said. We have to be brave until…" he can't finish the sentence.

Tears wash silently down her face. She pulls herself up on one elbow and pats the bed for him to sit down next to her. "Jozef, Papa's not coming back." Her voice is thick and gravelly.

"But we had an address Mama. Two days ago. Aunt Diny was here and she'd been to the council office and got an address for him. We're going to write a letter. You and me. That was the plan. This afternoon."

She wipes her eyes, shaking her head, and blows her nose again in one of his father's large white handkerchiefs. She pulls Jozef towards her in an awkward hug and he resettles himself under her arm.

"A letter came." She reaches across and picks up the half-folded piece of white paper next to her and passes it to Jozef.

He sees the crest of the Third Reich at the top. It's official. His German is rudimentary, but he scans the few lines and sees the last line: *'Sam Jacobs gestorben Oktober 31, 1941'*. His handshakes, it can't mean what he thinks it means. His head is buzzing now. His mother sits up and puts her arm around him. "Your father died a week ago Jozef, on the 31st October."

31 October 1941 – Mauthausen, Austria

A huge metal tank filled with ice cold water has been installed in one of the brick built annexes of the vast Mauthausen Labour Camp. The camp has up to 85,000 prisoners at any one time, many die within months of arriving. Most prisoners work in the nearby granite stone quarries, others are 'hired out', some assist in experiments. In the Reichssicherheitshauptamt (Reich Main Security Office) the camp is referred to as the Knochenmühle (the bone mill).

Water drips incessantly from a tap into the tank and the stone floor around it is wet. An SS captain takes off his jacket, hangs it on a hook and rolls up his shirt sleeves before approaching the barrel to look at the prisoner taking part in the water experiment. He has stopped thrashing about, there has hardly been a sound from the tank for... he checks his watch...five minutes. He checked five minutes ago, and he could hear the phlegm crackle in the prisoner's throat as he dragged in air. Time to check again. He steps onto a small platform along the side of the tank and reaches across the water, cautiously taking the hand of the prisoner. He doesn't stir, but the captain is still careful as he feels for his pulse. There is none. He takes a small mirror from his pocket and pulls the body towards him. He puts the mirror to the mouth of the prisoner to ensure he is not breathing. He looks at his watch to confirm the time of death and then checks the water temperature with a thermometer: it's just above four degrees centigrade.

The captain, who completed two years of medical training in Hamburg before the war, tells two prison orderlies to remove the body from the water. He notes that the prisoner survived for 74 minutes. Dr Aribert Heim, Dr Death as he's been nicknamed, is masterminding this 'experiment'. Dr Heim will be pleased.

The captain rolls down the sleeves of his shirt as he walks towards a table in a corner of the room. He picks up a flip chart and starts to make notes. They have carried out the same water experiment on 12 prisoners: immersing them fully clothed in tanks of ice-cold water to ascertain how long they can survive. The experiment will supply the Nazi military command with vital knowledge of potential survival rates for men stranded in the open waters of the North Sea following an attack on one of the Navy's ships or submarines.

He walks back to the inert body now lying on a cement table, water streaming from his clothes, his mouth gaping. The captain starts to record final details: body temperature, muscle mass, height. The captain notes the rubbery whiteness of the man's skin and sees that he is clutching something in his hand. How had that escaped his notice? Curious he pulls open the stiffening fingers of the corpse and finds a photograph, though the water has soaked away all but the faintest ghostly outlines of a woman and two children.

He asks an orderly already topping up the ice-cold water in the tank, to make a note of the prisoner's name so that the authorities can be notified.

PART 3

1942

Targeted

Hetty – Scheveningen – May

Where are they? Hetty watches the rain skitter down the windowpane, as she waits for her parents and her sister Loes. The few people in the street below the apartment are hurrying to get out of the rain, sheltering in doorways, a couple marching under black mushroom umbrellas, a peppering of Nazi soldiers.

She relishes the momentary peace. She checks her watch it's nearly 4. They must get back soon. She has to catch the 5 o'clock train back to the hospital in Amsterdam in time for her shift.

She has had a rare three-day break. It had taken her a week to get a travel pass for this visit and she wonders when, even if, she will manage to get back home again.

She checks her watch, it is already after 4. She looks up and down the Gentsestraat. The whole feel of it has changed; the bakery is still there, and the florists shop with bunches of tulips spilling out of buckets in front of the door, but the signs in German are depressing. Two wives of senior members of the German military have taken over the bookstore, now filled with

Third Reich propaganda; the dress shop has closed; someone has pasted a poster, a mean looking caricature of a Jew with a large yellow star on his lapel slapped with title 'the enemy within', across the empty shop window. Passing the shop on her way to the bakery this morning someone spat at her. It's the stars. It's been less than a week since all Jews were ordered to buy the egg yolk yellow badges, to sew them on their clothes and to wear them at all times in public. They're huge, ugly, unmissable. The effect has been devastating; people crossing the road if they see her, it; children staring as if she's something from the zoo. The spitting was the last straw.

'It'll change, it'll calm down,' her father had said without conviction at lunchtime. Her mother and Loes had got up to clear the table, take dishes to the kitchen, but as she started to push her chair back, her father had asked her to stay behind, he needed to talk to her. His tone changed as he passed her the business card of one of his suppliers in Amsterdam. "Keep it, remember this address, this man. We're going to send all correspondence here in future."

So, he too thought it was going to get worse. She looked at the card and realised she knew the street in Amsterdam, but not the man or his business as a perfume wholesaler.

Her father no longer trusted posting things to the Jewish hospital. She'd had her own suspicions that recent letters had been tampered with, others hadn't arrived. But that isn't all. She feels a tightness in her throat remembering his concern too that she might not be able to come home again. There were rumours that they were going to stop all Jewish citizens using public transport and so far all rumours had become fact. So how would she get home? Amsterdam was just that bit too far away. The train took an hour or more.

She'd asked about the man, the friend in Amsterdam.

"He's a business colleague, an old friend… he is a friend that we can trust as much as we can trust anyone. He'll oversee our business from now on…for as long as it keeps going."

He'd looked so sad. He'd spent a lifetime building up the perfumerie that as a Jew he was now not allowed to own.

"Just tell him you're Bram's daughter. OK?"

After lunch Loes announced she was going for a walk with her boyfriend Jacques, her cheeks pink with expectation; so in love her eyes were sparkling. And then when it started to rain her mother had suggested to her father that they go out too for an overdue visit to their friend the doctor, the huge black umbrella, protecting them from public view. They'd asked her to come with them, but she'd wanted to stay home, to be alone, to think. She'd sent the doctor her regards; he was a longstanding family friend and had given her the reference, which had supported her application to train as a nurse. She wonders what his view would be of her forced move to the Jewish hospital from the prestigious Hague teaching hospital. She wonders if the doctor knows her mother's not sleeping, if he has prescribed her any sleeping pills. Her mother is so calm, so controlled, so organised in the day, but she's heard her walking about the apartment in the middle of the night. Creeping downstairs she'd seen her pacing back and forth in the living room, head in hands, sobbing – for her brother Sam and for her missing son, Hans. She had crept back to bed, not wanting to invade her mother's private, endless worrying grief.

Where are they? She looks down the street towards the promenade, now heavily guarded and forbidden to all but those seconded to work for the Nazi occupying force. She has heard about the cement fortifications taking shape along the beach, embraced by a vast necklace of looped barbed wire, a warning to anyone thinking of going to get a closer look. Her father has told her about the lorries driving through the town with huge guns heading for the newly built army bunkers hidden in the dunes, filling the air with the metallic reek of gun oil. She'd seen one yesterday and couldn't believe the size of it. She wonders at the devastation to the once wide sandy spaces of the beach but has no desire to see what's happened. She prefers her memories: fine sand, wicker beach chairs, the world of happy holidaymakers and the familiar smells of suntan oil and ice-cream.

So much change. Someone she doesn't know is looking after the perfumerie, a young woman with a straight blonde bob and glasses. When did that happen? Did she work for the man in Amsterdam or for her father?

She's surprised to find that one of the things she doesn't really resent is her enforced move to the Jewish hospital; the PIZ is much friendlier than the huge hospital in The Hague and of course there is Phillipe, Dr Meyer, now more than a friend, something she won't tell her parents, probably not even Loes in case they disapprove. But it's a relationship of the time, nothing long term. But what is long term? Today is bad, tomorrow could be worse.

She's lucky compared to Hannah, the student nurse she shares a small room with at the back of the hospital. Her father, a watchmaker, had been arrested at about the same time as Uncle Sam and Hannah's mother had gone to live with her grandmother in Arnhem but Hannah had stayed to work in the hospital and to be close in case her father came back; from the hospital, she could keep an eye on their Amsterdam apartment. But the last time she had gone home, she had found the locks changed, a German woman at the door explaining that the flat had been requisitioned.

Where are her family's things, asked Hannah?

The house was requisitioned fully furnished explained the woman, looking at her incredulously, she had not bought furniture from Germany, there was a war going on. Where had she been, asked the woman, if this was her home why hadn't she been living in it? Hannah explained she slept at the hospital but the apartment was her home, her family home.

Well, the woman said, you have somewhere else to stay.

Hannah had asked what they had done with their clothes, their personal things before realising that the woman was wearing one of her sweaters, a soft pale pink cardigan her mother had given her for her birthday.

"That's my sweater." It was out before she could think and the woman had blushed, pulled the sweater off, tearing the buttons in her haste, flinging it at Hannah along with a clothes brush in the hall, hitting her in the face as she slammed the door.

She'd been inconsolable when she'd got back to the hospital, the sweater wet with her tears, the clothes brush lying on the bed. Hetty had done her best to comfort her, but she still cried most nights.

The rain is easing now, the sun striking the wet leaves of the poplar trees fringing the road, there'd be a rainbow somewhere. Looking down the street she sees Jacques and Loes holding Jacques blue serge jacket over their heads against the last drops of rain, Loes' curls bouncing softly on her shoulders, her arm tightly looped through Jacques, laughing and talking, eyes only for each other.

She likes Jacques and was glad to finally meet him having heard so much about him from Loes. He was looking for work but finding nothing and worrying that he would be sent to the Jewish work camp. He had lost his job as chief buyer for a huge fabric company in The Hague in February. It was a classic story, typical of what was happening to so many people said Jacques, not the director's fault, not that he was particularly fond of him. The director's teenage son had joined the youth wing of the NSB, the Dutch Nazi party. Comments had been made to the son about his father's continuing employment of Jewish staff. At a party celebrating the son's appointment as second in command of a small local NSB division, his father had been told by the NSB commander that if he wanted his son to do well then he should look to 'purifying' his staff, pointing out that a local cabinet maker with a Jewish partner had recently suffered a fire in his warehouse. Jacques had been dismissed the following day

Meeting him for the first time, Hetty had to admit her sister hadn't lied about Jacques good looks: square chinned, broad shouldered with a shock of light brown hair and a full wide mouth that curved easily into a huge smile. If looks were everything, he was certainly a catch, but so was Loes with her round smiling eyes and slightly pouting rosebud lips.

Hearing them come in, taking off their coats, she goes to the kitchen to make coffee, or a chicory-based excuse that they had been calling coffee for the last year. She takes small blue cups and saucers off the dresser and puts them on the scrubbed pine kitchen table and looks at her watch. She needs to leave in the next half hour.

Loes and Jacques are breathless, slide into chairs next to one another and Loes starts arranging and rearranging the coffee cups.

"Where's moeder?"

"Gone to visit the doctor, back soon."

As she speaks, they hear the click of the door, her parents arguing. Walking into the kitchen, her mother shakes out a red and green scarf and pats a stray strand of silver hair back in place. Her father is rubbing his hands to get warm. He looks at her.

"Worried about going back Het?"

"No...It'll be alright," she glances at her sister and her father catches her eye raises one eyebrow. It's beginning to feel claustrophobic around Loes and Jacques. She thinks of Phillipe. He'll be waiting for her.

The coffee bubbles up and Hetty takes it off the stove, her mother's talking about their visit to the doctor, seems he might help them if they need to get out of Scheveningen. Hetty catches her sister looking furtively at Jacques, a rosy blush spreading across her cheeks. Clearly she wants to say something.

She sits down as her mother takes over the pouring of the coffee.

"Well sis?" Hetty reaches across the table, taking Loes' hand squeezing it affectionately.

"Well what?" says their mother pouring coffee and looking pointedly at Loes.

Jacques clears his throat, sitting up straight as if he was in synagogue not in a kitchen, and they all look at him. "I asked Loes to marry me," he says a smile widening across his face breaking it apart, making the light blue pools of his eyes shine.

"Under a tree, in the rain," she laughs as she looks into his eyes. "And I said yes," says Loes quietly now, avoiding everyone's eyes, just looking into her lap, loosening her grip on Hetty's hand and sliding her fingers into Jacques palm.

Their father claps Jacques on the back, and there is general pandemonium and squeals of delight as everyone hugs Loes and congratulates Jacques.

"This is the sort of news we want to hear. This is great," says their father. "It calls for something special." He pushes back his chair and gets up to search the sideboard and finding nothing goes into the dining room, coming back with an almost empty bottle of *jenever*.

"I think a cup of coffee is all the excitement I need," says their mother refusing the tots her father pours for everyone and delicately lifting her cup and toasting Jacques and Loes.

"It's fantastic news, congratulations," says Hetty. But inside she feels the coming heartache of missing her sister; there'd be no-one to tease and talk to in the quiet of the night anymore when she comes home, if she can come home: no one to confide in. The passing of old times is permanent. She realises how she has clung to this vestige of their old life on her days off; despite the changes. She looks at her watch.

"Help, I've got to go. I need to make the 5 o'clock train if I can."

She hugs and kisses Loes and then Jacques and her parents, races into the hall and pulls on a light green summer mac, the ugly star prominent on the lapel, picks up a leather shoulder bag with her few things in it and calls out goodbye as she races down the stairs and out into the street. Better always to leave quickly.

The rain has cleared, and it is now a beautiful May day: sun sparking off wet puddles, late afternoon rays falling in shards of soft warm light through the trees dappling the pavement as she walks down to the end of the road and right alongside the park. She draws up the collar of her coat against a sudden crisp brush of early evening air. She passes a terrace of dark red brick houses, blinds being drawn, children being called in from a ball game, an old couple leaning on their gate talking to a neighbour.

She crosses the road just before reaching a little parade of shops. The shops are closing, and she can see the empty shelves in the bakery, her memory filling them with a pre-war display of apple tarts dusted with a snow of icing sugar, rich dark chocolate cakes and the creamy yellow cheesecake that was the baker's speciality.

She digs her hands in her pockets and smiles at a little girl skipping between her parents down the street in the opposite direction. The little girl grins back, but the parents keep their heads down walking on, no shred of recognition, though she is fairly sure she knows them, babysat for the little girl before she went into nursing. She pulls a headscarf out of her handbag, wraps it around her shoulders and neck, the ends dangling in the hope of making the star on her lapel less obvious.

She doesn't see the three soldiers leaning against the wall of the tailor's shop until she is almost upon them. She's sure she's seen one of them before: tall with short greasy black hair plastered to his skull and a nose too big for his face; he can't be more than 17 and looks out of place in the stiff grey green wool uniform that fits too tightly round his neck. She picks up her pace. The two other soldiers are older, a fat short man with full lips and short bristles of blonde hair and a taller, thinner soldier with small dark eyes and a black moustache. They are teasing the young soldier mercilessly. The colour has crept up on his cheeks as they playfully box him with their fists, the fatter of the two breaks into a wiry high pitched almost girlish laugh which catches her attention and makes her look up as she passes, straight into his eyes.

"Fraulein!"

She freezes, feels a gust of cold wind whipping around her legs. The fat soldier takes two paces towards her and grabs her arm; his fingers dig into her skin through her thin gaberdine coat, he spins her to face him.

"Fraulein, what were you looking at?"

She says nothing.

"Speak to me when I speak to you." He leans into her face and it is all she can do not to gag as the words spit out of his mouth in an acrid halo of chronic halitosis. He sees her draw back and pulls her closer, jabbing at the yellow star on her coat. He pouts, shakes his head. "You don't look at me like that." His eyes wander across her face and down her body. He breathes wetly into her ear. "Come and meet my friends."

His arm circles her shoulders as he pinches her to his side and pushes her forward. She can feel a bruise blushing up where he has poked her on the chest, the sweaty heat from the bulk of his body creeping through her. She tries to relax, to breathe, to stop her heart racing while inside she's screaming.

Fifteen minutes later they have gone; their boots echoing on the paving stone as they run, laughing, shouting, punching the air. She slips, helpless, to the ground, the agony and humiliation of the past quarter of an hour burning through her. She breathes, tries to stop herself shaking, pulling her knees up into a foetal position, wincing with the unremitting pain; the skin on the inside of her legs is torn and bleeding her blouse torn, her breasts bruised and scratched, but she focusses on trying to calm down. She hears footsteps coming towards her and rolls over, wants to be invisible, a heap of nothing next to the wall but the footsteps keep coming and she starts to shake again.

"Are you alright?"

It's not them. Relief courses through her. She lifts her head, opens her eyes, feels the bruise on her lip throbbing and swelling where one of them hit her across the face. It's the baker.

"Fine…. Thankyou…. I'll be fine."

He holds out a hand and she takes it gratefully as he pulls her up, stumbling as she realises her knickers are around her ankles. She makes a grab for them as the baker looks away. She pulls them up under her skirt which is damp and dirty from the puddle she has been lying in.

She looks up and sees his wife in the bakery door across the road, beckoning to him.

"Go. Go. I'll be fine. I'll just catch my breath." She smiles puts her hand against the wall for support, stands.

"Sure?" She nods and he leaves. She is shivering with cold and fear. She has never felt so broken, so dirty. But she's not going to let them win. She will not give in. She pulls her coat around her, the buttons have snapped off, and her fingers fumble as she pulls the belt tight, covering her skirt, her ripped blouse smeared with blood. She picks up her scarf which has fallen to the ground. It's wet and dirty but she rings it out, shakes and folds it and covers her head with it, pulling the scarf forward so her face is in shadow, the knot tight under her chin. She picks up her bag which has broken open in the scuffle, checks carefully through its contents. She takes out a hankie wipes at her face, her neck her hands, her legs until the thin square of cotton is a sodden rag. She needs to get back to the hospital. Now.

She tries not to cry, not to look at anyone, just to get to the station. The surprise is that there are people on the street, and they turn and look at her. Where were they when…? She can't think about it.

Getting to the station she hobbles in, shows her ticket. She's missed the 5 o'clock, but there is another at 5.30. She'll be late for her shift. She sits on a bench, waits for the train. Her head spins, what could she have done? How could she have stopped it? But there are no answers. She rearranges her scarf, ensuring the star is covered. When the train comes, she climbs into the first carriage and finds a corner where no one is sitting. Others get on and off, people look at her, but she keeps her head down. A plump woman in a brown coat sits next to her, tut tuts in her ear. "You better clean yourself up," she whispers. "You look a mess. A real mess. That's the way to get singled out around here."

The woman gets up, walks down the carriage to another seat.

Hetty closes her eyes. The hour-long journey is interminable. Finally in Amsterdam, she makes her way to the hospital, seeing nothing, acknowledging no-one, just putting one foot in front of the other, climbing the stairs. She needs to get to her room, needs to sort herself out, needs to shower.

"Hetty!"

Someone is coming down the stairs, rushing towards her.

"Hetty!"

It's Phillipe. She collapses against the banister, against him.

"Oh my God, Hetty."

Jozef – Laag Keppel – August

Jozef is hot. He sits under the apple tree in the far corner of the orchard, pulling apart a reed of grass and blowing through it, watching his mother walking down through the garden towards him with a basket over her arm. He jumps up.

"Casper is coming over for lunch; we've just had a message. Pick some plums for me?"

He takes the basket from her. "Is Jacob coming?" An afternoon with his cousin would definitely improve the boredom of the day.

"I don't think so."

He feels a lurch of disappointment: another day with the grownups and his little sister. His Aunt Diny is staying with them for a few days before going back to Scheveningen. She's been visiting his grandparents; Oma hasn't been well – and Aunt Diny wants a family consultation. Joseph had hoped that the whole family would come, as they had in past summers, and that they would eat in the garden under the dappled shade of the trees, kick a ball about after lunch. But now it looks like it will just be Casper and they will eat indoors and talk.

His mother and Aunt Diny spend all their time talking: sometimes about his cousin Loes' wedding three weeks ago, but more often about the occupation, the risks, what they should do. He is vaguely aware they are making plans, but what exactly they entail he has yet to find out. He feels annoyed, why is he always the last to know, the last to be told?

The situation sucks. His mother no longer even lets him go out to meet friends on the weekend. The star patches they now wear on their coats have changed everything…Trudi's the only one that doesn't have to wear one….and she's actually cross about that. Stupid. Most people in the village are fine, but there are one or two who now cross the road to avoid him. And their butcher's shop has closed. He remembers leaving for school one day and Trudi screaming when she saw someone had written *"Vuille Jood gaat eruit"* (dirty jew get out) in red paint across the front of the virtually empty shop and on the front door. That had been the last straw for their mother. It didn't matter that their neighbour, the greengrocer whose shop was opposite, heard Trudi scream and rushed over and within half an hour had washed off the paint with a bucket of hot soapy water, shaking his head, telling his mother it was some hooligan, she must pay no attention, she was respected in the village, all the Jacobs family were respected. But his mother can't forget. Now she is jumpy if she even thinks she hears a German truck or car rattling through the village.

He misses the bustle of the shop, the regular visits of his grandfather. The smell of the sawdust and the background chatter of customers.

Jozef picks the plums, cradling their dusky warmth in his hands, squeezes one in frustration until the skin bursts and the sticky juice seeps through his fingers. He throws it into the hedge and slightly ashamed licks his fingers clean before trailing back up to the house.

His mother and aunt stand over the stove. His mother is showing his Aunt Diny how to make sugar syrup from sugar beet, a trick she learned from one of the local farmer's wives. Aunt Diny wipes her hands on her apron and takes the plums from him. "I'm sorry that Jacob isn't coming Jozef – or the others. The twins are ill and Jet has gone to visit them in the sanatorium and has taken Jacob and little Frank with her."

His mother turns towards him unsmiling. She rarely smiles these days. "Help Trudi set the table will you?"

The two start taking things into the dining room for lunch, setting the table and entertaining each other with a game of I-spy.

Trudi is in the middle of guessing the answer to his latest challenge when he hears the back door opening; Casper has arrived. The kitchen always looks small with Casper in it. He is tall and lanky and wears a black skull cap under his hat, the centre embroidered with a red star and circled with a chain of green stitches. He's cycled over on his bike, taking farm tracks and back roads to avoid bumping into any Nazis and being questioned. Although visits to family were permitted, he takes the view that it is always better to avoid confrontation, so the seven kilometre journey had been an arduous 12. He is in his shirtsleeves, sweat beading on his forehead, his jacket folded over his arm and a slightly battered cap in his hand. His mother pours and passes him a glass of water which he downs in one and passing the empty glass back, pulls a handkerchief from his pocket to wipe his face. He hangs his jacket and hat in the hall and then sits in his father's old wooden kitchen armchair, and Jozef wants to tell him not to, but knows he can't and that some part of him likes seeing a man sitting there. Casper's talking about Jet and the twins who will be in hospital for another week or more, some unexplained chest infection, bronchitis or pneumonia. He looks at the kitchen clock. It is after one, he needs to be quick, he is keen to get back.

They pick up the remaining dishes of pickles, potato pancakes and a basket of bread and follow his mother into the dining room. Setting everything down and scraping their chairs back, Jozef thinks it looks like a feast compared to normal standards; there is cheese, liver sausage, and a bowl of tomatoes. Jozef's mouth waters; there would be no liver sausage if his uncle wasn't there. Casper takes the seat opposite his mother, his father's place but this time Jozef feels less uncomfortable about it.

"Begin. Help yourselves," says his mother settling herself into her chair and putting her napkin in her lap.

Casper pours glasses of water and passes them around while his mother serves the pancakes and Aunt Diny serves the liver sausage. Trudi slips from her chair and takes a dish of pickles, holding it with both hands, walking around the table offering them to everyone.

Jozef cuts into his pancakes, wishing there were more of them. He always seems to be hungry these days, surely it hadn't always been like that? He can't ever remember feeling this constant hunger when his father was around. He takes a careful bite, chewing slowly, making the food last.

"So, what do you want to talk about Diny. Is there a problem?" Casper stretches across the table for a slice of bread. "You've got Jet really worried I can tell you. She hardly slept last night worrying about the girls being ill and Oma not well. She was keen I come today, said I had to talk to you, that you had some plan."

Diny sighs, cutting a slice of bread into small pieces with her knife and eating each square with her fork. She starts to recount the discussion she had begun with Jet when they had met by accident at their parents' house two days earlier, the same conversation that she had had with their sister Roza who lives near her in The Hague, and with Bets, Jozef's mother.

Cautiously she outlines plans she and his Uncle Bram are making. Trade is now non-existent, even though they brought in outside non-Jewish help, so they have closed the perfumery business. They have put what they could in store with a friend but the message in Scheveningen is clear: the Nazis want everyone out, Jewish families definitely, but actually everyone.

"We do not want to be herded into Amsterdam – to the ghetto," says Diny looking Casper in the eye. The statement hangs in the claustrophobic heat; Jozef can feel the sweat blistering on the backs of his knees and his neck. Casper starts to say something, but Diny continues.

"Casper we hear about the Jewish Quarter from Hetty – it's an overcrowded unhappy place and now....now they are gathering people in their hundreds at the old Hollandsche Schouwburg theatre and taking them to the work camps."

"People were never just going to be moved to the Amsterdam Jewish quarter Diny – the move to Westerbork is logical. You know...."

Diny holds up her hand to stop him, she has seen all the propaganda about Westerbork and doesn't need Casper to add to it.

"They show those films, families sitting around picnic tables having lunch, posing in smiling groups, children playing games...I don't believe it Casper and neither do many people. And now they are being moved on: to camps in the East, in Poland and there are rumours...."

"Just rumours. They are work camps for the war."

His mother puts her knife and fork down, stares at Casper.

"Do you really think that?" says Diny.

"Sam died in a work camp Casper," says his mother, her voice husky with emotion. "Surely his death is a warning to us all." She pauses looking across at Jozef and then at Trudi and then down at her plate and says what she has been avoiding saying for days. "We have to disappear."

"You can't. The children."

"The children will be alright."

Jozef's mind is racing. Disappear, where are they going to disappear to? But he knows better than to interrupt. Casper takes another slice of bread and a chunk of the liver sausage.

Jozef drinks his water and eyes the remains of the feast on the table. Watching, his aunt hands him the squares of bread she hasn't eaten.

Casper eats and then fastidiously cleans his fingers with the napkin.

"OK Diny so what is your plan."

"We are going into hiding: Bram and I – up north – I am not

saying more, the less you know the better for you and for us –
and I want to take Mother and Father."

Casper shakes his head. "They are old people Diny. Is this
wise? Nothing is going to happen to them. What would the
Nazis want with old people? You do what you like but I think
they should stay with us or come with us. If it comes to that," he
hesitates. "If we are moved."

"Where? Where are you being moved to?"

"Wherever we are sent." Casper shifts in his chair, looking at
his watch and leans forward. "Diny, Bets, this will end. Maybe
not for a year or two or more, but it will end. Throughout history
Jewish people have been persecuted but we have survived. Look
at Moses…"

Oh no thought Jozef…he was going off on one of his religious
tangents, but Diny listens patiently for a moment and when he
hesitates, breaks in.

"Casper. We know the stories. But this is now. Nothing in
the Torah suggests that we should not think for ourselves, look
to our own survival. Maybe we see more in Scheveningen than
you do here. The town is swarming with Nazis…and they hate
us. There are signs and posters everywhere, we can go nowhere,
not into a park, not to play tennis, not into most of the shops.
They hate us…everyone hates us: neighbours, people we used
to be friends with, old customers. They call us names, cross the
street to avoid us. Many of them just wish we would disappear,
that they would wake up one morning and we wouldn't be there."
She is leaning across the table looking at him. "You know I have
lived in Scheveningen for nearly 20 years. It's changed. Not just
the place but the people. They are frightened. I'm frightened.
People – even old friends I used to have lunch with cross the
road now to avoid me, they are worried about being associated
with us in any way. Others…," she is shaking as she speaks.
"Others spit at me. They hate us.

"The Nazis are pushing people out, pulling houses down, building this defence wall – the Atlantic Wall. They are starting to push everyone out of Scheveningen. And us? We are not just anyone, any ordinary Scheveningen resident. We are marked as Jews." She pauses catches her breath, takes a sip of water. Jozef finds he can't eat any more, the bread is sticking in his throat.

"We are going into hiding. I want Mother and Father to come with us and I want your support. I am their oldest daughter, Roza our youngest sister is with me on this. Sam is not here to take part in the decision and Bets is making her own plans. But Jet needs to know what is happening. She's my sister Casper. I care about her. She wanted me to discuss this with you."

Trudi slips off her chair and goes to sit on their mother's lap. Jozef looks at her wondering exactly what the plans are for him and Trudi. Are they going into hiding? He feels slightly sick.

Casper leans forward. "It's dangerous Diny. They are old people. They can't hide, if somebody comes what is going to happen? You can't hide them under the stairs or in a cupboard. What are you thinking? If someone comes, they will be caught and the people hiding them will be caught and then… then what happens?" He cocks his head staring into Diny's eyes.

"Casper, I don't see another way. I don't think they would survive a work camp as you call it, do you?"

"Well, you will have to talk to them. It's not your decision or my decision. It's up to them. But I don't agree Diny." His hands bunch into fists on the table. "It's probably too late to change your mind but I see things differently. You and Bram have become a bit… detached from the community," his voice rises. "We are very much involved in our local synagogue. I am on the management board," he pauses, leans back looks at each one of them in turn. "So, I hear things that you and Bets and Bram don't." He takes a deep breath. "About a month ago a letter was sent to the synagogue from the Jewish Council in Amsterdam. The Council was set up to protect us. It is there for the Jewish people living in Holland, run by Jewish people liaising with the German Reich. To me that says something. To me that says that we Jews here in Holland, we have …we have some respect." Jozef looks at his mother and sees her head shaking almost infinitesimally as she rubs the top of Trudi's head with her chin. Diny looks at her plate. "The letter urges us to obey whatever summons we receive. They have told us we will be taken to work camps in the East. We risk much more by not doing what we are told."

Diny looks up suddenly. "You don't believe this Casper? You can't. I've just told you what's happening in Scheveningen, you have heard the rumours of what is going on in Amsterdam and you prefer to believe this….drivel?"

Casper sits back. "Actually, I do. We are law-abiding people. We need to get through this and, if we do what we are asked to do, go without fuss, then, yes, I believe we will be alright. In the end, we will be fine." He holds up his hand to stop anyone else speaking. "But the letter also warns that if we don't comply, arrests will follow, and the consequences…" He picks up his glass and finishes the water in it. "These are not Nazis telling us what to do. This information is coming from Jewish people. People I respect. People the synagogue respects: the Chief Rabbi, the President of the Dutch Jewish Congregation. They are good people. They are our leaders, and their aim is to keep us safe," he thumps the glass on the table.

"I am not suggesting it is going to be easy. But what is the greater risk? If the Council says just go quietly and you will be alright, then that is what I am going to do. That is what my family will do. Diny, Bets, I urge you to do the same. Be obedient to the law even if you disagree with it. Going into hiding is madness. What if you are caught, then what? Then you are not going to be treated nicely, not nicely at all and neither are the people who hide you. You are putting others in danger not just yourselves."

His mother pushes Trudi gently off her lap and folds her napkin and starts stacking plates, standing to take things to the kitchen, indicating to Jozef and Trudi that they should help. As they get up, Casper picks a plum from a bowl on the table. He eats it quickly, juice running down the side of his mouth, which he dabs with his napkin. He picks up another plum, cradles it in his hand but then puts it down and follows everyone into the kitchen.

"Bets I believe I can trust the Council. Who am I if I don't trust my own people?"

"The letter was signed?"

"Absolutely."

He starts to prepare to leave, going into the hall to get his hat. He turns to Diny. "Talk to Bram, Diny – persuade him to visit the Council. These are terrible times. But it will end. I believe we will be alright. I believe that."

Watching his uncle leave, Jozef feels his stomach churning. Things are happening, plans are being made but no-one is telling him what they are.

Hetty – Amsterdam – the same day

Hetty marches up the steps of the tall brick building on Marnixstraat overlooking the canal. She is wearing a short sleeved yellow cotton dress, a dark blue cardigan over her arm, no visible star…she never wears the star outside the immediate confines of the hospital and the nearby ghetto. Not since the incident in May. Never. There's a star on the cardigan but no-one can see that when she carries it inside out.

Going through the black front door, she barely glances at the polished brass name plate etched with different company names

and climbs the stairs quickly to the second floor, knocking on
the door of the perfume supplier and entering without waiting
for a reply. She breaths in. It smells like heaven, layers of different
perfumes, cinnamon, lavender, rose, musk, suffuse the room.
She breathes in the echoes of her parents parfumerie. A young
girl with tight blonde curls and glasses is bent over a desk in one
corner, deciphering something she has written in a notebook.
Looking up she recognises Hetty.

"Hi!" She smiles. "He's in, you can go through."

She walks into the inner office, knocking on the glass door
before entering.

A tubby middle-aged man is sitting behind the desk,
immaculately dressed in a navy-blue three-piece suit, his greying
hair slicked to one side, a pressed white handkerchief poking
out of his lapel pocket.

"Ah, Hetty! You are in luck, something came this morning.
So, two letters."

He reaches into a drawer and passes them to her. She glances
at the envelopes, recognising the writing, one from her father,
one from her sister.

"Are you ok?"

"Fine. Everything's fine. Thank you Henrich."

"You know your parents are…." He smiles at her.

"I know. I know what's happening. Sort of. Not really. But
whatever I am staying here."

"At the hospital?"

"Yes. They need me. And surely the hospital is…safe. No-
one is going to close the hospital."

He shrugs and picks up the pen lying on his desk in front of
him, ready to get back to work. He's always friendly but never
wants to get into a discussion. She leaves and thanks the girl in
the outer office who is looking through a box of small perfume
samples.

"You want one?"

"Mmm…no better not."

"OK"

She leaves, running down the stairs walking along the canal until she finds a bench where she sits and opens the letters. She should wait until she gets back to the hospital, to her room, but she can't wait, she's too eager for news. She opens the one from her father first, the one from her sister will make her cry, she knows that. She's missed the wedding, couldn't go, there was no way of getting back to Scheveningen.

Her father's letter is wrapped around two 10 guilder notes. She smiles and puts them in her purse quickly. The letter in her father's close script is just one page…the message clear.

"Dear Hetty,

"I hope things are still going well for you at the hospital. I doubt you would recognise Scheveningen, it has changed beyond recognition in the past two months and is now very clearly a frontline base for the Nazi forces and they want us all out. Not just Jews but everyone. Almost all the shops are closed now, we closed the parfumerie for the final time two weeks ago. Even the florist opposite has closed, only the baker remains open. I suppose everyone needs bread! It feels like a ghost town, something out of a nightmare, a resort turned into a military encampment. Lots of families have already left and more are going every day, cars piled high with boxes and suitcases.

"So this is to tell you we've been staying inside, waiting and we will go too, as soon as your mother gets back from visiting your grandparents. It's the best time with so many others leaving. We've got a lift, everything is arranged. We will be safe. I worry about you and enclose some emergency funds. Be careful.

"Vos will look after the place while we are gone. He seems to have some job in the army kitchens…so he will be able to look in."

Vos! Why her father trusts that greasy haired, pimply, creepy man who has on more than one occasion attempted to pinch her bottom, she has no idea. Something to do with debts owed from the past her sister thought whenever they'd talked about him and his unusual relationship with their father. They'd both disappear whenever Vos was about. She imagines him now strutting around the empty shop, around the apartment, as if he owned it. She shudders at the thought of him using their things, opening the chest of drawers in her room. She knows he'll do that, finger any clothes they left behind with his dirty hands. She finishes the letter.

"You can continue to get in touch with us through Henrich, but only if absolutely necessary. Still no news of your brother or what happened to him. One day we'll find out. I haven't totally given up hope.
"Stay safe dear Hetty. We think of you and miss you."

She folds the thin blue sheet of paper and tucks it in her handbag. She'll destroy it when she gets back to the hospital. The letter doesn't say where they are going or for how long but.... They won't come to the Amsterdam ghetto, she's sure of that. She looks down at the canal, water lapping lazily against the side of a barge, a broken branch carried by the current floating aimlessly out of view.

She opens the other letter and finds herself crying as she reads Loes description of the wedding, how despite everything it was romantic.

"Darling Hetty, they can't take that away from me, that moment when they ask you if this is the person you want to take in marriage and you say yes. Oh Hetty, I love Jacques so much."

She thinks of her friendship with Phillipe. Does she love him? She has been telling her friends that she and Phillipe were just friends; telling her room-mate that she had been downstairs talking to matron when she had been in Phillipe's room, making love to him, a man they all knew was married, whose wife had gone into hiding with their four year old daughter. Making love to him because she wondered if she would ever make love to anyone if she said no. She lives in the morality of the moment, their passion a distraction from the awful reality of each day. Does she love him? She turns her attention back to the letter.

"The only thing that was missing from our wedding was you dearest sister. I missed you. Always we have been together and you have been there for me. So I missed you. But I am with Jacques now and he will look after me. He has found somewhere for us, it's small but it is for us together. We will be safe.

Take care my dearest sister."

She hears footsteps and looking up sees a Nazi officer with a woman she presumes is his wife, walking down the cobbled street, deep in conversation. The man laughs and she stuffs her sister's letter into her bag and holds her breath as the couple walk past. She must get back.

She walks swiftly not looking at anything, ignoring the endless signs plastered across shops, cafes, restaurants, everywhere: *Joden Verboden, Joden Verboden, Geen Joden.* It takes her 20 minutes to reach the hospital. She stops short a hundred yards away, ready to duck into an alley to put her sweater on and freezes. It's happening again, outside the old Jewish Theatre. There are two trucks this time, children screaming as they are pushed roughly on board in the arms of their mothers. She is so close she can see the grim, lined faces of two old men as they grunt and heave themselves aboard the truck. A woman in a bright red scarf is waving at someone in the queue behind her, beckoning them forward, smiling brightly. A young boy, a teenager, head down looks up at one of the guards and suddenly breaks away, pushing the guard out of the way. The guard turns and in three paces has the lad in an arm-lock but the boy is struggling to get away.

"Isaac! Isaac – stop!" A woman is shouting at the boy while being pushed by another guard onto the truck. The boy is wrestled to the ground. He kicks out and the soldier, caught off guard, loses his footing and stumbles, falls, cracking his skull on an iron bollard as he goes down. There's a commotion, another soldier runs to see if he is alright. "He's killed him. *Er ist tot!*" Suddenly there are soldiers everywhere. The people on the truck cower as two of them grab the boy, shove him against a wall while an officer supervising the round up pulls out his pistol and without hesitation shoots the boy between the eyes. There's a collective gasp. The soldier they thought was dead is groaning now, pulling himself up, but the anger of the soldiers is palpable. They pull out another man, and another, an older man in a dark suit with a homburg, a boy in braces, another in a checked shirt and they push and pull them all against the wall. There are screams from the women and children. Someone is shouting "No! No! No! Freddy!". Someone puts their hand across her mouth to shut her up. Hetty shrinks back into the shadows, her heart thumping in her ears. She feels feint. She hardly dares breath. And then they are there, the hammering of their feet as they rush into line. The soldiers stop, raise their guns, shoot and the six men…boys fall dead to the ground.

The one in charge shouts at the horrified group waiting in line to get on the trucks, not daring to move.

"See! See that! That's what happens when you don't do as you are told. Get on the trucks. Quickly. Quietly. Now! Get on the trucks. Get on the trucks!"

All Hetty can hear now is the whimpering and weeping of some of the women, the almost imperceptible shuffling of feet as the last people in the road climb aboard the already full trucks, pushing their way in. And then with a grating of gears the trucks are gone.

The air is still. Others like her are staring at the place where the trucks were, at the soldiers picking up and throwing the bodies of the dead men onto a third truck which has appeared from nowhere. She sees two soldiers help the soldier who had been tripped up by the boy. He's complaining and rubbing his head. They go. They all go. The street is splattered with blood, pooling where the boy fell, and walls where the men were shot smeared with the history of what has just happened. It starts to rain; a brisk suddenly cold summer rain and she pulls on her sweater making a dash across the road towards the hospital watching the blood on the street melt into the rain and disappear.

Jozef – Laag Keppel – Three days later

Jozef kicks a large grey pebble along the rough earth path, knocking it back and forth with his feet as if it were a football and wishing he were at the match rather than walking over to his grandparents. Not that he would be allowed to go to the match these days.

His mother walks in front with Aunt Diny and his sister, talking about the lunch with Uncle Casper and then, again, about the wedding. He is sick and tired of hearing about the wedding, but Trudi can't stop asking about it. She is hanging on to his aunt's every word, repeating questions she has already heard the answers to, ears cocked to catch any tiny detail she might have missed before.

"It wasn't what we would have wanted for her," says Aunt Diny. "We got a pretty dress made from a piece of blue sprigged cotton Mrs van Daalder found in her attic, but not really a wedding dress. The florist was closing down but he managed to make her a little corsage of yellow and blue flowers and she wore it pinned to her jacket."

"Did she carry a bouquet as well?" interrupts Trudi.

Jozef wonders if Loes had the star on her jacket. That would have been a spoiler. But he doesn't ask. Kicking too hard, his pebble skitters into the ferns along the path and plops irritatingly into the canal.

He likes Aunt Diny; she smells of summer roses and has a habit of cupping her hand around your cheek as she bends to kiss you or when she wants you to pay careful attention to what she is saying. He thinks of past summers when he has gone to stay with her and Uncle Bram in Scheveningen. They'd borrow a bike for him and he would cycle along the promenade overlooking the beach, watching the gulls soar, and climbing in the dunes. In the evening he would play cards with Uncle Bram and sometimes with Hetty and Loes if they were home: Hetty was a terrible cheat. But he and Uncle Bram were really waiting for the click in the door of a key and the light drum of Hans' footsteps as he bounded up the stairs to join them for dinner. His unit was based in The Hague and he would wink at Jozef over the dinner table and say things like "we boys are so hungry" the 'we' being Jozef and him and he liked that, liked the feeling that he was in a team with Hans.

But there has been no visit to Scheveningen for three years, and still no one knows what's happened to Hans. Aunt Diny visits them though, mostly because of his grandparents. His mother is always a bit more cheerful, more as she used to be when his aunt is about – they talk a lot about Hans and about his father which is depressing but somehow it relieves the tension – talking about what is worrying them all the time, picking over any scrap of information. He is not looking forward to tomorrow when the doctor is coming to pick Aunt Diny up and take her home to Scheveningen.

Most days Aunt Diny walks over to his grandparents alone, but today they had all come with her. Jozef wonders whether they are going to bring up the talk with Casper. He wants to know what the plans are that are being made by his mother. "You'll know when you need to," she'd replied firmly when he'd asked again this morning. Why won't she trust him?

He finds a new stone and skiffs it from side to side, almost losing it, but diving off the path to retrieve it.

His mother turns. "Jozef!" She hates him moving even a few metres away from them. The path suddenly narrows through a copse of beech trees, before widening as it comes out on to the road on the outskirts of Doetinchem. They pick up their pace.

"Where did Loes and Jacques go on honeymoon?" asks Trudi wanting to re-start the wedding conversation.

"They didn't. Maybe they will one day when things get better."

"Where are they now then?" persists Trudi skipping to keep up with her mother and aunt.

"In a village, just outside of Amsterdam."

"What village?"

"I don't know Trudi. They're…" Diny doesn't want to tell her niece they have gone into hiding. Jacques was worried he would be conscripted to the Jewish work village and from there to a concentration camp. "They're in a village for honeymooners," she says finally. Jozef watches the 'oh' of delight crossing his sister's face and catches hold of her hand so they can move along more quickly, keeping out of sight, though he sees no one or no one that matters, only a man across the street walking his scruffy brown terrier which starts yapping at a black cat tiptoeing across a nearby wall just out of its reach.

His grandparents live in the bottom half of a small town house with a small garden in front and a larger one, dug over for vegetables in the back. He drops Trudi's hand and runs ahead as they get near to the house. The gate is open. Trudi is right behind him and together they run up the path to the porch and try the handle of the front door. It's locked. He pushes and twists the handle again, Opa usually leaves it open during the day. Jozef stretches up to the S shaped brass knocker and gives it two sharp taps.

His mother and aunt are now coming up the path behind them.

"Don't do that Jozef, just open the door and go in," calls Aunt Diny, "It's always open."

"It's not," says Trudi.

Diny stretches past them to turn the door handle, in case it's stiff but it isn't, the door is definitely locked.

"Has he gone out?" asks Trudi.

"No, Oma's not well he wouldn't go out and leave her on her own. Someone must be there."

Then they hear him, Opa clearing his throat as he walks down the hall.

"Who's there?" his voice is sharp.

"It's us Opa – Jozef and Trudi, Mama and Aunt Diny."

He hears his grandfather pulling back the bolt and chain, the rasp of the key in the lock and finally the door being opened. He is breathing heavily, unusually pale, bowed and taut, wisps of his white hair standing up on his head as if he had been running, his cheeks deep red.

Diny gently pushes between the children: "Is everything alright father? Is moeder alright?"

"Alright? No, everything is not alright. Come in."

Diny darts past him down the hall to the bedroom. The others stand and watch as Opa re-bolts and locks the front door calling Diny to come back, come into the living room. They follow him into the old-fashioned room: the red and black Persian carpet covering the table, the fine rosewood barometer on the wall, the intricately carved mahogany and brass clock tapping out the time on the sideboard. Having checked on Oma, Diny comes back and sits on the small green velvet couch next to his mother. Opa lowers himself with a sigh into an old spindle backed wooden armchair with an embroidered cushion that had been sewn by Diny when she was a girl. He sighs, leans on the arm rests of the chair, smooths down his hair with the palm of his hand, before looking up at the little group. "It's not your mother Diny. She's alright, just in bed with that really bad cold," he breathes in deeply pinching the bridge of his heavy boned nose.

He looks at Jozef and Trudi. "Children go and play in the back garden. Diny, Bets…I must talk to you. We must talk."

Reluctantly Jozef takes his sister's hand and leads her outside. Opa's garden wasn't one for doing much in.

"We'll water the vegetables Opa," he calls as they leave.

Jozef wants to know what has happened, what has really happened not just what he will eventually be told by his mother. He takes the watering can and fills it half full using the outside tap by the kitchen door. He watches as his mother goes into the kitchen and puts the kettle on the stove, the others following and sitting around the small round table. Diny has her hand over Opa's quietly talking to him. The basket of food has been placed on the side but it is clear they are going to have tea and talk before lunch.

Trudi pants up to his side, she's breathless after skipping up and down the path running between the rows of vegetables.

"Can I do the watering Jozef?"

He passes her the can. "Be careful, only a little bit on each plant." She heaves the can up and he helps her carry it to the first row of potatoes and watches as she starts to water them, the water forming a soup of mud around the dark green leaves. Trudi concentrates, not talking. She hums quietly and Jozef lets her carry on down the row.

"I'll watch you," he smiles and walks quietly back to the kitchen door.

It is hot and his mother has left the kitchen door ajar and Jozef can easily hear what is being said. You could have heard a mouse breathe, the air in the kitchen is so still, so tense with listening. They are all drinking tea, Opa stirring sugar into his and shaking his head.

"They came."

"Who came?"

"The police – the German police and Dutch. Captain Bellow – Gunther Bellow? He was with them."

"The police captain?"

"Yes."

"What did they want?"

"Like before. Like with Sam." Opa pushes his hands through his hair and across the back of his head and then sits up.

Jozef sees his mother spill some of her tea as she puts the cup back in the saucer.

Opa starts to talk again, his dark eyes looking directly into the eyes of the two women. "They told me they were taking all the Jewish families from here. I was to pack a small case and to go with them. It wasn't an invitation; it was an order. There was a truck just up the road, they'd pulled in and I could see inside the back there must have been 20 people? Men and women, families, I recognised old Isaac Cohen– he's the same age as me – and Irvin Frank. You know Isaac wears that crazy yellow beret and Irvin…well he is so tall you can always see him."

"So…but you are here? Thank God you are here. You didn't go?"

"We were meant to go to the station. We had a letter," he takes a sip of tea and bites his lip. "Yesterday, the letter came yesterday. Casper came over and said that we could go with them, but I told him we couldn't, not with your mother so ill. I couldn't leave her and she's too ill to go anywhere. I told Captain Bellow the same thing when they came here."

"And they left?"

"No, no, Gunther Bellow, he just kept saying that it wasn't personal, but I had to go. But I said I wouldn't. I couldn't go with Oma ill in bed. He said I had to go. He grabbed my arm. Can you believe it he grabbed my arm, hard, here! That boy – that young man! I've known him all his life and he grabs me like that!"

Opa pauses then, putting down the glass of tea and rubbing his arm just above the elbow. Jozef watches as Diny gently reaches over and pulls his grandfather's shirt sleeve up to look.

"You've got a nasty bruise there father."

"He was grabbing me and pulling me, trying to get me to go…But I was standing holding on to the handle at the back of the door. He could see he was going to have to drag me out. He got really cross. I could see one of the Nazis putting someone else into the truck and getting in it…and then they started the truck and someone shouts out to Bellow, shouting at him to hurry up, to get us and hurry up." He pauses and takes a thirsty slurp of his tea.

"Your mother had started to get up Diny. I could hear her coughing and crossing the bedroom floor. He could hear her. She called out to me and asked who was there. She knows him you know, Captain Bellow, she used to buy groceries from his father in law's shop every week and he was often there chatting. You know, she's always chatty. I think she went to school with his aunt."

"So, what happened?"

"He begs me much more politely now, not leaving go of me but still pulling. He says I have to go, and he's looking at the truck and someone is shouting at him again to hurry up. I looked down then and saw the pistol in its brown leather case strapped to his belt. And I said to him: 'If you want me to come with you, you are going to have to shoot me – shoot me now because I am not coming. My wife is ill and I am not leaving her.'"

"Father!"

"I told him. You want me to go you will have to shoot me, here in the street, in Doetinchem, everybody seeing. Old Michael next door had already come out to see what was happening… and that woman across the road, I could see her looking from her window."

Jozef can see Diny gently taking Opa's hand in both of hers and smoothing the back of it, comforting, soft strokes.

"And the men in the truck – must have been the officer in charge – just calls to Bellow to leave it, they must go, they need to get to the station for the train; they can come back." Opa rubs at his jaw, shakes his head and then drains his cup of tea.

"And then he left……running out of the gate to catch up with the truck which had started to move off."

Nobody says anything for a minute. Jozef can hear a blackbird on the wall and turns to watch it, sees Trudi skipping up the path with the empty watering can. "Jozef! I need more water."

He gets up to go to her and catches his mother's eye looking up and at him through the window. She knows he's been listening. He takes the can from Trudi and starts to fill it from the outside tap as the conversation begins again.

"And what about Jet and Casper?" asks Diny.

"They've gone. They took them."

"And the children?"

"And the children."

Jozef – Laag Keppel – September

Jozef is smarting with anger, his hands curling and uncurling into fists as he sits at the table half listening to his mother and his Aunt Lea. He has just come in from school and they have insisted he sits and talks to them, not interested at all in what has been happening to him.

"Are you listening Jozef? You must listen."

He shakes himself into the present, swallowing his anger and smiling at his mother: "Yes I am listening."

He's heard it all before, several times, and doesn't believe it, but for his mother's sake he has to pretend to believe it. They are planning their disappearance. Going into hiding. It is a secret, he understands that. But it is such an unbelievable plan that he wouldn't have told anyone anyway. They'll never do it.

He can't really understand why they are not all staying together, why she and Lea and his young cousin Trina are going into hiding and he and Trudi are going to pretend to be 'orphans'. His father would never have agreed to this. Never. She can't, she won't leave them surely.

He looks at his mother, her cheeks hollow, her hair clipped back by tortoiseshell combs. His father had given her those combs as a surprise gift on St Nicholas Day two years ago, hiding them in her shoes. He had said that St Nick had forgotten she was a grown up because she looked so young.... And he remembers his mother's laugh then, like a bell. She never laughs anymore and he can't really remember when he'd last seen her smile.

"Jozef?"

"Yes."

"So that's clear. We are going any day now,"

"This week?"

"Soon. They'll take you and Trudi to the Bandon's house. You remember him? You used to go to school with Johan?"

Jozef stretches out his fingers. This is unbelievable. How can he forget Johan. He had been there today. He had seen him. He used to be his friend but today he had done nothing, absolutely nothing, just stood there.

They'd been walking home from school, Trudi skipping ahead and he and David, another boy from Laag Keppel who'd been moved to the Jewish School walking behind.

It had been a strange day, two of the teachers had been absent and every week there were fewer pupils, amalgamated classes were amalgamated again. The teachers that were left wanted to talk, he had watched them during the lunch break, huddled together, arguing much of the time, one of the women constantly bursting into tears. The older children had been told to look after the younger ones in the afternoon while the teachers had a meeting. They'd split into two groups, most of the girls going off to chat and play a skipping game while the rest of them kicked a football about, eventually getting a five-a-side game going. He'd scored a couple of goals and he had felt almost cheerful walking home with David, planning another game.

Then he noticed that on the opposite path, coming in from the left, were a gang of about six boys with Frits Kuiper in the middle. And Johan was with them, hanging on. Frits was tall and broad and about a year older than Jozef. His father was in the police. He'd been kept down a year at the Laag Keppel school, and for six months he had sat next to him in class.

He had tried to be friendly at first, trying to help him with a maths equation that Frits had been struggling with, showing him his book. But Frits hadn't appreciated it, hadn't liked it at all, and had put his books away saying that he could cope on his own thank you. He had been delighted when Jozef and a few of the others had been moved to the Jewish School. 'Jozef the Jew. Jozef the Jew. Jozef the Jew' he had started to shout out at him whenever no adults were in view and he saw him out walking.

It was a pathetic taunt. Jozef ignored him, but the taunts had become worse over the months. And much worse since the summer holidays when Frits' gang seems to have grown.

"Silly boy," his mother had said when she saw Frits shouting at Jozef. "I'll speak to his mother. She'll put a stop to this." Jozef had pleaded with her to say nothing as it would only make things worse, but of course she didn't see things the way he did.

Today the taunts were relentless. Frits had started shouting and Jozef had deliberately ignored him, but Frits wouldn't stop. "Are you listening to me Jew boy? Scaredy cat Jew boy who went crying to his mummy. Can you hear me? Or are you so dirty that your ears are blocked up with dirt. Dirty Jew boy"

The insults were flying and Jozef could see Johan and the others just sort of smirking in the background. Not doing anything either way, just watching. Jozef had looked at them, looked at Frits, and said nothing, walked on his fists clenched in his pocket.

"Oh, oh, oh….we have made him mad. Jozef the Jew is mad! Jozef the Jew is mad!" Frits sang walking half-way across the road towards Jozef, the other boys surrounding him, laughing, beginning to join in and Johan watching.

Trudi had stopped and turned to look at Jozef, her eyes big with worry. "Run home Trudi. Run, we'll be ok. You go." And with a nod she'd gone. David suggested they do the same.

"No. Then it will get worse. They'll chase us. Let's just walk."

So they had walked, hearts pounding, as Frits came across the road and did what he had not done before, spat. He spat at them and encouraged the others to follow him. "Come on… he's only a Jew. My mother had to clean the house from top to bottom with bleach after his dirty mother came and knocked at our door."

Frits spat again, the glob of spittle landing on Jozef's knee, trickling stickily down. He wanted to scream but he kept his head down and carried on walking, they were at the edge of the village.

"Father was a traitor! Mother is a whore!"

That was it. He pushed Frits angrily out of the way. David had grabbed him by the shirt sleeve. "Don't!"

But he was so angry. He grabbed Frits by his collar. "That's a lie! That's a dirty lie!" But Frits hardly moved, he was so much taller, bigger. The gang was now laughing on the other side of the road, waiting for the fight.

"Oh big boy!" Frits spat his words into Jozef's face and grasped him by the arms pushing him down on the ground with his fist. Jozef kicked out catching Frits in the groin and jumping up as Frits bent over in pain. He stood ready to attack him again as the boys across the street shouted at Frits to go for him.

"Oi! You lot! What's going on?" It was the postman. Jozef swung his head round crashing into Frits who had just bent over to hit him.

"What are you doing? Jozef! Frits! Go home. Now! I'll tell your parents. We've got enough problems without you boys fighting." The boys, Frits gang, watched from across the road. "You should know better Jozef," said the postman staring hard into his face.

Jozef had been speechless with pent up anger. It wasn't his fault. He hadn't started it. But there was no point saying anything. And Frits had just smirked then, "Sorry," he'd said to the postman and just shrugged his shoulders before sloping off down the road with the gang behind him, laughing.

And then when he gets home, this, not a word about why he was late, why Trudi came home first.

"Jozef?" His mother is shaking him by the shoulder; he winces with pain as she touches a bruised spot. He shakes his head trying to forget the fight and to remember what she has said. Something about the Brandon's house, something about them being safer if the Nazis thought they were orphans. Ridiculous.

"Yes Mama. The Brandons. The orphanage"

"Jozef, what is the matter? This is important. You must listen. What has got into you?" She sighs not looking at him now but tracing the edge of her empty teacup with her forefinger. "We have to do this Jozef." Her voice softens; she waits for him to speak. He lets his anger go then, lets it all go, the fight was so small in the scheme of things, so small.

"Everything is fine Mama, everything is fine just thinking about school and things."

He watches her sigh. She tells him the plan again. Tomorrow or the next day or soon he will come home and she will not be there. He is to look after Trudi, give her a glass of milk and a piece of bread and butter.

"When will you be back?"

"Jozef, darling Jozef, we have to make ourselves safe now. All of us." Her attention drifts, he sees the shadows falling across her face. She had been close to his Aunt Jet and she'd relied on Casper after his father died. She misses them, they all miss them. And she misses his grandma and grandpa who have gone somewhere with Aunt Diny. They are the only ones left now.

"We have to keep out of the hands of the Nazis," Jozef adds appealingly – and a number of other people too, he thinks to himself. He smiles as she gives him her full attention. Lea is watching. She hasn't said anything.

His mother latches on to his words. "Yes...that's right. So we are doing what is best for you and Trudi. You will be safe in the children's home with the other children. They won't touch the children."

He thinks again how mad the whole plan is but doesn't argue. He can hear Trudi playing outside with their cousin Tina. If it happens what will he say to Trudi? How will she take it?

She's such a mamma's girl. But he doesn't argue, not while Lea is there. This is all Lea's crazy scheme, sitting there like a stone at the end of the table saying nothing, sipping tea.

He stretches out a hand and his mother grabs his fingers squeezing them in hers.

"Can't we come with you?"

"You can't come. It won't be as safe. We are doing what we feel is best Jozef. You have to trust me."

He doesn't really understand how he and Trudi won't be safe in hiding and she and Lea and Tina would. He's not sure she believes that either. She is crying now and she reaches across and pulls him towards her, he can feel the sticky wetness of her tears on his face. "I love you Jozef. You are my boy. You need to be strong now."

The following day he comes home and she is gone.

Jozef – Utrecht – October

Jozef is totally absorbed by the lesson. The teacher, a tall thin angular young man with short black hair and a pale checked shirt is always on his feet marching up and down as he talks, infecting the whole classroom with his enthusiasm. Not that long ago he had been a student at the university in Utrecht, now he is teaching a mixed age range of boys and girls about the solar system. He has been drawing the different planets on the board and naming them, showing their size and distance in relation to the earth. The enormity of the universe – the red globe of Saturn, blue Venus, the vast distances of space had enveloped Jozef's mind. For a few minutes he is lifted out of the minute-by-minute nightmare of his life. Life on earth seems so insignificant in the scheme of the universe.

The teacher is talking about Pluto, the biggest of the planets, when there is a knock on the door and one of the women who helps in the office, a short woman with round wire rimmed glasses that he remembers seeing when he arrived at the children's home, puts her head round the door.

The teacher stops talking, almost in mid-sentence, and turns to see who it is.

"Yes Mrs Mulder?"

"Is Jozef Jacobs here? He has a visitor in the entrance hall."

The words prickle his ears…someone for him? Here at the orphanage? His mother? He pushes the thought away knowing it is ridiculous, but it keeps popping back up, floating in his mind, refusing to go away.

"Jozef!"

"Yes Sir."

The teacher smiles and Jozef notices how bushy his eyebrows are and how red his ears.

"Go with Mrs Mulder and come back as soon as you can."

The legs of his chair scrape the floor as he gets up, the rest of the class watching as he slips out of the door and follows Mrs Mulder down the corridor. The orphanage is huge, and they eat, sleep, play and have lessons within its tall grey walls. Someone said it had been part of the university before the invasion. Mrs Mulder doesn't seem to recognise him. Why should she remember him, there must have been 15 or more of them arriving at the home at the same time and two girls had been crying inconsolably, Trudi had just gripped his hand as they waited, white with anxiety. He didn't blame the little girls for crying, he didn't blame them at all. But the tears inside him had dried up and only the damp salty wetness of his pillow in the morning told him he still cried at night.

At the end of the hall, Mrs Mulder turns to go into the orphanage office pointing to the large wooden swing doors leading to the buildings entrance where there is a small seating area. "He's sitting through there."

Who is 'he'? His father is dead, and his grandfather has disappeared with his Uncle Bram. There is Uncle Casper? But people didn't come back from the camps did they? Perhaps they'd got it wrong, perhaps there was another Jozef in the home and they had just got it wrong.

He walks into the waiting area where an old man sits, a brown felt hat in his hand which he turns slowly around and around. A wisp of grey hair stands up at the back of his head reminding Jozef of his grandfather, but it isn't his grandfather. He walks slowly towards the old man. He'll tell him there's been a mistake and go back to his class. But as he comes towards him the man looks up, puts his hat down on the bench beside him, his hands on his knees and turns and stares at Jozef.

"Jozef Jacobs?" His voice is gravelly.

Jozef's heart thuds. Who is this?

"Yes?"

The man pats the other chair next to him and throws Jozef a conspiratorial look with pale, ice blue eyes. Jozef sits, keeping to the front of the chair so his legs dangle down and he can reach the stone tiles with the tips of his shoes. The man puts his hand in his top pocket pulls out a small, folded piece of lined yellow paper and passes it to him.

Jozef trembles as he takes the piece of paper and unfolds it. His head swims. It's his mother's writing, definitely his mother's writing. He blinks back a tear and reads.

"Dear Jozef,
I am thinking of you and Trudi. Send me word of how you are? We are fine. I miss you every minute of every day. I love you. Be brave.
Mama."

Jozef's hands shake as he absorbs the soft breath of his mother's words. He thinks of the way her hair curls and bounces as she walks, her strong hands, her rare smile. He feels like he is floating in a bubble. The old man takes hold of his arm.

"It's ok, Jozef." The old man then takes his hand and Jozef can see the brown freckles mapping their way across the back of it. "Jozef?"

He opens his mouth but only a whisper comes out. "Where is she?"

"She is safe. That is what you need to know. That is what I am here to tell you."

He feels the weight of some of his nightmare lift from his shoulders and he realises that all the time, ever since they had arrived at the orphanage, ever since he had got home from school on that horrible afternoon and found she wasn't there, ever since then he has not really believed that she was alright. He's told Trudi over and over again that their mother was fine, she had to go away, and that they would be fine too. He's said it a million times trying to convince himself, but he has never really believed it until now: now he knows that she is safe.

He looks at the letter again, the smooth slope of her writing. The man reaches over to take it from him. "You can't keep the letter Jozef. That would be dangerous." He prizes the note from Jozef's grip and swiftly puts it in his pocket, then puts an arm across his shoulders, giving him a brief affectionate squeeze.

"Good boy." He looks into Jozef's eyes.

"Now tell me, how you are? How is Trudi? I want to tell your mother."

"We're fine," Jozef whispers, clears his throat. "I'm fine." He wonders what he can tell this man. What was fine anyway? Fine was that he was here and he was alive. He doesn't want to tell his mother about sleeping in a dorm with 20 other boys, or the fact that one of the bigger boys had stolen one of his two blankets so that he was always cold at night, or that he'd got into a fight and it had somehow ended up being his fault. He doesn't want to tell her that the water in the showers is never warm, the stone floors always cold and that they eat more cabbage soup than he has ever eaten in his life and that the whole place, the dorms, the schoolrooms, the hallways smell faintly of vinegary boiled cabbage and bleach. He doesn't want to tell her that the highlight of the day was occasionally finding a largish piece of potato or a teaspoon sized lump of fatty meat in his soup. He doesn't want to tell her how scared he'd been when he got home and she wasn't there and how he re-lived that moment every night: every night remembering it, waking up with the bile rising in his throat. He doesn't want to tell her how he dreams of the life before she disappeared, of the food they ate, of the touch of her hand on his head, her voice, the comfort of her. He doesn't want to tell her he is always, always hungry and cold. He can't tell her any of that.

He looks up at the old man. "Who are you?"

"I am a friend, that's all you need to know."

Jozef hears the clip of someone's shoes on the tiles and looks up to see the dark– haired matron walking towards them.

She addresses the man. "Hello? You are?"

"Smit, madam, Mr Smit," and there is something about the way he says it that makes Jozef realise that the old man made the name up on the spot. "Thank you for letting me see Jozef. He's a good lad. Wanted to see how he was. He lived in my village, would help me sometimes in the garden. Heard they had brought him here and I was this way, visiting my sister, and thought well, thought I'd see if he was alright, bring him a little present."

Jozef listens staring at his feet and then sees out of the corner of his eye the man put his hand in his other pocket and pull out a small bar of chocolate. He can hardly believe his eyes. He recognises the dark brown and gold pattern on the paper. The man pats him on the shoulder.

"For you Jozef," he passes it to him.

"That's a big treat Jozef. Be sure and share it with your sister," says the matron. He can feel the cold breath of her even though she is standing several feet away. Will she take it away from him? Clearly the man is thinking the same thing. "You eat a piece now Jozef. There are so many children here. You can't share it with everyone." Jozef opens the paper and stares at the chocolate, breaking off the first square and sliding it between his lips, not chewing just letting the chocolate melt in his mouth so he can hold on to the flavour of it for as long as possible.

He wants the chocolate to remind him of home, to remind him of birthdays and weekends and good times and yet all he can think of as it melts down into a thick cream in his mouth, is that the last piece of chocolate he had eaten was on the day his mother disappeared, in the house they'd been taken to, and it brought back all the memories of that day.

He remembers getting home, the day after the conversation in the kitchen, and walking into the house and finding his mother not there. He remembers Trudi putting her little red checked case on the floor and pulling out a drawing she had been colouring in at school, rummaging for colouring pencils, climbing onto the wooden chair, kneeling so that she can finish colouring her picture. She'd been talking about it all the way home, cross she hadn't finished before the bell went for the end of the day.

He'd watched her for a moment and then told her he was going to look for their mother and Trudi had said, without looking up: "I think she has gone somewhere with Aunt Lea. She said she was going somewhere with Aunt Lea and I wasn't to be worried and I was to stay with you. Didn't she tell you that Jozef?"

And he'd felt a stone sink in his stomach and raced up the stairs feeling the sweat prickle up over his body. Seeing his mother's bedroom door open, he'd run in. But she wasn't there, her black ebony hairbrush and comb was missing from her dressing table next to the window. And he remembers going into his room and seeing the case on the bed, his clothes and Trudi's clothes packed inside, the picture of his parents which had been in the living room lying on top. He remembers feeling a sense of panic and rushing downstairs to find Trudi still colouring in the picture of an apple tree, gripping the pencil tightly, her face close to the page as she coloured each individual apple red.

Aware of Jozef watching her she'd looked up: "Did you find her?"

"No."

"I told you. She's with Aunt Lea." She'd nibbled the end of the crayon in her hand. "Did she tell you where she was going Jozef?

"No, Trudi. Listen to me Trudi." He'd tried to stop her colouring in then to listen to him seriously, but she had just carried on, so he said it anyway. "Trudi, I think we might be going to a children's home now."

"This is our home Jozef."

"Didn't Mama say anything to you?"

"Not really," she'd whispered suddenly putting her crayons down and wrapping her arms around him. "Where is she Jozef? She said something about going to a place with lots of other children, but I told her I liked my school, I didn't want to go." She starts to cry then. "I don't want to go."

And then the woman, a friend of his mother's, had come and Trudi really began to wail, the sound keening through him, her face swelling with tears, her picture abandoned. The woman had knelt, put her arm around Trudi and told her to be good because there was something special for her at the house they were taking her to, some chocolate. And Trudi hadn't stopped crying: "I don't want chocolate, I want mamma!" But later after her sobs had subsided and they'd gone to the woman's house, they were still given chocolate.

Now in the hallway in the children's home in Utrecht, he feels very sick.

"Jozef? Are you alright?" It's matron, she's been chatting to the old man. Jozef wonders if he is going to faint, but the old man puts his arm around him, holds him steady.

"Put your head between your knees Jozef, you will feel better." He feels the old man's breath on his neck as he bends down, smells the faint remnants of tobacco and beer lingering on his jacket. He begins to feel better and sits up, but the old man keeps his arm around him.

The matron looks worried and Jozef fetches the necessary words: "I'm fine. I'll give the rest of the chocolate to Trudi."

"Catch your breath Jozef. Sit for a minute." The old man leans back but Jozef can still feel the circling warmth of his arm.

"Just brings back too many memories seeing me again I expect," says the old man talking to the matron. "It's difficult for these kids...hard work for you too. I'll come again another time."

"I don't know if we will be here."

"No?" The old man moves his hand and is fishing in his pocket, eventually pulling out a pipe and a small leather tobacco pouch, opening it and teasing out a few strands of tobacco then pushing them down with his forefinger into the bowl of the pipe. Jozef breathes in the sweet, warm smell of it, a memory of home.

"They want to move all the children to Amsterdam."

"To the Jewish Quarter?" asks the old man hesitating as he dips a second time into the pouch for more tobacco. "Why are they doing that then? That place is crowded."

"Don't ask me. Why would I know? They tell us nothing," the matron's voice barely contains her supressed anger. "We have to just do what we are told to do." Jozef feels her gaze on him again.

"Come on Jozef back to class. Say goodbye to Mr...?"

"Smit."

"Yes. Mr Smit." Jozef gets up then, turning to the old man who is still intent on his pipe. He looks up and Jozef sees a sadness in the old man's eyes that he hadn't spotted before.

"Thank you for coming."

"Good to see you again young Jozef. I miss your help. I'll see you another time."

"But…" Jozef remembers the words of the matron, they will be moving soon.

"I'll see you," says the old man stretching out his right hand and taking Jozef's firmly in his. "I'm often in Amsterdam for business."

Jozef – Amsterdam – November

Jozef pulls his cap down, feeling a cold wind whistling up from the Zwanenburgwal canal. He turns down Jodenbreestraat stuffing his hands in his pockets twisting a small stub of pencil around and around in his fingers, feeling the first spits of rain on his face.

It is Saturday, no school. One of the good things about the ghetto is the freedom that he and the older children in the orphanage have, to run about within its confines. Where can they go? The ghetto is mostly hemmed in by canals, its bridges guarded, barbed wire looped and snaking across other roads leading in and out. He walks behind two women in black headscarves, the worn heels of their shoes clicking along the pavement. They have linked arms and are huddled in conversation, hardly noticing the rain which is coming down harder now. He ducks into a covered entrance way and pulls the collar of his jacket up and his cap down hard over his ears. He is nearly at David's place. He'll wait till the worst has passed. Squeezing back into the doorway he looks up and realises he is standing opposite number 24 and hadn't even noticed. It is over a week since Simon and his family left. Looking up at the windows of the apartment where they lived, he sees three little girls looking out, one of them sticks her tongue out at him.

Jozef misses Simon, but he is getting used to missing people. He'd met Simon at the school in the ghetto. He had been told to sit next to him and they had quickly made friends, both loving football and Simon confiding that the last boy who'd sat in Jozef's seat had been constantly snivelling. Jozef had been surprised to learn that Simon lived with his mother and brother. Simon had taken him back to their flat on the third floor of a tall brick house. His mother had been nice, reminded him a bit of his mother, always in the kitchen: "I'm not cooking the food, I'm stretching it," she'd tell the boys as they watched her, while playing cards at the table after school. Jozef saw her take a large spoon of flour and mix it with a cup of water and stir it into the simmering pot. She was relentlessly cheerful and welcoming. He'd once asked what soup she was making and she had scooped a spoon from the pot and handed it to him.

"It's soup du jour Jozef?" He smiled as he remembered how she thought food, whatever it was, sounded better in French, more delicious and they would run around the flat shouting "fromage", "baguette", "tarte aux pommes" and more until they had run out of foods they could remember in French.

She'd serve the soup to Simon and his younger brother and would often give Jozef a small bowl too. Whatever it was it tasted better than the food in the orphanage. Simon's mother had been extra kind since she had heard about his father. Her husband had been taken in a similar raid. She still hadn't heard from him, still didn't know whether he was alive or dead or even where he was. She was just taking a day at a time she told him, hoping the trail was clear enough if he was alive, if he came back, if he started to look for them.

But then, just over a week ago Simon had told Jozef that they had been sent a letter from the Jewish Council. They were on the next train to Westerbork.

"It's alright Jozef. We will be fine," broke in his mother who was listening to the boys' conversation. "Lots of families we know have gone there now. Do you want to come with us?"

Jozef shook his head. "No. No, thank you, I must stay here with my sister."

"It's going to be like a children's town here! All the families gone and the orphans left behind," she'd said roughing his hair affectionately. Two days later he'd watched them walk over the bridge with other families to the meeting point at the Theatre Joodsche Schouwburg. Even today in the rain there are families being packed into trucks, he can see them in the distance. Someone is singing, Jozef recognises the song, something about summer, but then one of the soldiers tells the singer to shut up.

"Isn't it time you were somewhere else?"

Jozef jumps, he hadn't seen the soldier coming up the road, had hardly noticed the rain easing off a bit.

"Off with you now."

Jozef automatically runs towards the synagogue and the warren of an annex behind it where he and some of the other older boys have been lodged.

He and Trudi have been in Amsterdam a month. They'd been split up – Trudi was in a dorm for young girls in the main part of the orphanage and he was in one of several annexes set up for older children. The children far outnumbered the adults. His mother hadn't been alone in thinking that an orphaned child might have a better chance of survival.

He turns into Frederiksstraat and walks towards the other annex where David lives, his friend from Laag-Keppel. It's quiet and he wonders where everyone is; there is usually a game or something going on in the street? Maybe it's the rain. He pulls the collar up on his coat and runs towards the annexe as the rain turns from drizzle to downpour. It had been strange when he had bumped into David two weeks ago. It seemed like a one in a million chance that two boys from the same area would end up in the same place. But it's not so surprising really; it seems that anyone who is Jewish will sooner or later arrive in the ghetto. Finding David and making friends with Simon have been the best thing about Amsterdam – and seeing Hetty. He smiles as he remembers seeing her in the ghetto, standing there, looking at him. He had been so surprised. She'd been to visit a patient and was on her way back to the hospital – she'd spotted him playing football, but he hadn't recognised her at first, hadn't associated the nurses' uniform with the Hetty he knew in Scheveningen.

Reaching the door of the house on Frederiksstraat where David lives, he bangs on the knocker, turning the handle to go in.

An old man in a black coat calls out to him from across the street: "Not there sonny. They've gone."

"Where?"

The man smiles lamely: "Gone! Gone!" He pulls his black felt homburg down hard on his head and walks on.

Jozef pushes the door open, noticing that the hinges whine, he'd never noticed that before. An old woman is sweeping in the first room where the warden usually sat. He can see the blue veins in her arms as she pushes the broom back and forth, the darned fabric of her maroon coat swinging around her. Hearing him in the doorway, she stops and leans on the handle of the broom. "Who are you?"

"I'm looking for my friend."

"They've gone. They've all gone. They came this morning, early, and took them all." She squats down in front of a pile of papers on the floor and starts sorting through them. Tidying he thinks and then realises she's scavenging, separating out anything that could possibly be useful. She reaches forward to pick up a handful of pencils and he sees the white tendons at the back of her knees stretch.

"Where have they gone?"

The woman pockets the pencils and stands up. She cocks her head, eyeballing him: "Where do you think they've gone. On holiday? To the beach?" She chuckles wheezily then looks Jozef up and down like he was an imbecile. "Where are you from anyway?"

"I'm in the other boys' annexe, the one behind the synagogue."

"Well, you next then?"

Seeing that he was not going away the woman spoke again. "They've taken them to Westerbork, where they take everybody. Where else do you think they have gone?"

"I thought...."

"Don't think. We just have to put up with it. Go along with it." She turns back to her search mumbling to herself, coughing. "Go home, to whatever home you have today, but don't imagine it will be your home tomorrow."

He wants to run, to leave, but he must make sure and he walks on down the hall, climbs the stairs, peers into the rooms that had served as dorms – empty beds, blankets gone, nobody, nothing. The whole place abandoned. He turns on his heel, belts down the stairs and out into the street. It is still raining. He runs towards the synagogue, the water splashing up his shins. Head down he nearly collides with a couple coming around the corner with their umbrella. He ducks into a doorway to catch his breath. A woman neatly dressed in a fitted green coat with a velvet collar huddles in the other corner with her little girl. The cheap canvas square with the yellow stars looks garish against such a smart outfit. He smiles up at the woman and touches his cap politely. The woman smiles back and Jozef sees the cherry red of her lipstick and the whiteness of her teeth. "I forgot my umbrella. Looked like such a nice day earlier didn't it?" She looks down at the little girl whose face is framed by dark shiny curls.

"Yes," Jozef nods, not knowing what else to say touches his cap again, takes another deep breath and runs for the building where he lives, racing through the door and almost knocking over the matron.

"Oi! Jozef Jacobs. Hold up there!"

"Sorry mam." He stops, catching his breath and pulling his sodden cap off his head, waiting to be told off.

"Abe Krantz was looking for you. He said he had a message for you." She shakes her head, looking at his coat. "Take your coat off, you're drenched."

He starts to peel off his coat and she reaches a bony hand across to help him, taking it from him, hanging it on a hook. "Abe's upstairs."

Jozef takes the stairs two at a time looking for Abe and finds him playing marbles in the dorm.

"Hi Jozef, an old man was looking for you."

"When?"

"About half an hour ago? Maybe less. I was coming in and he asked me if I knew you. I think he sells smokes and stuff to the tobacconist shop? Said that if I saw you to say 'hi' and if he missed you, he'd see you next week? Who is he? Do you think he will give us some smokes?"

Jozef shrugs. "Maybe. I don't know."

"Well, a pity you missed him," Abe indicates the game, "Want to play?"

He steps towards them, tempted, then changes his mind: "No. You know the boys from the other annexe have been taken to Westerbork?"

"Never!"

"Yes, just been there."

"What the hell is…"

But Joseph is already going out the door running down the stairs. Someone leans over the banister.

"Where are you going?"

"I'm going to try to find the old man." Reaching the hallway he grabs his wet coat from the hook, pushing his arms into it as he makes for the door.

"Jozef Jacobs you can't..." he hears matron shout as the door swings shut behind him, but he can and he does. He just runs.

The rain has turned to drizzle and people are back outside hurrying about their business. He dodges into the road to avoid them and makes for the tobacconist's kiosk on the corner of the street. He must be there.

He darts in front of a family laden with heavy battered suitcases and into the shop. Nothing, no one is in there apart from an old man in a checked jacket and black hat, elbow propped on the wooden counter chewing the stem of his pipe. Jozef breathes in the potent smell of newsprint, tobacco and burnt sugar. He looks at the cellophane wrapped sticks of candy propped in a brown pot on the counter next to a tray of small chocolate bars like the one the old man had given him when he had visited him in Utrecht. Now what, but as he turns to leave the old man takes the pipe out of his mouth and turns his head towards the small curtain covering the entrance to the back of the shop. "Marc there is a young customer out here for you!"

"Coming!"

Jozef hears two voices behind the curtain and then a pale skinned tall youngish man with short blonde hair and a moustache comes out into the shop, one of the sleeves of his blue shirt pinned up where he has lost part of his left arm. Catching Jozef looking he smiles, "Unfortunately, not the result of great heroism, just an accident on my uncle's farm when I was a teenager. What can I do for you young man?"

Jozef didn't know what to say and then he sees the old man who had visited him in Utrecht coming through the curtain behind him. He'd seen him twice since that first Utrecht visit. He had appeared unannounced in the Jewish Quarter and seemed by chance to bump into Jozef. He always asks him the same questions: are you and your sister alright? Always giving him the same news; your mother is fine, she sends her love.

"Ah Marc I think young Jozef has come to see me. Hi Jozef, how are you? Wait a minute while Marc and I finish our business." Marc passes him an envelope which the old man tucks inside his pocket. With a wink at Marc he stretches out his other hand and takes two sugar canes out of the pot and puts them in his jacket pocket then comes around the counter, putting his cap on and his arm around Jozef's shoulders steering him out of the kiosk.

"Walk with me to the bridge."

The old man picks up the handle of a handcart he had left outside the shop and the two fall into step with one another. Jozef's heart is thumping, he breathes in the now familiar tobacco scent of the old man's coat. He still doesn't know his real name, he'd asked, but the old man had told him it was better for him not to know, then if anyone asks who he had been talking to he can quite honestly say he doesn't know. It is safer that way.

"Your coat's wet? Did you get caught in that rainstorm?" the old man asks as they walk companionably alongside the canal.

Jozef nods. "Well, you must get back soon and dry off. Don't want you getting ill. How are things? Everything OK? How's Trudi?"

"It's not good."

"Trudi's not well?"

"No, no, she's fine. It's just things are not good anymore."

The old man says nothing for a minute and Jozef looks across the canal at the people on the other side, not in the Jewish

Quarter: a teenage girl and boy strolling along with their arms around one another, a man cycling down the road in a red beret whistling, two soldiers standing by the next bridge chatting, looking lazily around. One of them looks across at them and Jozef ducks his head down.

"Oi, boy!"

The old man looks up smiles, puts a hand up, touches his hat.

"It's ok officer. The boy's not bothering me." The old man sighs and tells Jozef to go ahead of him, turn right and then right again. Jozef runs.

The old man catches him up a few minutes later, in the porch of an empty shop, a torn curtain obscuring it's dirty window, dead curling leaves blown up against the door. "These are hard times Jozef. You know that. You are probably as safe here as anywhere."

"I don't think we are safe anymore." He takes a breath and then tells the old man about David, about the other annexe and that the boys are gone.

"How old were they Jozef? Were they older than you?"

"Some of them yes, but not all, most were my age and some quite a bit younger...maybe 8? The really little ones are in the main orphanage, not in an annexe."

"And in the annexe where you live, behind the synagogue?"

"A mix. Some older, a few younger." Jozef feels a sudden cold breeze and wishes he had brought his scarf.

The old man scratches his head. "OK I am going to come back in a couple of days. The old man looks at his watch. "I could get you out but your sister..."

"I can't leave here without my sister."

"No, I know you can't. I'll be back on Tuesday. Meet me by the tobacconist at about 5. I'll try and come up with a plan. Think about what we can do."

Jozef nods and then remembers. "My cousin, Hetty, Hetty Van Leeuwen, she's a nurse… in the Jewish hospital. Maybe she can help?"

The old man smiles. "It's better to get as few people involved as possible."

"She goes in and out of the ghetto all the time. Like you."

The old man scratches his head. "I'll see you Tuesday." He dips his hand in his pocket and hands Jozef the two candy canes. "One for you and one for Trudi."

The old man turns down the next road towards a bridge. Jozef watches him trundling across, saying a few words to the soldiers, passing one some cigarettes as they wave him on. He sees the guard they all hate, the small one with the high-pitched voice, push an old man with a battered briefcase back into the ghetto before shouting at two boys teasing a cat.

Hetty – Amsterdam – November

Hetty holds the young woman's wrist, feels for her pulse, listens to the soft pumping of blood through her veins before picking up the chart hanging from a string behind her bed and marking it.

"Your pulse is good," she smiles as the woman wheezes a thank you. Hetty settles her gently back on the bed, plumping the pillow around her head and straightening the sheets. The woman closes her eyes, her face slipping back into some dream of another place, some other time.

Hetty looks across the ward at the dark face of the clock: nearly five o'clock. She has been on duty since 11.00. She is looking forward to her break, to momentarily putting her feet up and grabbing a cup of weak tea and something to eat from the small canteen at the back of the building. She'd really like a shower but that will have to wait until her shift is over.

A whiff of the strong disinfectant they use to keep the wards clean reaches her and she turns to see her friend Anki on her hands and knees cleaning beneath one of the beds.

"You ok?"

"Mrs Meir had a bit of an accident."

The bed is pulled back and Hetty starts removing the sodden sheets.

"Thanks."

"Where is she now?"

"Berta has taken her to the bathroom to wash her down and find her something clean to wear. " Anki looks tired, the shadows beneath her eyes marking the 11 hours she has been on duty.

"You're due off any minute."

"I'm staying on 'til 8. Vonneke is off ill again."

Hetty bites her lip: the same request to work late will inevitably come her way. She wraps the sheets into a bundle and walks out of the ward to the huge laundry basket in the hall, there is a gentle tap on her shoulder as she opens the lid of the basket. It is one of the porters.

"Someone is looking for you Miss Hetty."

What now? "Who?"

"No-one I know. He's in reception. Said it was urgent could I get a message to you. Said he was a friend of someone called Bets? "

Hetty stuffs the last of the dirty sheets into the basket and walks into the next door linen cupboard pulling a clean set off the shelves, noticing their fraying edges. So why is Bets trying to get a message to her? The porter is still waiting. "I'm off on my break in a couple of minutes. I need some fresh air. Tell him to meet me at the nurses entrance in ten. What does he look like?"

"Old, brown hat, dark brown coat, about my height, keeps chewing on the stump of his pipe.

"Thanks"

"He's not Jewish."

Hetty frowns. The porter pats his chest. "No star."

Hetty turns back to the ward her feet echoing on the polished wood, her mind scooting ahead. She gives Anki the sheets. It is 5.05, her break is seeping away. She goes to the nurses station to sign out, the ward sister looks up at her, her face pinched, her dark eyes red and watery with exhaustion. "Take an hour Hetty. Be back at 6.00. Vonneke's off ill so I am going to have to ask you to work a couple of extra hours and you won't get another break." The sister sighs. "Get something to eat."

Hetty leaves the ward and runs up the three flights of stone stairs to the top floor of the building where the nurses are quartered, taking off her cap and apron as she goes. In her room she quickly changes into a blue dress, the silky lining brushing her skin softly after the rough thick serge of the brown uniform. She unpins her hair and pulls a brush through it, and pulls on a dove grey felt cloche hat before grabbing her dark blue winter coat. She's removed the star. She settles a heavily fringed grey scarf she keeps in the pocket around her shoulders to disguise the deception. She is out of the room and running down stairs in less than five minutes, biting her lips to bring the blood into them and give them some colour.

Out of the nurses entrance she looks left and right, mentally clocking the soldier who keep an eye on the comings and goings of the hospital. He's chatting with someone and having a smoke down near the park. Across the street less than 20 yards away, an old man is leaning against a lamp post, brown coat, a pipe in his mouth. She crosses and walks slowly, cautiously towards him. He straightens up, removes the pipe from his mouth and breathes her name into the air almost as if he is talking to himself. "Hetty? Hetty van Leeuwen."

She turns, nods and they fall into step with one another.

"Who are you?"

"I am a friend of Bets… your aunt? Can we talk?" He puts his pipe in his pocket.

"I've got about 45 minutes before I have to be back on duty again. I need some fresh air but I must get something to eat."

He looks at her surprised but then realises she is not wearing a star.

"It makes things easier."

"And riskier."

She looks across at the guards who are deep in conversation and crosses the road, moving as fast as she can away from the hospital and the area around the ghetto.

"There's that big café on Amstelstraat"

She nods. "Perfect. Why did you want to see me?"

They walk quickly. "It's about your cousins. Jozef and Trudi?"

"Yes?"

"You know they are living in the ghetto?"

"Yes. I saw them… less than a week ago. I was in the ghetto, I had gone to visit one of our patients there." She remembers coming out of the tall black bricked house and walking back to the bridge, mildy depressed at how little she had been able to do for the old woman she'd been visiting. A shout from across the street and her eye catches a group of boys playing football, one has the ball and is dodging in and out of the other lads his feet flying towards makeshift goalposts made from upturned wooden boxes. As she'd watched, she'd realised it was Jozef, he'd grown, no longer the little boy she remembered. She was mesmerised watching him, thinking about her family, waiting for him, wondering where Trudi was, why he was there. And then when the game had ended he'd seen her and with a huge grin had flown across the space between them, flinging his arms around her, smelling of boyish sweat and carbolic soap. She'd walked with him back to the girls' home to see Trudi she tells the old man, a picture of the little girl's hopeful face haunts her.

"The ghetto gets worse and worse… I'm worried about them."

"With reason. They have started moving some of the orphans living there to Westerbork."

She shakes her head. "Not the little ones, not that I know of. Everyone thinks the children will be safe."

"Boys Jozef's age – and younger."

She feels her chest tighten, wonders at the naivity of their thinking the children would be spared. She realises that the fact that they are now moving them to the camps doesn't really surprise her. Nothing surprises her any more. Her eyes catch a moving shadow stepping out of a side street. Always shadows, always this fear of something following her. But it's nothing. She sees the café just ahead, a couple coming out.

"What can I do to help?"

"We need to talk."

Entering the café they are met by a warm fug of steamy air, noise crowding round them. Someone turns up the radio which is playing a tinny version of *Lili Marlene*. The old man leads the way between the tables, towards an empty booth at the back of the cafe. They slide into the worn plush red velvet seats and the old man passes Hetty the short menu. Hetty slips off her coat letting it fold around her on the seat. She orders a dish of leek and potato soup with a chunk of black bread and some tea. The old man orders a double shot of *Jenever*.

The soup comes quickly, thick starchy salty broth boiled free of flavour, with a decent hunk of bread on the side, but Hetty is grateful for its wamth and eats slowly, listening as the old man who leans forward, placing his elbows on the table, tells her what Jozef had told him. Her stomach churns but she keeps eating, she won't get anything else until breakfast and there is a long night ahead. The man leans across the table, his pale blue eyes piercing hers: "I need help getting them out. I can see how to get Jozef...but the little girl? Trudi? Never," he speaks almost under his breath. "Some people are....finding homes for the babies, the tiny ones."

Hetty says nothing but nods, they are all aware of the 'disappearing' babies being rescued by Amsterdam women, being given new homes, new families, oh god how she prays they are good families. Quite a few have 'disappeared' from the hospital, under cover of a large coat.

"But Trudi is not a baby, and she is too young to be allowed out on her own. They look after the little girls well at the orphanage. Too well to make this simple."

She remembers Trudi before the occupation, long plaits and plump cheeks and an infectious laugh like her brother Jozef's. The boy in the ghetto is taller, thinner, grown up beyond his years, his cheeks hollowed out. Trudi is a shadow of the little girl she had been, quiet instead of chirpy, strangely proud of the grey striped uniform she had been given to wear in the orphanage.

The nurses have freedom to come and go, but the atmosphere in the ghetto is depressing, a potent mix of fear, desperation and despair. She can't bear the thought of any harm coming to the children. She picks up the last crust of her bread and wipes it around the inside of the soup plate. "What do you want me to do?"

"Just wondered if there was some way you could help?" He keeps his voice level and smiles up at a fat man, pushing past their table. "See if you have some influence, you are their aunt. There is no way they will let me take them out of the ghetto, but you...well, worth a try? We can find somewhere for them to stay."

The noise around them covers the silence that now hangs

between them. *Lili Marlene* had ended and *That Old Black Magic* is playing. Hetty says nothing.

That old black magic has me in its spell
That old black magic that you weave so well

The old man leans back as she finishes her bread and pushes her plate away. He reached into his pocket for his pipe, turning it in his hands before putting it on the table, and returning to his pocket for his tobacco pouch. He doesn't want to meet her eyes, she can tell that.

She shrugs. "I'll help, don't worry, I'll try to help." He finally looks up at her and smiles so she asks him the question that has been niggling her while she was listening to him. "But what makes you want to help? You're not Jewish."

He hesitates: "My eldest son died during the invasion two years ago," he pushes tobacco into the bowl of the pipe. "We have to all do what we can to stop this," he glances up at her, briefly stretches across the table and touches her hand and speaking softly confirms what part of she knows. "Lots of people feel like I do….even if it sometimes feels like most people don't." He drinks his gin and places the empty glass on the table.

Hetty looks at her watch, it is already ten to six. She stands, buttoning her coat. "I have to get back. I can't be late. I've got a late shift tomorrow starting at 3.00. I'll go and see the children, in the morning. Can we meet afterwards, before I go on duty?"

He gets up: "Of course. I don't want to be seen with you in the ghetto or again at the hopsital though. Can you meet me in Kerkstraat, number 46? The home of a friend?" She nods and shakes the old man's hand, feels its firm warmth.

"I'll see you there."

"I'll be waiting."

She smiles and turns without answering, threading her way through the tables, leaving the old man to pay the bill.

Out in the fresh air she can hear her heart thumping. She is going to be late.

Hetty – Amsterdam – the next day

Hetty breathes in the damp earthiness of the fallen leaves from the plane trees fringing the pavement. A cold wind whips off the canal as she turns right alongside it deciding to cross into the ghetto over one of the smaller bridges. There are few people on this side of the canal: an old man walking a small black and white dog, poking its nose into dank piles of fallen leaves; two women, collars up, walking in step in the opposite direction, shopping bags over their arms. Almost at the bridge she looks to see who is on guard: the fat one with the red ears that stick out and a bulbous nose that's turned cherry red in the cold. Good, he was pleasant enough, it is one of the taller ones she finds difficult to deal with, something to do with the way he looks at her rather than listens to what she says.

"Guten Morgen." Hetty smiles, bright, breezy confident. The soldier smiles back, he loves it when the pretty girls smile, so many of the women coming and going look so angry, so ill. She hands over her pass and he flips it open with a plump thumb and looks at her under heavy lidded eyes, noting the nurses' uniform under her long dark coat.

"Who are you visiting?"

"Some children. The mother's in hospital having another baby. I promised I would look in on them."

He raises his eyebrows. "Too many babies." He holds on to her pass. He is cold and bored, the other guard on duty is reading a book and not interested in a chat, the nurse will relieve the tedium.

"So many kids. Do you have children?" He winks at her.

"No," she laughs. "All the children around here seem to get ill."

"Ill?"

"Yes. There are so many people. It feels as if sooner or later everyone gets sick."

"Well, its winter."

"Typhus. There is typhus going around at the moment."

The soldier frowns takes a step back and hands her back her pass at arm's length.

"That's awful. You can die from typhus."

"Poor little things." She smiles again at the guard as she puts her pass away. It's so easy to poke at the Nazi fear of typhus, of any disease. She finds pleasure in unsettling them, even the nicer ones.

"Let's hope they get better Fraulein," says the soldier dismissively, waving her on. She walks down the cobbled hump of the bridge and under the black and white ghetto banner strung high between two buildings feeling a small nub of triumph.

She remembers this part of Amsterdam from before the war, a rich quarter then of jewellery and antique shops, tailors, book shops, florists and a high-end chocolatier with a reputation of being the best in the city. From a distance it looks as if nothing has changed, that's what the Amsterdam residents on the other side of the Amstel think no doubt. But it has changed beyond recognition. Bleak boarded-up shops line the once bustling streets, the meagre displays of those that remain open are a constant reminder of how desperate the residents are now. She remembers the chocolatier when its windows were piled high with boxes and trays of different truffles, some dusted with cocoa, others glistening with strands of gold leaf or sugar crystals, the rich heady smell irresistible. Now the glass shelves are polished clean, a notice in the window says the shop is shut until further notice. Further along she notices the grocery shop, which used to spill into the street with piled high baskets of apples, plums, cherries and tomatoes, is equally bereft. A woman in a long tweed coat and velvet hat comes out cautiously as she passes. The shop is open then, but what little they have, they are keeping out of sight.

She walks further down the street, passing Levi's the tailor and dressmaker, the gold scrolled writing along the plate glass window flaking off. The tailor stands leaning in the door frame, a measuring tape hanging round his neck, smoking, his suit hanging loosely about him. She can hear people talking arguing inside the shop. The tailor had once had a reputation amongst the best families in the city, his window with its velvet swag displaying the highest fashions. But the swags have gone and all that is left is a red wool dress with a scoop neck, pinned stylishly back on a chipped plaster mannequin standing against a black card backdrop. A note in the bottom right hand corner of the window reminded people that Levi's were expert at altering clothes, turning hems. Keeping up appearances. A sense of personal pride in appearance reminds Hetty of her parents, never a dirty collar or a crease out of place whatever the crisis. 'Lose your standards and you lose the sense of who you are' her mother had once told her as she caught her trying to race out of the house in unpolished shoes.

As usual there is a gaggle of people chatting in front of the second-hand book shop, older men and women hunched over the rows of dog-eared books, bartering back and forth. She wonders if the old man who ran the shop made any money anymore, or if he even cared.

She turns left, towards the children's home, picking up the acrid stink of blocked drains that is rife in the ghetto, the odour heightened by the pile up rubbish which is rarely collected and too often finds its way into the canal.

Her heart thumps as she finally reaches the home, runs up steps to the door and carefully opens it. The smell of disinfectant and boiled cabbage engulfs her as she goes inside. The caretaker looks out of a small office next to the entrance and recognises her.

"Have you come to see the children? They're in classes now."

"No, I want to see the director."

"I will see if he is about."

Hetty follows him into his office, a small gas fire sputters in the corner, a desk is pushed against the wall with a range of different sized keys hanging on brass hooks above it, to the right a wall of numbered cubby holes.

"Remind me of your name?".

"Hetty. Hetty Van Leeuwen."

He points to a row of four slat backed wooden chairs marshalled along the wall closest to the fire.

"Sit there. Take your coat off, get warm. This is the warmest room in the building, so it's best to enjoy it while you can."

The clock on the wall reads 12.15. She checks it against her watch before leaning back, feeling the burning warmth of the fire on her legs. He picks up the phone and is talking to someone. She is so tired. She closes her eyes.

"Hetty?"

She snaps awake.

"He'll see you. Someone is coming now."

"Thanks," she smiles gratefully and looks up at the caretaker. "Sorry I didn't ask your name?"

"Frederik."

"Thanks Frederik." She smiles at him, noting his worn grey shirt, hollow cheeks and high forehead. "Have you got family here?"

"My sister and my mother, they live around the corner." He pauses and smiles at her and she notices his teeth are slightly crooked. "I used to work at the university, but of course not now. This was my father's job; he had a heart attack last year. I have taken over, keeps us going."

She crosses her legs. "Warm anyway."

"At least," he throws her a brief smile.

Just then a girl of about 12 walks in, her worn dress slightly too short but clean, her chestnut hair pulled back into two immaculate long French plaits.

"Miss van Leeuwen?" the girl looks at Hetty. "I'm Suzanna. The director has asked me to take you to his office."

Hetty gets up and with a parting nod of thanks to Frederik, follows the girl out of the room and down the corridor past rows of coats. Looking through glass door panes into the classrooms, Hetty can see the children sitting around large wooden tables, heads bowed in concentration listening to the murmur of the teacher's voice. Others queue against the wall, waiting to go into the refectory for their lunch, pausing in their chatter as she passes.

She follows the girl up a short flight of wide shallow wooden steps. Upstairs the institutional smell of disinfectant is overlaid with the warm woody smell of wax polish. They turn left down a long corridor. There are pale square shadows on the once white walls where pictures once hung. The paintings have probably been requisitioned by the Nazis along with anything else they perceived as being of value in the building. Someone has stuck a child's crayon drawing of trees and flowers half-way down one wall with a pin. At the end of a second corridor the girl stops and turns to Hetty before knocking on the door in front of her and immediately twisting the brass handle to open it, ushering Hetty in ahead of her.

Hetty finds herself in an office with two chairs in front of a large battered looking wooden desk. On the floor is a worn patterned red and blue faded Turkish rug, one wall is covered with shelves packed with files in labelled boxes, the other painted pale green and hung with black and white framed pictures of children standing and sitting in rows for unsmiling group portraits. The man behind the desk is bent over, writing intently, but as Hetty takes a step towards him, he put his pen down, stands up and stretches his hand out.

"Miss van Leeuwen?"

"Yes."

"I am the director here," he points to the more comfortable looking of the two chairs and invites Hetty to sit. "I hear you know some of our children?"

"My two young cousins Jozef and Trudi Jacobs are here, they were brought here from the orphanage in Utrecht."

"Ah". The man sighs picking over three ledgers on his desk. "Yes, if they were there they will be here." He opens the second ledger, tracing down a list of names with his thin heavily knuckled finger.

"Yes, yes. They arrived on October 15th. Would you like to see them?"

"Yes. Actually I have seen them, I met Jozef by accident in the street one day. Director, I am worried about them, about all the children. Are they alright? Is everything alright here? Are the children safe?"

A shadow passes across the director's face. "Is everything alright? I don't know. It's certainly alright here in the home. We do our best to give the children some education, ensure they are fed and have clean clothes and a bed to sleep in. That is what we do. That is all we can do." He scratches his neck.

"Someone told me that some of the children have been sent to Westerbork?"

The director looks coolly into Hetty's eyes: "How do you know about that? They needed some boys to help with some of the work they were doing. Just older boys...only older boys."

Hetty looks him straight back in the eyes. "But they weren't all older boys; some were only nine years old."

The director shifts in his seat, grimaces. "Nine is not so young anymore. We were acting on the instructions of the Jewish Council. These decisions are out of my hands. We have a lot of children here. Maybe it's a good thing some of them have gone to Westerbork. That's the way we see it; the way we have to see it." The director picks up a pen and turns it round and round in his hand, thinking "Is that what you came to ask?"

"No, I was just interested, concerned. I wanted to ask if I could take Jozef and Trudi to stay with some family friends. Good friends. I know their parents would be happy about it, they…"

The director cuts her off. "No, no, no. You can't do that. Are these people Jewish? If they are Jewish they will come here, to the ghetto, if they are not Jewish they can't have the children living with them. They can't." He taps the pile of registration books on his desk with his pen. "And more importantly we have to keep a record of everyone here. I am responsible for everyone in these books. Every child must be accounted for and stay here until I am given a different order." Sweat is now beading on the director's forehead. There are shadows under his eyes. He takes a white handkerchief from his pocket and wipes it across his face.

Hetty wonders if there has been trouble over the babies being smuggled out. The director straightens the ledgers, picks them up and thumps them into a pile.

"But surely, it's just two children…."

The director gives a breathy laugh. "They can't go. Not unless I get an order. These children are my responsibility; they must not leave. They are registered here and they must stay here. You want to get us all in trouble? All this should have been thought out beforehand, before they came into care. Now," he taps the pile of registers. "Now it is too late."

"But."

"What can I say? Maybe it is meant to be that they are here. Maybe they are safer here don't you think?" he leans back in his chair eyeing Hetty, raising an eyebrow. "I know these are hard times. A hard time for us all, but everything, everything in life is God's will. Don't you think? That is the only way I can see it. And we will get through this. We have the Jewish Council… they are good people, Samuel Cohen the leader of the Council, is a good man. He will lead us through this," he grimaces. "Like Moses he is supposed to lead us through this." He hesitates and leans forward across the desk until his face is centimetres from Hetty's. "You must have more faith!" He thumps the desk with his fist then sits back.

Hetty shivers. So, he won't let them go. So what is Plan B? She can feel a headache that has been hovering all day begin to pulse through her. She breathes in deeply. "I can see the children though can't I? Visit them?"

"You are a nurse…you can come and go," says the director bitterly getting up from his desk and looking at his watch. "Yes of course, see them whenever you like. The older children will be finishing their lunch now in the hall and the younger ones will be in the upper hall having a story read to them before class. The young girl who brought you to my office? Suzanna? She will take you."

He walks across the room and opens the door for her to leave. Standing, Hetty sees Suzanna leaning against the opposite wall straightening up when she hears the click of the latch.

"Take Miss van Leeuwen to the refectory and then go and get Trudi from Madam van de Groot". He turns to Hetty smiling now. "You can talk with them in the hallway downstairs, there are chairs there."

Hetty thought of the dark hall. "Can't I take them out for a walk?"

"A walk? Of course as long as you don't leave the ghetto. But you know that."

"Of course."

The director turns and walks back into his office closing the door firmly behind him. Hetty notes how thin he is, how his trousers and jacket sag around him.

Walking into the refectory a few minutes later where the boys are finishing lunch, the disappointment at the failure of her visit chokes her. Now what – any other plan to get the children out of the ghetto is risky, maybe impossible. She scans the room, searching amongst the sea of faces and clamouring noise for Jozef. The children sit shoulder to shoulder around the tables, boys on one table and girls on another, spooning the remnants of some sort of stew into their mouths. She scans the room again and then taps a blonde boy sitting near her at the end of a table on the shoulder.

"Jozef Jacobs? Do you know him? Is he here?"

The boy shrugs and turns back to the empty bowl he is licking with his finger. A teacher comes to speak to her, the meal is nearly finished.

"You are waiting for?"

"Jozef Jacobs"

"He's on the far table, but you will see him as they leave. They all use this door."

The boys finish eating and are stacking plates, passing them down to the head of each table who takes them to a hatch leading to the kitchens. Eventually, a tall woman with her grey hair swept into a bun stands and looks around the room before clapping her hands twice. Immediately the children shuffle into orderly lines and start to move out of the refectory, girls first.

A minute later Hetty sees Jozef. Someone has cut his thick hair brutally short; his ears stand out pinkly on the side of his face.

"Hetty!" He drops out of the queue. She bends down to kiss him, holding him firmly by his bony shoulders.

"Come. We are going for a walk. The director has agreed. We're meeting Trudi in the hall."

Jozef calls out to one of his friends and then walks to the front of the building where Trudi is waiting. She runs up to Hetty flinging her arms around her legs and rubbing her head against her skirt. "Hetty, Hetty." She bends down to the little girl only then realising that Suzanna had been waiting with her and now without a word was walking away, back past the coats, down the hall to a classroom.

She calls out to her "Thank you, Suzanna!" But the girl doesn't even turn around, just raises one pale hand in acknowledgement.

Jozef is already sorting through the racks of coats and pulling down his blue jacket and Trudi's dark green coat.

He shrugs on the jacket and pulls on a cap while Hetty helps Trudi into her coat lifting her chin to reach the top button. Trudi holds tightly on to Hetty's hand and does a sort of step skip as they go outside.

They walk through the streets to the canal so they can stand and watch the gulls swooping down looking for scraps amongst the rubbish flung into the murky water. Trudi skips off to collect autumn leaves falling from the elm trees fringing the cobbled pavement.

Jozef scoops up some pebbles and aims them at a can floating in the canal. Hetty leans with her back against the railings so she can watch Trudi. "How are things Jozef?"

"OK," he hesitates. "Not great. They took my friend…"

"I heard."

He looks into her eyes. "You've spoken to the old man?"

"Yes."

Jozef looks down, kicks at a pile of leaves, pushing up the pungent loamy smell of mould.

"We can't stay here." He whispers; he doesn't want Trudi to hear.

"I am doing my best to get you out Jozef. I will get you out. I'm going to see the old man now. We're coming up with a plan..." She pauses still not sure what the plan could be. "Just be ready?"

He nods seriously. "You will...?"

"You're going to be ok. We will get you out."

He nods, picks up a stone and throws it into the canal watching the circles pool around the point where it fell. He looks at her: "I wish I was a better swimmer. I wish Trudi could swim, then maybe we could just swim away." He looks up at her. "That's crazy isn't it?"

"No, just how we all feel. We all hate this situation Jozef, we all want it to end.

"Come on Trudi. Let's walk. I want to walk around the ghetto, along the canal."

"Why?" Trudi drops the fan of brown and orange leaves she has collected into the canal watching them flutter and fall, then float away.

Hetty smiles at her, grabs her hand. "Good exercise."

They walk, kicking leaves, talking about their memories of the time before. Jozef asking about Hans, about Loes, about all his cousins and Hetty tells him some of what she knows which isn't very much. So they remember jokes and games and the sorts of music her father always listened to in the evening and the taste of their grandmother's apple cake. Slowly they walk back to the children's home.

Jozef races off to the annexe where he lives and Hetty stoops to take Trudi's coat off, hang it on a hook. She gives her a hug and the little girl clings to her neck. "Don't go."

She unwraps the little girl's arms from around her. "I'll be back."

A wind has picked up as she leaves the orphanage, walks towards the edge of the ghetto, towards the city and crosses one the bridges, heading towards the hospital. She sees the same fat soldier who waves at her as she passes. He's holding onto the sleeve of an old man who he had been remonstrating with moments before.

"Everything alright?"

"Not so good. So much illness." She looks up at him. "Amazing you stay so well, standing out here, all these sick people in the ghetto."

The soldier tuts and then waves the old man he'd been arguing with back towards the ghetto.

Walking across the bridge, the shadow of the orphanage clings to her. It is nearly 1.30. She is late. She needs to get to the address the old man gave her and be back at the hospital by 3 when she's on duty again. She walks more quickly, head down, avoiding looking at people who avoid looking at her.

Unbeknownst to her or to the orphanage, the spectre of the Third Reich is stretching its claws towards them. Nazi General Otto Bene who is based in the Netherlands has been tasked with the responsibility of evacuating all Jews from The Netherlands within the next six months. On the 16 November 1942 Bene sends a report to German Foreign Minister Joachim von Ribbentrop that so far 45,000 Jews have been evacuated, and the programme of evacuation is to be dramatically stepped up to meet the Reich's 1 May 1943 target.

Hetty – Amsterdam – Two days later

"What the hell do you think you are doing!" Phillipe sits up suddenly, shaking his head, apoplectic with anger.

"What am I doing? I am doing what I have to do? Phillipe you know it is the right decision."

"Right for who? For you? For the children?" He gets out of the bed they've just been sharing, his bed, in his room in the attic eaves of the hospital. He pulls on underclothes, shaking his head.

Hetty doesn't get up but rolls over and props herself up on her elbow, pushing her hair behind her ears, pulling the rough cotton sheet over her breasts. Twenty minutes earlier they had been making love with an insatiable passion, like always, whenever they could snatch an evening or an hour, a sweet momentary release from the agony that surrounds them. Afterwards lying in each other's arms, limbs tangled, thinking, sharing a cigarette, Hetty had told him about the children, about the plan she had made earlier in the day with the old man to take them out of the ghetto and into hiding.

He paces the small bedroom. "This is reckless Hetty. Beyond reckless," he shakes his head in exasperation and leans back against the bedroom door looking at her. "You think they are just going to let you walk out of there with the children? First the orphanage won't let you…"

"They won't know." She cuts him off, leans across, picks up her watch from the side table and sees the time, then settles back against the headboard pulling another cigarette from the pack. She lights it and inhales deeply, pulling up her knees. "They'll just think I'm taking them for a walk."

"Second…crossing the bridge? Which bridge? You'll be stopped, there are soldiers everywhere on the bridges, on any road into the ghetto. What are you going to say when you are stopped? When Hetty, not if. And you think they are going to believe some crazy story about the children being ill? Are you mad? Half the children in the ghetto are ill!"

Hetty takes a long drag on the cigarette and blows out of smooth stream of smoke. Which bridge? Where to take them out? How to hide them? She'd been thinking about these things all day, deciding in her mind.

"Hetty?"

She taps ash into a tin ashtray on the side table and looks up into Phillipe's eyes. He's standing over her now, a frown furrowing his forehead. But she has already said too much, confessed too much, the less he knows the better. She smiles at him and inhales.

"I can't just let something happen to them. I can't. What would you think of me if I just said no, I can't help?"

"I would think no less of you." His eyes are soft and he lowers his voice, sitting next to her now putting an arm on her bare shoulder.

"Really? Well I would think less of me. I couldn't live with that…. that guilt. I know I am taking a risk but… I must. No other option."

"You could get killed. They'll shoot if they suspect something. They don't worry about killing people, killing us. Best case scenario you will get arrested and if you are arrested, if you are caught, you will definitely be sent to one of the camps."

"And? We might be sent there anyway."

"They'll never touch the hospital."

"We hope. You hope." She shakes her head, stubs the cigarette out and starts to get up, fishing around the bed for her bra smiling up at him. "You know, sometimes it does feel like a refuge here. We're part of the ghetto community…and not part of it, because we are here on the edge, on the other side of the canal. And there's this thing, this feeling that because we do what we do, and we are here not there, we are different. I think that gives us a false sense of safety." She smiles at him as she hooks the bra through her arms, reaches behind her back and does it up.

"You think?"

"I don't think any of us are really safe."

He lifts his hand to her face and smooths her curls back from her forehead, cups her chin in the palm of his hand. "I can't bear the thought of anything happening to you."

She looks up at him and takes his hand firmly in both of hers. "The thing is I can't not do this? Do you understand? I have to help these children. This is family. I can't, I won't say no."

Hetty – Amsterdam – the next day

She's exhausted, she's just finished a 12 hour shift and sits on the side of her bed, takes off her shoes and rubs the soles of her throbbing feet. Her body tells her to lie down, just for a minute, but she can't, she mustn't, she'll never get up if she does. She's been on the children's ward since 5.00 in the morning and now, twelve hours later, she has passed the point of exhaustion. Her ears are still ringing with the inconsolable crying of one little boy, his sobs setting off other children, some joining in and others burying their heads under their pillows and battering the bed sheets refusing to come out. She had been stuck attempting to do her work and that of Vonneke, who had now completely disappeared. She vaguely wonders where Vonneke has gone, but nobody seems to know.

Other staff coming in and out of the ward had winced at the relentless crying. Philippe had come in at about 3 to look at two of the children recovering from appendicitis and suggested they meet after work; a grateful patient had given him half a bottle of black-market gin, his room, about 6? And she'd had to say no, though everything in her wanted to say yes and he'd looked at her then, that knowing look and she'd lied, told him she really had to study, her second-year exams were a week away. She glances across at the dog-eared textbook by her bed. Well, no studying tonight.

She lifts her still warm shoes from the side of the bed and puts them back on, buckling them tightly. Standing up she unpins her apron and reaches into her wardrobe for her dark blue coat. She re-pins her hair and leaves. Her shoes squeak as she trips down the stairs, to the back door used by staff. It's cold: a bitter rainy gust blows into her face from the Amstel. In an hour maybe two it will be over. The plan seems straight forward enough if risky, she just hopes luck is on her side, no one gets too curious. But now it is happening, she is actually doing this, her stomach is turning somersaults. She wants to be sick.

As she walks from the hospital to the ghetto the rain lifts, to a light mist which drifts down coating her in a cobweb of water. The fat sergeant is on guard again, arguing with an old couple. She hears him shouting in the old woman's ear, his spittle spraying her face. "It's late. Time you were home, out of this rain." He jerks the old woman's arm, moving her off the bridge. The woman drops her bag, the contents spilling on to the pavement. Hetty needs the guard to see her so she stands and watches as the old man bends to pick up the contents for the old woman, the soldier watching, diving in, plucking out a silver pen. The old man helping her up, tells the guard to keep it and he slips it into his pocket as the couple wander off in an unhappy huddle. Hetty walks up to the guard, smiling, pulling out her pass to show him.

"Good evening Fraulein. It's late for you."

"Too late. I should be off duty, but those bloody children."

"The one's you saw the other day?"

"Not well, not well at all. The little girl is running a high temperature, they think it's typhus, and if she's got it the brother may have it too. And then the whole building will get it. I'm going to try to get them to the hospital tonight."

"Sounds awful." He steps back and turns around towards his colleague who's leaning on the bridge smoking. "I haven't heard anything about this have you Rob?"

The other soldier moves his weight from one leg to the other, and takes the cigarette out of his mouth, flicking the ash towards Hetty's feet.

"Nothing. But there is always some horrible disease in there. That place is a cess pit."

"We don't want the infection to spread."

The soldier leaning against the bridge steps forward. "Go and get them. Kids you say? Go and get them. We don't want an epidemic." Hetty's stomach clenches, her breathing quickens, could it be this easy? The soldier drops his cigarette to the ground, stubbing it out with the heel of his boot and steps in front of the other officer to usher her forward. "It's late. Be quick."

"I won't be long."

He shakes his head and spits on the ground.

Hetty tucks her pass back into her bag and starts walking towards the orphanage, feeling the menacing shadows of the darkening streets surround her. She walks faster. There aren't many people about. The impending curfew combined with the misty drizzle has chased all but a few stragglers into their homes. The old man locking up his book shop raises a hand to her as she passes. A young woman stands in a doorway halfway down the road, cheeks pink with rouge, red lips and a scanty dress, thin as a rake. She must be freezing as well as desperate.

Hetty races past her half not believing she is doing what she is doing. Finally she sees the children's home and makes a dash for the front door.

Frederik greets her in the entrance. "Hi there. What are you doing here?"

"I was over seeing a patient. And since I was yards away, I thought I would stop by and see Jozef and Trudi."

He glances at his watch, shakes his head. "It's really late."

Hetty smiles. "I know. Just no time for anything these days. I promised them I'd come."

"They will be getting the little one's ready for bed. Jozef's not here, he will be back at the annexe now, behind the synagogue?"

"Thanks. I'll go get him."

He shrugs indifferently, already closing the door against the November night.

She half runs to the annexe, why didn't she think to go there first. Minutes later a boy of about 13 opens the annexe door a crack.

"I am looking for Jozef? Jozef Jacobs?"

The boy stares out at her gawping.

"Jozef? Do you know him?"

"Yes. I'll get him."

The boy leaves her on the doorstep and disappears back into the house.

Stepping back into the shadow of the porch, Hetty checks her watch, and leans against the wall, feeling the damp November breeze curling around her legs. She could go now. Just leave. Go back and meet Phillipe, drink that gin, forget this madness. She holds her breath absorbing the deepening darkness, watching a couple walking along the opposite pavement, their uneven steps tapping along the cobbles. Out of nowhere, or so it seems, a sallow faced old man appears in front of her. "Are you a nurse? I saw you from my window," he points to the house opposite, to the second floor, a limp yellow curtain. "I need a nurse. My wife…my wife…"

Hetty smiles and is about to answer when the door behind her opens and Jozef comes out buttoning up his coat, eyes bright, face white and serious.

"Hetty?"

She grabs his hand and turns to the old man. "Sorry. I have to go. I can't come now. Tomorrow. I will send someone tomorrow." She smiles and walks past him as he grabs her sleeve.

"Don't forget. I'll remember you. Remember who you are," he thrusts his chin out, his fingers grip her like talons around her arm. "Second floor." He eyeballs her. "You'll remember that?"

"Second floor."

"Don't forget," he spits the words out and then abruptly lets go of her arm.

She grabs Jozef, "Come on. We need to get your sister."

Jozef talks as they walk. Her hands are cold. He's breathless, excited, nervous. "I've told her to come quietly to me if I put my head around the door. Just like the old man told me. Not to say anything. Just to creep out."

"Good."

He senses the tightness in her voice and looks up, eyes alert. "She'll do it. She will. No-one will notice. Not for a while. There are too many of them." She feels a tiny strand of hope sifting down through her fear. Maybe it will work. Maybe.

They walk in silence to the main orphanage, passing the tobacconists kiosk, Hetty raises her hand as Marc looks out of the door.

Going into the orphanage, Frederik looks out of his room and sees them.

"It's really too late. Jozef...!"

But Jozef is already half-way down the hall. Hetty smiles. "Jozef says Trudi has been crying; she misses their mother. It was their mother's birthday yesterday, I should have come then. Let me just see her for a minute? I just want to cheer her up, reassure her a bit." She leans against the door frame to the caretaker's room.

Frederik goes back and sits at his desk, stretches his arms behind his head and yawns before picking up the newspaper lying open on the desk. "Try and be earlier next time." He smiles sleepily at her.

"You're tired."

"Beyond tired, aren't we all? Sit down if you like."

"If I sit down, I won't get up again."

*

Jozef speeds down the long hall, through the double doors, past the refectory and up the wooden stairs. He knows roughly where Trudi will be. On their first few nights in Amsterdam, he'd come across every night to check she was ok and to say goodnight. Walking along the corridor, he sees Greet a girl from his class with a long white-blonde plait of hair falling across her shoulder. She inclines her head and smiles at him.

"Hi Greet," he slows down, smiles back, doesn't want to seem in any hurry. "Where's my sister? I came to say goodnight."

"In the room at the bottom of this corridor. The little ones are about to have a bedtime story."

"Thanks."

He can hear the rustle of chatter in the room before he gets there, and he opens the door cautiously. There were about 30 girls in the room, some sitting cross legged on the floor, others stepping around them to find their friends, several turning to see who was coming in. Trudi is sitting with her back to the wall across from the door, her legs crossed and her small elbows propped on her knees, her chin in her hands. She looks up when she sees Jozef at the door, then looks across at the teacher who has her arms around a little girl who's crying. Trudi gets up quietly and makes her way across to Jozef. One of her friends grabs her hand as she passes. "Where are you going?"

"My brother has come to see me."

"Oh. Sit by me when you come back?"

Trudi nods. Once outside Jozef grabs her hand, squeezing it tight. "Come on." He puts a finger to his lips and they run swiftly and quietly down the hall, down the stairs.

Hearing them Hetty stops chatting to Frederik and goes out to them. She bends down to give Trudi a hug and realises the little girl is already in her pyjamas.

"Where are your clothes?"

"It's bedtime."

She hugs her close and whispers in her ear. "You know we are going out now."

"But I'm not dressed!"

Jozef bends down, his face close to Hetty's and looks his sister in the eyes. "It's ok, Trudi, it's a real adventure. You'll be fine. We're going out for a treat!"

"Now?" She looks back down the hall towards the stairs they've just come down. "But the story..."

"There'll be better stories where we are going. Come on Trudi. This is what mamma wants. Hetty's here because she asked her to come." He looks at Trudi's pyjamas, the pattern of pale flowery stripes running down them, something she had brought from home, something his mother had made. The realisation makes his eyes smart. "Ok?"

Hetty holds the little girl close. "Now, you have to be good Trudi. You will be with me and Jozef. You must just do just as I say." She stands up, smiles down at her, at least Trudi has her shoes on. "Let's find your coat."

Jozef is already sifting through the rack of clothes in the hallway and Trudi runs off to help him, starting to chatter until Hetty puts her finger to her lips.

A bundle of coats falls to the floor and Trudi pulls out her green one triumphantly and starts to put it on as Jozef hangs the other coats back up.

Hetty helps her with the buttons and then stands and walks very quietly to the door. "Tiptoes," she whispers, trying to make it seem like a game for Trudi. "Hold hands, you must be quiet as mice." She opens the main door a crack wincing as the hinges start to squeak. She whispers to Jozef as she ushers them out. "Go to the tobacconist Jozef. Marc's expecting you. I'll follow."

He nods and grabs Trudi's hand but she pulls away.

"I don't want."

He bends down to her looking her in the eyes. "It's an adventure Trudi, a great adventure." He grins at her and takes her hand again looking up and down the road and crosses it quickly before running down towards the tobacconists on the corner.

Hetty steps back into the hallway and puts her head round the door of the caretaker's room. Frederik's engrossed in his newspaper, but seeing her puts it down.

"I'm off then."

"Trudi gone back upstairs, I didn't hear her? Jozef gone?"

"Yes, back to the annexe and Trudi was keen to get back to hear the bedtime story."

"She ok?"

Hetty shrugs. He smiles at her, leans across his desk and picks up an unmarked bottle.

"Want a drink?"

"I'd love one, but another time. I must get back to the hospital. I only came to see how she was really."

"Another time then?"

"That would be great."

Frederik stands up. "I'll lock up after you."

"Thanks. Thanks for letting me see them."

He opens the door for her and, as she crosses the road, she can hear him sliding across the heavy bolt.

Getting to the tobacconists she goes inside and sees an old grey-haired woman in a shapeless black coat and scarf leaning on the counter talking to Marc. She looks up when Hetty comes in then turns back to Marc, scratching her chin and dipping in her purse pulling out a guilder which she pushes across the counter. He deftly lifts a wrapped bottle from under the counter and passes it to her. The woman tucks the bottle away, nods at Hetty and leaves.

"Don't worry. She didn't see the children and she's got enough of her own problems to worry about."

Marc ushers her into the back of the small shop where the children are sitting on the floor. She smiles at them, checking their coats are done up, pulling a scarf out of Trudi's coat pocket and winding it around her neck. Jozef feels the tips of her fingers, cold and nimble, brush his cheek as she straightens his collar.

"Where are we going Hetty?" whispers Trudi.

"We are going to go for a walk. We are going to visit someone. Now you have got to be really good. Don't ask questions, just behave as if we do this every day, talk about anything. Don't look at anyone and keep hold of my hand. No rushing ahead, no skipping, no running. Just walk. Do you understand?"

Jozef reaches out and takes her hand. "Yes."

"I don't want to go."

Jozef looks at Trudi. "Mama has asked Hetty to help us Trudi. You want to do what mama wants don't you?"

Trudi nods.

Hetty examines the children's clothes. Jozef has pulled his hat down on his head and wound a blue scarf around his neck. Trudi's pyjamas are sticking out under her coat, but the coat is long...that would have been Bets idea, making sure they would have coats that could last them a while. Oh God this is it. She feels her body tense. She breathes in deeply and stands up.

"OK? Let's go." She looks at her watch, it is already after six. It is now or never.

Wordlessly Hetty grabs their hands and the three slip out into the light drizzle. They turn left down towards the canal and then walk alongside it, heading back towards the bridge that she had come over. Having been stopped on the way over, they might not stop her on the way back, particularly as it has started to rain. God she is grateful for the drizzle pushing even the soldiers under cover. She walks quickly, purposefully, the children keeping pace with her.

Her heart is beating so loudly she can hardly hear a thing until she realises Trudi is pulling on her hand. "Look Hetty!" And she points out two seagulls strutting one behind the other along the wall.

She smiles at the little girl. "They're out for a walk too."

Her heart is pounding as they get closer to the stone bridge. She forces herself on, trying to talk to the children as if this was something she does with lots of children. Looking up she sees one of the soldiers on the bridge talking to a member of the Dutch police, he laughs at something the soldier says, a high-pitched cackle and she suddenly realises the policeman is Mark van Herten, an old colleague of her brothers at college, someone too keen on the Nazis to be really liked, and one of the first to join the NSB. He'll stop them.

She turns away up a side street, dark wet shadows of the building crowding round them, the stench of a blocked drain. Did he see her? She guides the children along. Another way. Which to choose?

They walk back into the ghetto and towards another road leading out, but there are soldiers standing there and she doesn't know them and they'll wonder why she is going that way. It's not the way back to the hospital. She goes to another bridge that she sometimes uses but realises it will seem odd at this time of night and a detour if she was coming from the children's home. She spins back towards the first bridge. She'll brave it out. As far as they know she's going to the hospital. They have got to get out.

"Where are we going?" asks Jozef as they turn around and walk back towards the first bridge. "This is where we were going before?"

She smiles at him with a confidence she doesn't feel. "Just rethinking things for a minute." She grips his hand, smiles at Trudi. "This will be the best way. The soldier on duty knows me. But we'll just walk. Don't say anything just walk."

Jozef looks at her a confused frown on his face, but she smiles back at him.

"It'll be ok. Really."

They walk faster now, past a gap in a wall blocked with barbed wire shiny in the drizzle. She remembers the old man at that second meeting at his friend's house telling her again how he had thought he could walk out with Jozef, hide Trudi in his hand cart but she was just too big for that and anyway, they searched everything, the questions were interminable, the risks too great. The children were both too young and too old to smuggle out; she was their last chance, their only chance.

She breathes in as they reach the bridge. Approaching for a second time she sees Mark van Herten walking away off the bridge into the city, she wills him to keep going, not to turn around. That's such a stroke of luck and it boosts her confidence as they start walking across the bridge.

The fat solider is talking to his colleague again. They stop chatting as she gets closer, but she doesn't slow down.

The fat soldier looks up but doesn't step any closer to her. He turns to his comrade. "It's only the nurse from earlier. The pretty one."

The other soldier chuckles. "Let me see. Is she the one I like?"

"Maybe. But maybe keep away. She's got the children with her. I think she's taking them to the hospital." He smiles as Hetty slows ready to be challenged but not stopping, keeping a steady pace as if nothing could be more normal than walking across the bridge, as if they did it every day.

The other soldier takes the cigarette out of his mouth, smoke escaping in a soft stream from the corner of his lips, white in the cold November air.

"Ah but she's pretty." He winks at her.

"Typhoid. She was talking about a typhoid epidemic earlier."

"God, those Jews are so dirty."

The fat soldier waves her on. "Gute Nacht fraulein!"

"Good night."

She smiles, walks, holds the children's hands more tightly, doesn't look round, she is counting her steps, listening to the sound of their shoes on the cobbles. She feels the guards' eyes watching her as they walk on down out of the ghetto. She starts to talk to Trudi about the weather, about the trees, about a black and white cat she had seen earlier. The temptation to run tugs at her. But they don't run. They are on the other side of the bridge and she breathes, a breeze picking up from the canal and brushing her face, she feels the drizzle crawling down the back of her neck. She grips the children's hands more tightly turns left towards the hospital and then quickly right down a side street. The children are quiet.

Then there's a shout.

"Halt!" Heavy boots run across the bridge towards them. She yanks on Jozef's hand as he starts to run. "Walk. Just walk. Keep talking."

The rhythmic crack of metal heels on the cobbles comes closer and her legs feel like jelly. She is waiting for someone to grab her, stop them. And then there is a shot, it cracks through the air, but it is not aimed and them, and she realises the soldiers have run past the end of the road. Her head buzzes. Someone else, they are after someone else.

She looks briefly down at Jozef and sees a nervous smile break across his face, his eyes huge, he squeezes her hand hard and imperceptibly they all begin to walk a little bit faster now turning down a tree lined street of tall, terraced houses, slivers of light coming from between closed curtains, a feeling of a winter night shutting down. Near the corner of the street is a small service alleyway leading behind the houses. She pulls the children into the dark shadow of it.

"OK you two?" Jozef and Trudi nod as Hetty pulls off her nurse's cap, folds it and puts it in her bag, pulling out a pair of scissors. She bends down in front of Trudi and carefully snips the patch with the yellow star off her coat and then does the same to Jozef.

A couple, arm in arm under an umbrella, pass the end of the road and Hetty puts her fingers to her lips and they all hold their breath. She hands the stars to Jozef, puts the scissors away and pulls out a scarf draping it around her neck so that she looks more like a mother, less like a nurse, unpins her hair and shakes it out so it falls in dark curls on her shoulders. She takes the stars from Jozef and stuffs them into the fence behind them and stands up, pulling a grey cloche hat on to her head and adjusting Trudi's scarf.

She grins at them. "That was the hard part. Let's go."

They walk out onto the street. Two Nazi patrol officers are walking towards them on the opposite pavement, and she holds her breath and keeps walking, watching as they stop two women and ask for their papers.

She bends her head. Not now, not when they have done so well. Walk, walk she tells herself. They pass the soldiers, still busy chatting to the women, taking their time inspecting their papers. Hetty holds on to the children and they keep going. They turn down towards Amsterdam General Hospital. The houses here are smaller, and interspersed with shops, their windows dark, closed for the night. She looks up and sees a woman pull across curtains from the only lit window in the row.

"Hurry, hurry, hurry…why are you in such a hurry?"

Hetty turns around. She hadn't seen them: the policemen, two of them. Following her? Her heart stops.

"It's late. I must get the children home."

"Your identity cards please?"

"Yes," she lets go of Trudi's hand and starts to rummage in her bag. What can she do? What can she say? She keeps rummaging in her bag. "Sorry, too many things, just a minute." She suddenly feels a tug on her coat and looks down to see Trudi crossing her legs.

"I need to go to the toilet!"

"A minute Trudi."

"I need to go now," she whines.

The soldier shuffles: "Go on. Hurry. It's fine. Fine!"

Hetty looks him in the eye. "Thank you." She pushes her bag hastily back on her shoulder and grabs Trudi's hand. "Come. Quick, quick now children. We are nearly home."

They walk southwest, towards the cathedral. They will have to get over the Singel canal, then walk through the Vondelpark and then they have to find the address the old man has given her. Not until then will they be safe. And will they be safe then?

Jozef – Utrecht – November – later that evening

Jozef looks out of the window of the train as it picks up speed; his reflection stares back at him in the dark. He presses his nose against the glass and tries to see further out into the night, into the shadows of the flat landscape. He tries to make out houses, people, animals, and for a moment he thinks he recognises a redbrick farmhouse.

"Are we near Laag-Keppel?" He asks, still staring, keeping the farmhouse within site for as long as he can.

"No, nowhere near there," says the old man putting a finger to his lips reminding Jozef to be quiet. No-one seems to have noticed what he had said apart from the old man. The carriage is almost empty. A woman sitting in the corner with a green hat, reads a book, a young man sitting opposite her, taps his feet impatiently, twisting his cap in his hand, deep in thought. His sister sits opposite him, blowing hot breath on to the glass and drawing pictures of stick men and houses in the condensation.

Jozef is hungry again. He remembers telling Hetty he was hungry when they arrived at the house with the green door in Amsterdam. The old man had been waiting for them there and his aunt, his mother's sister, had been there too. That had been odd. She'd said so little to them. She was crying as she hugged them. And there was another woman with a gold necklace round her neck with a cross who seemed to be in charge. She had gone to get him a biscuit, and a glass of water. He remembers how everyone had laughed when he said, quite seriously, that he would return the favour, bring her biscuits when he had some. They were constantly told in the orphanage not to take more than their share, if one boy took an extra piece of bread then someone else went without. The lady who was wearing a red dress had given Trudi a biscuit too.

They'd said goodbye to Hetty then. He wonders if she is alright, if she got back to the hospital safely. The woman in the red dress had laughed when she saw Trudi's pyjamas and Trudi had begun to cry, but the woman had said how brave she had been, how brave they had both been and that she would find something for Trudi to wear. She'd disappeared and they could hear her climbing the stairs quickly and going into one of the bedrooms, opening cupboards and drawers and finally returning with a blue sweater. It swamped Trudi, but their aunt tied it at the waist with a piece of ribbon and with the sleeves rolled up it made a serviceable dress.

"Are we staying here?" Jozef asked the lady in red.

"No, grandpa there will take you somewhere safe. Somewhere special." He'd looked at the old man, but he had said nothing, just pulled two wool hats out of his pocket, squashed them on their heads.

"Come on, we have another journey tonight, we must get going."

They'd gone with the old man to the station and they had got on to the train headed for Utrecht. Joseph wonders momentarily whether they are going back to the old orphanage, but he knows in his head that isn't possible.

Looking out of the carriage window, he can hardly believe they have made it this far, that they are here in the train with the old man. He shivers at the memory of the walk out of the ghetto. He feels sick when he thinks about it, but he can't stop thinking about it. They could have been caught, they could have been stopped. It had taken only took 20 minutes to walk to the house where they met the old man, but it felt like hours. Trudi had been good though even though Hetty had rushed her to the loo when they got into the house. He is surprised at how quiet Trudi is now, it isn't like her, but she has become much quieter over the past two months. He realises he misses her annoying chatter. He looks across at her as she completes her melting picture on the window of two children, two adults and a house. She looks at him and smiles shyly, caught in her daydream.

The train begins to slow down and the old man begins to button up his coat. "Next stop we get out children. Start to get ready, do your coats up. Hats on."

The old man smiles in the direction of the lady with the green hat who has put her book on her lap and fallen asleep. He puts his fingers to his lips. Jozef leans across to help Trudi with her buttons and then does his coat up as the train slows and screeches to a halt. His stomach rumbles. He's so hungry. He hadn't liked to ask the lady at the house for more biscuits or some bread or cheese, what he would give for a chunk of bread and cheese. The old man reaches out of the window, undoes the carriage door and gets out first, then lifts Trudi down and holds the door for Jozef as he jumps onto the platform.

Half a dozen other people get off the train including a Nazi officer who has his arm around a woman in a brown coat and hat. He is walking their way, Jozef holds his breath, but the soldier doesn't stop. He doesn't even look at them.

The old man takes their hands and walks with them through the exit gate, handing in their tickets and then they are out and walking down steps on to an unfamiliar grey street. A short walk takes them to a tram stop where a tram is pulling in. Jumping on they walk down to seats towards the back. There is an old lady sitting opposite them looking disapprovingly across at them and for a moment Jozef wonders if she can see the place on his coat where the star had been.

"Those children should be in bed."

The old man shrugs. "I know, but their mother hasn't been well, so I went to fetch them, taking them to stay with me and their grandma for a bit," he sighs. "What can I do?"

The old woman clicks open her handbag and takes out a hankie. "Sick, everyone is sick." She eyeballs the old man. "You keep them near you, they might be sick too you know?" She settles back in her seat holding the hankie over her nose.

The old man stretches his arms out around the two children as the tram stops and three more people get on, two in the black uniforms of the NSB, looking up and down the carriage. Jozef closes his eyes, he doesn't want to see them. The tram rocks into action again. He drifts off to sleep against the rough wool of the old man's coat and then feels himself being gently shaken awake.

"Come on, just a short walk now."

They get off the tram and start walking, the soft cold drizzle waking them up after the warm fug of the tram. He remembers again how hungry he is, his stomach aches for the want of food. He wants to ask the old man how long a walk it is going to be but doesn't dare. He is too tired to do anything but put one foot in front of another, the hunger gnawing at his insides as he walks. The excitement of the escape has drained out of him along with the fear and all he can think of now is food, filling his mouth with bread and going to bed. He is so tired. The old man has hoisted Trudi onto his back, she's leaning on his shoulder half asleep, he holds on to her feet with one hand to stop her falling and her small arms hands are clasped softly round his neck. Jozef can see a damp tendril of hair sticking to her cheek, pink from the cold, her eyes closed with exhaustion.

They walk through a park, then out on to the street. It starts to rain more heavily and the old man walks faster, they pass a large pond, the rain freckling the surface. They turn left away from the pond, down a side street of terraced houses, and left down another much the same – J.S. Bachstraat. Each house has a small front garden, limp and grey in the November rain. Suddenly the old man turns into a blue painted gate and slipping Trudi to the ground, waking her up, fishes in his pocket for a key.

They go in and Jozef wonders if this is where they will stay the night. The old man starts to take his coat off and tells them to do the same. Jozef bends to undo his buttons, the fabric stiff with the damp, and then pulling his arms out of his sleeves looks up and sees his mother, there in the hall, in this house. He throws his coat down and walks into her arms, feels one arm fold around him, the other around Trudi. His throat is choking up, he thinks he is going to faint. She pulls him away from her and examines his face, her hand gripping his arm, Trudi is crying.

"Jozef are you alright?"

He looks up at her. "I need bread Mama. Bread. I am so

hungry." And he wonders afterwards why that was the first thing he says to her.

Jozef – Utrecht – the next day

Jozef hears voices as he walks down the hall towards the kitchen. "This is the best we can do Bets. The best." It's the old man. "I just wanted us to stay together," his mother. "That's just not…."

"Jozef!!" Trudi crashes into the back of his legs, flings her arms around him and pushes him into the kitchen. The smell of fresh coffee makes his eyes smart, brings back memories of home in Laag-Keppel.

Trudi runs and sits on their mother's lap, Jozef takes the chair next to them. "Did you sleep well?" asks the old man. "Fantastic!" bursts out Trudi. "Best sleep ever Opa."

They now know the old man's name is Jan Loggers, but he has suggested they call him Opa, just as they had on the train from Amsterdam. Easier if anyone finds out they are staying there.

His mother gently displaces Trudi from her lap and gets up to cut two slices of bread, giving each a scraping of butter from a covered dish.

Jozef watches. Opa Loggers looks up. "They must have something on their bread Bets – there's cheese in the larder, or a sprinkling of sugar?"

Trudi's mouth drops open. "Sugar? We haven't had that since…"

"Give them sugar."

His mother smiles and carefully sprinkles a scant teaspoonful across the slices of bread, before cutting each piece into four, putting the bread on plates and handing them to Jozef and Trudi, with glasses of water.

Biting into the bread, Jozef luxuriates in its sweetness.

The old man drums on the table lightly with his square fingers. "I think we should speak to them now Bets." The sugar in Jozef's mouth suddenly feels gritty. What now? His mind is still spinning from the escape. He reaches for his glass and looks across at Trudi but she is totally absorbed in her bread, taking tiny bites, making each piece last as long as possible, licking her lips after each mouthful. His mother picks up the coffee pot and pours a cup for herself, passing another to the old man.

Jozef feels the bread stick to his throat as he tries to swallow.

"What is it Opa?" asks Trudi wetting her forefinger and dabbing it around her plate to make sure not a grain of sugar escapes.

"Jozef, Trudi, you know it is lovely to have you both here." And? The old man takes a sip of coffee. Jozef holds his breath. "But you can't stay here. It is too many in the house and it is too dangerous."

"We can be quiet," says Jozef just above a whisper.

His mother clears her throat.

"We can be quiet," says Trudi, staring at Jozef, pushing her empty plate away.

"Of course you can." Their mother stretches her arms across the table and takes their hands in hers. "I know that. But we have to listen to Opa Loggers." Her voice shakes as she squeezes their fingers between hers before sitting back, picking up her cup of coffee, cradling the bowl of the cup in her hands, and sipping silently.

Jozef wonders if he has actually swallowed the sugar bread because there is such a lump in his throat. He wonders what will happen now? The plan was to get out so what now? Are they going to lock them in the attic or someone else's attic or... his mind starts racing. Last night they had slept top to tail in the same room as their mother. They are fine with that. It's all the room they need.

Opa Loggers takes his pipe out of the breast pocket of his jacket: "The problem is that the Germans regularly search houses around here. They will come here and there is nowhere in this house where you can all hide. We have a safe hiding place if they come to look," he looks up at their mother. "Tried and tested. But there is only room for two, maybe three."

"There are only three of us," says Trudi.

"You are forgetting your cousin and your aunt."

And Jozef had momentarily forgotten. He had seen Lea and Trina when they arrived, but they had been so excited at seeing their mother that he had paid them little attention. Of course, Bets and Lea and Trina had come to this house together. It made sense of all their hushed kitchen meetings in Laag-Keppel. He'd asked his mother the previous night why the Loggers were helping them, specifically them, and she had explained that Opa Loggers' sister was a good friend of Lea's, she had put them in touch, knowing they were looking for somewhere to go, knowing the Loggers would help and would hide them if they could, but the Loggers could only take the two women and one child. Jozef and Trudi had one another, Trina was an only child, and the youngest.

The cold ache of the past two months winds through Jozef. Where to now? Trudi starts to suck her thumb a look of concentration creasing her forehead. He puts his hand out under the table and takes her other hand in his.

Opa Loggers continues: "I am thinking of the safety of you all. Nobody is going far away, we are just talking about another house in this street." He chews on the end of his pipe. "Jozef will stay here. Trudi will go with Bets to the new family. They have agreed to take you for a month and then review things. If anyone sees you, they will say you are cousins from the country. But it is best if no-one sees you."

Jozef feels a mix of confusion, relief and disappointment. Pleased to be staying with Opa Loggers but unhappy to be separated from his mother. He watches his sister's nervous eyes darting between the two grown-ups wondering whether to be pleased or worried and he realises with an ache that she is no longer the little girl who played endlessly with dolls on the kitchen floor.

The old man is talking to him, telling him that he can help Oma in the house, fetch coal and make up the fires, get tea in the morning. He lights his pipe, drawing in the smoke, reaches out and pats Jozef on the shoulder. "You know I have three sons... well two now, one died. So, we like having boys about the house." He smiles at him. "You will be fine. We will keep you safe, look after you."

"What about moeder and Trudi? Will they be safe?"

Opa Loggers draws on his pipe again. "I think so... I hope so."

"We are going to move tonight," says their mother looking first at the children and then at the old man. She begins to get up from the table. "I am really grateful for everything you have done and are doing for us Jan. It is more than we could have hoped for, much more than we expected." She takes the children's breakfast things to the sink, washing them and setting them to dry on the wooden draining board. Drying her hands she walks towards the kitchen door and beckons the children to follow her.

"Bets?" Jan Loggers stops her as they leave the room. "I am sorry, but we will need to give the Bickers the money tonight. You have it?"

"Yes"

She shoos the children out of the door and upstairs. Jozef feels the soft warm pressure of his mother's hand on his shoulder. They go into the small twin bedroom they shared the previous night. His mother sinks onto the dark blue thick cotton bedspread and puts her arms out, folding Jozef and Trudi into her.

"Look we will all be together eventually," she whispers.

Trudi wriggles free from her mother. "Will you miss us Jozef? Will you be alright?"

"Of course he will be alright," says his mother before he can reply. "He's a young man now, 11 years old! You never know, it may not be for long. The Americans are now in the war and that could change everything. Opa Loggers thinks it will. We just have to keep our heads down for a while. Stay unnoticed."

Jozef looks at her. "But we don't know it won't be long... It could be years."

"Let's hope not." She ducks down and pulls a large brown leather handbag with a brass clasp from under the bed and puts it on her lap. She starts taking out the contents; her purse, a powder compact, comb, hankie, pencil and notebook – and puts them on a side table and then carefully untucks the lining in the bottom of the bag and brings out a wodge of 20-guilder notes. She peels off 8 notes and hands them to Jozef, putting the rest back under the lining, tucking it back into place and returning her purse and other bits to the bag before snapping it shut and dropping it on the floor.

"Who's the money for?" Jozef asks handing the notes back to her.

"It's for the people Trudi and I are staying with, the Bickers. This will keep us safe for a month, then we will give them more if they let us stay longer, if everything works out."

"Did you give money to Opa Loggers?"

She smiles and frowns at him all in one. "These people are risking their lives for us Jozef and we need to eat, we need space in their home and they need money. There is no shame in their asking for money and less shame in our being willing to pay for their help."

"What happens when the money runs out?"

"We'll deal with that when – and if – it happens. I still have some jewellery. Opa Loggers will sell it for me if necessary. And we can work too – even if we are in hiding."

"Doing what?"

"Lots of things – Lea takes in lots of sewing you know. And you are going to be a great help to the Loggers, you'll see."

Jozef's head swims. He wants Opa Loggers to be like real family not someone he has to work for. His mother looks him in the eyes. "You have a safe home here Jozef, a good safe place."

She puts the money in her pocket and then leans over and unbuttons her shoes and swings her dark wool-stockinged legs on to the bed, inviting them to do the same.

"Aren't you going to take the money to Opa?"

"Later. Let's just enjoy being together."

Snuggling up to her Jozef absorbs the shape and feel and smell of her. When will they be together again? Whatever their hopes, an insistent corner of his mind wonders if they will ever be together again.

Hetty – Amsterdam – the same day

Hetty is on the women's ward, clearing away the patients' lunch things when the ward sister strides into the room and calls her over.

"The director of the orphanage in the ghetto has asked, no demanded, that you go and see him immediately."

"Is someone ill? Why?" Guiltily she remembers the old man who had grabbed her the previous evening and made her promise to return. She'd completely forgotten about him.

The sister looks at her, annoyed and disbelieving. "Your two young cousins have gone missing. You were the last person seen with them." She purses her lips and pulls Hetty into the corridor outside the ward. "You realise the sort of danger you put us all in if you have done anything Hetty?" She looks her in the eyes, "When did you see them? What did you do? Children don't just...disappear."

"Look I am..."

"I don't want to hear it. I don't want to hear anything, particularly if it is not the truth." She sighs. "Just go... and come back as quickly as you can."

Walking into the ghetto Hetty is stopped by a soldier she hasn't seen before, ruddy faced with a flop of blonde hair, his breath rich with the smell of coffee. He shifts his feet as he flips her pass over, and she notices how polished his shoes were; black, shiny, new? He hands her back her pass and turns to watch a couple trundling a small covered cart behind them, beckoning them to stop, take the cover off the cart.

A group of men and women are arguing again outside the second-hand book shop; others are queuing at the bakery; the streets are wet from the rain the previous night and a cool breeze whips up the air and she feels as she hasn't felt before: a seeping, weeping cold fear that clings to her heels as she walks.

She passes a group of houses where people are congregating with suitcases: old men and women, couples and babies. She spots a young couple, teenagers, the girl in a pink coat and the boy with a chequered scarf, in an alleyway, locked in an embrace, nearby a woman gazes about her calling out: "Anna! Anna! We must go now. Anna!" A little girl sitting on a suitcase by her side is playing with a threadbare stuffed rabbit, whispering to it. It is another transport day.

The air around the group is rich with nervy panic, overlaid by hearty chatter as they prepare to walk across to the Jewish theatre. A group of Nazi soldiers, rifles slung casually on their shoulders, loosely surround the gathering group, while a woman in a grey coat with glasses ticks names off a list. Everyone watches nervously in case someone decides to break free before they leave; before they are herded on to trucks at the theatre waiting to take them to the transport train. Hetty tries not to remember the shooting she witnessed, but she does. She's haunted by it: the crumpled body on the ground, that moment of complete silence after it happened, a nanosecond when everyone held their breath. And then the scream from the boy's mother spiralling out across the city, the blood on the ground. It wasn't an isolated incident. There'd been others, lots of others but she hadn't been there, thank God. There'd been one the week before of a boy she had nursed when he'd been admitted to the hospital with appendicitis. He was 16. What a waste. She walks quickly past, holding her breath. Walk don't run she had told the children last night, walk don't run.

She shivers as she reaches the orphanage, shadowed by the memory of the previous evening. A plump man in a threadbare grey sweater looks out of the caretaker's office. Where's Frederik? God, she hopes he isn't in trouble. As if reading her mind the man looks up at her: "Frederik had to go home. I'm standing in for him."

"The director wants to see me?"

He points to one of the chairs in the hallway and tells her to wait. She watches him through the door of his office as he picks up the phone. She can hear children somewhere reciting a poem, the rhythmic chant of a normal school day. Lulled by the sound she hardly notices the girl walking down the hall towards her until she stops in front of her. It isn't Suzanna but a different girl with short brown hair clipped back with a brown barrette. Hetty notices the little girl's large feet, oversized against her small body as she follows her up the stairs to the director's office. The girl raps twice on the door before reaching for the round brass handle and opening it indicating that Hetty should go in.

The director looks up as Hetty approaches his desk and stands up. He gets straight to the point. "Miss van Leeuwen I regret to inform you that your cousins Jozef and Trudi have gone missing."

"Missing? When? How?"

"We don't know how, but they are not here. They disappeared yesterday evening." His eyes bore into her. "The matron has searched everywhere asked everyone." He sighs. "This is very, very serious."

Silence hangs between them.

"Any idea where they might have gone?"

"No." The man's face shuts down and he places his hands on the desk. "Sit down why don't you?"

She slips down on to the edge of the chair as he sits and leans back in his chair.

"Miss van Leeuwen?"

She looks up, sees the shadows under his tired grey eyes. He holds her gaze. "You were the last person to be seen with them."

"Me?"

"You came last night on your way through the ghetto. Frederik, the caretaker? He told me you came to see them."

"Yes, but he knows Trudi went back upstairs, Jozef back to the annexe. I told him. He locked up after I left."

"He told me that too, but he didn't actually see Trudi go back upstairs and Jozef never got back to the annexe. I've heard, been told this morning by one of the teachers that works here that she thought she saw a nurse…walking quite late…down by the canal with two children?" He keeps staring at her. "I've sent Frederik home. I told him to think about his job here. He's meant to pay attention, to monitor everyone going in and out."

"But…"

"He's meant to be looking after these children making sure they are safe." His hands curl around his fountain pen.

"Isn't that we all want?" Hetty speaks quietly, counterbalancing the rising anger in the director's tone. "Look this is very worrying, but Joseph is a sensible lad I am sure nothing disastrous has happened. Have you looked everywhere in the ghetto?" Surely this man, this Jewish man must know that the children might be safer somewhere else. But a small part of her wonders if she has got it wrong? Should she have left them here? But even as the idea occurs to her, she knows she had been right to get them out: she'd tasted their fear, seen Jozef's relief.

The director thumps the table with his hand. "Are you trying to tell me you know nothing about this? I don't believe you. How gullible do you think I am?

"What you don't understand is that we have to account for every child living here. That is my responsibility. When a child goes missing we have to tell the Jewish Council and they have to tell the German authorities and they investigate. You think it is just two children? They have got lists of every child here, every person in the ghetto. And every child, every person counts. I have to report to the Council at 6 o'clock this evening. What am I going to say?"

"This has nothing to do with me."

The director thumps his desk again. "This has everything to do with you! If they find it is you. If we find it is you. You will find yourself in the sort of trouble you don't want to begin to think about. You were the last person seen with them. You do understand I have to tell them that? You do understand, don't you?"

Hetty stands up. "I understand what you are saying. As I say, I had nothing to do with this."

She walks to the door looking around at the cracked paint and sagging chipped furniture that defines the orphanage. She turns back to the director. "I'm sorry. This is upsetting but I can only pray Jozef and Trudi are safe now…..safer." She looks defiantly at the director who starts to speak but she cuts him off. "I must go. I'm needed back at the hospital."

She walks out of the office and seeing the little girl tells her she will see herself out, knows the way. She marches ahead, the little girl trailing in her wake until she leaves the orphanage.

She walks back through the ghetto, across the bridge towards the hospital. As she turns towards it she sees the crowd now outside the Hollandsche Schouwburg, the Dutch theatre, volumes of shuffling shoes and erratic, helpless farewells pierce the cold air as families climb into flat bedded trucks. She doesn't want to see the tears, the last embraces. A German officer is shouting out names and the herd of people standing on the road wait to be called. Her eye catches the flash of the pink coat pressed against the side of the truck: the girl, but where is the boy?

A migraine is tightening like a band around her head. She walks on towards the hospital; a Nazi soldier is standing near the front door. That's unusual, but nothing is surprising anymore. He grabs her arm as she turns to go in, twisting her wrist and demanding her pass.

"Not so much of a hurry Fraulein."

"I'm late for my shift." She hears the blood beating in her ears, the rumble of the trucks moving off. She must pull herself together.

He taps the pass on the sleeve of his jacket, looks at her and looks at it again and passes it back. "Don't be late."

She has hours just hours before she will be reported. She has to go now; she has to get out to leave as soon as she can get away without being noticed. But where to, where to now?

Hetty – Amsterdam – The same day

Hetty sits on the long wooden bench in the middle of the station platform and feels the letter in her pocket and next to it the neat rough oblong of her ticket.

She looks up at the platform clock; the train for Zeist is due at 5.40. It is 5.30. She takes the magazine she has just bought from the newsagents outside the station from its brown paper bag and flutters through the pages before leaving it on her lap unread.

A man in a dark coat and grey cap sits down next to her, pulls out a packet of cigarettes and casually offers her one.

"No thanks," she smiles politely and picks up the magazine as if to read it. She doesn't want to talk. She tries to concentrate; to ignore the gathering crowd on the platform, but her head is teeming. Was it only yesterday she had gone to pick the children up? She'd felt like a bolting rabbit changing out of her uniform and packing an hour ago. She'd jumped when Hannah had walked in unexpectedly just as she was closing her suitcase. She'd told her almost nothing, just that she had to go. And Hannah had been amazing, leant against the door so no-one could come in. Given her, her hat because it was bigger, less recognizable, and not Hetty's, and wished her luck.

She touches the broad rim of the brown velvet hat and remembers the kindness of her friend. Hannah had done more too, gone ahead of her to see the coast was clear and within minutes she'd managed to walk out of the hospital behind a large family group and peel off quietly and make her way to the station. She hadn't said goodbye to anyone, not even Phillipe. But he'll work it out. She knows that. Gossip in the PIZ is rife, someone will tell him, probably even Hannah who suspects and probably knows what has been between them. She wishes him a silent goodbye, sends him a silent wish that he stays well, thanks him for all they have been to one another.

Where is the train? She looks at the magazine in her lap, *"Signal"* the Nazi propaganda journal with a picture on the front of Hitler talking to some scouts, standing ramrod straight. She hates the thought of what people will think, seeing her reading it, but it might give her some cover. She mustn't get stopped, asked for her papers between Amsterdam and Zeist.

Zeist had been the obvious, the only option. She'd go to the children's home where Rosa works. They knew her, if only slightly and in her last letter Rosa had complained of how short staffed, they were, said to join her if she was ever tired of nursing and Amsterdam.

Out of the corner of her eye Hetty sees two NSB policemen making their way down the platform, the waiting crowd parting to let them through as they approach. Nerves gather in the pit of her stomach as they come to a halt, just metres from where she is sitting. A voice over the loudspeaker echoes tinnily across the platform: "The train for Zeist is now approaching platform two. Stand back from the platform edge. All stops to Zeist. Platform two. Stand back."

Hetty stands up, rolling the magazine and pushing it into the top of her bag before picking up her suitcase as the train screeches to a halt. She walks forward stepping around and to the side of the two policemen and almost gasping when one of them puts his hand on her elbow.

"Don't I know you?"

She flashes him a look. "No," she smiles. "I don't think so." She pauses her heart pounding. "I'd remember." She smiles again. "I am catching this train if you will excuse me?"

"Let me help you. You are going to Zeist? I'll take your case on board." He plucks the case from Hetty's hand before she can protest and pushes through the crowd getting on to the train, beckoning her to follow. He marches down the carriage corridor looking for a compartment with seats and finding one with just three occupants, slides back the door and walks in. Someone has left their coat on a corner seat by the window and he picks it up and tosses it on the luggage rack along with Hetty's case before indicating to Hetty that she should sit. Then he turns, smiles, and with a click of his heels and a small bow leaves.

Hetty feels a blush rising up her face and speaks to the woman in the opposite corner. "Sorry, is anyone sitting here?"

"My husband. He has just gone out to get some air. But stay where you are, he can sit next to me instead."

Hetty starts to get up.

"Please," says the woman.

The other two occupants of the compartment are a middle-aged woman with blonde curls with a fox fur stole and an elderly man in a tweed cap reading a newspaper. Soon the man whose seat she has taken returns and sits down next to his wife as the whistle goes. Out of the corner of her eye, Hetty can see the platform guard waving a green flag. She settles back against the rough brown cord seat and is about to pull out her magazine, when the door to the compartment slides open with a bang and an out of breath young man pushes his way in, taking off his coat before taking the last seat in the compartment, next to Hetty. The train jerks into life, steam hissing up from its wheels as it moves forward, finally picks up speed before settling into a rhythmic rumble.

Hetty starts to pull her magazine out, but the young man who has just sat down starts talking to her so she tucks it away again.

"What are you reading?"

"Nothing, nothing important."

"I saw you on the platform. Where are you travelling to?"

"Zeist."

"Me too. You must be a visitor. I haven't seen you before."

He smiles, and she notices that his green eyes are flecked with brown. His attention unsettles her but then she sees a slight blush rising on his neck and likes him better. "Who are you visiting?"

"I'm not visiting. I've got a job there." It was a lie, but a hopeful one.

"Where?"

"At the Zonnehuis, the home, school for children with disabilities? Do you know it?"

The young man leans back in his seat. "Dr Lievegoed's place? Yes, yes I know it." He bites his bottom lip. "He's a good man. Do you know him well?"

"Not that well, I met him when the children's home moved temporarily to Scheveningen in 1940."

"Ah Scheveningen! Is that where you come from?"

Hetty nods at the man who she reckons must be in his late 20s. They talk about the evacuation from Scheveningen, how difficult it must have been for families from the town, the awful pictures of the barbed wire barricades and cement gun posts ripping across the elegant board walks and beach front. The Atlantic Wall for all that it was heralded as something great by the Nazis, was just an ugly tearing apart of everyone's favourite holiday resort.

"Did you ever go there on holiday?" asks Hetty.

"Yes, before the war. I had an aunt who would take a house there for the summer, up on the dunes."

Hetty thinks of her walks along the dunes, the intoxicating salty clean scent of a winter sea and wishes herself back home.

The young man breaks into her thoughts: "We had some great times there, memorable."

They talk about the ice cream parlour that was famous for its lemon sorbet; the baker who sold long twists of deep-fried, sugar-crusted dough; the amusement arcade, summer funfair and the brass bands that used to play on the terrace outside the hotel at teatime during the summer months.

"My aunt would never let us go."

"It was expensive. We didn't go either, but we would dance on the beach below the terrace." She remembers the noise of the band thudding out against the swish of the waves, the strings of lights, the couples dancing, and she and her friends dancing in bare feet, sand squeezing between their toes, it is a happy memory, and she is laughing as the train pulls into Amsterdam-Zuid. The old man gets up to get off the train and starts to pull the door back when a Nazi officer in the passageway grabs the handle from him, and then stands aside to let him out before walking into the carriage and taking his seat.

Everyone in the carriage stops talking. Hetty pulls out the almost forgotten magazine and begins to scan the pages when she feels long cool fingers touch the back of her hand and looking up sees the Nazi officer has reached across and is smiling at her. "An excellent read…Have you read the Fuhrer's speech to the scouts?"

"Not yet."

"I recommend it." He smiles at her. "May I?" He reached out for the magazine and flips to the appropriate page.

"Thank you." Hetty looks at the unsmiling face of the Fuhrer.

"You are travelling to Zeist?"

"Yes."

"I am going to our headquarters there. It's a good town you will like it." He leans back in his seat, stretching his legs out so the blonde woman sitting opposite him has to move her legs to the side. The young man next to Hetty picks up his book and starts reading.

Hetty looks out of the window as the train moves off and pushes into the flat countryside. It is getting dark, the November evening drawing in, and she wonders if and how she is going to find the Zonnehuis when she gets to Zeist. She hopes with every fibre of her being that Rosa is there, she hopes that they will take her in but if not she knows that Rosa will somehow let her stay even if it is just for a night or two while she thinks what to do. She tries again to read the article in front of her, picking up and turning the page, at least she no longer has the Fuhrer looking at her. She looks at her watch. Another 30 minutes before they get to Zeist, she leans back and closes her eyes, feigning sleep, praying the Nazi officer doesn't start to talk to her again. What seems like hours later, the young man sitting next to her taps her arm.

"We're coming into Zeist."

"Thanks." She sits up as the train slows, takes her hat from the rack and puts it on then stands to get her case.

"I'll get that." The young man smiles as he grabs the case and they shuffle past the other passengers following the Nazi officer onto the platform.

"Someone meeting you?"

"No, but I'll find my way to the Zonnerhuis don't worry."

He puts down the case. "I'd go with you, but I have to meet someone and I'm late. Will you be alright? Do you know Zeist?"

"I'll be fine. I'll get directions."

"Ask in the bar across the road. I think they've moved out of the centre of town, but the barman is a fount of local knowledge." He smiles. "I'm really sorry not to be more helpful. Maybe we will see one another in town one day and I can show you around a bit?" He smiles. "I don't even know your name."

"Hetty. And you?"

"Anton. Anton Janssen. Lovely to meet you Hetty." He picks up her case again. "I'll walk you across to the bar."

The barman tells her that it's a good half hour's walk. The Zonnehuis has moved into the woods on the outskirts of Zeist, a place called the Wittehul, their original premises in town seconded by the Nazis as an officers' club. Does she want to wait, maybe he can find someone in the bar to give her a lift? Does she want a cup of coffee to warm up after her journey? She accepts the coffee but declines the lift. It's late and there's no guarantee that there'll be someone to give her a lift and she doesn't want her arrival to be the source of local gossip, when she is not even sure whether she will be welcomed at the Zonnehuis.

The walk is dark and damp. She takes a wrong turning at one point and has to retrace her steps and it's nearly 8pm when she finally finds herself at the front door of the children's home in the Wittehul, down a long track leading into a dead end, into the woods. Her shoes are wet, her feet feel like lumps of ice and her arms ache from carrying her suitcase on the long, damp, cold walk.

A young woman opens the door and tells her Rosa is away for a few days visiting her parents. Hopes she'd had that the Zonnehuis could be her refuge begins to slip away.

"Is Dr Lievegoed here?"

"He's gone home for supper, but he's coming back later," the woman looks her up and down. "Do you want to wait for him?"

"Yes. Yes please."

The young woman asks her name and introduces herself as Truus, directing her to a low carved wooden bench in the hallway.

"I'll leave you here to wait," She smiles. "Warm up a bit. I'll get someone to bring you a cup of tea in a while. You'll excuse me. We're getting the children to bed."

Hetty can hear the going-to-bed noises of two dozen children: running water, bare feet padding along bare boards between bedrooms, the creak of bed springs, children's voices trilling out their good nights. Somewhere a child is crying, every now and then the painful rhythm of the sobs broken for a minute before beginning again.

Hetty calculates how long it will take her to walk back

to the station in Zeist and wonders where she will find a bed for the night, indeed if she will find a bed for the night if Dr Lievegoed won't let her stay. As these miserable thoughts crowd her mind, Truus appears with a small glass mug of tea and hands it to her.

She is cradling the tea in her hands, enjoying the warmth, when the door opens and Bernard Lievegoed walks in. She puts the glass cup down beside her and stands up as he shakes out his coat and hat and eventually, turning, sees her. She'd forgotten how tall he is.

"Hello?" he puts out his hand. "Don't I know you?"

"Yes. I'm Hetty, Hetty van Leeuwen. We met when you were in Scheveningen? I met you on the beach a few times...with the children...and Rosa."

"Ah yes! You are that friend of Rosa's aren't you? You were very good playing with the children on the beach. I do remember you. Did you come to see her? She's not here. Did someone tell you? Her mother is unwell."

"Oh, I didn't know. I'm sorry. Yes, I came to see her of course, but I also hoped to see you."

"Oh? Did you? Alright then, follow me. Come into my office and tell me how I can help."

She walks behind him down a narrow corridor and into a small office dominated by a huge desk and lined with bookshelves. A large bay window looks out over the darkening woods, that back onto the garden surrounding the Zonnehuis, branches cracking in the wind and rain. In front of the desk are two low worn leather armchairs and he directs her to one of them and folds himself into the other. He puts his elbows on the arms of the chair, interlacing long elegant fingers and looks at her. She'd forgotten how deep set his eyes were and how he had a way of looking at you that made you feel uncomfortably exposed.

"Tea? Have you had tea?"

"Yes, thank you." She feels in her pocket for the letter she has had for the past year from the doctor in Scheveningen, the friend of her parents who had encouraged her to train as a nurse.

"What brings you here?"

"I am looking for work. I have been working in Amsterdam at the hospital where I was training as a nurse. You know everyone has been evacuated from Scheveningen?"

"Yes."

"Amsterdam is too close. It is an unhappy place these days. Rosa said you needed workers here. I have a reference." She pulls the letter from her pocket and passes it across to him. He opens the envelope, takes out the letter and carefully reads it. Hetty feels the palms of her hands go sweaty.

She remembers telling the doctor in Scheveningen who'd written the reference for her on one of her visits home, that she didn't need a reference; that she would carry on training at the PIZ. But he had insisted that she take it. "Just in case Hetty, as back up. These are strange times."

And she'd taken the letter, kept it out of respect more than anything and because it was a letter that made her proud of the work she had achieved. It vouched for the work she had done first at the clinic on the downs where Wil had been treated, and then her work as a nurse in The Hague and then in Amsterdam. He had written it on his own headed paper and stamped it with a personal seal. The one thing the letter did not mention was her Jewish background. She had attached the certificate she'd received on passing her first-year exams to the letter.

Dr Lievegoed looks up. "It's a good recommendation, and we could certainly do with your help." He glances at the certificate. "But…this is all rather sudden isn't it? And this certificate, well it's nearly a year old. What have you been doing? Where have you been? Why have you not taken your second-year exams?"

He folds the letter and certificate and puts them back into the envelope, handing it across to her.

So, this was it. She'd come to the conclusion on the cold long walk to the Zonnehuis that if asked she had to be honest, to be straight, at least with him, if he was going to give her a job. She would be putting him and the home at risk after all. She twists her watch around on her wrist, pulling at the strap as if to ease it.

"I should be taking my exams next week, at the Portuguese Israeli Hospital, the Jewish hospital," she looks up at him. "But I had to leave."

"Why? What happened?"

And then she tells him about her cousins, the escape and the interview that morning with the director of the home – which seemed like days ago, not hours. She had needed to get away. Quickly. Rosa had often suggested that if she wanted, she could come to the Zonnehuis, that they were looking for more help. But she would understand if that wasn't possible, if he thought she was unsuitable.

Dr Lievegoed's face gives nothing away. She can't tell what he is thinking.

"I'm a hard worker."

He smiles and inclines his head. "What a day." He leans back in his chair. He points at the letter now lying in her lap. "I have great respect for the good doctor – we met several times when I was in Scheveningen." He looks her in the eye. "We do need help Hetty, so for now, stay. We'll see if this works out."

Relief floods through her. "Thank you, thank so much. I…"

"Don't say anymore and don't tell anyone else here in the Zonnehuis Wittehul what you have told me about why you have suddenly arrived. I'll just tell them that I asked Rosa to ask you to come and help us, and that with her mother being ill she had forgotten to say you were coming today. OK?"

He starts to describe how the Zonnehuis is run, the forty children, the different types of mental and physical disability they suffer from and his belief, his firm belief in his method of care and therapy which he trusts will give them a better more fulfilled and fruitful life. She tries to stay awake look focussed as he tells her it's based on Steiner's anthropomorphic system, looking at the inner life, the spirit of the child and using music, art and nature in their treatment and development.

He sees how tired she is. "Sorry, I get carried away. Look we will talk more tomorrow when my wife, Nel will be here. Let's get you something to eat and find you somewhere to sleep." He rings a bell and Truus arrives and takes her to the kitchen for bread and soup. She will sleep in Rosa's bed, tomorrow they will sort her own place out for her.

Truus chatters on about the Zonnehuis, about the children. Hetty asks sleepily about the other staff.

"We are co-workers not staff. We are all in this together," says Truus showing her to the attic bedroom where she is to sleep. Hetty collapses on to the bed, taking the combs out of her hair, unbuckling her shoes as Truus tells her where the bathroom is and what time she will need to be downstairs for breakfast.

"And you know about the camp?"

Hetty looks up. "What camp?"

"The SS barracks next to us in the woods? You probably passed it on your way here. It is set back a bit, off the road."

Hetty feels her mouth drop, her hopes sink. She had been so busy, so desperate looking for the sign for the children's home, the strange white house set back from the road described by the barman, that she hadn't really taken in the rest of her surroundings.

"You will see a lot of soldiers around." Truus smiles. "Don't worry they don't bother us. They don't question us because they think they know all about us." She looks into Hetty's eyes. "But they don't do they?"

Hetty – Zeist – ten days later

She bumps into him as she comes out of the library. She's flipping through the book she has just borrowed, head down, deep in thought.

"Hello?"

She looks up, shaking herself out of her thoughts, a surprised smile breaking across her face. "Hi! Anton?"

It had been ten days since her evening arrival in Zeist, ten days of trying to get to know 40 mismatched children of all ages and all mental and physical abilities and ten long days of learning about the unusual system of care practiced at the Zonnehuis. She likes the home, she likes Zeist, though she doesn't feel safe, she never feels safe. So much has happened that it seems an age since Anton helped her off the train.

Within days of her arrival, Dr Lievegoed had called her into his office, handed her new 'false' identity papers, an 'e' dropped from her surname, the *Jood* stamp non-existent. She'd been surprised and started to ask how and why but he had dismissed any questions. Two days later he had asked her to accompany him on an expedition. He wanted to introduce her to the local Nazi camp commandant. "When they know who you are and that you work here they won't bother you," he'd explained. She'd felt ill at the suggestion, but she'd gone with him and despite her insides churning and her head throbbing had shaken hands with the camp commandant at the right moment, even smiled back when he had made her 'welcome'. Dr Lievegoed told him that she been evacuated, had come from Scheveningen.

She'd smiled to herself passing the camp this morning, nodding to the guard at the gate, on her way to Zeist. She had gone into the library to find a book she had wanted to borrow, to read to the children, one she had loved as a child and which hadn't been in the rather limited selection of books at the Zonnehuis. She closes it as Anton leans across and looks at the title. "For the children."

"I imagined so," he grins. "You are settling in well then?"

"Yes…slowly. It's different from anything I have done before but it's a really friendly place, like a bubble in this crazy world….There is so much focus on the children, they need so much help, that sometimes, just momentarily, I actually forget what's going on in the outside world." She looks up. "Well not entirely."

"Have you had a chance to look around Zeist?"

"A little."

"Are you rushing back now or have you got time for a cup of coffee? Maybe I can show you round a bit."

"That would be great. I've got the afternoon off, but what about you? Don't you have other things to do?"

"An early finish for me too today. Come on."

It's an unusually crisp, dry almost warm November day, the final leaves of autumn clinging to bare tree branches stretching up dramatically against the blue of the sky, the town bathed in a soft afternoon light. They first walk through the park where an old man is turning over soil in the empty flower beds. They talk about nothing and everything, their families, their favourite music, favourite foods and books. Walking into the town centre they pass the huge red brick council building, people bustling in and out of the main doors. "Apart from the obvious, that is where I work – and it is also where everyone comes to collect their ration stamps."

She nods.

"Particularly important as I am usually the one handing them out."

She laughs. In the heart of the town he points out favoured shops; where he gets his bike repaired, the best butcher, the grocer who talks too much and finally a small bakery down a side street, the yeasty smell of bread lingering around the door. The bell rings as he ushers her inside where he is warmly greeted by a plump grey-haired woman behind the counter.

"Let me introduce you to my godmother, my mother's oldest friend, Vera. This is Hetty, she's come to work with Dr Lievegoed."

After enquiries about Anton's mother, Vera ducks behind the counter and brings out a neatly wrapped small package. "I know what you are really here for Anton." She smiles.

"Vera spoils me. Still thinks I need looking after."

"And you love being spoilt."

He tucks the package in his coat pocket as they leave the bakery.

"What's in the package."

"Apple cake. She's famous for it. Used to make loads. Now just makes a few when she can and always keeps some for me."

"Lucky you. What about your mother?"

"She's gone to stay in Amsterdam with my sister, to help her – I was on my way back from visiting them when we met on the train? My sister has two-year-old twins and a six-month-old baby – she needs help."

They walk back into the centre of town and to the Amsterdam bar. There is nobody there except an old man drinking beer and talking to Bram so they take a small corner table and order coffee.

"And two forks," says Anton, carefully unwrapping the package of apple cake.

He pushes the package towards her and passes her a fork and they both dip into the crumbling cake. Hetty luxuriates in the soft sweet texture and taste.

"What do you do at the Council Office then?"

"I'm a sort of clerk." He frowns. "I was at university in

Amsterdam but that's closed now, this job meant I wouldn't be conscripted to a munitions factory for the Nazi army." He looks up at her. "Which was the last thing I wanted."

"Were you in Amsterdam during the strike last year?"

"Yes…" He shakes his head.

"After the strike, we were all shaken. And after a few days I couldn't see the point in staying on there, that's when I came back to Zeist."

She cradles her coffee cup in her hands. "I had friends who took part in that march."

"Are they ok?"

"One of them got shot." She looks up and she can see the pain which has shot through her reflected in his eyes.

"I'm sorry." He takes her hand, gently smoothing her fingers. "It was a terrible time."

She tells him then about Dirk and Wil and Rosa, growing up together in Scheveningen, their energy, their vitality, the beach, the fairs, the concerts, the crazy tennis competitions they'd hold in the park and remembering eases her. Somehow the conversation shifts to her family, to Loes and Hans. And then she stops talking. She shouldn't be talking like this. She pulls her hand away, her brain spinning again with thoughts of her brother. Hans couldn't just disappear.could he? There was so much life in him. She takes a sip of her now cold coffee. "Anyway, a new chapter. I am here now." She shrugs wanting to get away from her memories, searching for what to say while her brain teams with memories and fears. Bram suddenly turns on the radio, something classical is playing, a Brahms concerto she thinks.

She looks up at Anton. "You know they have got me playing the recorder at the Zonnehuis."

"Can you play?"

"Well I did when I was at school. When I was nine… But

the Lievegoeds insist you play something if you can and that's the best I can do. Music is key to their therapy and the children love it."

"What else do you do," he shrugs and blinks "Sorry, am I being too nosy?"

"No, no," she shakes her head and with her fork splits the last edge of the apple cake taking half and eating it before answering, thinking of all that has gone on and what to say. "Well I just help wherever it's needed. Look after children when their carer is on a break for an hour or two….or even a day or two. It's a bit confusing because it takes time to get to know each of these children… but…" she looks up as the door to the café opens a sudden breeze whipping round her legs. A group of men come in chatting, ordering beer and she realises that a lot of tables have filled up while they have been talking. Two women at the table next to them deep in conversation, two young Nazi officers leaning on the bar drinking shots of gin.

She gets up. "I better head back before dark."

"I'll walk with you."

She protests but he comes with her anyway and she realises as he hooks his arm through hers that she enjoys being with him. They walk and talk and even sing one of the songs she's learned at the Zonnehuis with the ease of sudden, unexpected good friendship.

Back at the Zonnerhuis they arrange to meet again. Going up to her bedroom she hugs the memory of the day to her, the warmth of it. Should she feel guilty? The thought of Phillipe skids across her brain. She hopes he is alright, but in the same way she hopes that Hannah, that all her friends at the hospital are ok. God, she hopes they are all ok.

PART 4

1943
Hide and Seek

Hetty Zeist – January

Hetty feels tense as she stands in the queue at the Council Office for ration stamps. She checks her bag. Looks up at the red and black poster of Nazi soldiers. The poster has come unstuck, its message curling up and revealing an older poster of a girl on a bicycle but she can't see what its advertising. There's a couple sitting on the bench at the side of the large hall deep in conversation, the man looks at his watch, clearly waiting for an appointment. He's dressed in a suit and taps his foot as the woman talks to him and he nods. Wondering about them, she doesn't see the queue move forward and suddenly she is facing Anton across the counter.

"Hi there," he smiles, relaxed, encouraging. "Good to see you...We meeting for lunch later?"

"Yes, about 1? At the bar?"

"Perfect." He nods as he counts out the stamps for the Zonnehuis and slides them across to her in an envelope which she tucks firmly into her bag, looking up at him nervously. She can't believe how nervous she feels. "See you later."

She has been living in Zeist for just under two months, and yet looking at Anton, it feels like much longer and much shorter: thoughts of him fill her head, his slightly lob sided smile, his green eyes, the way his dark curly hair sticks up in the wind makes her smile. But she's nervous now as she walks out of the council offices, actually so nervous she feels jumpy.

Four days ago she'd been asked to go to Dr Lievegoed's office and had been surprised to find Anton there. They had soon explained why, Dr Lievegoed doing most of the talking, Anton interrupting every other minute to say "you don't have to do this Hetty". They wanted her help with work they were doing, helping the resistance. She remembers feeling slightly taken aback, surprised but not shocked and somewhere in her head rather pleased, rather proud that she might be able to help.

Now walking across to the bar where she has left her bike, she remembers how worried Anton had looked, how concerned that she might think he was taking advantage of her, of their relationship. But Bernard Lievegoed had reasoned that she was trustworthy, that she was the ideal person to ask. It was all quite straight forward: they wanted her to pick up ration books and sometimes other papers for the resistance when she went to pick up ration stamps for the Zonnehuis. She would take these extra ration books to an address in Utrecht, on her bike. She remembers how they had all repressed a smile at the thought of her rattle trap of a bike with wooden wheels, but it was a bike, one she'd found in a shed behind the Zonnehuis and cleaned up and oiled. They told her she wouldn't meet anyone and her only contact would be with Anton. But there were still clearly risks if she was caught. There was no doubt it was dangerous. But Hetty didn't hesitate, not because of any sense of obligation to Dr Lievegoed or Anton but because the thought of doing something constructive to help the resistance gave her a sense of purpose, of being part of the action not just a pawn of the occupation. She was by nature a doer, not one to watch and wait.

But now that it is happening, now that she is about to take the stamps to Utrecht her stomach is churning. She is going to be sick. After checking on her bike she goes into the Amsterdam Bar where Bram is uncapping bottles of beer for a group of soldiers lounging around a corner table.

"Can I get a glass of water?" she asks as she walks past, indicating the ladies' toilet where she is headed.

He nods "It'll be here on the bar."

Going into the toilet, the whiff of morning bleach springs up at her. No one's in there and she goes into one of the cubicles, and after throwing up takes a deep breath, sits on the toilet lid and opens her bag pulling out the manila envelope she'd collected from Anton and a tooled leather magazine cover, a 'gift' from the Lievegoed's, which currently holds a German magazine. She feels inside the envelope and pulls out a second envelope, more coupons and two identity cards. She flips the cards open and faces of two serious faced young men snap up at her and she wonders for a moment who they are, what their story is, how they are coping? She then removes the magazine from the leather cover and searches the watered green silk lining with her fingers for the seam running down the central fold which has never been stitched. Using a nail, she lifts the flap and slides the second envelope with the coupons and identity cards flatly into place under the lining before replacing the magazine. Leaving the cubicle, she rinses her hands and slews water over her face before drying herself and walking back through the café, towards the bar.

"Something to eat?"

"No thanks. I have to get going, Dr Lievegoed wants me to pick something up for him in Utrecht. I'll be back later; I'm meeting Anton for lunch." She picks up the glass of water he has put on the counter. "How's Berta by the way?"

Until a week earlier Bram's teenage daughter Berta had occasionally helped in the bar, waiting at tables with a dimpled smile and breathy speech. Her attraction had not been lost on the Nazi commandant and he had made her an offer to work in his office that she felt she could not refuse. But there were those in Zeist who didn't see it that way. Hetty's noticed there are fewer locals in the bar and an increasing number of customers coming from the Nazi camp and even from their regional headquarters in the Schloss on the edge of town.

"Fine. Doing ok, I think. I hardly see her."

"Send her my regards," She looks at her watch, it is nearly 11.00, if she heads off now she will be back in good time to meet Anton.

Bram takes her empty glass. "I'll save you young lovers a table eh?"

She smiles as she pulls on her gloves. The German officers are finishing their beer and looking across at Bram, one of them winks at her.

"I think you are wanted Bram."

Bram swings out from behind the bar and manoeuvres his not inconsiderable frame balletically through the tables, raising an arm to the officers. "More beer ?"

One of the soldiers puts up a pudgy hand with three raised fingers.

"Coming now sir."

Hetty walks out and puts her bag in the bicycle basket. The sky is turning slate grey. It looks like rain again.

She is pulling on her hat, getting ready to go, when a mangey black dog, ribs sticking out comes lolloping past with a piece of bacon still half wrapped in paper in its mouth. Careering after it is a woman, her coat flapping, shouting. She races past Hetty, catching her foot on the edge of Hetty's wheel, falling, her sudden weight yanking the handlebars out of Hetty's hands toppling the bike onto the ground and spewing Hetty's bag and its contents out of the basket.

Hetty gasps and then turns to help the woman up as Bram rushes out of the bar. The woman is wheezing in between sobs of anger and frustration, trying to catch her breath. She is bruised but not badly hurt. It has all taken seconds and Hetty turns to pick up her bike and sees that two of the Nazi officers who'd been drinking at the bar are outside collecting her things from the ground… her purse, her comb, her magazine. One of the officers is flicking through the magazine, looking at how to put it back in the cover.

Hetty holds her hand out, steps forward, smiling broadly, her heart thumping. "Thank you. Thank you so much." She takes the magazine and the cover, putting the one deftly inside the other and collecting the rest of her things, putting them in her bag. One of the officers looks more familiarly at her now as she nods her thanks and turns to get on her bike.

"A drink Fraulein? After all the excitement?"

"Oh," she looks at her watch. "I'd love to but I'm running late. Another time?" She smiles. They are about to protest when Bram reappears with a round of drinks. She hadn't even seen him go back to the bar.

"This one is always late," he shakes his head. "Drinks gentlemen?"

Hetty swings quickly onto her bike, pushing down hard on the pedals as the chain ratchets into place. It will take her less than an hour to get to the address in Utrecht that she has been given, a garage near the outskirts of the town where she will discreetly leave the envelope behind a toolbox left just inside the entrance for that purpose. If the toolbox isn't there, she will take the envelope back to Zeist, after picking up some medicines for the Zonnehuis from a chemist in Utrecht.

Within minutes she is out of Zeist, the flat landscape opening up into fields of stubble covered in a sugary white gauze of January frost, only a red roofed farmhouse on the horizon. She glances behind her, no-one there. No-one has followed.

Jozef – Utrecht – February

Jozef is in the cellar. He has been there all day, Opa Loggers shouting out instructions as he shoveled coal into the planked wood bunkers he had helped build a week ago, then measuring out and passing small 5 kilo bags up the stairs to Opa Loggers which he loaded onto a wooden trolly and would later distribute to his black market customers. The coal dust had gotten up Jozef's nose, under his fingernails, in his hair. He is relieved when Oma Loggers calls him to come upstairs for supper.

She looks at him as he emerges into the kitchen and tells him to go into the back kitchen and have a good wash.

But despite washing his face with soap and an old flannel at least twice and scrubbing his hands with a bristle brush, he can see from the look of mild disapproval in Oma Loggers face as he sits down that his attempt at getting clean had been only partially successful.

"After supper take off those filthy clothes and I will get them in the wash Joop." She calls him Joop rather than Jozef now. It's an agreement that the nickname is much less Jewish avoids any suspicion if someone comes to the house and sees him. 'Joop' can be explained away, his father conscripted to work in a German factory, his mother dead.

"We've still got more to do in the cellar yet," says Opa Loggers scraping back his chair. He catches a disapproving look from his wife and smiles. "But first give this hungry young worker some food." He winks at Jozef, slapping him affectionately on the back.

The coal had arrived in the early evening two days ago. They had taken a week to build the coal bunkers in the cellar which runs under the living room, moving old furniture and tools and pots of paint down to the far end to give them the necessary room in the area under the coal hole in the front garden. Two days ago, Jozef had been instructed to stand in the cellar as hessian bags of coal weighing 30 kilos or so were tipped down the coal hole in the front garden. The whole operation was over in minutes and the coal had scattered everywhere. It had taken him hours to shovel it into the bunkers. And then yesterday, was it yesterday he wondered peering at his watch in the gloom? Yesterday he had started to make up smaller bags of coal for sale on the black market. Opa Loggers had watched and given instructions. He had answered each of Opa Loggers commands with "Yes controller" making Opa bend over with laughter as he leant against the damp cellar wall chewing on the stem of his unlit pipe.

It was a family joke. Against all odds, Opa Loggers had landed a job as the part time transport controller (supplies) for the huge Utrecht bakery, less than two kilometers from the house. The bakery was one of the biggest in Holland and supplied bread for the occupying Nazi force. Coal to fire the ovens was imported from Germany by train. It was guarded with care, but coal had still gone missing: the slippage put down to the growing number of people hanging around the train depot hoping coal would fall, a bag would break, or a bribe would be taken. One of the station guards had been caught storing coal in the ticket office, taking it home in small canvas shopping bags and selling it on to favored passengers and friends, one of whom shopped him to the authorities when he felt he had been given a mean share of coal for his money. The guard had lost his job, but more than that, as a consequence of the theft, the director of the bakery had decided that they needed a coal monitor, someone to log in the coal as it arrived and organize its safe transport to the bakery. Hundreds of people applied, but a recommendation from a friend had eased Opa Loggers application to the top of the pile and to success, though his wife thought the long black boots, trench coat, grey felt hat, and a moustache trimmed square for the interview had clinched the deal. "You look like Hitler's cousin," she had told him with a mixture of disdain and approval as he left for the interview.

The first transport of coal had arrived at the depot four days ago. For two days Opa Loggers had stood, counting, stamping his feet to keep warm, clipboard in hand, collar up, watching as the coal was shoveled into hessian bags and loaded onto trailers destined for the bakery where it was logged in on arrival. It was dark by the time the final load was on the last trailer and covered with a tarpaulin, Opa had leapt on to the trailer with the bow-legged driver and the two men had rumbled off into the night, but instead of the bakery the trailer had changed direction and pulled up outside the Loggers house in J.S. Bachstraat. Speedily half the load was dispatched through the coal hole, into the cellar and into Jozef's waiting arms: the other half of the load was the 'bonus' belonging to the driver. The authorities would never know as the controller wouldn't log the coal's arrival.

The project has drawn Joop closer to the old man who misses his two surviving sons, one of whom has been conscripted to work in a German munitions' factory, the other hiding out and working on a farm somewhere north.

After supper he returns to the cellar to complete the day's coal orders before being told by Oma to go to bed.

"I don't care if you haven't finished, it is time you were in bed. It's time we were all in bed."

So he had left the cellar, bone tired with hardly the energy to hand over his dirty shirt and shorts before climbing upstairs to the attic which is where he now slept.

His aunt Lea is already curled up on her mattress, blankets pulled tightly up to her chin, fast asleep, she doesn't even stir when he collapses onto the mattress next to hers. He is beyond tired, every bone in his body aches, but he can't sleep. He listens to the even, unconscious breathing of his aunt on the mattress next to his: he looks at the hard curve of her back straining against the fabric of her black dress. It is how she always sleeps, turned away from him, pulled into herself but still much too close for either of them to be comfortable. They don't like the sleeping arrangement, but they can do nothing about it. Lea hardly speaks to him or to anyone, only to her daughter Tina. Endurance strains through all her words and actions. Even when she does say goodnight, he can hear an edge to her voice, dismay that it is him rather than her beloved sister, his mother, lying down on the thin mattress buttressed up against hers in the corner of the attic room. Well, he feels like telling her, he wishes it was his mother lying next to him too and his sister lying curled up on the little couch at the foot of Oma and Opa's bed rather than his cousin Tina. But she probably knows that. He turns on to his back, stretching his arms and legs to ease his throbbing muscles. He can still taste the coal dust in his mouth.

Thinking about the day, Joop remembers the way the old man had been pleased with his work, put his hand on his shoulder and squeezed it affectionately before sitting down to dinner. His father used to do that, squeeze his shoulder.

He thinks about how his life has changed again. Life in the Loggers house is so different, no school, no friends, no going out, not even into the small back garden. Even inside he has to be careful not to make any noise or even talk too loudly. He walks round in socks with felt slippers his Aunt has made for him as she has for herself and Tina, though he had put his shoes on to go into the cellar. Chores regulate his day; every morning he takes Oma and Opa their first cup of tea in bed and then cleans out the grate and sets the fire the way Oma Loggers likes it done. Then breakfast and he helps with the dishes, with setting and clearing the table, with whatever Oma asks of him, though not this week as he has had all the coal to sort out.

He turns on his mattress. He hasn't seen his mother or sister since they left. Opa brings him occasional messages, a sweater once that he is sure his mother has remade out of wool from one of her own cardigans, which somehow makes it even more special.

When he finishes with the coal he will get back to his book for a bit: tales of Greek mythology. He smiles at the thought of the books he had read in the past three months. His father would be astonished; a yearning floods through him when he thinks of his father. Opa Loggers had got him reading soon after his arrival. Seeing him sitting around, bored and idle, he had frog marched him into the front room, where a huge, crammed bookcase dominated one wall, the wooden shelves sagging with the weight of the books marshalled in rows, tucked in on top of one another, space at a premium.

'Read' said Opa.

'What?'

'Read it all, start there.' He'd pointed at the top left corner of the book shelf. "And read to there." He had swept his hands down to the bottom right corner. "And learn."

Right now, tired from heaving the coal, he longed for one of those afternoons, lying on the green Turkish living room carpet, watching a spider pick its way across a web that had not been discovered by Oma's duster. Opa had picked out the first book for him, flipping through it: "Flora and Fauna in Northern Europe. This book is by an eminent Dutch botanist. Look at this all the degrees he has and where he teaches." He'd run his finger along the closely typed lines. "This is how you learn. Read and learn."

Why can't he sleep? Jozef thinks of that first book. He can still remember the feel of the book in his hand, the title embossed in gold on the board cover. For days Opa asked him what he had learned. Joop told him about the wild purple orchids that could be found on the Wadden Islands in Texel and wondered if they looked like the orchids in the wood near Laag-Keppel. He had been about half way through the book when he recognized a picture of a soft blue butterfly, its scalloped edges rimmed with white, as one he had often seen hovering in the garden behind their house: the common blue Polyommatus Icarus. Trying to sleep he rolls the remembered name around in his mouth, thinking of the butterfly's delicate wings lifted by a summer breeze and finally he drifts off.

Hetty – February – Zeist

Hetty panics as she clutches the hand of the two little girls. Where the hell have the boys disappeared to: "Marten! Daan!"

Why did she think to bring them out here into the woods?

"Marten! Daan!" Nothing, only the feint rustle of wind through the trees. She looked up; rain, just to add to her problems, it definitely looks like it's going to rain.

It had seemed such a good idea. Britt was off sick with a bad cold, and she'd been asked to take charge of the children usually under her care; four children, two girls and two boys with a mismatched mix of mental and physical problems, the youngest Sophie just 7 suffered badly from epilepsy but she was a little sweetheart with long blonde hair and a gentle smile; the oldest Daan 9 was boisterous but always good humoured. Britt had told her between sneezes that they were lovely but not always easy children. But being cooped up inside with someone they didn't really know, the children had become fractious and bored and itchy with unused energy, so she had suggested a walk in the woods, some fresh air. She had done it with a larger group of older children and it had gone well, they had returned rosy faced, breath puffing out in clouds, singing some silly song she had taught them. She can't believe things had gone so wrong this time. She'd only taken her eyes off the boys for a minute…it had been only a minute hadn't it?

Sophie had been so excited, finding a cluster of snowdrops pushing out from under the fallen trunk of a tree and Hetty had bent down to see what she was looking at. The snowdrops had looked magical, white and pure and delicate against the rough bark and she had helped Jeanne, awkward because of callipers the result of a mind-numbing bout of polio when she was a baby, to bend down and look too. And when she stood up, the boys, who had been racing round and round climbing on and jumping off the tree trunk had disappeared.

Where are they? The forest is thick with pine trees and she can't see more than 50 metres ahead. "Maarten! Daan!"

If they boys have gone down the path they came on, they will be back at the Zonnehuis, but what if they have gone further into the woods? Or towards the SS camp?

"What's the matter Hetty?" Sophie pulls on her hand.

"We need to find the boys."

"I'm tired," says Jeanne.

"Already? Let's just look a little more. They might be hiding! You call them."

The girls start shouting for the two boys. A part of her wonders if the boys have gone to look at the soldiers standing at the entrance to the camp. Soldiers are soldiers whether they are Dutch or German and she knows that the boys are fascinated by them, particularly Daan who is always marching about pretending he is a general in the Dutch army, his father was or had been something to do with the military. But the SS Camp? "Maarten! Daan!"

"Hetty I'm cold. I want to go back," Jeanne pulls on her arm, tears welling up in her eyes.

Hetty feels the first spit of rain on her neck as she bends

down to talk to the little girls. But what will they say if she goes back without the boys? She looks up as Sophie pulls up the hood on her coat. She picks up Jeanne and hoists her on to her back and grabs Sophie's hand. "Come on Sophie, let's run, get out of the rain."

Dashing through the Zonnehuis gate, she sees the tall, rangy frame of Jan van Wettum, one of the older teachers at the school, standing in the porch, smoking a cigarette.

"I can't find the boys – Maarten and Dan."

"Where were you?"

"In the woods."

"In the woods! You left them there!"

"I.... look I didn't think..." She manoeuvres Sophie gently off her back and opens the door, tells them to go inside, out of the rain, to go to the kitchen, to get a warm drink. They run down the corridor shouting out: "We've lost Daan and Maarten!"

Rosa pokes her head out of a ground floor room and takes one look at Hetty who nods, fighting back tears. "I need help."

Jan van Wettum is already putting his coat on, grabbing a hat from a hook behind the door walking down the driveway. Rosa pulls a raincoat off another hook and grabs Hetty's arm and they chase after him.

Catching up Hetty runs ahead to the log where she last saw the boys, hoping they had returned. But nothing.

"This is where we were when I lost them. I just bent down..."

"We can talk about how this happened later...now we must find them," says Jan. "I'll go to the Camp; you and Rosa split up, go further into the woods." He looks at Hetty. "These woods are huge you know....huge."

Rosa grabs her arm. "It's ok. We'll find them." Hetty's heart is racing, she feels sick.

"Come on, Hetty it's going to be alright." Rosa pulls her further down the path and starts to call the boys.

They have only gone about 100 metres when they hear someone calling them. Turning they see Dr Lievegoed running down the path, raincoat flapping as he comes towards them and Jan van Wettum behind him.

Dr Lievegoed raises a fist, thumb up, waves to them, smiling. "They've been found. Daan and Marten are back at the house."

Hetty bends over with relief. "They came back to the house on their own?"

"No. Two of the junior officers from the SS camp brought them back. The boys were hanging around outside the camp, watching the soldiers. One of the riflemen on duty at the entrance asked them what they were doing, where they were from, and then these young officers brought them back. Maarten was in tears. He thought he was in real trouble. And Daan, he was just confused. I think they were quite scared."

"Thank God," says van Wettum.

"I'm sorry…I didn't think…" starts Hetty.

Dr Lievegoed turns on her. "No excuses. I don't want to talk about it here. Let's get back to the house."

Van Wettum puts a hand on Hetty's arm as they follow Dr Lievegoed.

"This was bad…really bad," mutters Hetty.

"It was a mistake. Don't worry. Dr Lievegoed is a reasonable man. He knows these things can happen – he'll just want to ensure it doesn't happen again."

But what will that mean for her?

They go into the house through the back door to the kitchen where two German officers stand drinking coffee and talking to Wilma the cook, one bending over to taste the soup she is making. Hetty takes off her coat and pushes her fingers through her hair.

"I think you have something to say to these gentlemen don't you Hetty?" says Dr Lievegoed.

"Thank you, thank you so much for bringing the boys back. You can't imagine how worried I was."

"It was Wolfgang here who insisted we bring them back, so he is the one to thank," says the fatter officer. "How come they were out in the woods on their own Miss...?

"Hetty. Hetty Van Leuwen," The abbreviated surname on her 'new' identity card rolls uncomfortably on her tongue. "They were not on their own. I was with them, but they ran off." She explains then, that she had taken them out because of the good weather earlier in the day, and they all laugh, looking out at the rain streaming steadily down, splashing on the kitchen windows. She realizes she is shaking. "So sorry to have caused you trouble." She looks down at her feet, her thick stockings splattered with mud and her wet skirt sagging damply around her legs.

"Boys will be boys," says the fatter of the two officers smiling. "They are safe now. That's what matters."

"Yes. The important thing is they are safe," agrees Dr Lievegoed. "We just can't thank you enough."

The fatter officer, who has undone his heavy wool coat, looks round. "Well maybe you can. I have been meaning to call on you. He walks over to the cooking range. This is a good kitchen; your cooker is so much better than the one we have set up in the camp."

Dr Lievegoed stiffens. "We are lucky, the range is built in, it was here when we moved in. We had to leave Zonnehuis Veldheim for your senior officers, so we are glad that this house was found for us." His smile is wintery as he clasps his hands behind his back.

"My comrade, Wolfgang, is in charge of the officers' mess," explains the thinner officer."

"Ach! The cooker in the camp is so temperamental!"

For one awful moment Hetty wonders if they are going to try to take the cooker but the fat officer is looking around; he clearly likes the kitchen. "You know this reminds me of my kitchen at home? In Berlin? I used to run a restaurant in Berlin. But that is long gone now and I am here. Maybe on occasion I can come here and use your kitchen? Your cooker?"

Dr Lievegoed looks at Wilma who nods.

"Of course. If we can be of any help."

"Only when it is necessary of course," he smiles.

Hetty feels dizzy with the unrealistic turn of the conversation. She realises then that the younger thinner officer is looking at her, appraising her. She looks at him and he turns away. She sees the scar running from his ear to his chin. "We must go."

And then they leave saying goodbye to the boys who are sitting quietly in a corner, drinking mugs of warm apple juice and being fussed over by Wilma.

As the door closes Hetty opens her mouth to apologise to Dr Lievegoed but he cuts her off. "You are wet through. Go and change, dry off and then come to my office."

Hetty – Zeist – ten days later

Hetty fishes around in the murky water for another potato, picks it up and starts to scrub it clean of the clogging winter mud. Her hands are red, cold, chapped, her fingernails cracked despite nightly efforts with a metal nail file. But this is her punishment she'd joke with Rosa as they crawled into bed at the end of the day.

The story of the lost children now makes everyone laugh, though Hetty never thinks it quite as funny as the others and the scene plays over and over in her nightmarish dreams. She feels guilty, lucky to have kept any sort of job at all after the incident. But Dr Lievegoed had been kind: yes it was a mistake, but it had been a lesson for them all and he didn't want to lose her.

He partially blamed himself for moving her between different groups of children, never letting here get to grips with the challenges of any one group. He suggested that for a few weeks she help Wilma in the kitchen. Wilma had been pestering him on and on about the volume of work she had to do and the lack of help since her assistant had left in December. The kitchen was the hub of life in the Zonnehuis and she'd soon get to know everyone well. Later she would have her own group of children to look after.

And she has to admit that working in the kitchen, she was getting to know the children and the staff a lot better. Wilma had been kind and just so pleased to get help. Her chatter is ceaseless as she bustles about the kitchen, telling Hetty what to do, complaining at the lack of one thing or another because of rationing and gossiping about her neighbour's suspected affair with the woman who helps in the bar on the corner of Bergweg and Gerolaan.

Hetty almost feels guilty that Wilma is so friendly, so easy to be with, her constant chatter taking Hetty's mind off other things, other thoughts: the whereabouts of her parents, Loes, Hans, Wil... Jozef and Trudi; every night she prays they are all safe.

She fishes around in the water for the last potato before emptying the sink, swilling out the dirt from the bottom and rinsing her fingers which are numb with the cold. She gives the brass tap a firm yank to turn it off and feels the warm press of a child against the back of her legs, arms coming around her. It is little Piet, she knew it just by the weight and feel of him; none of the other boys are quite as affectionate.

She stretches across to the striped-blue roller towel hanging above the sink to dry her hands before pulling his arms from around her and then squatting down and until her eyes were level with his.

Piet has grown since those days in Scheveningen three years ago when she remembers playing with him on the beach; he is taller, bonier, but still trustingly affectionate.

"What is it Piet?"

"When is Aline coming back Hetty? I miss Aline."

"We all miss Aline and Erika."

"I miss Erika too. But Aline made stories for me. When is Aline coming back?"

"I don't know Piet." None of them know. Erika, one of the helpers at the Zonnehuis, had been tasked with taking Aline home to her parents. Aline was a couple of years older than Piet and had been staying at the children's home for the past 18 months, placed there by her parents, a Jewish doctor and his Protestant wife from Eindhoven in the south. Their younger son, Laurens had been very ill, a Down's Syndrome child like Piet, he had caught pneumonia and become delirious and died. Aline had been close to her brother and become depressed and begun to stutter. Her father had thought some time away at the Zonnehuis, where she had sometimes gone with Laurens when he was alive, and where she had made a number of friends might be the answer. Dr Lievegoed had agreed. The quiet dark-haired girl had been one of the most easy-going children in his care and had taken to Piet who was much the same age as her brother had been. The two had become inseparable; she'd tell Piet stories and never stuttered when talking to the little boy.

But a message had come about a month ago from Aline's parents. They had gone to live on a farm working for an old friend of one of Aline's cousins in Tilburg and wanted Aline to join them. No one knew the doctor there and with false papers provided by the local resistance, everything was good. Aline already had false papers and it was decided that Erika should accompany her as she had a brother living in Eindhoven and was keen to see him, his wife and new baby.

The two had walked to the station. Hetty had gone with them balancing Aline's case across the handlebars of her bike. She had left them half an hour before their train was due to depart and gone to the Council offices to pick up food coupons. She had mentioned to Anton that Aline and Erika were going, and he had promised to walk down to the station to check they had safely caught their train. Then she had set off on her bike for her own weekly journey to Utrecht.

When she returned two hours later she'd met Anton at the café. He had been to the station and seen Aline and Erika board the train. Returning to the children's home she had reported their safe departure. But that was two weeks ago and there had not been a word from them since. Erika should have been back a week ago. Everyone was worried, and Piet was grieving for the disappearance of his friend.

Hetty took Piet's hand: "Shall I tell you a story?"

"Like Aline?"

"Sure. Maybe about you and Aline?"

"About me and Aline!"

They walk across to an old wicker garden seat covered in blankets which has been left in the corner of the kitchen, brought in to stop the frost from wrecking it, the seat was a favourite place for curling up. Piet tucks himself under her arm, and she starts a story about two children in a boat. She won't tell him about the news she had received earlier in the morning, or lack of news, about Aline and Erika.

Dr Lievegoed had sent a letter to Erika's brother and had received a very confused and distressed letter back, the contents of which had quickly been spread amongst the Zonnehuis staff. Erika had never arrived in Eindhoven. They had been expecting her and assumed that something had happened to prevent her coming to visit them, that she had been needed at the Zonnehuis.

Hetty is finishing her story – in which Piet and Aline arrive on a magic island and open a zoo – when Wilma comes in and squashes herself onto the other end of the seat. She pats Piet on the shoulder. "Young man do you need to be in class?" He shakes his head slowly.

"Then I need help making my pastry? I need a good assistant. Can you help me?"

Piet's eyes light up. "Can I?"

"Will you? I need you." She stands up stretching her plump lined hands out for his smaller ones and pulling him up. "Come on, Hetty has got work to do, she can't have all the fun!" She smiles poking Piet playfully in the stomach.

Hetty gets up listening to the instructions Wilma is giving her and wondering where Erika is, where her own family is, whether her brother is alive and who is safe and who is not.

Joop – Utrecht – April

Joop is beyond tired, his body aches, but he can't sleep. His aunt is snoring; he pushes her to make her roll over and stop and she does for a minute and then starts again. He picks up his watch trying to make out the time in the attic gloom. Two o'clock? He rolls on to his side and curls up putting his arm over his head to block out the snores. But then he hears something else; the grating metallic rumble of an engine turning into the street, a truck stopping, people getting out, a door slamming, marching, someone thumping on the door of a nearby house. He turns, grabs his aunt's shoulder and shakes her hard: "Aunt Lea! Aunt Lea!"

She wakes almost instantly, sits up, hears what he hears and pushes him off his mattress: "Move."

They pile the thin mattresses on top of one another, load boxes from another corner on top, grab blankets and open the attic door.

Someone is banging on the front door. The whole house is shaking.

"Up. Get up!"

Joop hurries down the stairs, Lea pushing him from behind, as they hear Opa Loggers, pull up his bedroom window. "What the Hell do you want! It's two o'clock in the morning!"

"Get up old man. Come and open the door." The soldier's voice is loud and hoarse, grating on the night air. "Get up now!"

"What do you think we've got in here? My wife's asleep. What's the matter?"

"Wake your wife up. Open the door."

Joop and Lea get to the kitchen; the rug is already pulled back, the secret trap door open so they can crawl under the floor into the foundations of the house. Every night they get it ready for a night like this one. Lea pushes Joop and he slides snake like into the space dragging his blanket and bundling it into his arms. Lea climbs in behind him and pulls at the trap draw until it drops back into the floor.

"The carpet!"

"Opa will get the carpet. Shshsh!" She puts her hand across his mouth. He pushes it away and turns and crawls forward on his belly.

He hears pounding on the front door again, then the rapid steps of Opa Loggers running downstairs. "Coming! Coming!"

They hear him in the kitchen. The table scraping across the floor. He must have put the rug back.

The rubble scrapes through Joop's shirt, grazing his skin as he pushes himself further in to the dark underbelly of the house, to the hollow they had painstakingly shoveled out under the kitchen floor, the canvas from two old deck chairs maneuvered into the cramped dug out space. There is just enough room for them both. With the grey blanket pulled over them, they melt into the ground. It is icy cold.

There are voices in the hall. Tina will be off the little couch at the foot the Loggers bed and hiding under the Loggers bedclothes, her tiny body looking like no more than a ruck in the blanket. Oma will pull Tina's blankets like a shawl around her shoulders and shift Tina under her knees. Joop had seen it rehearsed like a scene from a play and it works. He breathes in the dust of the cellar, pinching his nose to stop himself sneezing.

His aunt is breathing heavily after the race to hide; he's terrified they will hear her. The kitchen floor bounces as the Nazi inspection contingent stomp up and down the hall, open cupboards, pull furniture around, run down into the coal cellar, the coal they're selling hidden under old rugs and broken furniture. Their heavy footsteps send cascades of dust through the floorboards and down on to the blanket.

Someone is speaking to Opa. "We believe people are hiding here Mr Loggers. The penalty for hiding anyone is transportation to a work camp, for hiding a Jew the penalty is death."

The words rattle in Joop's ear, his heart races. He feels warmth between his thighs, he's wet himself and wonders if Oma Loggers will be cross. He slows his breath, tries not to breathe, not to think, not to make a sound, pressed up against his aunt, her elbow in his back.

The footsteps recede; they must be going upstairs, first to Opa and Oma's room, the spare room and now the attic. His mind races around the attic space – they'd be up there now, would they find anything, had they left anything? His book! They'd see the book. He tries to concentrate; remember where and how he had left it. What time is it? He looks down at his watch. It isn't there. He hasn't put it on. He's forgotten that too. He starts hyperventilating, his aunt reaches across and puts her hand on his, gripping it hard. He twists his neck to look at her and indicates his wrist. Her face asks the question, and he draws the face of his watch on his wrist. Her eyes darken with anger at the stupid slip.

He hears footsteps running down the stairs, footsteps in the living room, someone back in the kitchen, dislodging more dust into the cellar. The back door slams, somebody's gone to search the garden.

"Captain!"

Joop feels the shallow panic of his breathing,

"Sergeant."

"Nothing."

Joop doesn't dare breathe.

The front door opens, the footsteps recede, the clang of gate closing. They stay still. That is the rule, not to move until the trap door is opened into the kitchen. The search is continuing up the street. There is shouting and Joop closes his eyes praying this mother and sister are alright.

The house falls quiet and time stretches, his body chills. Eventually he hears the truck engine firing up, soldiers running down the street and jumping in, the whine of its gears as it rumbles away.

They still don't move. It will be a while before Opa comes to let them out. Aunt Lea grabs Joop's hand, smiles in the dark at him. Her relief is palpable, but she says nothing.

He closes his eyes and it is a shock when what seems like minutes later his aunt is pinching him gently and he wakes up, she is shuffling across towards the trap door which is open. He crawls out behind her.

Pulling himself up into the kitchen he sees Opa Loggers and then standing beside him Trudi, her eyes wide, her dress torn.

"Jozef!" pants his little sister softly stepping around Opa Loggers and opening her arms.

"Jozef!"

He pulls her into his arms and breathes into her hair: "Trudi! You have to call me Joop now Trudi, Joop."

Joop – Utrecht – the next day

During breakfast, between hungry mouthfuls of bread and
Oma Loggers' home-made apple jam, Trudi tells Joop what
had happened. How she had ended up in the Loggers' house
overnight.

She's been staying with the Smits four doors up the street, on
her own as their mother has been sent to the country to help a
farmer whose wife had fallen ill.

The raid had caught the Smits completely unaware. Trudi
had been woken by the rumble of the truck coming into the
street. She'd crept out of the cellar where she had been sleeping,
rolling and covering her bedding as her mother had shown her
and gone upstairs, going first to wake Anna, the Smit's daughter,
a year older than she is. Together they went to wake up Anna's
parents.

"Go back to bed," Anna's father had shouted. "It's nothing.
No-one's coming here." Anna had gone back to her room, but
Trudi had sat down on the stairs and started to cry. Then came
the thud of fists on the door and the Smits woke up, Mr Smit
shouting that he was coming, Mrs Smit pulling Trudi up by her
arm and pushing her down the stairs, out the back door, into the
garden shed, behind a wheelbarrow.

Trudi had waited there for some minutes, could hear old
man Smit arguing with the men coming into the house and
running upstairs. Then the shed door opened; it was Mr Smit.

"Run! Get out and run!"

She had been so frightened she couldn't move.

"Where?"

"I don't care, just get out of here or you will have us all killed!"
Then Smit had reached in grabbed her by the arm and pulled her
out and pushed her through the hedge into next door's garden.
There had been a hole at the bottom of the hedge; she'd pulled

herself through, scraping her knee and tearing her dress. There were lights on in the third house and she had hidden behind a bush until she thought she could run again. It was old Pieter de Groot's garden. She was sure it was his. He was a friend of the Smits and once he had said she could come and stay with him if her 'Aunt Smit' didn't want her, he clearly knew she wasn't the Smit's niece, and he'd chuckled and pinched her chin when he said it, but he had bad breath and she didn't like him, so she didn't want to go there.

"He plays cards with Aunt Smit sometimes when Uncle Smit is at work. Anna and I are sent upstairs when he comes but we sneak back down and watch. Sometimes they play for money! Once they played for the chicken the Smits kept in the back yard and Aunt Smit lost and Uncle Smit was furious when he realised the chicken had gone. And I got the blame. Aunt Smit said it was my fault, the hen had escaped because I hadn't closed the hen house properly. But I had. And I nearly said something but before I could open my mouth Uncle Smit had smacked me and sent me to bed."

Trudi pauses and takes a huge bite of bread, her mouth bulging as she chews and swallows. She finishes her story. Finally pushing her way through hedges, she had made it to the back of the Loggers' house, she remembered it because the back door was painted red; she had hidden behind the shed until she was sure the search was over.

"I didn't know where else to go. I'm not going back to the Smits. They don't want me." She looks at Opa Loggers. "Please Opa, not there without mama."

Opa Loggers pushes back his chair from the table. "A bath for you, young lady. I've got to go out. Joop, stay with your sister today."

Aunt Lea gets out the tin bath and soon Trudi is in it, squealing as soap suds are sponged over her while her cousin

Tina plays with stray bubbles. Wrapped in a towel, the girls and Lea go upstairs to find something for Trudi to wear as her clothes have been washed and are still too wet to put back on.

Oma insists then that Joop gets in the bath and gets clean too, a night under the kitchen floor boards and two days in the cellar sorting coal had left him filthy. She is washing his hair when Trudi re-appears wearing one of Tina's sweaters and a skirt, both slightly too small for her.

"Why don't you children go and have a rest? Up in the attic. Until Opa gets back." There is no argument from either of them, and they are both fast asleep when they are called down for lunch two hours later.

Opa is walking angrily up and down the kitchen. He has been to see the Smits. They are adamant they didn't want Trudi back, just as much as she didn't want to go back, the stress is too much for them said Mrs Smit.

Opa is cross because their mother had given the Smits three months money up front for Trudi's keep and the Smits are refusing to give any money back. They deserved the extra money because of the stress said Mrs Smit. "I bet she's lost it playing cards with that idiot next door," grunts Opa. "Just you wait till they come running to the door asking me for some of our coal, Joop." He chuckles. Joop only half smiles; he hates all this talk about where they going to hide, he feels like a tortoise without a shell.

Seeing his frown, Opa pats his shoulder. "You are going to be ok Joop. Don't worry, I am going to make sure you and Trudi are alright. We won't let those bastards get you." And then Opa goes out again telling them to wait for his return.

All afternoon Joop sits at the table reading stories, Trudi drawing and talking about Laag-Keppel, their friends, their parents, their grandparents, their school.

After supper Lea takes Tina to bed and they wait for Opa,

passing the time playing a game of checkers that Oma keeps in a cupboard in the living room.

Oma washes the supper dishes behind them.

"Help me a minute Joop."

He slips out of his chair, pulling the tea-towel from the peg by the oven and starts to wipe the plates steaming in the drying rack. Aunt Lea spends her evenings sewing for Oma Loggers who has built up a little repair business: turning collars, shortening and lengthening hems, letting out dresses, making something out of nothing. The guilders Lea earns with her sewing supplement the debt she owes to the Loggers. But it means that Oma is left washing the dishes and Joop is detailed to drying duty. She chats to him about her sons while Joop dries and piles up the plates and dishes on the table. Trudi is resting her head in her hands half asleep.

Jozef wonders where Opa has gone. He has been thinking about it, how he has the safest place to hide, safer than his sister and his mother, and he feels as if all their troubles are his fault. If he hadn't panicked in the ghetto, if he had just kept calm then maybe everything would have been alright. They might be sent to the Westerbork camp, but what could they do? Nothing, nothing bad would happen. That's what his Uncle Casper had said; Casper could have been right. By the time he has finished drying the dishes he has convinced himself that he could offer to go back to Amsterdam so that his sister could stay with the Loggers.

Chores completed he gets his book back down from the sideboard and starts to read. He has hardly got past the first sentence when he hears the click of the door latch: Opa is back.

He joins Joop at the table while Oma gets his supper out of the oven where it has been keeping warm. They wait as he eats, eventually pushing his plate away. "OK. I have made some new plans." Joop gently shakes Trudi awake and she sits up rubbing her eyes. Opa Loggers looks at her.

"Trudi you have had a difficult time. You have been clever and brave."

"I don't want to go back to the Smits."

"You won't be going back."

"Am I staying here?"

"No, you can't stay here either," his voice is firm. "You are going on a real adventure."

Trudi looks as if she might cry but she doesn't, instead she smiles tentatively at Joop, and then looks intently at the old man.

Opa Loggers speaks to Trudi as if there is no-one else in the room: "It is a bit of a journey. You are going to go North to Friesland to stay with a family we know. They run a bicycle shop up there in a town called Dokkum and keep a few cows. It's a big house, lots of room, and it is safe. Really safe."

"But how far away?"

"It's about three hours journey, maybe more."

"Three hours!"

"I know. A long way – a real adventure for a young girl like you. But it is a really, really, safe place and that has always been your mother's wish that you go to the safest possible place. A man I know will take you in the back of his van tomorrow. You will take a letter I'm writing tonight. I know this family will look after you, treat you like their own daughter, and they won't betray you. It will be great. There really isn't anyone much up there, very few Nazis, there's no point, Friesland goes nowhere, but it means that you can have a freer life, a much better life. No more hiding all the time. There is a big garden too."

"Like our garden at home?" asks Trudi.

"With apple trees?" asks Joop.

"Maybe."

"It sounds nice," Trudi speaks softly. "But where will mama be and Joop?"

"Joop stays here. He is helping me with some things. Your mother will stay with the farmer for the time being."

"Can't I go to the farm with mamma?"

"No. The farmer needs someone to help him. His wife is ill. He needs someone to look after his wife and their boys. It's not a good place for a little girl."

Joop watches his sister biting her lip, and nervously doing up and undoing one of the buttons on her sweater. He notices how thin and bony her wrists have become.

Joop looks up at Opa Loggers. "I have an idea Opa." He makes the offer then, to go back to the orphanage; he's nearly 12 now, he'll survive, whatever happens. Trudi can then have his safe hiding place with the Loggers.

Opa Loggers folds his hands together and leans forward.

"Joop the children's home isn't in Amsterdam anymore. It's gone. They've gone."

"Where?"

"The home has closed. All the children have been taken to Westerbork, some straight to the camp at Sobibor we think."

"What? Even my friends? Even Maartje and Roza and Wilma?" gasps Trudi her eyes enormous, her mouth open.

"Everyone."

Amsterdam to Sobibor April 1943

The director of the Amsterdam orphanage leans against the cold mettle of the cattle truck as it jerks into life, lifting his head and searching for a crack of cold air from the metal slits in the side; he has to get away from the stench. He still can't understand why they are in a cattle truck and not in a passenger carriage. The others had left on a train last week, a proper passenger train. A creeping sense of foreboding which has been scratching at his conscience for months now stares him in the face. So, this is it, is it? Thank God his parents had not lived to see this. Thank God for that.

He feels someone grabbing at his sleeve and looks down and sees her. And seeing her he lifts his hand and feels the small damp curve of her head.

"We'll be alright, won't we?" she asks staring up at him. "You said we would be alright."

"Of course," he smooths her head. "Of course we will, when we get there, we'll be fine."

He smiles down at the little girl's trusting face and reaches out to hold her hand, something he would never have done before, not before now, not before this day.

The letter had come to the children's home the day before. He had expected it, opened it quickly, sent for all his key staff. In the previous weeks thousands of families from the ghetto had been rounded up and taken to the station to be transported. It had been incredible to watch them pouring down the street, a crying, calling, lumbering human river of people, the ghetto emptying out like a sieve.

The organisation, the military style organisation of the exodus by the Jewish Council now horrified him. He had trusted them. He wonders if Cohen was still sitting behind his mahogany desk, still issuing instructions, smug bastard, or whether he too would be on a train to Westerbork. But they weren't going to Westerbork, they would have been there by now if that had been their destination, but they had been travelling all day, the carriage getting hotter, people fighting over scraps of bread, children crying. Where are they going? His thoughts just keep getting darker.

He strokes the little girl's hand, remembers her shy smile as she conducted visitors to his office at the children's home. All that trust!

They had taken the boys first from the annexe at the end of

last year. That had worried him, but he'd told no-one about his fears. He had made enquiries, spoken to the Jewish Council, and they seemed to think everything was in order, there was nothing strange, not really, about the boys being conscripted. And then ten days ago an order came that 100 of the older children where to be transported out of the ghetto. He remembers the children's brave chins and frightened eyes as they were escorted by rifle carrying soldiers to the collection point outside the Jewish Theatre. He had walked with them, being careful to stand far enough away not to be swept up in the tide of flesh pushed on to trucks bound for the station. He had felt guilty then and gone back to the home and drunk a whole bottle of gin that he had been keeping to celebrate a hoped for liberation, the end of occupation. And today it has been his turn along with the remaining children from the home, several hundred of them of all ages, but mostly younger children the five– and six-year-olds holding hands, lined up crocodile fashion in the hallway as if they were going for a walk in the park. He can see their faces, their trusting eyes, their odd excitement at doing something different at going where their friends had gone, whispering about who they might see.

The stench on the train is getting worse. An old man slips down to the ground, a yellow stream of vomit sliding over his coat, the vile smell mixing with the stale acrid stink of urine, human sweat and fear.

He had been surprised by the cattle trucks. They had been standing on the station, trying to keep staff and children together waiting for a passenger train; they had thought that the metal cattle train was just passing through. He had been amazed when it had stopped, and soldiers had slid back the heavy metal doors to each carriage and told them all to get on.

He had been so gullible! He had urged the staff to get the children into two adjoining carriages and stood back, ushering them forward, but the pressure of people around him had resulted in his being pushed aside, as he shouted to the staff to mind the little ones, hold their hands, help them up. He had somehow got pushed down the platform into another carriage with older people, and the girl. How had she got here?

"I can't breathe," she says, gasping. He elbows an older heavy-jawed man next to him and leans down until he can get his hands under her arms and lift her up so she can feel the cold air coming through the slits in the sides of the cattle truck.

She puts her arms round his neck. "Thank you."

"It's alright. We'll be alright." He speaks softly. Her warm breath tickles his ear, makes him want to cry. He pats her back, feeling the fragile warmth of her bones beneath the skin. He's been trying and trying, but he still can't remember her name.

*

Between 5 March and 23 July 1943, 19 trains containing 34,313 Jews from the Netherlands, arrive in the Sobibor Extermination Camp in Occupied Poland after a journey lasting, on average, three days.

The first two trains consist of passenger wagons; after 10 March the deportees are transported in cattle cars. One transport contains 1,266 children. Some deportees are selected for work details within the camp, others sent to labour camps in the region, but the vast majority are killed within two hours of arrival.

Hetty – Zeist – July

She's been dreaming and in the dream she is sitting in the dunes with Loes and Dirk and suddenly there had been no Loes and Dirk had stretched across and pulled her towards him and she could feel the cool boniness of his arms and that feeling inside of not knowing quite what was going to happen but at the same time knowing and everything around her sharpening: the colour of the sky, the blinding light on the water, the smell of salt air and warm dusty sand, the high mewling cries of seagulls chorusing above them. And then she looked across and it wasn't Dirk but Anton and she reached out to him feeling the warmth of her love for him….when she realised that someone was shaking her.

Someone outside of her dream, was telling her to get up, was pulling at her hand and their hand was small and pudgy and warm. She opens her eyes, only half awake, to see Piet, still in his pyjamas bending over her bed a smile cracking right across his 9-year-old face.

"Get up Hetty! Get up! We are going today. We are going on holiday!"

His excitement is usually infectious, but it's too early, she reaches on to her bedside table and grabs her watch; it is not yet 6 o'clock, she needs another half hour at least in bed.

"Piet?" She limply squeezes his hand. "It's not getting up time yet."

"It is. It is. It's sunny!" He sits down and starts bouncing on her bed. She puts her arms around him to make him stop, feeling the warmth of his small body through the worn fabric of his pyjamas, he wiggles delightedly in her arms and she whispers in his ear: "Go and get dressed Piet. We can't go until we're all dressed." He jumps up and runs across the room, his bare feet thumping merrily on the floorboards, as he rushes out and down the stairs waking everyone up.

Hetty lies back for a moment, closes her eyes and tries to recapture her dream, but nothing. The dream is over; she wants to weep for the normality of it, the sad impossibility of it. She opens her eyes, fully awake. The sun is sliding through the curtains bathing her in its warmth as she drags herself out of bed; there is a huge amount to do before they leave 'on holiday'.

Two months have passed since Hetty was moved from the kitchen and asked to look after a group of older boys who were based in a long low wooden building, sitting on its own, up against the garden fence behind the main house. They had been Erika's group, but Erika had never come back.

"They can get a bit noisy," said Dr Lievegoed when he'd told her she'd be taking on the older boys. He had once interrupted the group playing their own invented game of 'indoor football' with a balled-up piece of old newspaper. But that was mild she soon learned. A week later she was describing the boys' antics always racing around playing different games, knocking furniture, paint, everything over, to a local farmer Vincent Brouwer and his wife Marie over a cup of weak tea. The farmer had been good to the Zonnehuis. When he could, he would give them extra cheese and milk or small sacks of vegetables, knocking on the back door of the kitchen with the booty. Hetty had made a friend of him when she had been working in the kitchen. He reminded her of her Uncle Sam in a way no-one else could, his easy ways, smiling eyes, and the smell of fresh windblown air and fields that he seemed to carry with him. She'd promised to visit the farm and, soon after taking on the boys' group, detoured there on her way back from an Utrecht run. Marie had been fussing round the kitchen making a pie when she got there. Listening to the stories about the boys, washing and wiping her hands after sliding the pie in the oven she suggested Hetty bring the boys to the farm for a break.

"They need space, boys do," she said raising an eyebrow and looking at her husband.

He'd chuckled. "She's thinking of our three."

There was a moment's quiet then: two of their sons had been conscripted to work in a German munitions' factory and the third, the youngest was somewhere in Scotland, they thought. He'd got out with a group of Allied soldiers who had hidden in the barn for a few nights.

"Bring them. Come for a week if you like. Now the weather is fine, they can all sleep in the hay loft, help with the animals, bring in the cows, ride on old Harold the plough horse and run through the fields until they fall asleep," said Vincent. He'd looked up at his wife and she'd nodded her agreement. "There's plenty of room for them to play in the barn if it rains. The boys' old rope swing is in there somewhere, I'll put it up."

"I'd enjoy cooking for some boys again," said Marie patting her husband's shoulder.

Hetty had talked to Nel Lievegoed about the idea during a picnic lunch in the garden. They were surrounded by children – one little boy snuggled on Nel's lap, her own son leaning against her. Nel was all for the trip.

It was decided that Jan van Wettum would go with her, she'd need another teacher there and he was the most experienced they had. He had a natural authority with all children; nothing ever phased him. He also had an easy way with the boys, humoured their antics when they didn't go too far and laughed at their terrible jokes. Although he was more than twice Hetty's age they had become good friends since the day she'd lost the children in the woods.

A date in late June was agreed for a week-long visit to the farm. Vincent was coming after breakfast with a horse and cart to pick up Hetty, Jan van Wettum and eight boys.

Hetty dresses quickly, pulling the thin blankets from her bed and folding them to take with her. She drags an old canvas rucksack out from under the bed that she had packed the previous night, tucking in her hairbrush and toothbrush before yanking on the strings to pull the top tight, pushing her feet into canvas lace ups, she runs downstairs to join the others.

Piet calls out to her as she walks into the kitchen for breakfast, his face covered in jam. "Hetty! Come and sit with me. We are sitting here together!"

She pulls up a chair up between Piet and André whose head is bent in concentration over a piece of half-eaten bread which has been cut into squares, his jaw rhythmically chewing.

"You alright André?"

The eleven-year-old twists his head to look at her, and swallows giving her one of his strange half smiles, the left side of his face completely frozen following an accident when he was a baby.

"Will we have food there?"

"Of course!"

"Will we be safe? I don't think we will be safe outdoors. I don't think so."

"We will be safe. We will sleep in a lovely hayloft and you will have your own blanket and pillow with you," she smooths back a dark lock of hair falling into his eyes. "We will be very, very safe. Mr van Wettum will be with us."

"And Hetty is with us," said Piet putting his sticky hand affectionately on Hetty's arm and bouncing in his seat, nodding his head back and forth in excitement as he tries to eat and speak.

André looks at Hetty steadily and she wonders again about the boy's background. He had been brought to the Zonnehuis by his grandmother who lives just outside of Utrecht. She'd delivered a card once to the grandmother made by André. He'd spent a week bending over it, drawing tiny flowers of yellow and red and blue against wispy blades of grass with a deep blue summer sky. It was a beautiful thing when he had finished it and he had gravely gone to Dr Lievegoed's office and asked for it to be delivered to his grandmother 'for her birthday'. Hetty had taken it to the address on her way back from Utrecht. The grandmother, hair pulled back in a bun had answered the door. Hetty could hear a woman call from inside the house.

"Who is it mooder..."

"It's a woman with a card from André."

"For me?" shouted the disembodied voice from inside the house, collapsing into giggles joined by the deep throaty laugh of a man.

"No, for me."

"So, my imbecile son remembers you and not me?" A much younger woman in a black petticoat had sauntered out of what must have been the living room, a cigarette trapped between bright red lips, dark circles under her eyes. She'd taken the cigarette from her mouth blowing smoke into the air and stared at Hetty but spoke to the older woman.

"Show me."

The grandmother had started to push the front door closed, shutting Hetty out, already talking to the younger woman. But as Hetty got to the garden gate the door opened again and the old woman had poked her head out and called out to her. "Thank André. Tell him I think of him every day. Tell him to be good." Then banged the door shut.

She had repeated the grandmother's words to André not once but ten times and was curious to find that he didn't ask about his mother or about anyone else living in the house because clearly there had been others there. She had seen soldiers' boots lined up in the hallway.

She watches as André quietly chews his last mouthful of bread, picking up her cooling cup of coffee and taking a final gulp.

"Come on, clear the table. Get your luggage – don't forget anything."

The boys scramble out of their chairs, put their plates on the sideboard and disappear to collect their things. There is a vague hope that while they are away the peeling green striped wallpaper in their room will be stripped off, the walls whitewashed over and a broken window frame fixed.

Five minutes later they are all tumbling out of the door with their knapsacks, jumping up and down in the porch as Jan van Wettum appears with the two oldest boys who had their own tiny attic bedroom at the top of the house and Vincent drives the cart through the gate.

The excitement at the sight of a huge cart horse in front of the Zonnehuis is intense and children and teachers pour out to see it. It is then that Hetty sees someone walking behind the cart, an SS soldier from the camp. He taps the side of the cart with a stick, walking around it. Hetty slides behind Jan van Wettum and the bigger of the two teenagers.

"What's happening here?" asks the officer.

"We are just taking some of the children camping. Mr Brouwer has kindly invited us to his farm," replies Jan van Wettum casually.

"How many are going?"

"Just ten of us, myself, Hetty here, and eight boys."

"These boys," he points at the boys now standing quietly in a group, suddenly drained of all excited energy.

"Yes, these are the boys."

The SS officer walks up and down in front of them.

"And no-one else?"

"I think eight children is enough?"

The soldier looks in the back of the cart, turning over some sacking Vincent has put there for the boys to sit on.

"And when will you be back?"

"In a week."

The soldier continues walking around the cart, slowing down to look under it as well as in it. Eventually when it seems he will never finish checking the cart, he stops. "You better go then. Please tell Mr Lievegoed that he should always inform us of things like this. Any movement, any change."

"Of course. I am sorry you weren't informed. The farm is not that far away."

"Still." The SS soldier spins on his heels and leaves as quickly as he had come.

The boys climb into the back of the cart. Jan van Wettum climbs up on the front holding the reins while Vincent ensures the tailgate is secure. Hetty wheels her bike around from the side of the house.

"Aren't you coming in the cart?" asks Vincent.

"No, I'll ride alongside on my bike," says Hetty.

"I saw Anton on the way through," says Vincent rummaging in his pocket. "He asked me to give you this." He hands her a roughly folded piece of paper.

"Thanks Vincent."

He jumps up into the driving seat and takes the reins. The boys are yelping like puppies with excitement. Hetty quietly unfolds the piece of paper. She reads it quickly, feeling the blood drain from her face. She scrunches the paper into a ball and puts it in her pocket.

"You OK Hetty?" asks Jan van Wettum, turning round and catching her eye as the cart moves out of the drive, the boys waving and shouting to the children staying behind.

Hetty feels the blood in her ears and leans forward on her bike, forcing herself to smile. "I'll be fine."

"You sure?"

"Yes, yes… I'm fine." She pushes down on the pedals of her bike. She won't, can't think about it now. The message has confirmed her fears. She focusses on the boys who are pointing things out along the way, waving, and shouting out to everyone they see. She breathes in and starts whistling to entertain the children, some of them laughing and whistling back.

The day sweeps by: a picnic in the fields of cheese and bread and a plum cake that must have used a month of the farmer's sugar ration; building a den in the woods; games in the field. Tired an exhausted, nested with blankets in the hayloft, they are all exhausted. Sleep takes over, but Hetty wakes breathless, as if she was pulling herself from drowning, to find Jan van Wettum, kneeling by her side, shaking her shoulder to wake her. "Hetty! Hetty!" she can feel his breath on her fac.

"What…What's happening?" She pulls herself up from her stupor.

"You were crying…you are waking the boys…you were crying and…you were shouting," he looks gently at her. "In your sleep." He smiles.

"Sorry. Just a nightmare. I get them sometimes." She sits up lifting her hand to her face which is wet with tears, wiping them away with the back of her hand. "A nightmare… That's all. Thanks for waking me. I'll be fine now." He shuffles back to his makeshift bed on the other side of the boys.

But it was more than a nightmare. All those people. She had been thinking about them all day in the back of her mind. Thinking about the hospital, the old man who kept the fires going, the matron who always told her off, her friends. She had been thinking about Phillipe and Hannah, sweet, kind Hannah. All those people. Her dreams had taken her back to the wards full of patients, the noise and clatter and smell of disinfectant and boiled cabbage and then she had turned a corner to go into another ward and it was empty and she had raced through that ward and into another but all the wards were empty, the beds unmade, spiders spinning grey webs across the windows. And she had gone outside, and they were there, walking towards the station, Hannah calling to her, telling her she misses her, telling her to come too. They were going on holiday. They were going to a camp. And in her dream she had tried to stop them, telling them it wasn't a holiday camp. They mustn't go, they had got that wrong and she had looked down and seen she was holding a red plastic bucket half full of shells. It is not a holiday she had shouted, but they kept going…and then they were all gone the last one turning around as they disappeared into nothingness her face hollow, fleshless, charred black, teeth in a rictus smile, a finger beckoning her.

Awake, Hetty relives the dream, her heart beating fast, sweat on her brow. She leans out of her makeshift bed and finds her neatly folded clothes, fishes around for her sweater and the piece of paper in the pocket.

A week ago she had asked Anton to find out what had happened to the hospital. She had read about the intensified clearing of the ghetto, people being sent in droves to Westerbork and other camps. There were pictures in the underground press and in the German sponsored press, but there had been no mention of the Jewish hospital, and she had hoped the hospital was safe. Surely sick people would just be a burden in the camps? But she had wanted to know for sure. Anton's message was clear.

"Hospital no longer there. All gone – patients and staff – not sure which camp."

She crumples the message in her hand, lies down and pulls her blanket up and over her head. She isn't alone, she knows that. She can hear the boys turning and snuffling in their sleep, but right now, right at this moment, she feels like the history of her life has been wiped away, that she is the last survivor.

Joop – Utrecht – July

Joop huddles closer to the green painted back door; the rain is pelting down, splattering against his legs. He puts the package down, leaning it against the door to protect it from the rain, and examines his hands, picking coal dust out of his fingernails.

He smooths down his hair, and then picks up the package and knocks. He can hear her inside, moving about, going into the living room and coming back. He waits, then, finally, tentatively knocks again. This time the door is opened.

Mrs Lodder looks him up and down and then stands back to let him into the house. She doesn't smile, she never smiles. He steps past her, into the kitchen, rubbing his wet shoes on the mat in front of the door and handing her the package. She places it on the small scrubbed kitchen table and waves him through to the dining room. Mr Lodder is already there, sitting at the polished table, reading a book, stroking his greying moustache.

"Ah, Joop," a smile slants across his face.

"I brought meat." A memory scratches at him of the butcher's shop and his father, and his father's hands.

"Yes, how kind. Thank Mr Loggers will you? Sit down. Sit down there and we will continue."

Joop sees the pile of textbooks, just as he had left them the previous day, the grammar on top, a blue covered exercise book by the side. He pulls back the chair covered with a towel in front of his place. No-one says anything, but he knows the Lodders think him dirty; they don't want him sitting on one of their plush red velvet upholstered dining room chairs. Opa Loggers had laughed when he had told him about the towel, thought it was the funniest thing he had heard in a week, and Joop had laughed too, but he didn't really find it funny. He slides into the seat and the lessons begin.

For all his oddity Mr Lodder is a good teacher, indeed had been head of one of the major schools in Utrecht before his retirement the previous year. The deal, made as if by second nature by Opa Loggers, is that Mr Lodder will teach Joop, three or four mornings a week, and bring him up to the necessary educational standard for his age so that when the war ends – "when Joop not if" Opa Loggers had stressed – Joop can return to school without being behind in his education. In return for this schooling Mr Lodder and his wife benefit from the valuable goods stored by the Loggers: coal from the basement, bartered food from their larder.

Opa had been delighted at the deal, rubbed his hands together and sucked in his cheeks when he told Joop. And, in the undercurrent of unvoiced emotions, Joop understood that the demographics of his relationship with Opa Loggers had changed. The lessons, which had begun two months earlier, somehow signified his affection and interest in him beyond the agreement to give him a safe place to hide. Not that anyone said anything. His aunt had been indifferent when he told her, just carried on sewing, pinning the hem she was shortening on a blue dress. "That's nice for you Joop," she'd commented tersely out of the corner of her mouth jabbing another pin into the dress. "Perhaps you can then help Tina with her reading?"

Joop had not immediately warmed to the gaunt faced teacher, who had inspected him like a spider would a less than perfect fly when they had first met. But after a week or two he began to develop a begrudging respect for the old man, sometimes even enjoying the education that was unravelling in front of him. His real problem was with Mrs Lodder.

He settles himself on the towel covered chair.

"OK Joop we will start with English today. The green book." Mr Lodder points at the pile and Joop pulls the book out, opening it as directed. He scratches his head idly as Lodder starts explaining the intricacies of the past tense and the lesson glides forward. After twenty minutes of explanation and repetition, Mr Lodder takes the textbook and flips through it to an exercise at the back. "Let's see how you do. Translate this." He passes the book across the table and looks at his watch. "Ten minutes."

Joop picks up the pencil with the rubber on the end that Oma Loggers had given him when he had started lessons and starts to write. He struggles for the right words as he translates the paragraph about summertime from Dutch into English – *in the summer the boys had camped on the beach*. Mr Lodder is a stickler when it came to accuracy. He starts to write. Who can possibly camp on the beach these days?

Thoughts of Scheveningen fly through his mind, the chatter on the promenade, dogs barking, bicycling along the seafront, a summer breeze blowing through his hair, the gulls wheeling and crying overhead. But the beach would be empty now. In fact Scheveningen is empty. He wonders briefly about his aunt and uncle and cousins.

He shakes his head trying to concentrate. There had been a raid the previous night and he and his aunt had spent most of it tucked in under the kitchen floor listening to Opa Loggers being interrogated about the whereabouts of his sons.

"They are in Germany. They were conscripted like other men their age, you know that," the old man had claimed impatiently. "I haven't heard from them in months."

"They are not in Germany," came the guttural reply.

"Well, where are they then?"

And the search of the house intensified. After a while Opa Loggers had invited the officer in charge to share a shot or two of Schnapps and although the search had then dissipated, the officer had stayed for a second drink. Waking up still underground Joop had felt a sudden wave of claustrophobia. Sometimes it just got to him, that feeling of being caged, trapped, however kind the Loggers were. This wasn't what life was supposed to be like; his normal life had seeped away like sand through his fingers.

"How are you doing?" Joop jumps as he realises that Mr Lodder must have gone into the kitchen to get a drink and is now looking over his shoulder.

"Yes, just finishing." Joop grips the pencil and guesses the last line of translation, then passes the work to Mr Lodder.

The teacher traces the lines of writing with his finger. "No, no, Joop. You have made a mistake here. A silly mistake," he sucks in his cheeks. "Let's go through this again. You are not a stupid boy, you can do this." He pulls a crumpled white handkerchief from his pocket and blows his nose as he goes to sit on the opposite side of the table.

Joop is tired and just wishes the lesson over. Mr Lodder pulls the yellowing foolscap notepad he uses for teaching Joop towards him as Joop glances at the clock, the minute hand dragging its way around the hour.

It is another half hour before Mr Lodder finally lets Joop put away the English grammar and open a history book. History is Lodder's favourite subject; it is amazing how many history lessons Joop gets in comparison to others, and any history class eventually leaches into a discussion about the war. Mr Lodder is convinced that the entrance into the war of the Americans the previous year will change everything. He has a real admiration for the Americans. It is his ambition to move there when the war is over, his only son had moved to New York in the late 1930's to work for an international trading company and they will join him.

But today the conversation turns to the final expulsion of all Jews from Amsterdam. Joop had seen the paper that morning, read it over Opa's shoulder, caught sight of the picture of a little girl forlornly clinging on to her mother's leg. He was sure he recognised the little girl. He'd looked at the headline: "Last Jews deported from Amsterdam". The story took up most of the front page, with a quote from one of the Nazi officers in charge of clearing the ghetto that he hoped Holland would soon be *"Judenrein"* free of Jews. Joop couldn't imagine it, gape mouthed he had wondered what had happened to all the thousands of Jews in the ghetto. How could they move all those people? Why? The mother in the picture is dressed in a dark coat with a headscarf wrapped tightly over her hair waving desperately at someone unseen with a gloved hand, ignoring the little girl who is staring straight into the camera, oblivious of the crowd around her, men in Homburg hats and caps, tousle haired teenagers and right on the edge of the picture a tired old man half bent over his cane, older than Opa, a Nazi officer standing by him, holding him up by the collar of his coat, twisting the fabric.

He discusses the article with Mr Lodder who had been surprisingly sympathetic. He's read the article too. The last line had been chilling, warning any Dutch citizens of the dire consequences of hiding Jews.

"It's not right, Joop. We are and always have been a tolerant nation. Consider our history." He looks Joop in the eye. "This will change Holland. I'm sorry, I truly am," It was a rare acknowledgement of who Joop was, and he blushes.

"OK lessons over," said Mr Lodders pushing back his chair.

Joop puts his pencil down next to his exercise book and gets up, carefully pushing the chair under the table. He'll leave Mrs Lodder to straighten her stupid towel.

"Thank you, Mr Lodder."

The teacher nods and smiles.

He leaves the room, speeds through the empty kitchen and out of the back door. The rain has eased to a drizzle and pulling up his collar, Joop runs into the small garden and pushes his way through the gap in the hedge into the Loggers' garden. He runs into the kitchen. Opa is sitting at the table filling his pipe. Aunt Lea has come down from her room at the top of the house and is sitting with him, Oma Loggers is busy making lunch and his cousin is sitting on the floor, playing an imaginary game with a rag doll.

Opa looks up scraping his fingers back through his hair.

"Hello Joop! Good lesson? Sit down. I'm just giving your aunt some news about your mother. You should hear it too."

He clears his throat and wraps his hands together, rubbing his thumbs against one another.

Joop slides into the chair next to his aunt.

"There is no easy way of saying this. Bets has had to move again."

Lea's head drops onto her folded arms on the table. "She was with that bloody farmer, wasn't she? The one in Werkhoven whose wife was ill?"

The old man nods slowly and Joop can see the warning in his eyes, but his aunt goes on. "Oh please, you know what happened? I can guess what happened. I can imagine anyway. He was a dirty old man. And Joop is not a child anymore. He's 12 years old. He's nearly a man. He knows what goes on."

The old man puts his hand up to stop her talking.

"Look Lea she has a new place. She is with a cousin of hers in hiding. She is happy about it. The fact is that she is now in a safer place."

Lea starts to sob. "This was a safe place."

"Lea! Enough."

Joop feels the blood drain from his face, he feels the sides of his mouth sticking together and wonders if he can actually speak, his mind is spinning, please don't let anything happen to his mother.

Lea gets up from her chair, her voice calmer. "I'm sorry," she mutters under her breath. "I'm going upstairs. I've got work to do." At the kitchen she turns and catches Joop's eye; the accusation in her face makes him wince.

He hasn't seen his mother since the move to the farm. Unbidden a memory rolls around in his head: they are all in the kitchen, his mother teaching Trudi to walk, standing behind her and walking like a penguin, feet splayed out, his sister's tiny feet rocking into each accidental step forward. After every few steps his mother picks Trudi up and shouts "hooray, she's walking" and it makes Trudi giggle and Joop laugh. He always wonders whether his mother had done the same thing with him when he was a baby.

He is pulled from his thoughts by Opa talking to him again. "Your mother wants me to tell you not to worry Joop. The most important thing to her is that you and Trudi are safe. Do you understand that?"

"You saw her?"

"Only briefly."

"Can I see her?"

"No."

"But this is the third time she has had to move?"

"So, let's hope it's the last."

Joop feels guilt sift acidly through him: he didn't even need the look from Lea, he feels it all the time, would feel it until the day he died. His mother has given up her safe hiding place for him.

The old man gets up from the table with a sigh. "Come on Joop. I promise you she is fine." He taps the table. "Come on now. There's someone in the front room waiting to talk to us."

"Who?"

"My son, Victor."

Hetty – August – Zeist

They creep up the stairs like guilty children suppressing giggles, holding hands. Reaching the door of his room Anton winces as he turns the handle and hears the metallic click as the lock disengages echoing into the quiet of the corridor. He turns and Hetty feels the warmth of his arm going around her, holding her closer.

"You know I love you?"

"And I love you back."

She lifts her face to his, smiling, reaching up to kiss him softly on the lips.

He lives with his uncle in a small redbrick house on a quiet road just outside of Zeist. The house is half hidden by a cherry tree in the front garden, a neat brick paved path leading to the front door. It smells of old furniture and tobacco. Coats hang in the hallway, a grandfather clock, keeping noisy time.

They can hear the uncle's snuffling snores as they push open the door to Anton's room.

She remembers meeting his uncle for the first time, tall, broad-shouldered with an unruly head of grey hair and wide smile which wrinkled his face as he gripped her hand almost too tightly, insisting she call him by his first name, Jacques.

He had ushered her in to the kitchen with Anton and made them sit and talk to him while he cooked a supper; potatoes and carrots and some sort of concocted egg dish. He opened the back door to show her his garden, neat rows and rows of vegetables and a small hen coop at the back.

"We eat well, don't we Anton?"

Anton had smiled and agreed and gripped Hetty's hand whispering in her ear "He likes you."

They'd had supper together at least once a week ever since and it always made her think of her family, sitting round the table, arguing, eating. Anton and his uncle were more casual, ate in the kitchen more than the dining room, but the warmth was there, the feeling of being family. After supper they would wash the dishes while his uncle smoked his pipe and reminisced about the past or talked about the day's antics of his two chickens who he has nicknamed Beaky and Pecker, unbelievable stories made up to make them laugh. He avoids talking about the war, the occupation.

After he has gone to bed, she and Anton sit in the darkening garden and talk about life now and life how they want it to be before retreating to Anton's room as quietly as they can.

Anton now pulls her through his bedroom door, pushes it closed and wraps her tightly in his arms. The closeness, the warmth of him makes her pulse race.

He reaches for the light, but she stops him turning it on. She looks into the speckle grey green edges of his eyes, lifting her hand to his face, catching his soft direct gaze, that is what she loves, the honesty in his face. She wants children like that with strong faces, honest eyes.

Later, much later, as she lies in bed and he lies unconscious beside her, she breathes him in, the earthy, soapy smell of him, the comforting warmth of his skin next to hers. She daydreams about a future she hopes they might have together, if and when the war ends, if they both survive it.

She knows she wants to stay with Anton. She dreams about a small house of their own like his uncle's, a garden, children, a family, a normal life.

They have talked about the 'when's' and if's that can be once they are no longer fenced in by the occupation, neither wanting to believe it can go on for ever or even for very much longer. He wants to marry her now, but she has told him she won't marry until after the war is over, until she knows they are safe. What she doesn't tell him is that she doesn't want to entangle him and his uncle in the complications of her life, of her being Jewish. She's told Anton little of her life in Amsterdam, the cruelty and poverty she witnessed, the hospital....it's the past and she wants to keep it in the past. She knows, he knows that it was a bad time, a terrifying time and that is enough.

Afterwards, after the war, when, not if the Netherlands are liberated, she's promised, they will get engaged, plan a wedding, celebrate. Only then will she know if her family are still alive.

Turning over in bed, she conjures up their faces, imagines their delight; her father pouring everyone celebratory glasses of Jenever, her mother's happiness, her sister's joy. She prays her brother will be there too. Hans would tease her mercilessly about Anton but she knows he would embrace him like a brother.

But until that time comes when they can all be together again, Anton and Jacques are her family. She looks at his sleeping face, the soft curve of his cheek, strong nose. He is her everything. She snuggles up against him. He half wakes and turns and spoons her into his arms, falling almost immediately asleep again.

She weaves her hand into his as it falls across her stomach and for a rare moment, just before she falls asleep, she feels as if everything could be alright.

Joop – Utrecht – August

The stuff looks disgusting thinks Joop as he peers into the buckets under the table in the cellar. He watches the dirty beige liquid, pieces of rye floating on the surface alongside a few bloated Juniper berries. He admits it's beginning to smell a bit alcoholic, but it looks like it will never turn into anything even vaguely drinkable. He isn't going to tell them that though – not the old man or Victor who arrived back in the middle of the night and is still asleep.

He watches the creamy grey surface for bubbles. Nothing. He wants to wake Victor and tell him, but he will have to wait.

The three buckets, one wrestled from Oma Loggers back kitchen and the other two somehow obtained by the old man, have been filled with a mix of ground germinated rye, yeast, and water. He'd watched the unpleasant mix ferment over the past few days and now that there are no more bubbles, the "mash", as Victor calls it, is ready for distilling into gin. The gin distillery is the latest crazy money-making scheme indulged in by Opa Loggers, this time at the instigation of his son Victor.

Joop had warmed to Victor the moment they had met

four weeks ago when he had risked coming out of hiding on his uncle's farm 80 kilometres away in Doesburg to visit his parents. He looks like a younger version of his father, but with lighter brown hair. Within an hour of entering the house on Bachstraat he had started outlining his idea for distilling home brewed gin to Opa Loggers and to Joop whose active participation in monitoring and mixing the fermenting liquor and its subsequent distillation would be key to its success. Victor had been inspired by a night-time visit to a farm near to his uncle's where, to his surprise he'd been offered a tot of gin. It was good, or at least more than passable, and with a few sincere compliments to his host and a little persuasion, he had eked out the formula, as long as he could get hold of the two key ingredients – rye and yeast – he could have a go. On his uncle's farm they had plenty of rye and his father had access, through the bakery, to yeast. On a second visit to the neighbouring farm, they had shown him the still.

Joop admits to himself that the project couldn't have come at a better time, the summer has meant a drying up of demand for coal, so he'd been given the very boring task by Opa Loggers of wearing down an important forged Nazi seal used by one of the underground groups. If it was to pass inspection it couldn't look too new and so for hours on end he would be told to use the stamp repeatedly on one piece of paper, wearing the sharp edges down, his arm aching with the effort and his head with boredom. The gin business was much more exciting.

Joop looks at the rather shaky contraption made from an old copper pan and bits of pipe that is their gin distillery. He doubts its ability to produce anything like the gin in the red and silver labelled bottle that used to sit on the sideboard at home. Expressing this hesitation two days ago Opa Loggers had just clapped him on the back with a grin. "We can but try Joop. We can but try."

Joop crouches down to stare into the buckets again, daring the liquid to bubble up. He is about to stand up when he hears someone coming down the cellar steps and turns to see Victor, a broad grin on his face.

"How's it going partner?"

"I think it's ready. It's stopped bubbling. Have a look."

Victor crouches down next to him sniffing loudly. "Smells good doesn't it?"

"Sort of," says Joop doubtfully.

"Time to start straining it, Joop," Victor stands and stretches looking at the makeshift still. "And then we get to use this little beauty."

"Today?"

"Why not today?"

Victor disappears upstairs and then returns with a strainer and a large saucepan he's purloined from his mother and a piece of muslin. He puts the saucepan on the table, the strainer inside and lines it with the muslin.

"You hold the strainer steady Joop, I'll pour."

Victor ladles the liquid through the muslin, but even decanted the liquid in the pan looks like dirty bath water. By lunch time they are ready to start the distilling process.

"What if there's a raid?"

"We give them a drink," jokes Opa Loggers. But it is no joke and Jozef knows that in the unlucky event of that happening they will have to find room for Victor under the kitchen floor boards and someone will be squeezed on the rubble between the rafters as there isn't enough room for three of them in the makeshift dugout. That unlucky someone is bound to be him. He doesn't really mind, he likes having Victor about.

The three of them gather around the makeshift still after lunch and using a flame of gas from a supply rerouted to avoid the gas meter, they start to steam the alcohol through the still.

They watch the first clear cup of liquid fill and then a second, pouring the cups into a jug and then into sterilized bottles.

Victor is rubbing his hands with delight and looks up at the old man who is turning one of the bottles around in his hands. "I think it's time to taste."

Victor runs upstairs and comes back with three glasses passing one to his father and one to Joop.

"Me too?"

"You too. You've done the work," says Victor. The old man just shrugs.

Victor pours them all shots.

"OK. Together." Victor swigs back the alcohol at the same time as the old man and after a second's hesitation so does Joop. It feels like liquid fire, running through him, burning his mouth and his throat. He gasps and they all start to cough and the old man grimaces and shakes his head. Catching his breath, he turns to Victor. "There's something wrong with that Victor. We will kill off any customers we get with that stuff."

"Maybe it needs to be distilled again?"

"After supper."

After a hurried meal, Victor and Joop return and put the liquid through the still a second time. It is after midnight before they finish. The old man has gone to bed and Victor pours Joop and himself a small shot of the new gin. They drink it down at the same time. Joop's throat burns with the taste but Victor is smiling. "That's the stuff!" he nods his head with delight and pours them both a second shot.

Joop drinks it back. His head is thumping, he isn't sure whether it's from tiredness or the alcohol as he holds out his glass and they both take a third shot.

"*Proost*" He laughs and claps Joop on the back. "I'm taking a couple of bottles of this back with me to Doesburg."

September – Utrecht De Meern

It is completely unexpected. The two women, Joop's mother Bets and her cousin Dina, are washing clothes in the outhouse when they hear the front door bang and footsteps running through the corridor. Carl, the youngest of the three boys in the house where they are hiding, looks at them, breathless.

"Go. Father says go. They are coming. The Nazis are coming."

Bets drops the shirt she is wringing into the pile of wet laundry and feels a churning in her stomach.

"Go!"

"Come on Bets get your coat. We'll get out of here."

"We can't."

"We can. We will just walk away as if we do that every day."

Dina throws Bets coat at her and pulls her towards the front door. Doing up buttons and pulling on hats, they walk out of the gate. Glancing down the road, Bets can see the commotion; the truck, a clutch of policemen and SS officers banging on doors, a baby crying, an old woman leaning against a fence shaking her head, two dogs barking. She takes it all in as her cousin loops her arm through hers and pulls her in the opposite direction towards the bridge crossing the canal, leading out of the village.

"We don't have any papers."

"No-one will stop us."

"They might."

As they walk towards the bridge, they see an old couple coming out of the house on the corner, looking curiously at them.

"People don't know us. They know we don't belong."

"Shut up. No-one will say anything. We just have to keep walking."

"The old couple?"

"They can't make out who we are. Calm down Bets. Keep walking."

Bets is aware of every sound around her, of her own breathing, the slapping sound of their feet as they walk. In her head she wishes she'd hidden in the house or the cellar. Turning a corner, she sees two Nazis, standing chatting in the middle of the road. She draws in a terrified breath, yanks her arm away from her cousins and turns back. "I can't do this Dina. Sorry, I can't". She starts walking back towards the house, head down, and collides into a Nazi officer.

He grabs her by the arms.

"Who are you?"

Bets freezes; her mouth working, no words coming out.

"I asked you. Who are you? Where are your papers?"

"I....I...."

Later squatting in the corner of a police cell, surrounded by the stench of other prisoners, an old man chanting a prayer, she wonders what had possessed her to turn back? Why had she been so stupid? So afraid? She puts her head in her hands and prays; God help her children, God help them wherever they were. Waking and sleeping she thinks of them, thinks of the life they had, thinks of the life she wants them to have, thinks of Sam. She prays that Loggers is as good as his word; that Jozef and Trudi are safe.

Joop – Utrecht – September

When he hears about his mother's arrest Joop buckles in two, as if Opa Loggers had punched him hard in the belly. He races out of the room to the privy outside the back door and throws up; his body shaking with fear. He wants to scrape back the past hour to the one before, when he didn't know. He wants the knowledge to disappear to the transparent nothingness of a nightmare; for it not to be true. He feels tears rolling down his face, sobs racking his body. It is nearly half an hour before he can pull himself together enough to go back into the house.

In the kitchen Lea sits at the table, her head in her hands, muffled sobs shaking through her. Joop creeps past her and down to the cellar, the only place his aunt won't go. He crouches on the floor next to the gin still. His head spins with questions without answers, scraping for hope from somewhere in all the despair.

It is days before Aunt Lea speaks to him again.

It is days before he can speak about it at all and then only to Opa.

"Is there any chance?" the question squeezes out when they are decanting a new load of gin into bottles.

"There is always a chance."

But Joop knows; he has been told more times than he can count, that the penalty for a Jew found hiding will be hard, will be final. His hope for his mother is more fragile than a soap bubble.

"Can we do anything? Anything at all?" he asks Opa a week later.

"We wait. You keep safe. You work hard." Opa faces him square on, looks him in the eye. "Whatever Joop, we'll try to keep you safe. One day it will be over. I am sure of that. And when that day comes it is up to you. You have a responsibility to make something of your life – for your father, for your mother, for all your family. You survive for them. And you succeed in life for them."

PART 5

1944
Hell's Fury

Hetty – Zeist – June

She doesn't see him. She is coming out of the council office, carefully putting her purse back in her bag, deep in thought, when she bumps straight into him.

"Sorry, so sorry." She steps back as he steps aside and then, recognising her, grabs her by the elbow.

Closing her bag, she apologises again. "I wasn't looking."

"Hetty! It's me! Don't you recognise me?"

She looks up into the ice-blue eyes of SS Sergeant Wolfgang Hoffman and her good mood plummets. He's back.

He grins. "We meet again!" He doesn't let go of her arm and fumbles for words: "What are you doing in town?"

"Shopping." She feels her skin prickling uncomfortably. She knows he's trying to be friendly, more than friendly; he was trying before he left for Paris a year ago. She'd met him after that awful incident in the woods, losing the children, a memory she wishes she could erase.

She disengages his arm and tries a brief smile: "Welcome back sergeant." She steps around him, but he steps in front of her.

"Do you want to have a drink?" He flicks his wrist and looks at his watch. "I have to go to our headquarters, but I have some time now?"

Hetty looks up and out of the corner of her eye sees Mrs de Graff across the road walking her dog, furtively looking at them, her face shrivelled with disapproval. Mrs de Graff had been forced to move out of her home when the SS commandeered it and all its contents – her silver, her furniture, her beloved piano – for one of the SS officers and his family. She has moved in with her daughter, who plays the piano for singing lessons at the Zonnehuis. But the older woman has found it impossible to settle in her daughter's home and is known to take her distress out on everyone. She glares across the road.

Hetty turns to Sergeant Hoffman: "I really don't have time to stop." She walks to the bike stand, empty except for her old wooden wheeled bike.

She pulls it into the street and Sergeant Hoffman grabs the handlebars: "I'll walk with you."

They turn down the road and are now walking parallel to Mrs de Graff. Sgt Hoffman starts to recount his movements over the past year; the delights of Paris, the difficulties of war, the terrible losses in Normandy, his belief that, despite Allied advances into France, the Third Reich will recover, will win. He shakes his head and suddenly asks about the children – and particularly the ones she 'lost' in the wood.

It was in the months after the boys' rescue that the sergeant had sought her out, inviting her to go for a walk or a drink. She was beginning to run out of excuses when he'd been posted to Paris. The relief had been immense. She had been sorry to hear rumours of his return from Wilma the cook. For the past 18 months Wilma has occasionally shared the Zonnehuis kitchen with the fat SS mess sergeant who accompanied Wolfgang in returning the boys. He comes over to bake pies and cook stews –

enjoying the huge cast iron range in the Zonnehuis kitchen and probably the company of a like-minded foody like Wilma. He gets in the way, but Wilma holds her tongue, listens, passes on information and, when possible, he slides scraps of fat and meat from the SS camp supplies into the Zonnehuis stew pot.

Hetty's bike rattles along the cobbled road. "God knows how you ride this heap of junk," complains Sergeant Hoffman as the bike jerks under his hand. Hetty says nothing but she knows that if the bike had been much more than a repaired wreck it would have been taken by the Nazis months ago, like every other good bike in town.

Despite Wolfgang's suggestion that the Normandy landings are just a blip, the Allies sweep across France makes her blood tingle with a sense of a possible end. It has injected the once disparate Dutch resistance with renewed energy. This afternoon, for the second time in a week, she will cycle more than 80 kilometres through woods and along muddy canal paths to Zwolle to deliver false papers to Allied airmen shot down and in hiding. Her nerves are stretched by the thought of the journey ahead– bumping into Wolfgang Hoffman is the last thing she needs.

Deep in these thoughts of her own, she realises she has not been paying full attention to Wolfgang who is talking about his sister. She's a pianist, a student at the Berlin Conservatoire before the war. They are halfway down the avenue leading east out of Zeist. She glances across the road; Mrs de Graaf is still there. Hetty wonders if she is shadowing them but then looking up at the street sign realises that of course, Mrs de Graf's house is on this road. She's going to check on it, to bitterly gaze at the roses climbing over her garden wall and watch the comings and goings of the SS officer's family.

As they approach the house Hetty sees a flatbed lorry sitting outside it, the tailgate down, furniture being packed inside.

"The captain is moving back to Germany," explains Wolfgang. That'll please Mrs de Graff thinks Hetty glancing across the road at her. But Mrs de Graff has stopped still, her mouth tight; she is winding the dog's lead around her hand, deaf to his whimpering as he rises on his back legs, hanging from his collar, front legs paddling as they search for solid ground.

Wolfgang follows Hetty's gaze.

"I think something's wrong. Maybe I should…."

Wolfgang cuts her off: "She is just a miserable old crow Hetty. Stay here. Someone else is going to her." And as they watch a young woman approach and puts her hand on the old lady's arm, loosen her grip on the lead.

"The captain's wife and daughters left yesterday, once they have loaded up this truck and the captain has left, she can go and look around the house. She should be happy. Who knows, she might be able to move back in if the house isn't needed." Wolfgang smiles "There's a nice piano in the house. The Captain thought my sister might like it. He's taking it back to Germany for her. Such a thoughtful man. He told me that he met my sister once, heard her play. He was impressed."

"But its Mrs de Graf's piano."

The soldier looks across the road. "She doesn't play it does she? I thought it was her daughter who played." He sighs, the white bone of his knuckles appearing as he grips the handlebars of the bike more tightly. "Weren't you listening, Hetty? My sister's house in Hamburg was badly bombed, her piano damaged beyond repair. It's lucky she is alive, lucky that she was visiting our mother at the time of the attack. She is talented. She needs a piano."

"Yes, but."

"But what?"

"They seem to be taking most of Mrs de Graf's furniture, not just the piano."

"He probably needs it. I don't know. You forget how lucky you are here. Many families in Germany have lost everything. Absolutely everything."

Hetty reaches across and takes her bike from him. "I have to go... We're short staffed." She glances across at Mrs de Graff. A little boy crouches down on the pavement playing with the dog while two women talk to Mrs de Graff, trying to persuade her to be quiet, to go with them.

He follows her gaze across the road. "That woman has got nothing to complain about – her home is still standing."

There's a shout and they both swerve automatically round towards the house. Two men carrying out a polished dining room table had let it slip and the legs slam down on the pavement.

"Be careful, for God's sake you idiots," shouts the man in the doorway.

"That's the captain," says Wolfgang.

"That's her furniture," says Hetty. Wolfgang flushes, she doesn't know whether from embarrassment or anger and she doesn't wait to find out. The blood pounds in her ears as she grabs her bike, gets on it and sets off, the soldier's eyes boring into her. She doesn't look back.

Hetty – Zeist – July

Hetty lies on her back in the garden of the children's home, looking up through the canopy of trees, leaves twisting and rustling in the relieving breeze. She feels the sun on her bare legs but has carefully positioned her head under the dark green shade of one of the camellia bushes edging this side of the garden. She feels dozy, half asleep in the sun, enjoying the quiet hum of a lazy afternoon, the gentle chatter of the two boys sitting on the lawn next to her.

She shuffles up on to her elbows to look at them They are playing an invented game with the pebbles from the path: Luuk and Tim, one so physically handicapped he sometimes has difficulty feeding himself, the other so painfully shy he hardly ever speaks. Most of the staff and children have gone to the wedding of one of the teachers in the Catholic Church in town, setting off in the finest clothes they could conjure up, flowers pinned into the girls' hair, the mood merry as they piled into the back of a horse-drawn cart. She and Mina, one of the younger local helpers, have volunteered to stay behind with those too young, too disabled or too shy to go.

Tim is collecting handfuls of pebbles, Luuk separating them into different colours and handing them back to Tim who is stringing them out in competing rows. They have been completely absorbed in the task for more than half an hour.

"So, how is it going boys?" ask Hetty. Breaking their companionable silence, the boys look up at her and smile.

"Don't know yet," says Luuk. "The pale grey ones are the ones we have most of, but it might be different in different parts of the drive."

Hetty smiles at the delicious pointlessness of their game. She looks up at the back of the house and sees Mina through the window rocking a crying toddler and waves to her. She half wishes Rosa had stayed behind rather than Mina, she hardly ever gets to spend time with her old friend, they're both working or sleeping or she's out with Anton or on a mission. She misses her laughter, her ordinary comradery.

She feels a drowsy sense of ennui, the soft grassy smells of summer lulling her into unusual calm. A small part of her wishes she was at the wedding, just the feeling of celebrating something would be good. But she hardly knew Maartje, who takes craft classes with the younger children twice a week. She twists the thin silver ring she keeps on a chain around her neck thinking of Anton. When the others get back she is going into town to meet him, she hugs herself with the thought of it, the sweetness of the love they have found with one another. She so wants him to meet her family. Part of her wishes she knew where they were, how they were; the other part of her not wanting to know in case they have been found and sent to one of the camps. She watches the boys, looking up when she hears the crunch of wheels on the front drive: a car, a lorry? She sees Mina through the long hall window speeding down the stairs, her white-blonde plait bouncing against her tall straight back. Hetty starts to stand up wondering who has come and is brushing strands of grass from her skirt when Mina races across the lawn. The boys stop playing their game, handfuls of pebbles dropping on to the ground.

"What's the matter?"

"Officers. From the camp. They have asked to see everyone here." She is breathless, her cheeks red from running.

"It's probably nothing." Hetty leans down to put an arm around Tim who has started to hyperventilate, breath searing through him in desperate gasps. He is petrified of the SS.

"No, no. They want to search. They are looking for people in hiding. Someone said…" She stops seeing Tim's panic and waits until he is calmer and then speaks firmly, quietly: "I told them no-one was here. That everyone was at a wedding. Just you. And me. And the children. But they want to see you. They are adamant about that." Her eyes flick back and forth with panic.

Hetty swallows. She isn't the only Jew living in the children's home, she knows the music teacher Jan van Zijl is also Jewish, as are two of the older children. But they are at the wedding, Jan van Zijl is playing violin for Maartje.

She starts to walk towards the house when the back door opens and two SS soldiers stride across the lawn towards them.

"Hetty! Hetty!" Luuk shouts. She turns, his face is creased with worry, Tim is curled into a ball, hugging his knees, rocking back and forth, a strange high animal cry comes from him searing the air. Hetty turns back and squats down, putting an arm around him. "It's alright Tim. It's alright..." She smooths his arm gently and kisses his damp sweating forehead. He'd watched his parents being interrogated then tortured and shot by SS officers, convinced they were hiding something other than the leg of ham they'd found under the kitchen floorboards.

Hetty stands up as the soldiers come to a halt in front of her. One of them is Sergeant Wolfgang Hoffman. She speaks calmly: "Good afternoon. What can I do for you?"

"We have information that there are Jewish people hiding here." Wolfgang speaks as if he has never met her, never spoken to her, his voice clipped, divested of friendliness. "We need to search the premises."

"We would like to see everyone's papers," says the weary voice of the captain standing next to him.

Her resolve turns to jelly, but she speaks calmly: "There is no-one hiding here. This is a residential home and school for children with physical and mental problems."

"Our orders are to search the premises. What is your name miss?"

"Hetty van Leuwen. I am one of the staff here."

"Please go and get your identity card." Wolfgang makes the order, takes a step closer, dislodging the neat rows of pebbles into the grass.

Tim is crying, heaving sobs, Luuk pulls himself closer, finally yanking Tim's arm as he stretches towards him. "Sit with me Tim," he whispers and the little boy shuffles towards him, tipping over into the lap of his disabled friend who puts a small arm around him, strokes his back.

Hettty speaks to the captain. "Come with me" She wants to get the soldiers away from the boys. She turns to Luuk "Look after Tim. You will both be fine. It is nothing to worry about."

She smiles at them before turning and walking briskly back towards the house. Wolfgang and the captain follow.

Stepping into the cool of the hallway, she can hear soldiers shouting to one another as they swarm through each room. She walks into the kitchen to see one officer tearing a chunk of bread from a newly baked loaf and stuffing it in his pocket. She turns and comes face to face with the captain.

"Your papers?"

"In my room. Would you like to wait here? Mina can get you a glass of water. It's so hot. I am sure you know Mina? Do you want her to get her papers?" She gabbles.

"We have seen hers. Just get yours." There is rising irritation in the captain's voice.

Hetty feels dizzy, her stomach churns. She climbs the stairs, hoping her legs won't give out, feeling their eyes on her. On the first floor she stops at the bathroom, leans over the cracked wooden toilet seat and throws up. She sits on the loo, her bowels emptying desperately. She stands, washes her hands, rinses her mouth, wipes her face and is then sick again, this time the acid bile stings her throat. She rinses her mouth and goes back into the hall, up the second flight of stairs towards her room. The wardrobe is on the left, she opens it, pulls her handbag from the shelf, slides her hand into the side pocket and pulls out the identity card, flipping it open, she feels dizzy. She hears steps behind her and spins round to see Wolfgang in the doorway.

"Why is it taking you so long? Have you got it?" She holds up the card. With a jerk of his head he indicates the stairs. She passes him, careful not to brush against the rough serge of his suit. She grips the stair rail to steady herself as she goes down.

No-one has ever scrutinized the card before. She has flashed it for cursory inspection for a guard on a train once or twice, once or twice when on her bike. But in Zeist she is known, official statistics show there are no Jews in Zeist anymore, all have been deported to Westerbork, so no-one ever asks for identification, no one has examined her card for its authenticity.

Hetty's ears are ringing, she's screaming inside. The papers are genuine, created just for her by the local Council, but she can't help thinking that somehow they will see that she is not who she says she is. She stops on the stairs to catch her breath: she has to keep calm, no-one knows – apart from Anton, Dr Lievegoed, Rosa and Jan van Wettum – and they wouldn't, they couldn't, they wouldn't…tell? Her head swims with impossible nightmarish thoughts.

"Move." Wolfgang is behind her as she steps down the final flight of stairs and wordlessly hands her identity card over to the captain restlessly tapping his foot. He has taken his cap off and put it under his arm.

He flips the card open, looks carefully at it and at her, trying to match the grainy image with the more attractive reality in front of him. He holds out the card to Wolfgang.

"What do you think?" he barks.

Hetty takes a step back, leans against the solid oak hall table and steadies herself. Wolfgang walks towards the window, holding the card to the light. He looks across at Hetty. He looks at the card again, turning it over in his broad hands. She can see the fine hairs on his skin shine in the beams of sunlight as he turns and turns the card as if turning it would reveal its secrets. A frown flickers across his forehead, mild confusion in his eyes. Finally he closes the identity card and hands it back to his superior.

"It seems all in order sir." He clicks his heels.

"Thank you," says the officer taking the card and turning, smiling now at Hetty holding it out to her. "It's routine you know. There have been a number of arrests today." He pauses, looking into her eyes. A question almost forms on his lips but then he sighs. "We must be thorough." He turns on his heel and barks at the soldiers, most of who are now congregated outside the front of the house, smoking and chatting, one balancing the heavy onyx desk clock that Dr Lievegoed keeps in his office in the meaty palm of his hands. Hetty hears the children crying upstairs and Mina slides past her to go to them, blowing her nose. She spots the soldier with the clock and comes back down and walks over to him.

"That belongs to the doctor. He needs it."

The soldier laughs and hands it back to her dropping the clock heavily into her much smaller hands with such speed that it slips and falls to the ground, crunching as the corner cracks off. Mina stoops, picks up the clock and the broken corner and without a word takes it down the hall to Dr Lievegoed's office.

Hetty looks at the soldier who is laughing. "Excuse me, the children," she says to no-one and everyone and runs up the stairs, two at a time, racing down the corridor to the crying children, breathing more deeply at every inch she puts between herself and Wolfgang Hoffman.

Mina joins her minutes later in some distress about the clock and they pick up the two smallest children and rock them; their cries die down, soothed by the motion. They gaze out of the window of a first-floor bedroom as the truck that had brought the SS delegation turns noisily in the drive and leaves.

"Let's all go downstairs," says Hetty, stroking the sweaty blonde head of the two-year-old she has hoisted on to her hip. "Let's find Luuk and Tim."

She finds the boys almost where she had left them, sitting on the ground, re-arranging their rows of pebbles. Tim has calmed down and it is as if the SS visit had never happened.

An hour later they hear the pony and cart coming back from Zeist, the noisy chatter and the laughter of the wedding party syncopating with the tired cries of one of the smaller children. Hetty gets up as they come into the garden, slips away as they come to report on the festivities. Drained, she climbs up to her room, lies on her bed, closes her eyes and breathes deeply, until her heart finally stops pounding and her body stops shaking and she falls fitfully asleep.

It is an hour or more later when she hears her name being called up the stairs: Dr Lievegoed wants to see her in his study.

He is leaning over his desk in his shirt sleeves when she walks in, the grey jacket of the suit he wore to the wedding hanging over the back of his chair. He gestures for her to sit down by the fireplace: a colourful child's drawing of brightly burning logs sits skewwhiff in the middle of the cold grate.

He sits down opposite her, propping his elbows on the arm rests, lacing his long fingers and rubbing his thumbs together. "Are you ok? I heard about this afternoon." He has this way of looking at you as if he sees not just the expression on your face but everything inside your head thinks Hetty.

"Fine." She doesn't tell him about the sickness she still feels seething through her. She knows it will pass. She wonders if he has talked to Mina, if he wants to hear from her what happened, or if he wants to suggest she leaves the Zonnehuis before another search, a more 'successful' search takes place and puts them all in danger.

But he wants to talk about something completely different. He gets up to check his office door is firmly shut before returning to sit opposite her.

"Jan Schep has been arrested, as have several of our other friends."

She can't breathe. Jan was central to all that happened in the underground movement in Zeist. It was Jan who used his position at the council to create 'clean' passes for dozens of Jewish families in the region. It was Jan who ensured there were enough ration stamps for all those in hiding.

From somewhere she finds her voice: "How? Who?"

"This afternoon. I saw it. Some of it. Two SS officers were standing outside the church, after the wedding. I could see Jan Schep in the back of their lorry. They have been arresting people all day. They were pulling people from among the guests, shoving them into the lorry." He shakes his head.

"And Anton?"

Joop – Utrecht – 5 September 1944

First thing in the morning, straight after a hurried breakfast, Opa Loggers sends Joop to the attic to monitor news on the radio they have set up there. "Report back anything Joop as long as it's a fact. I don't want to hear what people think is happening. I want real news."

Joop takes the stairs two at a time, ducking into the attic, and swinging briefly on a rafter before hunkering down into the corner where they keep the radio hidden inside an old suitcase under a pile of linen. He pulls it free and sets it on the floor as he has dozens of times before carefully turning it on and manipulating the dial until it is tuned to Radio Orange: nothing only static; they don't usually broadcast before 9 in the evening, but it was always worth checking in case something dramatic happened, something amazing. Joop dares to think about it for a second: freedom, liberation from occupation. Delicately with his forefinger and thumb, he turns the dial again tuning in to other stations across Europe. He picks up the news coming from Reich Broadcasting in Germany grating through the airwaves and gently twists the knob again. There is crackling on the line but he can hear something coming from Radio Belgique. Something's happening, the newscaster sounds excited, breathless. Belgium is definitely being liberated. It's happening! He waits between gaps in transmission and bursts of music, for news. Just the excitement in the broadcaster's voice makes his heart soar. He is willing them to say that the Allies have crossed into the Netherlands. But nothing definitive is said, just rumors and he knows that Opa Loggers hates rumors. He waits, tunes and retunes, listening to every scrap of news.

An hour later, he stands up and stretches, nearly hitting his head on the roof rafters. He's stiff from sitting in the same position and his legs tingle as the blood rushes into his veins. He wraps his arms around one of the beams and clinging to it, bends his legs until his feet lift off the floor so that he can swing back and forth. Closing his eyes, his head spins with imagined freedom.

The night before, when he'd been listening to the news coming from Radio Orange, he'd heard that the Allies were crossing into Holland. He had almost fallen down the stairs in his excitement to tell the old man.

Slapping him on the back, almost knocking him over, chuckling with delight, Opa had put on his coat and gone to gather some of the other local resistance members. They had brought the radio downstairs; drinking and talking, listening for further dispatches, switching from one station to another. One of the others had heard Seys Inquart, the Reichskommissar appointed by Hitler to oversee the occupation and administration of The Netherlands, announce a "state of siege". He had threatened locals caught "fraternizing with the enemy" or "hindering the German Reich" saying that perpetrators would be shot.

"They are on the run!" Loggers had punched the air with delight. Someone else reported seeing a group of Nazis trundling up the road with a horse and cart loaded with bikes and household goods, two women in headscarves sitting on the side of the cart, heads bowed, hands gripping the sides as it jerked its way out of Utrecht. Everyone laughed, the mood had been infectious, and Joop had been sent to get a bottle of homemade gin from the cellar.

"Nearly over, eh Joop?" said one of the men pouring himself a tot of gin and passing the bottle on. "Your father will be home soon." Joop's mood dropped like a stone, but he didn't correct the man. It was better he believed his father had just been conscripted to Germany, his mother ill, Opa doing a good turn to old family friends.

Joop had eventually been sent to bed, but he had hardly slept. Breakfast had been a hasty affair, and he is pleased to be back on listening duty. He can't take it much longer, the waiting, cooped up in the house, day after day, month after month, year after year. He feels his life is slipping from him and he hasn't started to live it. He is desperate for news, confirmation that the troops have entered the Netherlands, but today there is nothing, nothing new, nothing specific.

Settling back down in his corner he hears the door to the attic open.

"Joop?"

"No news, Opa…just the same information repeated again and again. The Allies have pushed into Antwerp, that's confirmed." He blinks up at the old man hopefully, biting his lip.

"It can't be long, Joop. Be patient."

Joop – Utrecht – 9th September

It's a week later when Joop and the old man put together the events of the previous ten days taking information from the reports on Radio Orange, and from Victor who had come for a visit, as well as from underground newspapers and the Third Reich's own broadcasts.

On the 4th September Allied forces had liberated Antwerp. Rumours blossomed overnight: it would be days, hours before they marched north, entered Holland and liberated the Dutch people.

Lieutenant-General Brian Horrocks, Commander of the British XXX Corps spearheaded the British advance. Morale was said to be high, France and Belgium had been liberated, the Nazis were on the run, the border with Holland almost within sight.

It was reported that General Montgomery had told General Eisenhower that "one big and energetic push in the direction of Berlin" would quickly end the war.

The first rumours spawned others: reports that the American and British troops had taken Rotterdam, Dordrecht, Delft, The Hague, Leiden. But they weren't true. Even before they crossed the border into the Netherlands, the British troops had been told to halt. Supply lines had not been secured, a further advance could be fatal.

Lieutenant Commander Horrocks was reportedly furious. The force under his command had plenty of fuel, the morale of his troops was high, they were keen and ready – supplies would catch them up. But he was trained to obey orders, so obey orders he did and the advance stuttered to a halt.

Two days later, on 6 September they are told to resume the advance – but they had lost their advantage. Forty-eight hours had given Nazi forces time to regroup, to stiffen their resolve. After four days of hard fighting, Allies still had not reached the Dutch border.

News that they were still under occupation, still in Germany's power, filtered down slowly.

The Dutch underground were already saying that Tuesday 4th September would go down in history as 'Dolle Dinsdag' – mad Tuesday – the day Holland was nearly liberated.

But the Allies were not retreating.

"That's good news Joop. Really good," said Opa Loggers trying to bring a smile to Joop's leaden face.

Slowly the Allied troops were picking off towns and cities in the South, but the north of Holland was still firmly in German hands.

Already they knew that the brutality of the occupying Nazi force would become even more brutal, not an inch would be given, everything would be taken. One of the Loggers' good friends, a man he relied on, had been found breaking the 8pm curfew and was shot.

Jozef was bitter with thwarted hope. Nothing had changed.

Hetty – Zeist – one week later

There is still no news of Anton. It is two months since the raid on the Zonnehuis, the arrest of Jan van Schep and the disappearance of Anton and other members of the local resistance.

With every fibre of her being Hetty waits for news, searches for fragments of information, asks everyone she can if they have seen him or heard from him. She's been to his house, his office, to see his friends and friends of friends. But nothing.

Jan Schep is behaving like a hero. He could have told on the other members of the underground cell, but he doesn't. He refuses to give the Nazi authorities any information, refuses to be tempted by offers of a softer sentence – imprisonment rather than death. They are known to be frustrated by his lack of cooperation: he is a good catch, but not the larger catch they anticipated. The network at the Council is still out of reach, disabled but undestroyed.

During the day Hetty works long hours wanting to make herself so tired she can sleep without dreaming. But it doesn't work. At night the memories crowd in on her, the way his hair curls on his neck, the way his green eyes lift when he looks at her but when she sinks into a dream and reaches up to put her arms around him, he is ripped screaming from her arms and she shakes herself awake out of the nightmare. She prays to a

God she has never believed in. She even walks into the Catholic Church on Rozenstraat wondering if she could find an answer there, but the church feels cold and unfamiliar, her words hollow in the stone pillars of the nave, so she cries; bitterly, silently, desperately kneeling on the hard tiled floor.

Some of those caught in the August raid have been taken to a concentration camp at Amersfoort and she tortures herself with thoughts of their treatment. Red Cross workers sometimes visit the camp, returning with tales of deprivation and cruelty. She needs to know for herself if Anton is there and offers to help on their food and clothing runs. She doesn't think of what she will say or do, just hopes she might find Anton. When Jan van Wettum hears she is going he gives her a list of names of people who have disappeared to add to the Red Cross list she is to take, to which she has already added Anton.

"Find out if they are there. Just ask."

She is accompanied by one of the regular Red Cross team, a man called Lars.

They set out on a surprisingly warm day, their bikes laden with parcels and letters for the prisoners. Lars had been an ambulance driver before the war, retired in '35 he tells Hetty as they cycle companionably side by side on a particularly open stretch of road. Hetty tells him about the list.

"Well just pray they are not there. It's a slum of a place – hell on earth," says Lars, flicking ash from his roll-up on to the road.

But Hetty doesn't want to hear that. She has put together a parcel for Anton, just in case, with a warm sweater, a book of poems she knows he likes, and a cake made by Wilma. The ride from Zeist to Amersfoort takes an hour and, deep in thought, she is surprised how quickly they find themselves in the town, a tidy street of shops, people going about their normal business, women queueing for bread. Lars is cycling ahead of her now and shouts back that they are nearly there.

The town centre ends abruptly. They cycle through a short stretch of woodland until unexpectedly the camp looms up in front of them, huge gates covered in barbed wire, behind the gates acres of beaten barren dirt dotted with wooden huts. The whole camp is surrounded by a double layer of barbed wire fencing which stretches impossibly into the sky, spiked tendrils of loose wire waving menacingly in the light September breeze.

Lars gets off his bike grumbling, takes the handlebars and wheels it towards the entrance gate, and a small black painted guard room. Hetty gets off her bike and follows him. Hit by the stench: a sour mix of dirt, sweat, faeces and rot she covers her face with her hand. As they draw closer a thin red-faced sergeant walks out of the guard room towards them chuckling at her obvious discomfort.

"You get used to it fraulein." He looks her up and down but speaks to Lars "What do you want old man?"

"We've got some parcels for some of the prisoners, letters too. And we wanted to check who was here from Zeist, we have a list of people who have gone missing."

The guard laughs, spits on the ground and shakes his head indicating the group of men that are starting to assemble in the yard behind him. They are pouring out of the huts, a grey mass of skeletal frames, dishevelled and dirty walking into the bare quad in front of them, forming lines; someone shouts against the piercing sound of an electric bell calling them outside. Hetty scans the grey mass of unidentifiable ragged unwashed men, caked in dirt. She thinks for a moment she sees Jan Schep but she has been told not to ask for him. He has been given the opportunity to escape but has refused it; if he did escape the reprisals would bite deep into the Zeist community and affect his family.

Lars stubs his cigarette out on the ground and reaches into his pocket for his battered pouch of tobacco and unfurls it, three carefully rolled cigarettes lie inside and he offers one to the German sergeant, who takes all three.

Lars says nothing and tells Hetty to hand him the list. "Know any of these?"

"Who's the girl?"

"Someone just helping me out," says Lars indicating the bags hanging from the back of both their bikes.

"She can help me out any day," says the sergeant chuckling.

Hetty feels her cheeks go red but says nothing. Lars shrugs. "Can I give you the parcels?"

The sergeant looks at him. "Unload them here. I'll get my list."

They unload paniers laden with letters and parcels, and bags of food. Hetty stops and looks at the men in the quad. They have formed a block and a Nazi officer is marching up and down between the lines. She scans the faces again.

Lars pinches her arm. "Hetty stop. Help me." She turns to pull out the last of the parcels, piling them all neatly by the gate, she holds the wodge of letters in her hand.

The guard returns and squats in front of the meagre pile of packages and starts to rummage through them, opening some as he goes. He picks up a bag of apples, takes one with his bony fingers and bites.

He continues to crunch the apple while looking through the other packages, calling to someone in the guard room to help him, come and take some of them. He stands and looks at Lars: "We'll take them in, see they get to the right people."

Hetty hands the guard a small pile of letters and he sifts idly through them, keeping a few, handing the rest back. He turns away dismissively, squats down and picks up more of the packages.

Lars starts to leave, walks towards his bike, but Hetty stands still and calls out to the guard: "The list please, you were going to check the list." She holds her list of names out to him. The guard turns his mouth full of apple and looks at her as he chews.

"Missing people. We just want to know if they are here." She smiles and walks towards him. "Please?"

The guard swallows and picks a piece of apple skin from his teeth and then puts out his hand. She hands him the list. He retreats into his box taking the bag of apples and the list with him. She sees him through the doorway, putting the bag of apples down on his desk and picking up a well-thumbed pile of papers clipped onto a board and scanning the names, comparing them to the ones on the list. He pulls a pencil from his pocket and strikes some names out. He comes back and wordlessly hands it back to Lars, all but three of the 20 names has a line through them. A fourth name has a cross by it indicating he had been there but had died. He turns to go back to the guard box.

"Are you sure?" Hetty calls after him.

He turns and looks at Hetty, picking at his teeth again. He speaks to Lars. "Go."

"Can we see these three?"

"No." He shakes his head irritably, then suppresses a laugh. He indicates the men in the quad, a sergeant walking around them shouting, cracking a riding whip at anyone who moves. "We're busy today."

Lars grabs her by the wrist and pulls her back to the bikes. "Don't push them," he spits the words from the corner of his mouth. "They can get nasty." He pushes up the sleeve of his shirt, two livid scars run the length of his arm. "From another time," he says as he swings on to his bike.

They cycle in virtual silence back towards Zeist. On a quiet bit of road skirted by a canal, cows in the field, a few red brick houses on the horizon, Lars slows down until he is cycling next to her: "I know what you are thinking Hetty. You think that was a pointless visit? You think they won't get the food we delivered.

Maybe, maybe not, but three families in Zeist will tonight at least know that their husbands, fathers, sons are alive thanks to us."

"And the family of the man who has died?"

"They will at least be able to mourn. They will have an answer however dreadful that might be."

But she has no answer about Anton.

Joop– Utrecht – September 19

Joop is in the attic, twisting the radio dial until he is tuned to Radio Orange, tucking a bag behind his head and lying stretched out with his ankles crossed, notebook and pencil by his side. Opa Loggers has 'friends' coming round later, and he is in charge of giving them a clear report about the Allied attacks on Arnhem. Work on gin making has been temporarily abandoned. Opa is listening to the German station on the family radio downstairs, a huge rather crackly mahogany box affair. They will compare notes later.

The raid had started on Sunday and Joop has hardly been able to sleep since the first reports came in. Every fibre of his being is twisted into a knot of hope.

He wishes he could have been there, seen them dropping out of the sky. So far over 1,500 aircraft and 500 gliders have been involved in the onslaught, carrying troops and guns and all necessary armoury to smash through the wall of grim resistance from the Nazi military.

Field Marshall Sir Bernard Montgomery had favoured a single thrust north over the branches of the Lower Rhine river, which runs through Arnhem, and then a push forward to a final victory in the Ruhr. His hope, his expectation is that this final thrust, Operation Market Garden, will bring an end to the war.

Joop can think of nothing else: an end to the war, an end to his 'imprisonment' in this small house. There are reports on

Radio Orange of the magnitude of the operation, the welcome the Allies received from Oosterbeek residents who had climbed onto their rooftops to welcome them, waving and shouting, plying them with tea, coffee, bread, pears, apples, – emptying their meagre store cupboards to greet their liberators. They cheer, throw flowers, blow kisses to the troops. There is even a report of some people singing not just the Dutch national anthem but also "God Save the King" in English, tears streaming down their cheeks. Joop thought this so wonderful that when he went down to give Opa Loggers the news he started to sing it himself marching around the living room – even though he didn't know the tune and had only heard the first line. Hearing him, Tina had poked her head around the door and come in and started marching behind him, causing Opa to double over with laughter.

Yesterday he had believed that now was the time, now the long vicious occupation of his beloved Netherlands was about to end.

But that was yesterday. Today the news is not so good. Joop sits up and writes everything down. The Allied forces had come face to face with the 9th and 10th SS Panzer divisions, crack forces at the top of the war game, troops that are not ready to give in.

There was going to be no walk over, there was every chance now that there may not even be a victory.

*

Less than a week later, nine days after the attack began, Joop climbs down the ladder from the attic, Opa Loggers is standing on the landing. Joop falls into his arms and cries.

Arnhem is devastated, its destruction total. In all 1,485 Allied troops are dead as well as unrecorded numbers of Dutch civilians; more than 6,000 Allied troops have been taken as prisoners of war; the shattered remains of the Allied Airborne forces have withdrawn.

Holland remains under occupation.

Hetty – Zeist – Two weeks later – October

Hetty hardly talks about her trips to Amersfoort. She doesn't want to contaminate the sanctuary of the children's home with the ugly despair of the camp which has infected the very core of her being. But she still goes back and back again and again, sometimes without Lars who gets sick. But she has little success.

Zeist is suffering, every day there are new raids as old men some in their 60s and young teenage boys are forcibly taken to assist the Nazi war machine. They aren't being sent to Germany but to the front line at Arnhem to dig trenches for Nazi troops and to provide cannon fodder for Allied forces who can't distinguish between them and the Nazi force they are fighting. It's a death watch.

The woman who has taken Anton's place in the council offices distributing coupons tells anyone who will listen how they have taken her son.

"They took my boy…., my 13-year-old boy. He's tall, so they said he looks older. I told them they had no right. He was still a boy." She shakes her head, wipes a tear from the corner of her eye. "I was polite. I did nothing to antagonise them, but they just pushed me, broke my glasses, told me to do my duty," she spits out the last word and lifting her spectacles Hetty can see the dark circles of sleeplessness bruising her eyes and a nasty livid gash under her eyebrow.

Coming out of the Council offices an elderly man approaches her.

Hetty looks up and smiles. It's Jacques, finally, Anton's uncle. He looks worn, his coat sags and there is a patch of stubble under his chin he missed when shaving. She has tried so many times to get hold of him, to ask if he had any idea where Anton had gone, but a trick of fate had meant they always missed one another. He had never been in when she had called at the house and she had no idea where else to find him. They had left messages but never met. Has he got news? Her heart races and seeing her eyes so filled with expectation he shakes his head.

"No news Hetty." His eyes film with sadness but he asks her to walk with him.

"I don't know where Anton is. Some think he was taken on the raid – or he could be hiding somewhere. Better not to know perhaps?" Jacques looks up at her, his eyes mirror her pain but then his face suddenly breaks into a gentle rueful smile. "Shall we walk a bit? Are you in a hurry?"

"No particular hurry, it's my half day." She swallows a lump in her throat, it's one of the days when she always met up with Anton. "I was going to go by your house."

"Let's sit in the park."

He walks unevenly beside her with a stick. The lines of age scarring his face like the uneven rings on an old oak tree, seem to have deepened over the last month, but she can see his resemblance to Anton and her heart lurches with longing. Jacques' limp is the result of an injury in the first world war. Anton had told her that the day the war ended his uncle had returned home and married his childhood sweetheart, and a year later, she had died giving birth to their stillborn child. He had never married again and Anton, his sister and their mother had become his family, moving in with him after his father died in an accident when Anton was six.

The park is busy with children playing some sort of hide and seek game in and out of trees, two mothers picnicking on the grass, a mangy dog barking. Late summer roses, pinks and yellows scent the air as they look for a quiet spot to sit. They find a bench up against the hedge of mock orange bushes.

They watch a family trudging along the path, the children straggling behind their mother pushing a pram loaded with their worldly goods, rolls of blankets, battered suitcases, pans tied to the handle. A girl of about 12 dragging a toddler along in a cart follows behind.

"More refugees from Arnhem."

After Operation Market Garden, the Nazis demanded that all residents evacuate the city, now the front line of the interminable war.

"There are so many refugees, too many. People were welcoming them at first, but now I've heard people shout at them in the street to go on, not to stop here…it's terrible."

"I've taken in a family, two of them are sleeping in Anton's room, I've told them that if…when he comes back…."

Hetty takes hold of his hand. "Anton would be pleased about that."

He clears his throat looks down at his hands, folded in his lap. "I've heard about your trips to Amersfoort?"

She shakes her head. "I'm not sure they do much good."

"More than you think." He looks up as a ball bounces across the grass towards them. It rolls under the bench and Hetty leans down and picks it up, throwing it back to the boy in blue shorts waving at her from the grass bank.

Jacques speaks softly. "You know about the raids: the men and boys taken to Arnhem to dig trenches?" Hetty nods. "They won't survive. They will work them until they drop dead of exhaustion, hunger or disease or until they get hit in the crossfire." He pulls his pipe out of his pocket and turns it in his hand. "We must do something."

"What can we do?"

Jacques tilts his head to look at her. "We are meeting in an hour at Oma Anja's house in Stolberglaan. Do you know it?"

"I know Stolberglaan."

"Well it's Anja's birthday," he chuckles and puts the pipe back in his pocket. "A good excuse for a get together. Will you come? Number 34. About 3?"

Hetty scratches the back of her hand, wondering what help she could possibly be, some irrational part of her imagining that Anton will be there. "Sure. I'll be there."

Walking later to Oma Anja's house she is uncomfortably aware of the distress and disappointment that cloaks the town. There are Arnhem refugees everywhere; camped in the park and in the woods, whole families squeezed into spare rooms. But food supplies are beyond short and tempers are frayed by hunger, exhaustion, and despair. One man whose two oldest sons had been shot during one of the raids had poisoned the refugee family staying with him after they stole bread from him and when confronted by his deed had poisoned himself and his wife. The energy to survive is draining. Some talk of the end being close, but it looks as if Armageddon will come first.

Reaching Stolberglaan Hetty can't decide whether to go in. Her mood seesaws between hope and despair. A woman in a blue coat walks up behind her, gives a sharp knock on the door and pushes it open.

"You coming?"

Hetty follows her into the small corridor, coats hung against the wall, a pervasive smell of polish and mothballs. An older woman pokes her head out of what must be the parlour and beckons Hetty and the other woman inside.

Oma Anja sits by the cold fireplace in a red plush chair, looking bewildered by the mix of people who have invaded her home. A young woman with tight blonde curls, her granddaughter someone says, sits on the floor near her feet playing with a toddler in red shorts who keeps hiding behind the old woman's chair, his thumb firmly stuck in his mouth. The room is stuffy with forced cheerfulness.

The old woman looks up and smiles vaguely at Hetty, but before Hetty can say anything she feels a firm tap on her shoulder and turns to see Anton's uncle who has clearly been waiting for her and with a slight movement of his head he beckons her to follow him.

Back in the hallway he heads to the back of the house, to what must have once been the dining room. There are about a dozen older men and three women crowded around an old polished oak table, the air thick with tobacco smoke. Three of the men and one middle aged woman puff on pipes, while half a dozen younger woman share three cigarettes, inhaling with deep concentration before blowing out the smoke. The table is littered with glasses, some half full of a brownish liquid that Hetty recognises as homemade beer, others with the dregs of coffee.

Hetty vaguely realizes she knows some the men, that she has met them at one time or another in town, though never realised they were involved in the resistance. One of the women is from the library, another she recognises as the girl who helps in the dressmakers. She can't place the third woman though she looks familiar. There is the elderly ticket collector from the station and two silver haired men who regularly play chess outside the local bar. She has deliberately kept out of these planning meetings in the past, just carrying out whatever Jan Schep or Anton asked of her. It was better that way said Anton…safer. But now?

Someone passes her a small glass of watery beer and she takes a sip carefully before placing the glass on the tiled mantelpiece she finds herself leaning against. She looks across and sees a bald-headed man she has occasionally seen at the Zonnehuis where he comes to teach flute to one of the older girls who is an asthmatic, the breath control helping her strengthen her lungs. She loves the warm woody sound of the flute floating through the Zonnehuis when he is there. He has an awkward limp – a hip damaged by an accident in his youth – and someone told her he was once a member of the Amsterdam Royal Orchestra. What was his name? They nicknamed him maestro at the Zonnehuis. He smiles and raises his glass to her as he takes a sip of beer. There seem to be at least three different discussions going on. Jacques is talking to a woman who appears to have taken charge of the gathering. She is sitting in a wide curved back wooden armchair at the head of the table. The conversation rattles around the room, people talking over each other with ideas of how to rescue some of the Zeist men. Hetty wonders why she is there. She should get back to the Zonnehuis.

Someone, a pale faced boy who looks as if he is barely in his teens says he knows how to get hold of an ambulance. They could pick them up in that. She sees the daring in his eyes. Well not as easy as all that she thinks, just drive up in an ambulance and pick up a dozen Dutchmen working in a ditch.

But the woman at the head of the table nods. "OK Gerrit that is a good idea. We can find some justification for getting some of them back. I can use the hospital paper, draw up a list."

Hetty realises now why she vaguely recognises the woman, she's the administrator at the small local hospital.

The maestro speaks up. "I am happy to drive but that won't be good enough. Someone has to come with me. You don't see ambulance drivers just turn up on their own."

There is silence. "It needs to be someone with some experience of medical care," says the woman who works at the library.

"I'll go." The words are out of Hetty's mouth before she has really considered what she is saying.

Everyone in the room turns to her and the woman smoking at the table blows a cloud of smoke into the fetid air.

"I worked as a nurse in Amsterdam before coming here," she explains tightly. Questions won't be asked but she feels she has to explain herself.

The woman from the hospital looks at her, a memory lighting her face. "Are you sure? You've already helped," she pauses. "Going up to the prison camp at Amersfoort?" Hetty remembers that one of the names confirmed on one of the lists she has brought back is that of the woman's brother.

The maestro looks at her and she watches his hooded eyes half pleat into a smile. "Well Hetty, we will be a team." She is surprised he knows her name.

"Yes maestro."

"You better call me Frank."

Joop – Utrecht – October

It is seven in the morning. Joop drags himself out of bed, pulls on a sweater and trousers and with a cursory glance at his aunt who is stretching, rolling her shoulders and beginning to wake up, leaves the attic and goes downstairs in his stockinged feet to make early morning tea for Oma and Opa as he does every day of every week.

While they drink their tea, Joop leans on the wall or sits on the floor and Opa tells him the plans for the day. There are always things to do, Opa Loggers has little time to spare between his job at the bakery, his resistance work and varying black market operations.

But when Joop gets to the kitchen to put on the kettle Opa is already there, sitting at the table, a cup of tea going cold in front of him as he chews on the stem of his pipe.

"What's happened?"

The old man takes his pipe out of his mouth. "Trouble."

Joop stands and waits, knowing better than to say anything. He will be told.

The old man stretches out a hand pats the seat next to him. "Sit." He sighs as Joop sits down. "They've got Victor."

A moan escapes Joop's lips. Victor is the nearest thing he has to a friend these days.

"How?"

"He was outside. Careless. Bloody boy can be so careless sometimes."

"But...but I thought..."

"We all thought. The SS are going mad out there. Mad. They are taking everyone and anyone who looks vaguely fit....so Victor, well Victor would have been a catch! Young, strong."

"Won't they wonder why he didn't...."

"I'm not worried about that. Victor will come up with some story, some reason why he didn't go to Germany when all young men were conscripted. He'll invent some essential job, some spurious illness. Victor has always been a good storyteller Joop." He chuckles despite himself.

"So there is nothing to worry about. He won't be sent to one of the camps."

The old man looks at him sadly. "There is everything to worry about Joop. Everything. They are sending him, like they are sending everyone to Arnhem, to the front line, to dig trenches....to get killed."

"He'll survive Opa."

"Maybe...but maybe not. This is one time when he can't charm his way out of things." He bites his lip and looks up at the ceiling; on the floor above is his bedroom where his wife is still sleeping. "And what do I tell her? She doesn't know yet. I got the news this morning." He picks up a piece of paper with a short message on it that must have dropped through the letterbox during the night. "I heard someone coming up the path. I came down. I found the note."

"Victor will survive Opa." Joop doesn't know what else to say, not believing anything he does say, just knowing it's the only thing he can say.

Hetty – Zeist – Two days later

The day is unremittingly grey, wintry cold for October and wet. The slish-slash of the one working windscreen wiper on the battered ambulance marks time as they rumble along the potholed road. Frank says nothing, his eyes set on the strip of grey tarmac ahead; every now and then he swings the old ambulance to the left or right to avoid the worst of the potholes.

Hetty has on a borrowed nurse's uniform, mud brown dress, long black wool stockings. It reminds her too closely of the Amsterdam hospital, the smell of it clings to her with its memories, and paradoxically strip her of any fear she has of what lies ahead. She's pulled the belt of the dress tight, pinned her hair up under a cap; she's a nurse.

Before leaving, she had checked the contents in the back of the rusting ambulance, sorted through a much depleted first aid kit with a pair of scissors a couple of crepe bandages, which had seen better days, and a half bottle of iodine. She's folded the blankets which have done long service, noticing the faint brown blood stains in the grey weft of the rough wool.

She hasn't said anything about the trip at the Zonnehuis but she suspects Frank has told them something. By the day after the meeting everything seems to be planned. Frank has come to the Zonnehuis to teach his pupil and passing her on the stairs told her to meet him at the back of the cottage hospital the following day. She had gone to see Dr Lievegoed, knocked on his door, and been forestalled by his wife coming down the hall. "I hear you are going off to visit friends tomorrow. Bernhard is not in. He told me to tell you to come back quickly."

Hetty looks across at Frank focussing on the road ahead of them and wonders at his life before the war. Everything has changed; there's been a seismic shift in their lives, will they ever get the pattern of it back? Can it ever be as it was after all of this?

They have been on the road for half an hour, only passing people going in the opposite direction; family after family struggling along the road: two women wrapped in sagging coats pull a cart with a young girl sitting in it holding a baby crying mournfully into the rain; an old couple limping along in their best Sunday clothes, carrying a battered suitcase he in his black Homburg hat, and she with an incongruous feather in her green cloche; another woman pushing a pram with a baby and a toddler leaning over the side. They keep going against the flow of people, towards the place they have all come from. Hetty wraps her cloak more tightly around her. No turning back.

Frank starts to hum and some part of her recognises the tune.

"What's that?"

"What?"

"What's that tune?"

"It's from Vivaldi's Four Seasons. The largo from Winter."

He shuffles in his seat, leaning forward to see through the windscreen. "It reminds me of other times. And it complements the rhythm of the rain. Sorry did it bother you?"

"Don't stop."

Frank is quiet for a minute and then starts up again and Hetty closes her eyes listening to him hum against the rattling of the van. She falls into a semi-doze and is somewhere back in Scheveningen on the beach when she is jolted awake by grating brakes and a wiry hand shaking her gently.

She realises they are approaching one of the villages on the outskirts of Arnhem, some of the buildings have been wrecked by recent bombings, roofs have disappeared, gaping holes in walls reveal the lost detritus of the families that once lived there, broken tables and chairs, blackened laundry flapping in the rain. She winds down her window and the dank acrid odour of spent gun fire and burning buildings fills the air, the rain lifting the smell into the ambulance.

There's a guard ahead. She sits up as the ambulance slithers to an uncomfortable halt in the mud.

Frank winds his window down and she finds herself looking at the face of a boy, acne peppers his skin and a pale, unshaven down brushes his chin; his uniform hangs loosely round his waist and is too short in the arms, his wrists clearly visible, reddened by the cold and the wet.

"Where are you going? Nobody is allowed through."

"We have come to collect some Dutch patients."

"No-one has time to be sick here." He spits and chuckles at his own joke, then coughs.

Hetty leans across Frank and speaks to the lad. "But these men are contagious. Better get them away before anyone else becomes sick eh? Really sick."

The lad shakes his head. "I have been told not to let anyone through."

"We are not anyone are we…?"

The boy eyes the ambulance suspiciously.

"Wait."

He ducks back towards a doorway leaving his partner who is shorter, blonder and possibly even younger, standing at the front of the ambulance, nervously gripping a rifle hanging by his side.

They hear laughter from inside the house and then the boy returns, red in the face with an older Nazi officer behind him.

"OK. You've been told. Turn around. You can't go through. Why are you arguing?"

Hetty leans across again. "We are from the hospital in Zeist. We believe some men have been taken to work here who are contagious. Typhus, we've got a typhus epidemic." she shrugs. She tries to look sympathetic. "I have a list."

The officer spits on the ground and looks in at her. "Do I care if these men are ill?"

"You'll care if you get ill."

"This is crazy. You want to be crazy? Go through. When you get into Arnhem, what's left of it, head for the centre, the town hall. The commandant has made his headquarters there. If he wants to let them go, that's his business."

"Thank you officer," says Frank, winding up the window and jerking the ambulance into gear.

They drive ahead, the rain easing a little now and the windscreen wipers squeaking on the glass. It's a ghost town, buildings smouldering, walls torn down, no one is about. Frank turns the wipers off as the ambulance rattles forward jerking over potholes in the road. Everywhere is deserted. The lack of people is eerie. An old woman watches them from a doorway, there is little left of her house, two of the walls have gone, the furnishings and curtains look like the entrails of a dead animal, flapping wetly in the breeze.

Driving on it is hard to believe they are coming into a city, so much has been destroyed; houses, shops, buildings all around them are cripplingly damaged, some obliterated, others with jagged walls like rotten teeth, more with windows blown out, roofs smashed; piles of rubble cleared to the side so that tanks can pass down the road. Hetty sees a couple of soldiers taking shelter in an archway, sitting on a stone, smoking, leaning on a gun. Frank has stopped humming, his mouth hangs open, focussing just on the road ahead, on reaching the square, or what had been the square at the centre of town. He pulls the ambulance to a halt. Neither of them says anything. They can hear the ackety-ack of distant gunfire. Hetty looks at Frank, all colour drained from his face, his eyes mirroring the pure evil awfulness of what surrounds them.

"You stay. I'll go. I'll get them. I don't think we should leave the ambulance unattended," she says.

He looks her in the eyes. "You sure?"

"Yes."

"You have the list?"

"Yes"

"I'll wait here....if."

"No ifs. Wait here."

She steps out of the van into the muddy square, the nauseous smell of open sewers mixing with the heavy wet dust of destruction makes her gasp. She picks her way across the square, or what is left of it, towards the red brick town hall which is still standing, though half the windows have been blown out. It is deathly quiet; she can hear her footsteps echoing on the cobbles. She goes through an arch into a courtyard where a group of soldiers are teasing a cat that one of them has caught, holding it up in the air by its tail, the cat twisting and snarling, clawing the air, trying to get free. They see her and wave the screeching animal in her face.

She says nothing, and they laugh: "It's just a cat! Food!" They laugh. "Cat food!" And with that one of them pulls a knife from the hilt on his belt and slits the cat's throat. The cat shudders and is then deathly still. Blood streams down its mangy grey fur and drips on to the ground. There's a moment's silence, everyone's breath caught, and then two of the soldiers start to giggle helplessly watching her.

She takes one step towards them ignoring the cat: "I want to see the officer in charge. Can you tell me where I can find him?"

"She wants to see the man in charge?!" chants the youngest of the men in a falsetto voice. But one of the older soldiers suddenly sobers.

"Through that door." He points to a half open door in the far corner. She turns and as she walks away hears one of the others shout. "Come back and eat some cat!"

Ignoring him, she goes through the door and finds herself in a surprisingly wide pillared hallway. A young corporal sits behind a huge desk.

With a polite nod, she shows him the letter from the hospital with its attached list of names. He asks her to follow him and he gets up and walks down the hall, his feet marking time on the chequered tiles. He raps on a large mahogany door, halfway down, opens it and goes in, holding the door for her to follow.

"Commandant – this nurse has asked to see you"

The man sitting at a desk looks up, there are bags under his eyes, his grey hair is thinning, his mouth sags. Two soldiers standing near him argue about something. The corporal hands the commandant the letter and the list.

One of the other soldiers turns and she recognises him, a sergeant based at the camp in Zeist for a while, tall with a prominent jaw, and a misshapen squab nose. Someone told her he used to be a boxer. He looks at her and she can see from the way he looks at her, that he is trying to work out where he has seen her before. He turns to finish his conversation and then swings back to face her and she notices how blue his eyes are as he looks straight at her.

"Don't you work in Zeist?"

"Yes, at the hospital." It takes all her energy to stand still, to stop herself from shaking.

The commandant looks up at her. "You have had a wasted journey. You must be crazy to think I am going to let these men go." He screws the letter up and then stops before throwing it in the bin and looks towards a half-boarded window. The scream of a mortar hitting its target shakes the building.

"Do you hear that? That's them. That's the bloody English. They don't give up." He bends his head, raps his knuckles on the table. "We need these men, we need everyone here to help us fight and that includes the idiot Dutch."

She is startled but doesn't move. She waits.

"Who sent you on this pointless journey?" He doesn't look at her for a reply, but turns again towards the window, a muscle working in his cheek as he hears another burst of gun fire.

She clears her throat.

He turns back. "You can go. Go back to Zeist where you came from."

She draws in a breath, looks the older man in the eye: "You would be crazy to keep these men here. This is a list of sick men, most have typhoid, they will pass it on to other prisoners, to your soldiers. Another is still getting over pneumonia, one has a heart condition, they'll collapse just when you need them. They are of no use to you. They will hinder rather than help you." She pauses and sees a flicker in his eye. "They are a risk not an asset."

No-one says anything. In the silence they hear the intermittent sniping of guns nearby, the distant crump of another mortar. The scream of battle.

The officer holds her gaze. He shouts for one of the soldiers in the hall who dashes in, clicking his heels "*Sieg Heil!*"

The commandant passes him the list. "Take this – get these men. Find out where they are. They can go."

"All of them?"

"All of them." The commandant turns to her again and now the pain in his eyes is raw. "A good deed today? We save some Dutchmen?" His chuckle is empty. "Do I care? I really don't care. But you want these men. Take them. Today. Tomorrow, who knows what tomorrow will bring eh?"

Hetty starts to move but he stops her. 'Wait.' He turns to the sergeant that recognised her. "Is she a nurse? Is she really a nurse?"

The sergeant looks at her "Yes. She's a nurse from Zeist." He looks her up and down and Hetty feels her flesh creep.

"Show her out."

The sergeant takes her elbow and walks her towards the door. She picks up the vinegary smell of his sweat mixed with mud, his warm breath on her ear as he opens the door and follows her along the corridor. He grabs her arm: "I did you a favour there didn't I?" He breathes into her ear. "Perhaps you can do me a favour some time." He pulls her towards him, pressing his body against her until she can feel the hardness of him.

She coughs. "I think your friend is coming back."

"Who cares?" He moves his hand down over her buttocks pressing her more closely.

There is a shout then from outside and the commandant's door bursts open as he strides into the corridor. He sees the sergeant. "What the hell? Let her go! Keep your pants on. There's no time for that nonsense." There is fury in his voice as he slaps the soldier across his face. "You," he points at Hetty. "Go! Get out of here. Now!"

Hetty walks quickly out of the building, across the courtyard, not stopping, not looking, heading straight for the place where she had left Frank and the ambulance. She hears men running down the street, the hard metal heels of their boots ringing loudly against the cobbles. The bitter smoke of endless battle permeates the ruins around her. She sees a dead soldier half buried beneath rubble, his head lolling back, mouth open and then another and another. But she doesn't stop, she can't stop. The dead don't need her.

Getting to the rusted ambulance she climbs in, breathless.

"They are getting them."

"Where from?"

"Come with me."

She walks back, running now, worried now. And then she sees him, the young corporal who had been sent to get the men and she races towards him.

He looks at her and laughs. "*Sieg heil,*" he says, the witticism not lost on her, she blushes. "They are finishing their shift. Meet them at the camp in half an hour." He hesitates. "Two of the bastards have been coughing their guts up for the past two days. They'll be glad to see the back of them."

"Where?"

He lifts his arm as he turns back towards the headquarters, points behind him and to the left, shouting as he goes. "You'll find them. Just follow the stink!" They've got the list.

They walk back to the ambulance in silence. It takes them half an hour to find the camp. It's easy enough once they spot a line of dishevelled men shuffling away from the front line. One of the men meanders exhausted out of the line, and a guard shouts as someone else hauls him back into place, another man suddenly makes a run for it towards a clump of trees, and the guard pulls out a gun and shoots aiming for the man's head. Without a sound the running man crumples to the ground.

They park the ambulance up against the fence of what must have been an old farmyard just outside the town. The main building is destroyed beyond recognition, though the walls of some old stone barns still stand. Other makeshift buildings and improvised tents squat around the walls. The whole encampment is circled by a roughly erected barbed wire fence with a crude entrance which the men are now shuffling through. It's a desperate place. Someone is trying to cook an insipid soup on an open fire in a huge cauldron, but it does nothing to mask the smell. Men are sitting and lying in amongst the ruined walls, crowded in the few corners left with any kind of roof, desperate to keep out of the unforgiving rain.

"Are you the nurse?" says the guard at the entrance. He is painfully thin, his skin like paper, his jaw scarred by a livid burn, his eyes bloodshot with exhaustion. He looks at the short list of names. "We are all sick you know. Sick to death" he laughs bitterly as he spits out the words.

"Yes."

He hands her back the list. "It's up to you to find them." He spits and turns away.

She walks into the camp. All eyes pivot towards her. There are hundreds of men here maybe thousands and she has come to rescue just five.

Someone walks up to her, a middle-aged man, his clothes hanging on him like rags, his face streaked with dirt but he speaks politely, with seeming genuine concern: "What are you doing here? What do you want?"

She explains and shows him the list. He nods his head.

"I'm....sorry," she says as she realises from the look on his face that he is not on it.

He smiles weakly. "Sorry?" he coughs roughly, phlegm rises into his mouth and he turns and spits it out before turning back to her. "At least someone might sleep in a bed tonight. If I help you to find them will you take a message for me?" She nods and he takes the list from her.

They walk through the body of men, some reach out to touch her with small cries of "please" and, at first, she stops but her guide takes her by the arm. "If you stop you will never get out of here and it will be the worse for them." She glances back and sees one of the Nazi guards watching her, watching who she talks to what she does.

They walk into the roofless shell of an old barn and she is shaken by some of the order within the stench and chaos: neatly folded dirty blankets, men sleeping curled up, resting their head on their arms, breath heaving out of skeletal bodies. Her body screams with the futility, the inadequacy of her efforts. She passes an old man, his leg caked in blood and grime and he calls out to her...but she is pulled forward. The man who has taken her into the barn stands on an outcrop of rubble and starts shouting out the names on the list. There are whispers, one or two shuffle forward someone shouts from a corner, his voice rasping. Outside she can hear the call being echoed by others and slowly the five she is looking for shuffle forward, two of them leaning heavily on others.

The man explains that they are to go with Hetty as they are sick. There is a bitter laugh from someone crouched on the floor by Hetty's feet and she looks down.

"We are all sick young lady. All sick and on the road to Hell." He pauses. "This is a death watch. The Nazis watch and we die."

Her guide pulls at her arm, pulls her back outside, the dishevelled gang he's called together follow in a ragged string, coughing and spitting.

She takes the moment to ask the man about Anton.

"Anton? From Zeist?"

"Yes." She describes him, his curly hair, green flecked eyes, his height. The man nods.

"He was shot, I am sure it was him...maybe a week ago? He was caught trying to help one of the British airmen hiding in the woods. They brought him here. Shot him in front of all of us. To show us you know?" He shakes his head. "Terrible waste. It's all a terrible waste. You knew him?"

She can't answer, can't say a word. So. That's it.

"Did you know him well?" he asks.

"Yes." She chokes.

"A good man. Sorry about that."

She's not sure how she gets to the gate but she does and one by one the guard lets the men behind her through, marking them off the list Hetty has handed back to him. Frank is there to help them into the back of the ambulance. After the last man is in the ambulance, she turns to thank her guide and puts out her hand. He takes it in his and she can feel the square of paper he is pressing into her palm, but the guard sees and pulls the piece of paper from her….reading out the name of a woman – Gerda and a nearby town. He reads the message to himself, laughs and tears it up, then takes his rifle from his back and using the butt, hits the man on the chin. He stands, a livid streak of blood down his face and looks at Hetty: "It's alright…" But he doesn't finish the sentence before the guard hits him twice again, then as he stumbles pushes him on to the ground with his boot.

"Go. Get out of here." He shouts at Hetty, turning with the rifle and aiming it at her. She stumbles over one of the sandbags stacked against the fence and nearly falls, reaches out a hand to steady herself and feels flesh. She looks down and to the side and realises that the sandbags stacked against the fence are not sandbags, but men, dead men, piled up like a wall. She tries to wipe her hand on her skirt, wipe away the smell.

The guard shouts at her as she hesitates. "Get out!"

She goes, gets into the ambulance parked feet away. Frank slams the door on the men in the back, jumps into the driver's seat and cranks it into gear.

They pull on to the road and start the long journey home. Rain starts to pelt down, and they slow down as the windscreen wiper starts to jerk, constantly stopping halfway across the window.

She looks blankly outside as the ambulance gets stuck behind an overturned cart. She sees a little girl scrabbling in the ruins of a building which has been torn apart by a shell, still smouldering, bricks scattered like toys. The little girl squats uncomfortably, her hair pulling out of once tidy pigtails, one yellow ribbon lost the other untied and flapping against the back the of her dirty brown coat. She is looking under the bricks, moving them aside, on the ground, in front of her a headless doll with one leg. Near her a woman is retrieving pieces of furniture and broken pictures from the mess, piling them into a small wooden barrow. "Come away Nella, you are going to get hurt!" Her mother pulls at her as more bricks topple from the pile scattering at their feet hitting the little girls leg. "My baby's dead…my baby's dead…" cries the little girl. The ambulance jolts back into action and as it moves Hetty sees the tear streaked face of the mother and wonders whether the little girl was talking about her doll or a real baby.

She winds down the window puts her hand out, lets the rain wash through her fingers until they are freezing cold. But she feels nothing.

Hetty– Zeist – November

Hetty keeps her days as busy as possible, she doesn't want to have time to think, if she thinks, she will sink into an emotional hole she might not be able to come out of. She goes to the hospital to see how the Arnhem men are recovering – four of them are seriously and unexpectedly ill, the result of days of exposure to driving cold rain, non-existent rations and hard labour. They are grateful and exhausted and on their physical brink. She keeps thinking of the dead bodies.

She sees a middle-aged matron at the hospital coming out of her room, closing the door behind her, closing the door on one of the SS guards from the camp, lounging in a chair, the neck of his uniform undone, a cigarette in one lazy hand, his boots propped on the desk. The matron has the good grace to blush. She looks at Hetty pointedly.

"You've come to see the men?"

The scene disturbs her and when she has a chance, she tells Dr Lievegoed, leaves the knowledge with him.

Two days later her friend and colleague Jan van Wettum is caught up in an SS raid of what is left of the male population in Zeist.

Despite his authoritative height he had cut a sorry presence in the town square, rationing had peeled away the once plump layers of his figure and his coat had become too big for him, his hair was grey and thinning and time had drawn deep lines in his skin. There is total consternation at the Zonnehuis; after the Lievegoed's, Jan van Wettum is the lynch pin of the home.

Hetty cannot believe it, cannot believe this can happen to her friend and cycles to the work camp in a desperate attempt to get him released.

"He'll just be a burden," she tells the weary looking Nazi officer with a lick of blond greasy hair pasted across his bald head. "He has a serious heart condition and he just won't last for any time at all if he is put under any physical strain. He is also vital to the children's home, he is needed there." She says more, but later can't remember what, just knows that at all costs she wants to take Jan van Wettum back to Zeist.

He is released with two others she also asks for and Hetty realises that it all depends on who was in charge: her success see-saws with the mood of each officer, some are sympathetic, others brutal, some just tired, as exhausted with the battle as she is.

She goes to the hospital again to visit the men she rescued. She wants to see them well. It seems a small price to ask for rescuing them, for hearing Anton had been shot. If wishing alone could do it, they would be up and about by now, playing cards and making jokes. But they are not. Seeing them, the smell of despair in the camp washes over her, clings to her. She resolves not to go back.

Nothing will make anything better. There is no better; she is haunted by memories of Anton on every corner of every street in Zeist.

She has a painful meeting with his uncle and they cry helplessly in each other's arms.

She is dizzy with exhaustion and grief. When will this end? Will this ever end?

The official letter from occupation authorities arrives at the Zonnehuis a few days later. It is both a sentence and a blessing. In it Hetty is instructed to report for duty as a nurse at the emergency hospital in Vaassen north of Arnhem; it's an order. It's not that much of a surprise. She'd known that her trips to Arnhem would mean that knowledge of her nursing ability is bound to have been noted.

She tucks the letter into its envelope and walks down the corridor to Dr Lievegoed's office. She can hear him on the phone talking in German – probably to the SS officer in charge of the camp next door – he continues to make it his business to get on with them.

Hetty knocks on the door. She can hear him putting the receiver down before calling her in.

She hands the letter to him across his desk and watches as he scans its contents before putting it down and looking up at her. "What do you want to do?"

"I don't have a choice."

He puts the letter back in its envelope and hands it back to her. "The children will miss you." He looks up at her, a tired smile crosses his face. "We'll all miss you."

Neither of them say what they feel; that the timing is fortunate. She knows they don't need her any more at the Zonnehuis, where every extra person is an extra person to feed as rations are cut and cut again. Her involvement with the now skeletal resistance movement in Zeist is also beginning to strain the delicate film of the relationship Dr Lievegoed needs to maintain with the SS if he is to keep the children safe.

"When are you going?"

"I am to report there by the end of the week. It's Wednesday – so tomorrow?"

PART 6

1945

Hunger games

Joop – Utrecht – January

Joop pulls up the collar of his coat, shivering briefly against the icy wind, tucks in a rough wool scarf and pulls a grey woollen hat over his ears. It's freezing. He sees Opa at the end of the garden pulling out his bike.

"Joop. Come. We must go."

He hurries down the path and opens the wooden gate. Opa wheels his bike out into the passageway at the back of the house as Joop grabs a chipped old blue scooter hidden in the hedge and follows. The scooter is too small, but the wheels are solid and the handlebars steady. He's not sure where the old man got it but it serves its purpose. Joop hunkers over the handlebars and pushes off down the rough path behind the old man disappearing into the darkness ahead of him.

He doesn't care that the scooter is too small, or that it's freezing outside. He's out and away from the house and he can breathe in the expanse of the world around him.

They slip right and left, through streets of dark terraced houses, curtains drawn tight against the cold night. A freezing mist fills with fine drizzle that spits against Joop's face as he scoots along. Soon they are down by the canal and the old man picks up speed. Joop follows, his knees sore from being cramped on the scooter. It's late, a sudden gust of wind and a tin can caught in the breeze rattles and spins across the road. Joop switches his head round to see if anyone is following them. Nothing, no one. He speeds up.

Half an hour later they arrive at a small copse of trees on the edge of the frozen hard Loosdrecht Lake. The old man leans his bike against the dark wet bark of a huge plane tree and Joop rests his scooter next to it and helps the old man unload the paniers on his bike: fishing rods, a net, some rope, a tin of bait.

The old man ties the rope around Joop. "Secure?"

Joop nods and tucking a small hammer and a chisel into his coat, pulling his hat firmly down over his ears, he crawls out on to the ice, the bitterness of it cutting through the rough corduroy of his trousers, soaking his gloves, numbing his fingers. The rope tightens and he stops, gets out the hammer and hitting the chisel drives it hard into the ice, holding the handle tightly as it suddenly gives into the water. He creates one hole, and then crawls across a few feet and chisels out a second. The water splashes up as the ice disks plop and disappear into the dark depths of the lake. His teeth are chattering and his ears ache with the icy breeze. He yanks on the rope and the old man starts to pull and he slides and crawls back to shore, scraping a faint line with the chisel from the holes.

Loggers holds the first rod and hands him the line, unspooling it, Joop goes back to the first hole and drops in the bated hook; the old man pulls him back, takes the second rod and they repeat the process.

Joop is jittery with the cold when he gets back to shore. He jumps up and down beating his arms and hands against one another to try to get warm. This is the coldest it's been. He takes one of the rods from the old man and hunkers down beside him and they start to fish. This is the third time they have come to this spot. It's a good one. The first night they caught two large bream, on the second they stayed out almost all night and caught half a dozen trout. But tonight it's so cold they won't stay for more than an hour maybe two. They sit silently, companionably and wait.

The fishing expeditions have played an increasingly important role in their food supply. Even the old man, with all his wheeling and dealing, has begun to find rations hard to come by. Joop dreams of meals once served at his parents' table; roast chicken and beef stews, remembering the rich glutinous, peppery taste. But now they are lucky to see a small fatty piece of meat once a week. Food supplies to the Netherlands have been cut off: first because of Nazi retaliation following a train strike, now because of the ice. Even the Nazis have started complaining.

There are rumours about a further cut in rations. They drink more water to try to feel full. It doesn't work for Joop, but he says nothing. On very cold nights, Loggers pours each of them tiny shots of their home-made gin topping them up with hot water to make them feel warm before bed.

The fish are a godsend. Fish had never tasted so good. Oma even boils the heads and bones to make a grey, oily, watery soup, it tastes awful, but no-one says anything; everyone scrapes their bowls clean.

After two hours Joop can't feel his hands anymore and they've only caught one fish, a reasonable sized silvery scaled bream. The old man gets up stamping his feet to get warm. "Let's go. It's too cold."

The old man wraps the fish, already stiffening in the freezing weather, in a piece of newspaper he's brought for the purpose and they start to pack everything neatly away. There is a rustle in the copse behind them and they both look up as a man and woman, thin as rakes and white as ghosts appear. The man brandishes a carving knife and grabs the handlebars of Joop's scooter which he has picked up from the ground.

"Give me the fish."

The man is covered in dirt; they can smell his rancid breath from where they are standing. The woman stands behind him, holding a smaller knife shaking, terror sparking her bulbous grey eyes.

The old man holds up his hand. "I'll split it with you." He pulls the fish from the newspapers and calmly puts it on the ground, slowly reaching into his pocket for his pen knife.

The man jumps forward poking the end of his knife into the lapel of the old man's jacket, bringing the blade up to Loggers' face, and scratching it. Joop sees a small trickle of blood run down his cheek.

"Put that knife down! Give me the fish."

The old man looks up. His face is implacable. Joop feels the handle of the hammer still in his pocket, he pulls it out and raises it in the air ready to strike. The woman screams, the man turns around, letting go of the scooter as she drops her knife and runs behind a tree.

"I said, I'll split it with them Joop."

Moving slowly now the man edges back not sure which one of them to attack. Reaching for his knife for a second time, Opa Loggers swiftly splits the fish in two, the blade is razor sharp. He tosses the tail end at the man who falls to the ground scrabbling to pick up the fish. Opa stands slowly re-wrapping the other end of the fish. He looks the man in the eye: "Hard times eh? But do your own fishing next time." He backs up towards his bike, packs their half of the fish into the panier and not taking his eyes off the couple swings on to it and cycles away from the lake, shouting at Joop to follow.

Joop still holding the hammer in one hand, grabs his scooter and follows, skidding on the icy ground, but keeping his balance until they are out on the road. He tucks the hammer back into the pocket of his coat and pushes hard to catch up with Loggers who is speeding ahead in the gloom.

Joop – January – Zeist

Joop listens to the radio at night longing to hear news, any news. There's a report on Radio Orange that Queen Wilhelmina from her home in exile in the English countryside has appealed to US President Roosevelt for help, for food, for something for the starving people of the Netherlands. He has, after all, got Dutch ancestors and he is godfather to her youngest granddaughter.

But nothing comes. Doesn't anyone understand they are starving? Doesn't anyone care. They are desperate for food. Opa says you have to rely on yourself. It is never any good looking for handouts even in a crisis. He'd gone on and on at him. "Haven't I taught you that Joop? That's important. Think for yourself. Be self-reliant."

It's snowing outside, but he knows Opa is going to suggest another fishing expedition, but they are taking a gun, not, Opa says that he will use it except to scare people. But Joop has seen him cleaning it, making sure it works. He'd been so cross when they got back last time. Not because of the couple with the knife, he sympathises with them, but because he was unprepared for any attack. "But even if I'd had this gun I would have given them some fish...."

There's another report on Radio Orange saying that an appeal has also been made to the British government for help and another letter has been sent to President Roosevelt.

*

A fortnight later on 28th January, food arrives in Holland from an unexpected source: two Swedish ships anchor in the port at Delfzijl on the northwest coast with food and medical supplies for the Dutch people. The Nazis prevent its distribution.

Hetty – North of Arnhem – February

The door bangs and Hetty looks up to see a tall greying man leaning heavily on a pair of crutches, his whole body bent in concentration as he makes his way down the ward, swinging his one leg forward. She sees the sweat beading on his forehead, but she doesn't go to help him. Finally he collapses on to one of the iron framed beds and lets the crutches fall to the ground.

He looks up at her as she passes his bed.

"Pick them up for me will you, love?"

She looks at him, the livid scar on his cheek, his clothes limp and ill fitting, he'd been digging out a ditch in Arnhem when he was caught by the edge of a blast, his leg smashed into bloody pieces. Even without the leg he is still one of the lucky ones. What was the death toll someone had told her: 1,500 Allied soldiers and airmen, 500 civilians, 3,000 Nazis? And she wonders whether anyone has yet bothered to work out how many people had died in the work camps. All the camps. The rancid desperate smell of death haunts her.

"Do it yourself."

The man rolls over and reaches out, his body contorting with a sudden bout of coughing. He can't pick the crutches up.

"Come on Hetty, please help me?"

She picks the crutches up and props them against the side of the bed.

"You've got to do things for yourself Albert. You'll never...."

He cuts her off: "Leave me alone." He collapses back on the bed, the worn springs squealing in protest.

The ward is half empty. In November there was no room to move, the doors of the hospital banging constantly as a bloody, broken stream of casualties arrived from a makeshift Red Cross station a few kilometres north of the fighting in Arnhem. The hospital close enough to hear an attack and watch the flak flash in the night sky. Days had bled seamlessly into one another without pause. Hetty had hoped the exhaustion would stop her endless screaming nightmares, block out the loss that fills her. But it didn't and it doesn't. She still wakes each day to find her face wet with tears, her body shivering with fear, grief rebooted by the night, hollowing her out.

Sometime at the end of December the hospital had begun to get less busy; key action moving to the Belgium border, but the Waffen SS still hold grimly on to Arnhem.

The problem now is food. Hunger is all consuming. A watery soup is made daily at the hospital to hand out to the desperate who queue outside the kitchen door. Children whimper as they wait and are handed thin crusts of dried bread – as much straw as wheat – to nibble.

Early in the morning Hetty finds a woman rake thin, hair combed and pinned up, sitting on the hospital steps. She is crooning to a child, swaddled in a blue blanket.

"Is the baby ok?"

"She's quiet now." The woman smiles, holds the bundle out to Hetty, her hands are raw and chapped. Hetty takes the baby gently into her arms, feels its stiff cold limbs. knows it is dead.

How long before they all just drop down dead? There'd been a hope a month ago that someone, some other nation – the Americans, the British – someone might find some supplies to send them, but she had read a report that the Allies have said that feeding the Dutch people under occupation is Hitler's responsibility. That's as good as a death sentence.

The woman reaches out for the child and Hetty hands the

bundle to her, then stoops and helps the woman to stand.

"She's beautiful isn't she," the woman says. She smiles. "My baby is beautiful."

Hetty ushers her into the hospital.

"She is."

Hetty – North of Arnhem – March

Hetty stands at the back door of the small house. The ground is covered in frozen waves of snow, the crisp early morning breeze brushes her skin, goose bumps flush up her arms. She watches silk black rooks preening in a nearby tree, its bare black branches glistening with ice.

A concerned neighbour, cough hacking, waiting in the hospital queue for soup had asked if someone could go; if someone could see if the old couple living in the cottage were alright. And Hetty goes. The neighbour said she hasn't seen them for a day or two, maybe three, wonders whether they are ok, doesn't want to interfere, not with her cough and all. They hadn't been well either, she didn't want to catch anything from them.

The front door of the cottage is locked, so Hetty goes around the back, the kitchen door is on the latch so she walks in, calling out as she goes. The house is cold and sparsely furnished. The kitchen is tidy and empty, a folded washcloth hangs over the sink, two cups draining on a wooden board. The small living room is equally spartan. She calls out again but nothing, so she climbs the stairs.

She finds them in the second bedroom, huddled together in their coats on the bed, his bony arm circling her waist. They are not much older than her parents. Their bodies are cold and a faint odour of death comes from their skin. She finds a blanket and covers them gently.

She walks back to report the death of the couple. Turning in at the hospital gate she sees someone has posted a notice on the board outside. She rips it down, still wet with glue. One of the doctors is putting his coat on to go out as she takes hers off and puts the torn sheets into a wastepaper basket.

"You heard about Woeste Hoeve?" He indicates the notice she has torn apart.

"I heard."

"Did you know any of them?"

He waits but she doesn't answer the question. Who knows? Probably? Maybe? Yes? 117 men shot, dragged from different villages, from hiding places, from farms and shops. The youngest is a 17-year-old Jewish boy who had been hiding on a local farm – the oldest a grandfather of 75. The killing is retaliation by SS troops for a bungled Dutch raid: hungry people trying to steal a rare consignment of pigs on its way to Germany. Retribution had been swift and extended into Amsterdam and Utrecht as well as the nearby village of Woeste Hoeve.

The poster was a warning to others, plastered on the hospital wall. One of many.

"One of them was my nephew," says the doctor.

Hetty – 29 April 1945

"Come on Hetty, come on!"

She chases after Charlie, a Canadian soldier admitted to the hospital after being injured in a skirmish in Arnhem. He is limping down the path out of the hospital grounds, racing towards the field where canvas bags of food are dropping from the air...tins of sardines and ham, packets of dried beans and peas and bars of chocolate.

It had started in the morning when they had heard the roar of a low flying aircraft overhead. One of the nurses had gone out to see what was happening, gazed up at the sky and watched these huge packages tumbling out of low flying aircraft; RAF planes; the liberation force. She'd run to see what had been dropped, coming back breathless, waving a bag of dried beans in the air.

"That's it guys! That's the food, they promised!" shouted Charlie dragging himself out of bed and into some shoes, sweating with the pain of his exertion, but not stopping. He had been listening to the radio and been telling everyone that food, real food, was coming. The liberating Allied forces pushing their way through Holland, pushing out the Nazi occupiers, had now witnessed the starvation and screamed up the line of authority for help.

The liberation had finally begun in earnest by Canadian forces in early April; and despite the hunger that clawed at them day and night, everyone was poised for the end. First to be liberated was Deventer on 10th April, Nazi forces, destroying the bridge across the Ijssel as they retreat. On 12 April three infantry brigades of the II Canadian Corps leapfrogged through the ruined city of Arnhem. By 16 April Arnhem was totally under Allied control and the Canadians advance North, East and West into the remaining occupied territory. By 18 April Epe is under Allied control.

And now on 29 April Operation Manna has begun; 145 RAF Mosquitos and three Lancaster bombers undertaking 3,298 sorties across the Netherlands flying as low as 120 metres, dropping 6,680 tons of tinned food, dried goods and chocolate.

It's not enough. An American Airforce Operation, codenamed Chowhound, compliments the British air relief. It is still not enough, so convoys of aid are sent in by road as the army fight on. The Nazis are on the run, but they are gripping on to their final strongholds in the West with grim determination: Amsterdam, Rotterdam, Utrecht and all that lies between remain under Nazi Command.

Joop – Utrecht – 5 May 1945

Joop nibbles the edge of his thumb nail. He is lying on the wooden floor of the attic, the dust tickling his nose. His other arm stretches around the small black case of the radio, his right ear inches from the receiver. He can't quite catch what the man is saying.

Something....the sound dips in and out, cracking at every second word. He reaches up and gently moves the aerial slightly to the right then delicately with his thumb and forefinger turns the tuning knob until the sound is clearer. He checks his watch – two minutes before 7 – the news would come then. It must be time. It must happen. The Nazis are leaving Utrecht in droves, Loggers has told stories every evening for a week about their antics, laughing when he sees two soldiers, balancing on one bike, desperate to get back to Germany, terrified of what would happen as the tables turn against them.

It must be time. The end must now be here.

"This is Radio Orange. This is Radio Orange. Coming to you from London. The Netherlands are free. Today General Charles Foulkes of the Canadian army and German Commander-in-Chief Johannes Blaskowitz reached an agreement on the capitulation of German forces in the Netherlands in Hotel de Wereld in Wageningen. Holland is no longer under occupation. The Netherlands are once more free. The occupation is over.

"The long days of darkness are over.

"This is Radio Orange. This is Radio Orange. Coming to you from London. Holland is free. The capitulation document will be formally signed tomorrow. This is Radio Orange. Holland is free."

Joop's ears burn. Giddy he gets up, slides through the hatch, down the bannisters. His heart is bursting. He is crying out, shouting for them all, throwing open the front door, standing in the road, blinking back tears. Everyone is there. Everyone has heard. Everyone is laughing and shouting and happy, like they have never been happy before, men and women hugging in the street, children spinning around with sheer joy. And crying, crying with relief and exhaustion and the horror of it all. He wants to see a Canadian, to touch a Canadian truck or soldier or something, to know that it is really, really true, really happening. And he wants his mother and his father and his sister. He wants to tell them. He wants to be with them. And he knows now that what he wants he will never have again. And he can't stop crying. He wipes away the tears, but they still come. The tears keep coming.

Hetty – May – North of Arnhem

It is a spur of the moment decision.

For weeks before the liberation motorcades of Nazi soldiers have passed by the hospital, booty spilling from cars and trucks, trigger happy soldiers in the front. At first Hetty is too busy to care, scarred, wounded, bloody victims of the liberation still demanding her attention.

But then things calm down, and the day after they finally hear that the Nazis have capitulated, and they have danced through the night with any semi able-bodied patients, she sees a flat backed lorry, packed high with paintings, carpets, and velvet upholstered chairs pass by. Two soldiers and a woman in a headscarf sit amongst the booty one of them holding onto a clock as the truck bumps over a pothole. The clock jogs her memory: the shape, the carving, she wasn't sure what, but it reminds her of home. And she realises that is what she must do, as soon as she can: go home. If the others have survived that is where they will go. The realisation breaks something within her: a part of her, one of the deepest parts of her, the part that has been holding on, holding her in for the past five years, and suddenly she breathes in and it feels as if it is the first real breath since the occupation began, as if she has been living without oxygen and tears of relief stream down her face with the realisation that it is finally over. That now she can be who she is, that she can stop being someone else, start living her life, her own life.

Leaving the hospital is the easy part. After a flurry of activity in April, the hospital is emptying out and food supplies are finally getting through. Things are not back to normal, will not be normal for a long time, but the sense of desperation is abating. Thousands of people are tumbling out of hiding. Nazis are escaping back across the border; the exiled Dutch military are back and in charge. She still needs permission to leave, to cross the country. It takes her 10 days to get a pass signed by Captain A.A.A. Dickers.

She ties her bag securely to her old bike and sets off West. She is soon pushed off the road and on to a canal path by a motorcade of Allied jeeps and trucks. She cycles down by the Lower Rhine but feels too exposed and returns to hug smaller paths through woods and by small canals, enjoying the sweet smell of the pine needles crushed by her wheels, the fresh muddy newness of late Spring. She manages over 80 kilometres on the first day, a good run on wooden wheels.

She stops at a farmhouse where a Dutch flag flutters from an upstairs window and asks if she can sleep in the barn. They invite her in, regale her with tales of the food drop at the local airfield the previous day, the crowds of people, the tins of beans and chocolate. They offer her a piece of chocolate and she lets it melt slowly luxuriously in her mouth. She tells them she is heading home to Scheveningen, doesn't know what she will find. They sympathise, they know about the destruction of the seaside resort by Nazi forces, hope for her that her home still stands. They wrap up a whole bar of chocolate, half a loaf of bread and a tin of beans and give them to her: provisions for the rest of her journey. They lend her a blanket and a pillow, and she makes herself a bed in the hayloft. She sleeps until the sun breaks through the wooden slats of the barn door, then gets up, splashes her face from an outside tap, and is on her way before the household is awake.

It is four in the afternoon when she arrives in Scheveningen, or what had been Scheveningen: her head telling her she was on the edge of the town she called home, her eyes revealing a desperate vision of hell, thousands of buildings destroyed, deep trenches and huge walls of rubble tearing through the ground where elegant houses once stood proud. She picks her way across the park which has turned into a wilderness, wheels her bike around potholes in half familiar streets. She is surrounded by memories of the fear she felt, sickened by the destruction. She holds her breath as she turns into Gentsestraat. It is a ghost of itself but mostly undestroyed, too close but not close enough to the sea front to fall victim to the Atlantic Wall destructions, escaping the ravishes of occupation and liberation. The bakery is still there and a clothes shop she recognises with a one armed undressed mannequin in the window, she waves at a half familiar face sweeping the pavement outside what used to be the florist's shop.

The boarded-up window of her parents' perfumery is plastered with propaganda. She feels in her pocket for the key to the front door, the key she had kept in the bottom of her case all this time and sets it in the lock. The door opens.

She runs up the stairs, her footsteps echoing against the wood, the carpet gone. The living room is stripped of furniture, shadows on the walls where paintings once hung. She goes into the kitchen, even the kitchen table has disappeared. There are two dirty encrusted plates and cups in the sink, nothing in the cupboards but half a packet of caustic soda and a dirty rag.

There is no-one and nothing there. Where are they? Are they alive? Will they come back?

She walks back into the empty living room. She notices one picture still hanging in an alcove, a funny little print of a windmill that her sister had brought back from a holiday in Epe and she goes and straightens it on its hook, dusts the frame with the edge of her cardigan.

She sinks down on to the bare floorboards, leaning her back against the wall where the mahogany sideboard had once stood. She fills the room with her memories, the laughter of her family, the clock ticking on the wall. About to get up thinking she will go and talk to the florist, see if he has any news, knows anything, thinking she should start tidying up, sweeping exploring the rest of the house seeing if there is anything left in the cellar, she sees the corner of a postcard caught between the skirting board and the wall. She pulls it out. It's a picture of snow topped mountains, blue skies and a clutch of fir trees. She turns it over and immediately sees the address in his neat sloping handwriting: Hans. It was from Hans, sent to her mother from Switzerland two years ago. No message just a signature 'H'. He's alive, that must mean Hans is alive.

She breathes and traps the card between the palms of her hands, feels tears rolling down her face.

Tomorrow she will start to clean the house, from top to bottom, to make it new again. She closes her eyes, and dresses the room with the clock, the plush velvet couch, her mother's chair. She wills them back – her parents, Loes and Hans. She wills them all to be alive and to come home.

In 1939 there were an estimated 140,000 Jews living in Holland, some 25,000 of these were German Jewish refugees who had fled to Holland from Nazi Germany during the 1930s. A census in 1946 showed that just under 35,000 Dutch Jews survived the war. 75%

of the Jewish population of the Netherlands was wiped out, more than in any other Western European country. During the Dutch hunger winter of 1944-45 20,000 people died of hunger.

Epilogue

Hetty – June 1949 – Jakarta

Hetty stands by the door of the open topped jeep tightening a headscarf round her chin. It's a beautiful day. It's been the most beautiful day. Peter opens the door of the jeep and she slides in looking up at him, smiles as wide as they can go on both their faces.

The cinched leather belt around her tan trousers emphasizes how thin she is, boniness hinting at her past. They have a pact, not just to love and cherish in sickness and in health, but to 'draw a line' under the dark years, the war years, to pursue their own new beginning.

Four years earlier after the war there is euphoria when her parents' and sisters' return to Scheveningen. And then within weeks Hans arrives home too. The family holds fast to one another. At first there is the relief of being free, of not watching people watching them, then the challenge of starting again; Hetty goes nowhere, stays home and helps her parents rebuild their lives, their business, their home. It takes time, lots of time and there are days and nights when they all have to stop and shake themselves to realise they are alive. And days when they all talk about where they have been, and the family and friends they have lost. "So many people…." says Hetty face buried in her hands as they talk. Hans tells them of his escape; Loes and Jacques are soon expecting their first child.

After two years, the parfumerie is thriving again, the seaside smells and sounds of Scheveningen returning to an even norm, and Hetty yearns to leave. She wants to find a new beginning away from the Netherlands which are filled with too many memories of those she loved and lost. She applies to join the newly formed Women's Corps of the Royal Netherland East Indies Army and before the end of 1947 she is on her way to Batavia.

There she meets Peter at a friend's dinner party in Jakarta, a young British diplomat with twinkling blue eyes. He walks her home and asks to see her again, and again, and again, until a bitter jealous captain posts her to a remote part of Sumatra. For a year they keep their love alive with letters. Every day she gets a letter from Peter.

"I am waiting for you," he writes.

"Straight as an arrow I'm coming to you," she writes back.

And she comes back and leaves the army to marry Peter.

"Shall we get married in Dutch or English?" she asks him.

"Whichever is quicker." says Peter.

"Dutch."

The wedding is small. The British consul's wife gives her a length of white Japanese silk for her dress. The icing of the wedding cake is so hard it turns to nougat. But no one minds, everyone laughs. It is a joyous occasion and now the laughter, the ceremony and the traditional toasts are over they are going away.

The late afternoon sunshine glances off the windscreen of the jeep as they drive under the rustling palm trees. Hetty spots the startling turquoise breast and red beak of a kingfisher; an old man dragging a cart, waves at them, the jerry can tied to the bumper of the jeep bounces out a discordant tune celebrating their marriage.

They will drive into the mountains, into the cool green trees, away from the heat.

Peter reaches across and holds her hand. Today is the first day of the rest of their lives.

Joop – June 1950 – Utrecht

The school hall is packed with students, teachers, parents. It's the end of the year, there will be wise words of advice, certificates and prizes handed out to graduating students and a rising rendition of the National Anthem to conclude.

Cramped between two of his best friends in the second row, Joop feels a mixture of excitement, nerves and sadness. It's been a good year, a good few years. Unbidden the thought suddenly comes to him of the old headmaster who taught him during the occupation. He doesn't think of him often, he was such a pain in the neck, but his pedantic teaching had given him an academic grounding that stood him in good stead. Silently he thanks him.

What he wants now, what all 50 students in his year want is the academic cup. It is given to the student who achieves the best results in the exams and has kudos with universities and businesses. There's a wooden board in the entrance hall of the school that carries the names in gold of all previous winners. Three runners up will get certificates that are almost equally prized; it is, after all, a fluke which student lands up half a point in front and gets the coveted cup. It goes to a tall thin dark-haired girl called Yvette who wears glasses. Joop gets second prize. There is clamorous cheering and clapping as he goes up to collect his certificate from the headmaster; friends thump him on the back as he sidles past them, down the aisle and up the wooden steps on to the stage. His teacher sitting in a formal black gown at the back of the stage smiles broadly.

Then it is all over and everyone is leaving, chatting and hugging and swearing never ending friendship. He feels happy and sad as he says goodbye to his friends. He must find the Loggers.

He stayed with them after the war. Where else was he to go? His mother and father are dead. His mother died in Auschwitz, was sent to the gas chamber on the day she arrived, 22nd of October 1943, less than a week after being arrested. The news cripples him, but he knows deep down that it is something he has thought for a long time, it just extinguishes the last tiny bit of hope left in him. His Uncle Jasper and all his family also died in the camps. The litany of death piles up in his heart and he knows will be with him all his life. But Opa Loggers talks to him man to man – he must not bend under the news, he must stand, he must live and succeed for his parents. He must show the world that he will not be defeated.

He had asked the Loggers if he could stay with them after the war, not go to the Jewish orphanage, so when his aunt and cousin move out, his aunt barely speaking to him in her ongoing grief, he moves down into the spare room, goes to the local school, waves goodbye to the retired headmaster next door who goes to live with his son in America.

He sees his sister who is taken for a short time to live with another aunt but she was unhappy and asks to go to the Jewish orphanage.

Walking away from the school, out in the sunshine he sees the Loggers and walks across to them, Oma hugs him, congratulates him; the old man shakes his hand.

They walk back to the house in silence, leaves of the elm trees skirting their path rustling in the light breeze. Joop thinks of his place at university to study veterinary science, his final parting from the Loggers family looming. They have been good to him.

As they get to the house, the old man turns to Joop. "You know, if you came second, you could have come first."

Joop feels momentarily hurt, will Loggers never be satisfied? But he smiles to himself, the old man's determination that he do well, do better than anyone else, never stops.

In less than a week he will leave for Scheveningen to see his aunts and to work along the seafront during the summer before setting out for university. Hetty won't be there, she's in the Far East, but whenever he thinks of his family, he thinks of her; her tears when they were reunited weeks after the end of the war; the relief that against the odds they at least survived. He knows he will hold her closely in his heart for the rest of his life. He knows that without her he too would probably have died.

After university he does better, achieves more than almost any member of his surviving family; ambition and determination knotted within him, entangled inseparably with the sadness and loss which sits deep within his heart.

His sister Trudi, with other Dutch Jewish orphans, eventually emigrates to Israel, but for Joop the Promised Land is The Netherlands and will always be The Netherlands; he cannot leave his past, the birthplace of his father and his father's father. He is there to stand up for all that was lost. He is ready to help protect the land and the people who protected him. He will play his part in the rebuilding of a nation.

Left: Hetty aged about 20.

Above: Jozef in his early 20s.

Below: Jozef, his mother and sister in 1940

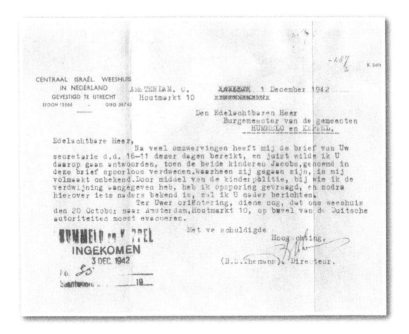

Letter from the occupying authorities looking for Jozef and Trudi

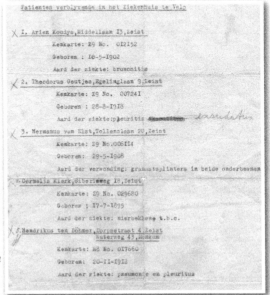

List of Zeist men rescued by Hetty from Arnhem in 1944.

About the Author

Ann Donovan (Morris) is a journalist and author and has worked for the Observer, The London Evening Standard, The Daily and Sunday Telegraph, Harpers and Queen and the Daily Mail amongst other publications. She is the author of three non-fiction books and curates exhibitions on Arabian explorers. Don't Look for Me is Ann's first novel. She is married and has two grown up daughters. She lives in London and Cornwall.

Made in the USA
Coppell, TX
28 December 2023